Jon~~athan Gash is the pen name~~ also
wrot~~e under the~~ name of Graham Gaunt. Born in 1933 in
Bolton, Lancashire, Grant trained as a doctor and worked
as both a GP and a pathologist. He also served in the Royal
Army Medical Corps, where he rose to the rank of Major,
and was head of bacteriology at the University of London's
School of Hygiene and Tropical Medicine. His first Lovejoy
novel, *The Judas Pair*, won the Crime Writers' Association
prestigious John Creasey award in 1977. Grant lives in
Colchester, Essex.

D1100006

The Lies of Fair Ladies

A Lovejoy Novel

Jonathan Gash

Constable • London

CONSTABLE

First published in 1992 by Arrow Books Limited

This edition published in Great Britain in 2018 by Constable

1 3 5 7 9 10 8 6 4 2

Copyright © Jonathan Gash, 1992

The moral right of the author has been asserted.

A CIP catalogue record for this book is available from the British Library.

ISBN 978-1-47211-952-0

Typeset in Berleley Book by TW Type, Cornwall
Printed and bound in Great Britain by Clays Ltd, Elcograf S.p.A.

Papers used by Constable are from well-managed forests and other responsible sources.

Constable
An imprint of
Little, Brown Book Group
Carmelite House
50 Victoria Embankment
London EC4Y 0DZ

An Hachette UK Company
www.hachette.co.uk

www.littlebrown.co.uk

For:
Charlotte Grace

To:
The Chinese god Wei D'to, who saves books from scoundrels

Thanks:
Susan, as ever

Lovejoy

Chapter 1

Time to get rid of her.

Decisions about women creep up, don't they? They can even reach in, where antiques rightfully rule. I'm an – *the* – antique dealer, and I know.

Joan made love when her husband Del was talking at us. I'm a patient bloke but there are limits. She spat insults at him, jeering until her moans came and oblivion ruled. Can you imagine?

I'd given her the best years – well, two days – of my life. The reason was this antique she hadn't got.

Joan was filthy rich, in a praiseworthy way. That is, she honestly thought everybody else was rich, too. To me, antiques are one of the ten reasons for money; the other nine don't matter.

'What do you think?' she'd asked me brightly at the auction. First time I saw her. She gave me a dog to hold, silly cow. I gave it her back. It yawned, thinking what a hell of a day.

'Dog looks fine, lady.'

I wasn't particularly happy. I'd had a lousy day, St Edmundsbury. The worst job in antiques is being a tax hiker. You stroll into some auction. Then, obviously suppressing excitement/glee and whatnot, you bid for Lot No. X – some duff painting, whatever old dross you've been hired to hike up. Rival dealers see your eagerness, and get drawn in. The more the merrier. The price soars. Guess who eventually buys it? Why, Lot X's owner himself! Then he donates it to some museum, and claims tax relief *on the price he bid.* Good, eh? The painting was one I'd faked, a John Constable *View of Dedham, Late Sun.* Quite good, but wrong canvas. I'd got his greens just right, though mixing Prussian Blue like J. C. is a swine. The owner was Barry Dimmonson. He met me in his Rolls to pay.

'I'll need you again soon, Lovejoy.' He fumed carcinogens from his bulbous cigar. 'This time knock me up somefink else. A pot.'

'What sort? A Ch'ien Lung vase takes—'

'Any frigging sort.' He cruised off snarling into a car phone. Like I say, a tax hiker's a rotten job. I hurried to the viewing day at Wittwoode's Auction Temple, to meet destiny and Joan.

She was exquisite. One waft of her perfume was worth Wittwoode's Auction Temple plus all the crud that lay therein.

'I don't mean Jasper!' she cooed. 'I mean *that.*'

The onyx cameo, Lot 66. Passing dealers listened with their directional ears.

Now, there's an obligation among dealers to support each other against the common enemy. And the good old C. E. is you. Punters, buyers. Anybody who wants what dealers want, namely antiques. Auctioneers don't count because everybody hates them. Reason? Because they know nothing, and do nowt. *And* get a rake-off. Makes your blood boil.

The question worried me. Was this bird honestly asking for honesty? Then my mind smiled.

Over in the corner of the draughty old church Wittwoode has the nerve to call *his*, not God's, Temple, Denny was trying to sell this very cameo to a woman called George Danson. A word about terminology here: a 'woman' to the antiques trade is a non-dealer, man or woman. A 'lady' is anyone with money, pure and maybe not so simple. George Danson was a poor old gaffer with a kindly soul. Denny's a shark, that is, an antique dealer. He didn't own the lovely cameo brooch, of course. (Tip: people who try to sell you an item in an auction viewing never, ever own it, so watch out.)

I'd seen Denny come in out of the rain. He tried to con me once, a royal Worcester framed oval porcelain plaque painted by John Stinton. Not really antique 1928 or there-abouts, but worth a small car. Denny's was a dud. Fake porcelains are stamped out in Germany these days; the colours are wrong. I decided to blame Denny and do this ladylady (sic) a good turn.

'That, lady?' Decibels bring audiences. 'Fake.'

'Fake?' She stared at me. 'I mean the cameo.' Emphasis was needed. 'Duff. Neff. Fraud. Sexton Blake, fake.'

'But . . .' She had a lovely high colour of a sudden. Jasper growled, bad vibes. 'The catalogue says genuine Etruscan.'

The power of the written lie always astonishes me. And nobody lies like a cataloguer. Except an auctioneer.

'Balderdash,' I boomed. 'Auctioneers cheat. Some pil-locks – er, sorry. They hope to deceive.'

'That's positively shameful!' She eyed me. 'You can tell?'

Somebody passing chuckled. Bernese, a luscious dealer in doll's houses and Edwardian domestic furniture. She hates me. We once made smiles.

'Lovejoy's divining rod's famous, dear,' Bernese said with malice, crashing across to up-end a small occa-sional table, 1906 or thereabouts. She wants me to go into partnership. I won't because they don't last. Her husband runs a Civil Service school.

'I'm a divvie, love. I feel it. But get a MacArthur microscope. Even a handlens'll show the surface scratches from an electric micro. Modern fakers have no patience. It's supposed to be nicked from Florence's Archaeological Museum. Cosimo de'Medici's collection of ancient jewellery.'

The dud cameo was well-nigh perfect. It showed Hercules and his missus Hebe. 'Beautifully done. See how their profiles are cut, the brown layer as his hair, beard, cloak?' The bluish underlayer was left in various thicknesses for the gods' features.

She wasn't taking any notice, just staring. 'You hadn't seen it before,' she accused. 'Yet you . . .'

People never believe you, first time round. Yet they believe promised tax cuts, the lies on food labels. Amazing. She looked me up and down, registered (a) shoddy (b) wet through, so no motor and (c) resented by all dealers and auctioneers present.

'Right, Lovejoy!' Wittwoode steamed up, frothing. He's a great frother, walrus moustache and bottle specs. He thinks nobody knows he fiddles his books. A pillar of the trade. 'You've done enough damage. Out!'

'I'm going, I'm going.'

Then the lady uttered magic. All froze in reverence.

'I have a valuable original cameo.' She smiled. Jasper whimpered, knowing trouble. 'Would you . . . divvie it, Lovejoy?'

Police or profit? A gorgeous bird, or Wittwoode's goons?

'Well, all right.' I'm good at surrender.

Joan's cameo was a similar fraud. She'd paid a fortune for it. I explained the sad news.

She heard me out. First time she'd listened to anyone for

years. I talked on, scams I have known. I came to when it was almost dark. We were served tea by a grovelling serf. I made to go. She restrained me with skill.

'I have more jewellery, Lovejoy. In my boudoir.' I'd never heard anyone use that word except in the music hall.

And that was that. Except that, when we were just on the point of serious smiles, she breathlessly cried to wait, for Christ's sake. Just another minute . . .

She clicked a radio on at seven o'clock. Everybody's talk-show favourite, Del Vervain, came on, poisonous with affability.

Joan turned to me, face suddenly haggard. 'See, Lovejoy?' she asked, in tears. 'My husband's famous boyish charm. Isn't it wonderful?'

'Er, very wonderful.' I didn't want any part of this. The bloke was connected with grimsville.

She said, abruptly savage. 'Don't go. It's a live show. He'll not be home for hours.'

Sloshed out of his mind, by all accounts. Her dress fell, her breasts appeared. She took hold of me, fingers working. I started a lucid denial, based on pure logic.

I managed, 'Ooooh.'

My second evening with Joan – Del Vervain's show broadcasts between seven and eleven – I escaped by saying I'd go for a present for her. She was thrilled. As her cameo was fake, wouldn't it be luvverly if I wangled her a genuine Etruscan cameo? She wept sincere tears.

'You're wonderful, Lovejoy.' We were still in the afterthroes. I was dying to slip into the little death that comes after. Joan, typical bird, talked non-stop.

I filled up. She was right. I am. Emotion's catching, to sensitive blokes like me.

'When do we meet, doowerlink?' My cover.

'Coffee. Joynson's, Sudbury.' She owns Joynson's.

She sent me off in her chauffeur-driven Rolls Royce. I had him drop me at the Antiques Arcade. Closed at that hour, of course. The chauffeur wasn't deceived. His eyes kept giving me sardonic glances in the mirror. I don't like people who are sardonic. What's wrong with trust?

That night at my cottage I slept the sleep of the just.

By eight next morning I was up and whistling, feeding the robin his cheese, the bluetits their nuts, and me fried tomatoes, dry bread, tea with brown sugar. My cottage is Lovejoy Antiques, Inc. – to sound American and affluent, all Americans being rich. Our own humbler description 'Ltd' sounds sternly not-got-much.

An elderly lady was on the doorstep as I launched out to face the world. I sighed. Today, I especially did not want a Yank researching her family tree.

'Morning, Miss Turner.'

She's from Virginia or somewhere. Started haunting me after we met in the grotty town library. Like a fool I'd taken pity on the dingy old crone, corrected a library lass who was telling her wrong about birth certificates.

'Morning, Lovejoy!' She's an eager ninety. She dragged notes from a handbag like a leather trunk. 'I'll only trouble you a moment. Your advice worked! The people at the General Register Office in Saint Catherine's House were charming.'

'Sorry, love, I've no time.' Everybody's always after me for a hand-out. Didn't the shabby old biddy know Americans are millionaires?

She trotted alongside, adjusting specs to peer at some scrap. 'My parents, John Turner and Mary Ann. I have their birth certificates *right here!*'

'Glad you made it. So-long.'

'No, no!' she cried. 'Lovejoy, I'm desperate!'

What now? I cursed myself for a fool. And halted so she could wheeze into the punchline. She looked threadbare as me. I was worn out and I'd only got ten yards. I gave her my last note. Anything to get rid.

'Marriage certificates at the GRO, Kingsway. Alphabetical order. Different coloured form. Guess your Grandpa's marriage date, work back. Only takes half an hour. Ta-ra.'

'Thank you,' she called after, smiling. Daft owd bat.

I yelled over my shoulder, 'Put the right volume number on the form, for God's sake.'

'Thank you, Lovejoy.' Tears of gratitude? Silly old cow.

Our village bus was late – not an all-time first. I was still waiting at the chapel when the Plod stopped and offered me a lift. Not where I wanted to go, but police are poor on direction. I've often found that. We drove in monosyllables to a huge moated house near Manningtree, set in a vast flat cornfield, a small river snaking indolently past. My heart sank when I saw who the head ploddite was.

'Morning,' I offered heartily, going to stand beside him at the drawbridge. 'Black Knight challenged yet?'

He snorted non-amusement, stood there examining the edifice. Lovely turreted windows in serried ranks.

'Ever heard of pace, Lovejoy?'

Drinkwater's some sort of inspector. Though the Bill come heavy with titles these days. Ever noticed? The more titles, the worse they behave. Odd. I'll have to think about that. It may be a universal law or something.

'Pace?' Be helpful. 'Speed? Alacrity?' His cadaverous features didn't improve. 'That poison gas?'

Drinkwater's a Midland's reject. He has four spoonfuls of sugar in each half-pint mug of tea at the nick. His false teeth clack when he talks. His left ear twitches.

'That's Mace, you prat.' He never sits either, even during

7

interrogations, just walks about, hands in his trouser pockets. I've never seen him without a mac. His Adam's apple yoyos hypnotically. He focuses attention. A one-man carnival. 'P.A.C.E., Lovejoy, Police and Criminal Evidence Act.'

'No. Have . . . ?' Maybe he had? I coughed nervously.

His bleary eyes took me in. 'This interview will be deemed to have satisfied that Act's requirements, Lovejoy. Follow?'

'Yes.' I wasn't to complain.

'Did you pull the robbery herein?'

Herein? Trust the Plod. Archaisms deceive the innocent. 'What's been nicked? Looks empty to me.'

He chuckled, gave me the benefit of his features face on. You know he's chuckling because his skeletal chest jerks.

'Not empty, Lovejoy. Gutted. Fireplaces. Balustrades. Tiles. Wallpaper, even. Pelmets. Kitchen ranges. Chandeliers.'

This is called a turkey job in the antiques trade. Whether Turkey specialised in them, or cleaning out as in your Christmas fowl, I don't know. Drinkwater waited. A uniformed bobby lit a fag discreetly.

'Must have been strong lads,' I offered. Silence. Another bobby lit up, coughing in the morning stillness.

'You see my problem, Lovejoy?'

Quite honestly I didn't, but you daren't disagree. Then I began to wonder.

'Left empty some time, eh?'

'Six months. Council conversion, planning offices.'

Late Georgian, it was imposingly set, moated amid this flat field. No trees lined the little river's banks. I began to smile, trying hard not to. The only road ran straight as a die across the field to the mansion. No cover. No way to creep close.

'How'd they get pantechnicons and robbers in?'

'*And* the antiques out, Lovejoy. A wheelbarrow would be spotted a mile off, let alone a van. The river's out.' He indicated a cottage where the road joined a narrow wooded lane. 'The security specialist house. Three men, on shifts.'

Then I did smile. It was the old locked room mystery, for the most unlockable site in the known world.

A smile's dangerous to Drinkwater's kind. 'You know something, Lovejoy, you frigging dross.'

'Me?' I said indignantly. 'I've never even seen the blinking place before, Drinkwater! I didn't even know—' . . . *I didn't even know Prammie Joe was out of gaol.*

The change in his eyes warned me.

'. . . this building was here,' I finished lamely.

He stared me down. 'Know what, Lovejoy? I wish you was one of them crets as boils shredded soap and diesel, for homemade bombs. But you're a chiselling shagnasty, living off any woman with enough in her purse.'

'Here, Drinkwater. I don't have to put up with—'

'Sooner or later, lad, some item from Cornish Place will turn up in your hovel. And I'll fit you for life. Follow?'

'My cottage isn't a hovel,' I tried indignantly. He simply walked across the drawbridge, left me to make my own way home. Ten miles, through the dullest countryside you ever did see. I got a lift from a sales rep disappointed I wasn't going to Norwich.

Prammie Joe out of nick, though. Well, well. He must have worked like a dog, doing a turkey on that huge place all on his own. Good old Joe. Class tells. I decided oh-so-casually to meet up with Prammie Joe. Maybe his brilliant theft was a commission job for some big roller (= rich antiques buyer who doesn't really care what stuff he buys, for swift resale). Then I'd best keep out of it. But if it was

9

a loner, I'd cut in for a share. And why not? The only loser would be the taxpayer. And local politicians, of course. That made me smile wider still.

Chapter 2

Things surge up or down in antiques. Never two days alike. Antique dealers live on their wits – they possess none, hence their vaunted penury. In fact, most dealers couldn't make a living at all, were it not for the honest old public, which lives for greed while pretending the opposite. This is why I like women. They *know* they're greedy, that everybody else is too. But it's okay as long as you keep up appearances, like offering your last macaroon to a visitor, hoping she won't take it.

So that fateful day I strolled hopeful into the Antiques Arcade (think a dingy covered walk of counters offering dross) because, remember what I said? Antiques are either on a down spiral, or soaring. Even in Ancient Rome, with barbarians howling at the gates, antique dealers made a killing, street stalls getting priceless valuables for a song, burying the loot in the yard. My advice: Don't waste pity. Save it for the starving. Antique dealers are born with a whimper, like those terrible Christmas dolls that wet the bed. And the whimper goes: 'Times are 'orrible bad, guv'nor, so please don't quibble about the price; this is a genuine Van Dyke I'm practically giving away . . .'

They also hate talent, as the chorus of abuse I received testified.

11

'How do, Lovejoy.' Gunge was waiting. 'This big ring any good?'

'No.' No, because the answer's always no. At first. If you don't believe me, take that precious heirloom your Great Aunt left you – let's say a genuine Hepplewhite shield-backed upright chair. You *know* it's genuine because you have a portrait of your own great-grandad posing beside that selfsame brilliant piece of crafted wonder. Take it to any – *any* – antique dealer. Pretend you want to sell. You ask, 'Valuable, eh?'

What does he reply? *'No. Sorry.'*

He gives reasons to knock down your reasons. He has a trillion put-downers – sneers, scorn, sighs, reproach. You have documents? He sneers, Lady, everybody tries *that* on. Your chair's in Gloag's *Dictionary*, and its vase splat (the middle bit where your spine rests) is identical? Faked, he sighs, and offers you a pittance. Lovejoy's Antiques Rule One is: *It's always no.* Tell you about exceptions later.

'The ring is Jeff Dalgleish's. I'm on ten perk.'

That made me hesitate. All about, dealers were making crude comments on my dishevelled state. A happy band of siblings, all cut-throat.

'Watch your language,' I shouted down the Arcade. 'I'm the only customer today with any money.'

That shut them up. Their ribaldry faded. It might be true, antiques being the ultimate switchback ride.

Perk is per cent. I took the ring. It was genuine but fake, if you follow. Some antiques truly are both. 'Papal' rings would fit no finger except some panto giant's. They are so huge, they rattle around even on your thumb. Mostly gilt bronze, with a prominent bezel and a stone of rock crystal or plain-coloured glass. They're pretty common, and not much sought. For all the world like a child's idea of an impressive dress ring. We aren't really sure, but suppose them to be worn on a cord round some ancient legate's neck, symbol of authority. They never have a seal die, for impressing wax on documents. I weighed Gunge up.

Gunge Herod, like me, suffers from his name. His first means unmentionable, his second slaughter. His nickname comes from his usual response: 'No; it's gunge.' He's disliked because his barrow blocks the Arcade entrance. A barrow exempts him weekly dues, so you can imagine. He does jewellery and household antiques.

'Jeff's got a weird one here, Gunge.'

Usually papal rings aren't valuable. But unless I was mistaken this monster was solid gold, and the stone was brown topaz. Don't knock topaz; its pink, honey-yellows and blue varieties are some of the loveliest of gems. I saw most of the other dealers were carefully not watching, and took out my polaroid sunglasses. Every jeweller carries them. Mine are simply lenses from an old pair somebody chucked away. The trick is, put the gem on one polaroid lens, and look at it through the other. Rotate the top one. If the stone stays dark for a complete rotation, then it's one lot of stones, including diamond and simple glass; if it alternates light and dark, then it's a group including topazes, sapphires, rubies and a million others. Mind you, the polaroid trick only tells you what a gem is *not*. Like, if a gemstone shows dark-light every quarter turn, and a jeweller is trying to sell you this amazingly cheap genuine diamond, you know he's lying. And if an auctioneer invites bids for a spectacular 'antique sapphire pendant', and the gem stayed dark to your sunglasses ploy, then that auctioneer – perish the thought! – is a crook, and the 'precious sapphire' is probably just a chunk of polished bottle.

The stone changed, light to dark, light to dark. I was honestly surprised.

'May be honey topaz. Done the gold test?'

· 'No.' He shuffled in embarrassment. I moved aside so he could shuffle without crushing me. He's a huge bearded bloke, six feet eight, wide with it. Has to go in pubs sideways. Size always amazes me. I mean, Gunge comes from my county, and we're average everything.

This annoyed me – not Gunge's hugeness, but that the miserable sods in the Arcade wouldn't do him a gold test. It only takes a second. There wasn't one who didn't have a gold-testing kit. I looked along. Connie was in.

'Connie? A favour, love.'

'No, Lovejoy. You owe me for those boots.'

'Boots?' I did a theatrical start. 'Ah, yes, I remember. I got a fair price. Settle up in the Bricklayers Arms tonight?' She'd got me a pair of Victorian ladies' boots. A Dulwich collector pays me on the nail. I'd forgotten to pay Connie. Well, who can remember every damned thing?

She dithered, a delightful sight. She's about twenty-two, comely, dresses classy instead of this current shopsoiled fashion. High heels, swinging skirt, spends two hours every morning in front of her bedroom mirror . . . I mean, I'll bet she possibly does. Has rich parents who fondly think their daughter's beavering at Manchester University doing astrophysics. To me, women and lies are unknowable. I mean, why didn't she pretend she was doing sociology, a phoney subject nobody cares about? Then she could carry the lie with total conviction. Real sociologists do it all the time.

'Gunge's shy his dues, Lovejoy,' she lectured severely, drumming her fingers prettily. 'It's cheating.'

Which was rich, from an astrophysicist running a crummy antiques stall among a load of deadlegs. But pointing out a lie to a female's considered impolite.

'Just a bad patch, dooowerlink. One dropper. Please.'

'You'll divvie some stuff for me?'

Sigh. I took the papal ring to her stall – three feet of

14

plank, a homemade glass case, a strip of black velvet. 'Deal. Where is it?'

'They're not here, Lovejoy.' I brightened. They is plural.

'Bring them along to the Bricklayers.'

She shook her head, a lovely sheen. 'They're not handies.'

A quick look. The dealers had lost interest. 'A lot?'

'Several. I'll take you. It has to be tomorrow.'

No longer mere plural, but multo. I swallowed. I wasn't sure if my throat was dry from her astrophysical nearness or the thought of a dream warehouse crammed with antiques.

'Here.' I passed her the papal ring. She didn't examine it immediately, another surprise. I go by feel, some inner bong that homes me on to genuine antiques. But other dealers have to look, scrutinize, weigh. And she wasn't doing any of that. Preoccupied with her cache of antiques. Must be worth a mint. I warmed to her. No, honestly. I quite like astrophysics. For all I knew, so did she.

'Deal, Lovejoy?' She gazed straight at me. Not exactly Drinkwater's look, but with a hint of the same quality. Judging, goading even. For the first time I felt something wasn't right. As if Connie'd only come to the Arcade that day waiting for me. But Lovejoy Antiques, Inc. was a supersurvivor.

'Deal, love.' I was starving hungry. I'd have touched her for a pasty or two, except I owed. Mistrust is catching.

I left the Arcade, blithely irritating the dealers by yelling for them to stick at it, customers. They bawled outrage back. Lovejoy's Rule Two: Always look on your way to a terrific bargain. It depresses rivals no end.

Prammie Joe isn't on the phone. Some say he isn't even on Planet Earth. He's a true loner, living on this promontory on the banks of the Orwell. Waterman born and bred, he makes a meagre living among the waterways. Canals, rivers, estuaries are his world. He isn't quite the scruff I suppose I'm making him sound. He's impeccably clean, always shaved. He was a sailor once, and they're precise of habit. He's a worry to any antique dealer, is Prammie Joe. Has a disturbing habit of coming up trumps from nowhere. Bound to dismay the Arcaders, when you think.

Like, once, Prammie showed up with two serpents – musical, not fire-breathers. The serpent is six feet of carved walnut, or even sycamore, with a brass mouthpiece shaped like a, well, guess. You hold it crossways, a phenomenal boa constrictor on your lap, and play it with breath and finger-holes. First showed up in France about 1590. A lovely sound. They are unbelievably rare. Prammie Joe's two antique serpents – just one would have left the Arcade thunderstruck – were both true as a bell, about 1635. I actually played one, to round off my feeling. Everybody was asking where the hell an old swamp tromper like Joe found them, for heaven's sake. None of us found out. You never do, with blokes like Prammie. One-offs.

No hope of the taxi fare from the railway station, so I set off along the by-pass thumbing a lift. I got one after trudging three miles, a schoolteacher rabbiting about educational precepts. I went 'Mmmmh' and similar until we reached the river. He was pleased to meet an antique dealer, and gave me his address to call and see a genuine ancient coffee pot with a perforated spout. 'Maybe it's an early teapot,' he said brightly. 'Know what I mean?' I did, and thanked him most sincerely.

'Look,' I told him as I alighted. 'I'm on reconnaissance. Christie's of London. Keep it under your hat.'

'Right!' he exclaimed. 'That why you're dressed shoddy?'

'Er, yes.' You can go off people pretty quick. 'I'll send one of my deputies along.'

'Splendid!' He drove off beaming.

A carter's wagon gave me a lift at 2 mph down towards Prammie's marshy abode. It was getting on for four o'clock when I plodded through the hedgerows. Prammie was at the water's edge with his pram. Not pram as in perambulator, that vehicle you shove babies about in. Pram as in short, blunt-prowed dinghy, propelled by a single stern oar. Shallow of draught, it floats joyously on any piddling stream, unseen and silent. Hence my reason for thinking of him and Cornish Place.

'Wotcher, Prammie. I covered my tracks at the hedge.'

He crouches like an Aussie, one leg thrust out before. You wonder how his arms reach. He was mending his lever. Lying supine, he can scull the pram forward. He sighed. I was narked. I'd suffered a lot of sighs.

'Thought you'd be along, Lovejoy.'

'Don't you sigh at me, Prammie. I could've shopped you.'

'Drinkwater have you, did he?' He has one of those moustaches that fluff in and out with each snuffle. It looks borrowed off a dog. What with him and Drinkwater, I'd had enough chuckles, too. 'Burk, he is.'

Confidence makes me uneasy. It never lasts. Like good health, it's on a loser.

'Take care, Prammie. He's a nutter.' A nutter is a bobby of singularly malevolent disposition. No rarity, but functions unimpeded by law, justice, similar myths.

'Bad as those security blokes.' He almost tumbled into the river with merriment. 'Know what? They *wired* that cornfield!'

Well, some things do make you laugh. I'm no countryman, but you've only to glance at a field of standing grain to see the tracks of every newt that wended through.

'Searchlights for hang-gliders, eh?' We fell about.

Sobering, I reverently asked how long the robbery had taken. You have to admire class.

'Every night bar Sundays, eleven weeks, Lovejoy.' He doesn't work on the Sabbath. He's churchwarden at St Michael's. His old eyes misted over. 'Know what, son? I'm really proud. My swansong.' He rolled and lit a cigarette. Strikes the match on his thumbnail. I wish I could do that. I once tried but burnt my thumb.

'Anybody would be, Prammie.' Praise where it's due.

'Had two rafts. Towed them. There are spin-offs. I saved a little lad in the—' He paused, chuckled, having nearly given a location away. He pointed down to the shallow creak. 'Lucky I went at Cornish Place from downstream, eh?'

Well, that really set us rolling. We finished up in his hut with a drink, wiping our eyes. You need only watch a great mansion in a river moat in the middle of a plain from upstream. One watcher there, the place is impregnable.

'Marry that lassie yet, Lovejoy?'

That set me thinking. I remembered. 'Well, no, Prammie. I would have, but . . .' I couldn't even recall her name. Blonde? Or not? Harriet Something was it, strong opinions on celery juice and pollution? 'Er, Harriet moved away.'

'Pity.' He sobered, eyeing me. 'A nice girl, Lovejoy. I don't think you played fair.'

The reason I'm the only dealer in the Eastern Hundreds who'd know that Prammie Joe did Cornish Place was that I'm the only one ever seen him in action. And that was pure accident.

Harriet – if I've got her name right – was a carnivore from Wapping. On a sweep for some Antiques Road Show. (A sweep is scavenging ahead of the main shoal of predatory televisioneers.) She fell on me, lit. and met. Knew nothing about antiques. I had to stop the lads selling her collections of pre-1842 trademarks and French Revolution photographs. She and I were making heavy-duty smiles on the banks of the Deben, when a gentle rhythmic shushing disturbed the rural peace. I thought it was Harriet, until somebody ahemed in my earhole. And there was Prammie Joe, in his modified boat. His bare foot worked steadily at his stern-mounted oar. He lay on his back, holding the gun'ls.

That would have been a quick embarrassed adjustment of clothing, and the usual sheepish conversation until he'd gone by. But in the prow of his pram stood a Martinware jug. I'd seen the same one sold seven days before at Southwold. Martinware is grotesque – salt-glazed stoneware, mottled as hell, so grey and muted you wonder why the Martin brothers bothered. Anyway, they're no earlier than 1873. The Martins packed up in 1914. The jugs often feature hideously contorted faces, or supposedly comical fishes and ducks. Horrible.

'Mister Martin, I presume,' I managed, as Harriet squealed and we rolled apart. I thought that pretty witty in the circumstances, on the Deben, in flagrante delicto.

Prammie had paused, peering sideways at us. He nodded, sussed fair and square. Simply mentioned a tavern near Woodbridge, saying he'd be there about eight. We all three then resumed our activities, some more carefree than others. I christened him my secret nickname Prammie that very evening.

'You could have been anybody, Lovejoy,' he told me inside his hut. 'A godsend it was only you.'

That 'only you' stung. He could have met a blackmailer, is what he meant. He's got a sense of fair play which should tell you straight off he's no antique dealer.

'I feel it too, Prammie,' I said most sincerely. Harriet had mauled me bog-eyed. I was almost at death's dark door when she had to move on. She wrote to me hourly for five months, made sudden unnerving visits. My guardian angel made sure I saw her Ferrari coming. 'I was heart-broken, Prammie. Truly. Her mother's an MP. Well, my face didn't fit.' I sniffed, quite overcome by cruel fate and Harriet's snooty bitch of a mother who came between us. In the nick of time I remembered I was making this up for Prammie's benefit.

Prammie murmured, 'Never mind, son. Time the great healer.'

Sometimes you have to stare. I mean, this old goat'd just pulled off a robbery anybody would be proud of, and deep down he's a sentimental softie.

'Er, ta, Prammie.' Kind, though. 'Got any tom handy?' I was dying to see the stolen stuff.

'Nar, Lovejoy.' His rheumy eyes were shining. He's a tee-totaller, non-wencher. 'Know why I risked it, son? My plan. You know I breed?'

Breed? I didn't even know he had children. I was just about to say, when I looked out through the window.

His cabin is an old reed-cutter's hut. Low down among reeds and bullrushes. You haven't a hope of seeing it unless you know it's there. He has a way through the hedgerows. He uses the waterways for getting anywhere. For proper journeys, he uses a proper dinghy. His night-stealing's all done on his pram. He keeps it buried in the reeds. Even anglers don't come down this marshy stretch, and they're daft enough to go anywhere there's a tiddler. Breed. He had mentioned waterbirds a few times with passion.

'Ducks and them?'

He smiled. 'That's Lovejoy,' he said. 'Yes, ducks and them. Migratories, transients, indigens. I foster and propa-gate them all.'

'Well, Prammie,' I said, rising quickly. 'Nice seeing you—' Passion for antiques and women, inevitable. But passion for pigeons? 'Time I was off.'

'Stay, son. Tea's ready.' He poured out of an old tin teapot. He explained, 'Notice how I brewed up?'

Almost worth another sigh. 'Kettle,' I observed shrewdly. Living on your own sends you bats.

'How?' He was amused. 'Coal fire? Logs? Primus stove? Paraffin? Gas?'

'You plugged it in, Prammie.' Humour a loony, I always say.

'Electricity, Lovejoy. Pinched from the mains.' He chuckled with flaps of his doggie moustache. 'No smoke, see? No National Insurance card. No tax. No post. No family, save my birds. I'm not even here!'

'I know you're here, Prammie.'

'Ah, but you're as barmy as me, Lovejoy. If you hadn't been . . . admiring Harriet that day, you'd not know either.'

'You got gaoled, Prammie.'

'Bad luck, Lovejoy.' He was tranquil. He makes good tea, for all his rustic isolation. 'Taken for wrongful possession, a Daniel Quare clock. Caught in football traffic. Two bobbies helped me across the road. Saw the label, next day's auction at Gimbert's. I'd no fixed abode . . .'

'Rotten luck.' My heart bled for him. Remove the label, you lower an item's value to any decent fair-minded receiver of stolen goods. 'Still, if it was Daniel Quare, it might well have been a fake, eh? Look on the bright side.' The other favourite clockmaker for fakers is Breguet of Paris. It's joked that clockies – fakers of anything that tells time – can sign Quare's and Breguet's names better than they can their own.

'No, Lovejoy.' He was serious. 'The Lord's work. He moves in mysterious ways. It was in gaol I met the scammer.'

I saw light. He'd met a blackguard. 'On commission?'

'Flat fee, son.' He spoke with eyes glowing, doubtless seeing a million migratories, or whatever, laying eggs and nuzzling mud. A really great vision. 'I'll have enough to buy this stretch. Can't you see it? A sanctuary!'

'Lovely, Prammie.' I ahemed. 'Can I, er, help?'

He shook his head, still friendly. 'Lovejoy. I took every fireplace, every Speer and pelmet, with my own hands. I *know* every item is genuine. I hand the last over Monday.'

'Sure? Be careful, eh?'

His smile was beatific. '*You* are telling *me*, Lovejoy? It was me caught you in the very act of—'

'Yes, well.' I stood with finality. 'No harm asking.'

He saw me away from his hut. At the hedge I turned to look back. Only eighty feet away, you couldn't see a damned thing. A few cows grazed, providing yet more cover. It was true. He was the careful one all right.

And that, said Alice, was that. Goodnight, Prammie.

Chapter 3

That afternoon was murderous. Not death. Money. Some people spend, spend, spend and gain nowt. Like Big Frank's joke: 'If I won a trillion on the sweepstake, I'd just carry on being an antique dealer until it was all gone.'

Think of the price of stamps and melons. I was having a blazing row about a melon. Savvy Savvy's a supermarket. Their only superlatives are their blinking prices.

I'd reached the till girl after only ten years of battling through hordes. 'Four quid? For one measly melon? You're off your frigging nut!'

'That's the price, Lovejoy.' The girl was heated. People behind were murmuring angry agreement. 'It's marked.'

'It's still not fair, you silly cow!'

'Our melons are not measly!' The manageress, steaming up with more falsehoods. 'Lovejoy. You're barred from shopping here,' this boss hood thundered. 'Savvy Savvy's for respectable shoppers. Get security, Nelly!'

'Barefaced robbery!' I'd only come in for some cheese and tomatoes. They don't do pasties. I get those from Barm In The Barn near the railway, Tuesdays. 'Don't come to me when you go broke. Thieving cow.'

The town was crowded, mostly with people delightedly grinning through Savvy Savvy's windows at the chiselling within. I dumped their grotty cheese and tomatoes, yelled, 'They used to be four shillings, proper money.' Pre-decimal prices always get to them.

'He's right!' an old crone cheeped. 'I can remember . . .'

The babble of reminiscence rose to a hubbub, which let me out unscathed. No, though. It makes my blood boil. These posh shops'll have us in our graves. Cost-efficiency tactics never work, do they? Prices'd go down if they did. I headed down East Hill to Sandy's Dutch Treaty, fuming. Same with antiques. Look at stamps. I pick stamps because they're utterly boring. Yet they're the classic example of antiques holocaust. A lesson to all antique grabbers, like you and me.

Lately, there'd come a mighty flood of philately. It was worrying me sick. In fact, this was the reason I'd gone to the arcade, to suss it out. Somebody said Sandy – more about him in a minute – was offering a whole stamp collection portfolio. In this day and age! Can you believe it? A caution: avoid stamps.

Back in the fabled Good Old Days, when singers sang the words and gold was simply colour at Christmas, bureaux used to bring out catalogues listing prices of British Colonials and Persian Commemoratives and whatnot. That set the scene for ever and a day – or at least until the next catalogue. Then things changed. Inflation (remember that old thing?) happened. Currencies wobbled. Oil did, or didn't, do something vital. Stock markets seethed. One fateful dark day in 1980, London awoke jubilantly to the Stamp World Exhibition. To find the floor had vanished. Nobody wanted stamps.

Prices fell like a stone. Stamp empires were engulfed. Down through the widening cracks plummeted dealers, traders, speculators' portfolios. Amsterdam to Tel Aviv, Geneva to New York, the philately world went crunch. This is my point: if you want to speculate, fine. Anything you like – gold, stocks, shares, land – and good luck. But speculate in antiques? Stick, please, to those *where collectors provide a permanent floor to market prices*. Better still, don't speculate at all. Be a pure collector, you can have the top brick off the chimney.

The Great Stamp Catastrophe of 1980 was odd. All portents were favourable. Times were mindbendingly boomy. Wasn't the 6 May the 140th anniversary of the first Penny Black? Wasn't the Cold War dissolving? Everybody was over the moon, joyous with profits.

You see, nobody bought.

Dealers wept, gnashed, pleaded. But the only sound was the popping of speculators' bubbles, the splashing of tears.

Since that date, there are two markets in old stamps. One's the top market, where unique stamps still bring buyers for the yawnsome little things. Here sells the 1849 vermilion tête bêche for a fortune, and the American 1918 24-cent airmail with an upside-down middle. The other market is down here, you and me. Forget dealers, portfolio managers, that lot. Think only of Joe Soap next door. How often does he come home rich and rejoicing? He's your market.

See? Not boring at all. I wish it were. It's something far worse. It's really rather scary. Because there's a terrible hidden question here: What *exactly* turned the floor into Scotch mist in sunny old 1980? Answer: *Nobody knows.* Which is when fright creeps night-stealing into the soul. It crouches, chewing its nails and blubbering every time the door goes. Antique dealers want straight upward graphs, not ones that nuzzle the lino.

If I knew all this, what was my problem as I fumed down East Hill? The sudden influx of old stamps. Like swallows at midwinter, they just don't, aren't, can't. But they'd come to town, via Sandy. And he truly is your rare bird.

*   *   *

Sandy was alone. This was the other meganews of the century. He was determinedly showing he Didn't Care by setting up shop near the Ship tavern. He'd rowed with Mel – cerulean taffeta for a wall hanging – and ended the only permanent partnership our local antiques scene has. Had.

The door blared 'YMCA'. I blocked my ears.

'Wait, too lay mond!' a voice trilled. 'Coming!'

East Hill's a trailing string of small dumps. Never been any different since the Emperor Claudius slithered cursing down it on his decorated war elephant, the Roman legions grinning him a safe journey home. For a king's ransom in rent you get a square room, and a curtained back the size of a confessional.

The curtain slowly opened. A recording blared 'The Arrival of the Queen of Sheba'. Sandy emerged. I watched, irritated. It's gormless. He wore a sequinned bolero, a caftan, scarlet Cossack trousers. His T-strap ribbon-trimmed high heels were French, 1920s. His turban was beige velvet decorated with Mameluke points and pearls. He spun, eyelids fluttering. His cosmetics could have filled a pint pot. Ridiculous.

'The music, Sandy,' I bellowed, suddenly embarrassed because it silenced in the middle of my yell.

'You adore, Lovejoy? Worship, positively drool?'

My tongue almost spoke the truth. Then I remembered. I wanted his help. I managed a feeble smile.

'Magenta?' I said. Doubting colours works with women. By extension . . .

He leapt to the half-cheval mirror, advertised as a genuine Sheraton and priced for any passing tycoons.

'Scarlet! You dare *doubt*, Lovejoy?'

'No. Honest. Maybe it's the light.'

These vague things are what you've to say when you've

not a clue. It saves you knowing what they're on about. Sandy's inspection satisfied him. He perched on a high stool, eyes twinkling maliciously.

'Face it, Lovejoy. You're not Beau Brummel, are you, dear?'

You have to hand it to Sandy. His sense of decor is superb. The grotty shop was tasteful. Style comes with wit and elegance. Him and Mel could make an alcove in a garret into a cathedral, just by panels, mirrors, lights, textures. Sandy had a small bar counter, spirits, wines.

'In spite of all, you may deliver your message, Lovejoy.' He gushed coyly, fingers glittering striped plum and madder nail varnish.

'Don't *tease*, Lovejoy!' He actually blushed. I thought, Oh, Christ. 'Mel's sent you, hasn't he? To apologise?'

He lit a cigarette in a rotating ivory fag-holder. It chimed 'What Shall We Do with a Drunken Sailor?'

'Don't make excuses for him, Lovejoy. I *know* he's headstrong. He *begged* you to make the peace. Poor lamb.' His lip quivered as he struggled not to cry. 'Give him this letter. Tell him it *won't* be easy. Not after what he said about my carpet.' He glared, spitting spite. 'I mean, you've only to *see* what he *did!* Chandeliers like Woolworth earrings . . .'

'Sandy.' I felt stricken. This was serious stuff. I'd never known them part before, though they're always swearing lifelong malice. 'I've not seen Mel.'

He paled. He gathered himself and swept grandly into the back room. The curtain closed. Then he wept, sobs so total they almost shook the walls.

'Sorry,' I called after a bit. I honestly was sorry for him. I mean, where love flourishes and all that. But I hadn't got time for all this. Gunge Herod's speciality is household pre-Victoriana. Was he in with Prammie Joe? Today wasn't one of Connie's usual days at the Arcade. That papal ring business felt a put-up job. By Connie? She alone offered to do a dropper. And she'd seemed unnaturally tense. Or was it my imagination?

'Er, I'll come another time, Sandy.' I was leaving gingerly, when the curtain swished aside and Sandy stood there dramatically attired in a black sheath dress, beret with a diamond clasp.

He swished out, sat smouldering on a cockfighting chair.

'Ay shell neffer foor geef 'eem, Loofjoy.' He snapped out of it instantly, doing his eye-shadow with stuff from his handbag, and said, 'Right. Who was I?'

'Ginger Rogers? Betty Grable?'

'Marlene Dietrich, buffoon! Don't you know *anything*?'

'Mind your fag ash. That reading chair's Sheraton.'

'It is?' He was suddenly all dealer. I never know when he's being Sandy or not himself, if you follow.

'It's a reading chair, Sandy. See how narrow the back is? You sit astride it, facing backwards.' The rear ledge sticks out for a book. 'The mistaken name, cockfighting chair, comes from engravings of blokes watching cockfight mains seated in them.'

'Anything else, Lovejoy?'

'Your half-cheval's dud.'

'*Bitch!*' He examined it. 'It's eighteenth century!'

'It's last month, Sandy.' Giving bad news always wears me out. 'Free with some crummy magazine, I shouldn't wonder.'

A cheval ('horse') glass is so-called because of its 'horse' pulley for swivelling the mirror to different angles. The plate-glass revolution brought in the 'full' cheval, instead of the mirror in halves. This faker had used chunks of genuine old mirrors, a common trick.

'Spiteful beast! You're saying that to buy it cheap!'

Enough. I opened the door. 'See you, Sandy.'

'Please, Lovejoy.' He looked stricken. I didn't go back. It might be another mercurial mood switch. 'I'll behave. What?'

'Those stamps. You tried touting them ten days ago.'

'Flat fee, Lovejoy.' He simpered. 'My friend had a dreadful terrible time in gaol, poor dear.'

Flat fee? My slow neurones clunked into gear. Another ex-gaolbird? Nobody likes selling antiques for a flat fee. Like, fifty quid if you sell this antique turk's head hourglass. You lose money, if it goes for a thousand.

'Did they sell?' They couldn't have.

'No. Parcelled them into job lots, Wittwoode's next auction. Best I could do, dear.' He tittered. 'He'll be furioso!'

So would anybody. Sending antiques to auction is an admission of failure. So why do it? Because somebody was desperate, that's why. Somebody who'd come out of nick after a number of years.

'Didn't you warn him?'

'It was all he had.' Sandy shrugged, admiring his reflection. 'Got this horrid dollop broker to store his stamp cache until he was released. Lovejoy, do you think I should go platinum blond? Mel would *rage!*'

That adjective meant the dollop broker was a woman. Sandy's vernacular. Also Sandy's ex-convict pal was desperate for money.

Time to scarper. I risked one last dig. 'Wish Mel's friend good luck with his Penny Blacks.'

'Mel's friend?' Sandy cooed after me. 'With *his* colouring?'

So Mel also knew who it was. My mind was working out: this old lag emerged from a stretch of long porridge. He wanted money. So he unearthed his portfolio of stamps – they must have seemed a cast-iron investment, way back when. He gives them to Sandy to sell. Sandy can't, because the floor's vanished. Sandy sends them to Wittwoode's, for costly auction. Flat fee, too. The cheap way. Any dealer on earth would hang on for the market to recover.

And, surprise surprise! Monday the massive haul of household goods from Prammie Joe's turkey job *had* to be handed over. Joe said so. And Connie wanted me to divvie a load of heavy antiques without delay. A pattern? With the conviction of the unlearned, I went to meet The Great Marvella and her talking snake. I like her. Not sure about the snake.

Chapter 4

There's a joke: antiques is the hobby God would have, if only He had the money. Like all cracks, there's a grain of truth. Antiques is a bottomless well. This parable proves it:

A bird bought a small hotel hereabouts. She made a go of it, started discos, bingo, resident band. Then bought a garage, import concessions for foreign motors, flashy dress shops. A ball of fire. The town hadn't seen anything like Gervetta. Then she got antiques, like people get beri-beri. A deficiency disease.

In her case, she wanted paintings. I mean hungered, craved, would do anything for. Now, paintings are the one antique everybody *knows*. We look and go 'Yuck!' or 'Yes!' We may not react the same, but we do it. Gervetta looked, waved her bulging chequebook. Paintings flowed in. The trouble is that liking is light years away from being able to *recognise* that Rembrandt, that priceless Turner or Monet. Paintings are the frightening game of Spot the Dud.

Gervetta knew she *knew* she knew paintings. She didn't.

She started on scenic English watercolours, pre-1851. This expansive market is one where, dealers sadly remark, a collector can't go wrong. Oh, fakes abound: David

Cox, Samuel Palmer, Turner, John Constable even, the Rowbothams. But usually a competent friend can more or less guarantee good odds of authenticity. So, dearly beloved, Gervetta drained the countryside. Dealers scavenged for watercolours like maniacs. Then on a whim she changed – old Irish and English drinking glasses. She'd have been wiser to choose American blown-three-mould glassware, which is classy, identifiable, and plentiful. And not much faked – yet.

Our fakers had a riot. They sold her recycled glasses barely cool from the furnace. In sets of six, would you believe. They sold her Jacobite drinking glasses so rare nobody had ever seen their like – meaning, the faker had got it wrong but was reluctant to chuck the damned thing away. Then by mistake Gervetta came to me. I'd heard of her. Who hadn't? She wanted to sell her precious antiques.

'You understand, Lovejoy,' she explained after introducing herself in my workshop, a tumbledown ex-garage in the overgrown garden. 'It's tax write-offs.' She smiled winningly. 'The Inland Revenue's caught up, and wants a cut.'

'Why me, lady?'

'You're the only dealer in the Eastern Hundreds who hasn't sold to me,' she said frankly.

Aye, well. I'd been away overseas. Still had the scars. Anyhow, crooks don't trespass. We – I mean, *they* – daren't.

She watched me work. I was repairing a worm-eaten Charles II cane-bottomed day bed. For all the world a low chair with the seat inordinately stretched. They're unbelievably rare. This lovely piece was 'relic', too far gone to be anything but firewood. All six worm-holed scroll legs were shredding sponge.

I use that thin plasticky stuff shops use for packing porcelain. Here's how wormy furniture's restored: make a cup of this, and fix it beneath the moth-eaten wooden leg with elastic bands. Pour in a thick cream of rabbit-skin size, chalk, and plasterer's whiting, with a drop of formaldehyde to kill the woodworm. Let it set a couple of days. Harden it off three or four days.

The leg I was working on was the fourth. I test the stuff with a pin. Hard as stone. Then you can file it, like real wood. I include a few artificial cracks, of course, filling them with stained beeswax. This trick is unnecessary, but legally allows you to advertise the furniture as 'restored'. The buyer then has no legal claim on you.

'You're good, Lovejoy.'

'You're beautiful, love. But your antique glass isn't.'

She stared. 'How do you know it's glass?'

'You lifted the box out of your motor like, well, glass. And I'm the only real antique dealer on earth.'

It was all beyond her. 'But you haven't seen it unpacked.'

'Don't bother. It's fake.'

Naturally, being a bird, Gervetta was all doubt. I had to show her the simple glass trick. Put a fake antique glass down. Stand a brand-new glass, bought today, next to it. Shine an intense light at both, equal illumination. Look at the rims. The new glass rim seems whitish. So will a fake. The antique glass shows lovely greyish crescents.

'Yours, love, are white. See?' She also had some Stuart crystal, ho ho ho, engraving white as snow, edges sharp. 'Born yesterday.'

'Me? Like the glass?'

She took it well, give her that. But women are fifty times more practical. She wouldn't believe that all her 'antiques' were duff. She asked me to come and check. I said no.

'Why not?' She was outraged. 'I have to know, stupid!'

'Can't you see, you silly bitch?'

We were in the cottage. Her Rolls Royce besmirched the garden. Inside, bare flagged floor, no furniture, no fire, no light, bare windows. She looked, the bewilderment of wealth.

'You said your Carolean bed was highly valuable, Lovejoy.'

'It's somebody else's, missus. Now clear off. I've done you an expensive favour. Free. Now let me earn my next three meals.'

That was when she hired me, and learned the ghastly truth about her collections. Her real heartbreak was an antique David Wolff glass. He was a Dutch bloke, whose stipple-engraved glasses are famous. He worked on English drinking glasses shipped to Holland, his tiny dots so fine you need a lens. This fake (*white* dots is a give-away) even had an English shilling of 1782 in the glass as 'proof'. It's the oldest trick in the book.

Me hired meant we moved on to other kinds of linkage. The dealers wouldn't speak to me for ending their spree. Women dealers were doubly scathing. Females don't like other birds. Dunno why.

Gervetta and me were friends for almost a fortnight. She suddenly sold up and went to live in Charlottesville, USA, among the ineffably rich. She left me a fake Ch'ien Lung tea-dust glaze bowl, having paid a fortune for it. The five phony certificates – British Museum, Sotheby's – were still stuck on. You didn't need to check the absence of that curious green hint to the dark brown glaze, or peer through a surface microscope to see the unnatural smoothness. It *felt* dud. Poor – poorer – Gervetta .

The lesson? Bottomless wells take any amount of gelt and echo for more. Parable ends.

So I went to see Jeff. They call him a different nickname, but he's Dalgleish. Geordie, from the Tyne. He lives with Eleanor, blind and bonny since birth.

* * *

The bus got me down the estuary in time for dark. Jeff teaches tense people relaxation. Antique dealers always do a spare-time catchpenny. Jeff's was the easiest I've ever heard of. 'Sit down, lady. Nod off. Next.'

'Wotcher, Jeff. I warn you I want a lift to the Bricklayers Arms in a few minutes.'

'Come in, Lovejoy.' He called my arrival ahead. They live in a cottage. He's levelled off every floor so there are no ledges, no sudden steps. The lights are always apologetically dimmed, in self-rebuke for Eleanor's misfortune. 'Glad to see you.'

Jeff has the lowered gaze of the blind minder, forever checking protrusions. They never lose it. Eleanor on the other hand has the strange merriment of the afflicted, her laugh straight poetry. She's lovely, vivacious. Makes me wonder what the rest of us have done. She immediately was up to buss me, hurrying to make tea. I always dawdle at Jeff's, never move anything. I'm clumsy enough.

'Jeff. You sent a ring through Gunge Herod?'

'Yes.' He looked too hopeful. I sighed inside.

'Take a hint?' He hesitated. I'd been right to come. He had it bad, lured by some big scam. 'Yes or no, Jeff?'

'Anything wrong, Lovejoy?' He glanced to the kitchen door.

'I think so. Suspect.' I corrected.

'I own the ring, Lovejoy.' A guarded little speech.

'Jeff. Before Eleanor comes back.' We both spoke softly. 'My guess is, you've been asked to put some money in a scam. Big. Cast iron. The money's needed fast, tomorrow. Am I right?' Silence. 'Cut out, Jeff.'

He licked his lips. He doesn't have much savvy. I should talk. He's the one with the gorgeous bird.

'You don't understand, Lovejoy.' He indicated Eleanor's

trilling. 'I'm her mainstay. I'll need help as we grow older. A nest-egg's vital.'

'What if the nest-egg's a myth, Jeff? You in clink?'

He searched my face. I've seen that look a million times, the ineffable hope of the wistful buyer.

'You two conspirators done?' Eleanor came swishing in, carrying a tray. I think she hears everything, and pretends not to.

'Yes, Ellie.' Jeff smiled, as if she could see him. Did she feel smiles? 'Lovejoy's come to warn us. No unwise investments.'

I felt rather than saw her hesitation, speaking of feelings. She said evenly, 'Thank you, Lovejoy.'

And the chat turned from antiques to innocence, which is never worth reporting. Over and out.

The Great Marvella and her talking snake is (you'll see why the singular in a sec) an institution. We've had our wizards, sure. But TGM and HTS hit us like a typhoon. Nobody quite believed her, until they actually clapped eyes on. Then, worryingly, some people did. And she was made.

Jeff dropped me at the door, by St Botolph's Priory, one of the ruins that Cromwell knocked about a bit. I could see torchlights among the gravestones – a local amateur drama rehearsing towards catastrophe. I bumped into Acker Kirwin. He's an affluent buyer from Nine Arches, village of specialists in tax evasion. He carried something that pulled my bellrope. My chest went boiing.

'Acker!' I cried, shoving him into the lamplight to see. 'Great to see you! Musical box? Nicole Frères?'

'Shhh, Lovejoy, you burk!' Acker's the only dealer who always sounds furtive. He wore an alpaca overcoat, lined by camel velvet. Done up like a dog's dinner. Women say he's a handsome devil, with his Errol Flynn tash. To add insult to injury, he deals money in your hand. I don't like him. He has connections among the grim, same as others.

'Is it mint?' A musical box in mint condition's worth four times the amount you'd get if it has a tooth missing from its comb – the metal bit that plucks the tune from prongs on the revolving drum.

This box was just over two feet long, the right size. Get one with a fat cylinder, with the names of classical pieces on the lid's escutcheon, and you've found a genuine long-playing 'overture' box. Top value. They are wound by a simple key.

'Yours for a year's wages, Lovejoy.'

'Eh?' I gasped at the price. We talk in fractions of the nation's average annual wage – monetary values being the shifting sands they are. I mean, King William III – of William and Mary fame – bought all Kensington Palace for 14,000 quid. See what I mean? 'That's robbery!'

Acker sniggered. 'You know it's a steal, Lovejoy.' Acker means a.k.a. – 'also known as'. He uses aliases.

If he wasn't going to sell me the Nicole Frères box for a song I'd annoy him back.

'Marvella in? Had a chat with her snake?'

'Not seen her, Lovejoy,' Acker said, and strolled off.

Odd. The only doorway with a light on was The Great Marvella's. I'd seen him emerge from it. I'd never heard so many lies in one day before. A record even for the antiques game.

A buzz on the door's voice box got an aloof, 'Who?'

'Never mind who's out here, Vell,' I rasped back. 'Who've you got in there?'

The grille laughed fit to burst. 'Geronimo's caged, Lovejoy. Promise.'

'Okay,' I said, peeved. All very well for the silly cow to laugh, but a snake's a snake. 'Good evening, Marvella,' I began again, politely. 'It's Lovejoy. May I come in?'

Chapter 5

Stairs are the most boring structures on earth. You can't do a thing except go up or down. Sometimes what's at the top is less than pleasant. I mean Geronimo, not The Great Marvella.

Her upstairs flat is over a florist's, facing the chip shop (Fantle's chippie. Not bad, but it's gone curry-with-pasta and other uncontrollables. Plastic spoons are the end of civilization). It was still open. I'd no money. The aroma wafted in after me and clung. A pause is always wise at a top step.

'Hello?' I knocked. I'm pathetic, but snakes are definitely not my scene. Although I remember an auction duel over a stuffed cobra that brought the house down.

'Come in. Coward.'

Her voice is unnaturally whispery, a come-on, maybe past trauma. You don't ask.

Slo-o-owly I entered. There she was, sixty inches of female, flowing dark hair, dressed only in a man's buttonless jacket. That's only. Not even shoes. She was reading elegantly on a sofa. She pointed to the table.

Geronimo's cage, Geronimo coiled inside. I sweated relief.

'Look, Vell. Can't you put him away?'

She raised her eyebrows. 'What *are* you suggesting?'

Cages look secure. But snakes can wriggle, can't they? And climb. Ugh.

'Don't muck about. Lock him away, Vell.'

She asked, 'What d'you think, Geronimo?'

The snake replied, 'If he'll come in with me, Marvella.'

'Geronimo agrees, Lovejoy. On one condition—'

'I heard, I heard.' It's only Vell's voice-throwing act. She says she was on the professional stage, really quite famous. We don't believe her. Ventriloquists aren't, are they? I mean, you can always see their lips move. They're embarrassing. The audience all want the act to end.

'Going to stand there all evening, Lovejoy?'

There's nowhere to sit. A straight chair, opposite her couch. Perching on the table was definitely out. She has a bedroom and a kitchen, sumptuous by comparison. But this was her intro room for clients. She tells paranormal fortunes in her inner sanctum, the Marvella Revivification Clinic. She revivifies by massage and asking Geronimo what next, and other symbolically penetrating questions. Unbelievably, people actually pay money. They bring real problems – about Auntie's cancer, should the daughter get the cottage, is he sincere, the wide world's moans. The snake diagnoses. Vell interprets, to satisfying massage.

Many antique dealers, Connie among them, have regular appointments. My reason for risking Geronimo.

'No, Vell. I'm just going.' I shuffled uncomfortably. She was all but naked, the big jacket hopelessly inadequate. 'Heard of any big antique scam, love?'

'My clients' disclosures are confidential, Lovejoy.'

That old one. Everybody – insurance companies, charities, governments – claims your secrets are 'confidential'. They mean they stick your precious secrets into files clerks read for a laugh when the office is slack.

'Did Acker Kirwin say owt?'

Puzzlement on her brow. Quite good acting. Maybe she had been on the stage after all.

'Come to bed and I'll tell you, Lovejoy.'

'Er, ta, Vell. But I'm . . .'

'Running for a train?' Getting mad. Not my fault. I'm the one should be narked, not her.

It was from a time she and I nearly made smiles. We'd met at an auction. I'd actually sold her a lovely circular supper Canterbury, 1810, beautiful mahogany though not Sheraton. I'd mended the railing round the top myself. Four legs, and very rare, with two drawers in the railed drum layer between the legs. Castors original. She'd got in my way when I carried it into Wittwoode's. I got narked. She made slighting remarks back. She and I swiftly became polarised as well as passionate – until I knocked over a cage on her bed table, reached down to pick it up. And found myself staring into the stony eyes of Geronimo while his tongue flicked in and out. I was off like a cork from a bottle. I'd babbled, hurtling out of the bedroom door, that I was running for a train. Vell's hated me ever since.

'Sorry, Vell.' I backed out, eyes on Geronimo.

'Don't be stupid, Lovejoy.' She rose, her bottom dragging my eyes. She strolled indolently to a wall hutch – modern crud, veneered chipboard – and poured some wine. 'I thought it was only me scared you.'

'I'm not scared.' I declined the wine. 'Got anything to eat? Snake and onions?'

'Cut that out, Lovejoy,' the snake said. Vell's throat moved, her lips stiff. I wish she wouldn't do it.

'The chippie's open,' Vell said. 'Nip out and get some. We can chat.'

'No, I won't bother.'

Her eyes shrewded up. 'Broke, Lovejoy?'

Women nark me. Nothing but criticism. Like when you're ill. It's a real excuse for them to go to town bullying you back to health.

'No, I'm not.' Her accusation stung.

'No,' she agreed quickly. 'I *know* you're not *broke*. I meant you'd forgotten your wallet. Look.' She brightened. 'I've not had anything yet. I'm peckish. Would you slip over to Fantle's? Fish and chips twice.'

I shot out with her gelt. This was lucky. If she hadn't been starving . . . I ran across the rain-glistening black road, and wolfed two lots of chips, brown sauce, before returning sedately with a scalding hot newspaper parcel for us both. Geronimo watched as I dined regally from the fat-soaked paper. Vell luckily had lost her appetite, so I had hers as well. Anyway, women never eat much.

Vell watched me nosh with that patient detachment women bring to observe appetites. She was kneeling revealingly.

'Geronimo has to go away, Lovejoy. For a day or two.'

I paused. This was worth thought. 'Got relatives?'

'His medical's due.' She was smiling. God, but women are cruel. I mean, it's basically unfair for a gorgeous bird undressed only in a jacket to sit near when you're full.

'I thought he looked peaky.'

'Nerve,' Geronimo said, through Vell's tight lips.

Even tight lips aren't fair in these circumstances. I mean, tight lips make you think of loosening them, and what with.

'That rich bitch Mrs Vervain left your scene, Lovejoy?'

'Who?' I never blab. It's the road to dusty death.

Vell nodded slowly, her smile returning. I screwed up the empty newspapers. Actually, this was another fluke. Because if Vell wouldn't disclose what Acker Kirwin was up to, maybe she would if I stayed a while? But I could only come, so to speak, when Geronimo wasn't here.

'When do you go?' Like a fool, I asked the snake.

It flicked its reptilian tongue, dead eyes swivelling my way. Said, 'Soon. What's on your mind?'

'Nothing,' I told it quickly, and smiled weakly at Vell, who smiled back and handed me the wine, which I took.

The rest of the evening was uneventful. I got nothing out of Vell about Acker or Connie, though I tried. I left, backing round the wall as if pinned in a searchlight, to keep clear of Geronimo. Vell waved bye bye, her breasts making me groan with lust as I hopped it. I'd promised to come next evening for supper. We'd be alone.

Outside in the cool drizzle, the shoe-black night sheened on the town like polish. I drew breath. A motor swished past, spraying my legs. Fantle's was shut. The florist's was lit by a single fluorescent strip. Farther down, the night was lit by an orange sky glow from the town's ring road.

The bus station's a couple of hundred yards, through a narrow gateway in the Roman wall. I went along the alley that passes the Priory ruins.

'Is that you, Lovejoy?'

'Martha?' I couldn't see a damned thing. They've cut street lights for efficiency, so we can all break our legs after dusk. 'How's the show?'

She's a pleasant lass. Acts with the St Hilda Players. A pleasant lot on the whole, though each'd kill to get the lead part. Summer performances in the ruins with floodlights. She has a boutique out in the villages, and a husband.

'Fine, thanks. We're doing *Titus Andronicus*.'

'Comedy? I'll come.'

She put her arm through mine. We walked along. 'Why

do you, Lovejoy? Pretend you're thick. I've seen you, creeping in.'

'I can't afford a ticket. Who can?'

'Our prices are cheap!' The actress's dictum: it's proper, charging people to admire me.

'You're rolling, love. I've heard about your new benefactress. Cassandra Clark, isn't it? You should make the plays free.'

And suddenly it fell into place. Acker hadn't been coming out of The Great Marvella's doorway. He'd been ducking *in*, hoping not to be seen, when Jeff's car had dropped me off. He hadn't come from the shuttered pawnshop, Fantle's chippie, the florist's. The only other place was the Priory ruins. And the rehearsal.

'Just because we've found somebody public-spirited in this God-forsaken town, Lovejoy! People are unwilling to pay to see a wonderful show. Yet they watch endless grot on telly—' Et yawnsome cetera.

'I agree, love,' I said.

Astonishment stopped her tirade. 'You do? I *knew* you approved of us, really.'

'Cassandra Clark there tonight, was she? Only, I saw Acker Kirwin take an antique . . .'

'Came briefly.' Martha's tones had the reverence actresses reserve for people who put up money. 'Cassandra's wonderful. She never interferes with the artistic side. A *true* philanthropist.'

We entered the bus station to the sound of heavenly violins, Martha waxing eloquent about philanthrophy and me thinking there's no such thing. Waiting for the last bus out to our respective villages, I got a rundown of those present at rehearsal, and the loan of the fare home. Martha didn't explain why a lovely rich lady would pour money into shamateur drama in an ancient ruined priory.

Bits were adding up. I wished Prammie Joe was on the phone, or that message bottles flowed from my river directly into his. But it was late. Countryside frightens me at the best of times, let alone when bats do fly and trees start watching you. So I didn't go to Prammie's marsh. Wrong again.

Chapter 6

The day dawned with brilliance. One of those that makes you understand why some folk actually like countryside. I've even heard some take country holidays. A white frost, hard as iron, the grass stiff with the spittle of a full moon, sky blue as childhood, air still. The birds were nodding the ground as usual. A squirrel fooling about, dashing along branches. I yawned at the window, perished with cold.

Telephones are counter-productive. Their absence is the same. I considered this philosophy while cooking my breakfast. The swine had cut me off, non-payment of debts to robbers. The gas and electricity were temporarily off – a disagreement about fiscal policy with energy barons. I used my home-made stove. A tin bowl half-filled with sand. Put in a little oil or petrol, drop in a match. It woomphs into flame. Perch on it your pan containing margarine, sliced tomatoes, bread, and dine like a king.

The trick's dangerous, so I do it between two bricks in the garden – a wilderness of fecund greenery engulfing my cottage. The birds stay away.

I washed – standing at the sink, on a towel to protect the valuable Wilton carpet (joke), towelled myself dry, gasping at the cold. Cold permeates like nothing else. Odd, that. Warmth doesn't, so why should cold? The bare flags set me shivering. My underpants were dry, thank God. Socks were barely damp, though frigid with that cunning old cold. I was down to my last tea bag. An apple – plenty of those – and I was off to my daily slog singing that Tallis *Sanctus* everybody else gets wrong.

My garage is deep in the foliage near my back door. It functions without any modern aid – the only way to fake antiques. The greatest workshop of the western world, sez I.

It was a relief, getting back to real life. Joan Vervain had taken it out of me. Drinkwater was worrying, though the Cornish Place robbery was more recycling than theft. I mean, our local councillors don't *own* the buildings, do they? They only look after them for us people. If they can't be bothered, they must take the consequences.

This train of thought narked me, as I set up the lathe. I'd make an issue out of it next local election, and vote against everybody.

My lathe's a dentist's old treadle drill. I use a Singer strap, gears from a machine spindle. I've given up sitting on a stool when turning wood. You have to move about. I was repairing/restoring/faking a small tripod table. Not the most profitable antique, because small genuine antique tables are still cheap. It's a question of the things that can be done *in the way they were done* that matters. A decent fake has dignity. It's trying to be as superb as Hepplewhite.

This tripod table had been shattered during its theft from a Lowestoft antique dealer's. Not by me, I hasten to add. There was only the top and tripod feet left. The single pillar was broken to smithereens as the lads hoofed it. A tripod table's so simple it sounds cheap, but don't be fooled. No antique is easy.

A woman was watching me. I didn't look, kept going.

Tripod tables – actually split three ways between me, Desdemona Sands from Rowhedge, and her cousin Luke

Brennon the thief – are simple. Flat circular top, stem, three small feet radiating out. It sounds easy, doesn't it? Dealers still speak of a 'claw foot' table, as in the eighteenth century. Nowadays you don't hear that term. The public gets confused. (The feet are usually plain, turned in, smooth, or merely bulbous. It just resembles a bird's claw.) Mahogany's the wood. My job was to make a new pillar, to be its single leg. It would look 1780, give or take a yard. I'd got a piece of mahogany, brand new, uncured. Which needn't stop you nowadays. The woman still didn't speak.

There's this stuff called PEG. Means polyethyleneglycol. Fakers call it peg. You put granules into water. Drop in your new wood, and forget about it – two days to six weeks; depends on thickness. Mop it with a dishcloth and start work. Simple. The new wood becomes easy to work, hardly ever flakes, and planes like a dream. Normally you need eight years of careful curing in the open air. Monks used to pee on new timber in lined pits, but they didn't have PEG to speed things along. I'd pegged this mahogany piece, and it was ready.

Odd feeling, to be lathe-turning new wood when it feels old. Slippery, too smooth, yet the chuck bites as if the wood . . .

'No tongue, missus?' I hate creeping people.

'Lovejoy, isn't it?'

Cassandra Clark, as ever was. I sighed to a stop, elbows on the work. I approve of lovely women. They bring a glow to, well, a drossy workshop. Hair lustrous, skin blooming, eyes to dazzle. Clothes that make other women swivel with that up-down rake of instant envy. Which raised an all-important question.

'To whom might I have the pleasure of addressing?'

She smiled. 'Where are they, Lovejoy?'

Stumped, first go. I thought hard. The place was bare

except for tools. Maybe she wanted a fake, I thought hopefully.

'They're here, love.' It was true. Whatever I had was here.

'Your antiques, Lovejoy. The ones you make. Fake?' She smiled, not hard to watch. 'Create?'

That was more like it. 'It's this tripod table.'

She inspected my crude lathe. 'Ordinary mahogany, Lovejoy?'

This ignorance is typical. Untrained, unlearned, unread. Hoodlums have more sense.

'There's no such thing. Mahogany's more than sixty different kinds. Matching them up is a pig. Three genera are mahogany proper. Others say only *Swietenia* is the true stuff – Cuba, Honduras, Guatemala. It's unbelievably rare.'

'I know. Rose mahogany.' She was narked, tapped her foot. I really love ignorance. No, honestly. To be that thick needs genius.

'Rosewood's not mahogany, love. It pretends to be . . .' I beamed, hoping to annoy her into some relevation '. . . something it isn't.'

That set her wondering whether to march out, forget this little encounter ever took place. Or stay . . . and what?

Time to needle. 'Duckeggs – meaning you – don't know a thing, love.' I got fed up, resumed my treadling. 'Auctioneers at least dig out a few glib phrases.' I knew I was getting to her. Any woman who hangs around the town's antique dealers and buys not a bauble is up to something. And this one didn't hang around by accident. She'd had to clump through the undergrowth in high heels, for a start.

'For somebody who's broke, Lovejoy, your arrogance is—'

'Don't buy this table, love. It'll look like a Chippendale.

Everything matching. Dealers call anything that vaguely looks right "genuine mahogany". But you know what?' I lowered my voice, all furtive.

'What?' she was caught in the pull of a secret.

'They're lying.'

She tutted, decided I wasn't worth a candle. 'And to think that I was actually con—'

'Good morning,' Joan Vervain said sweetly. 'Considering what? I do hope I'm not interrupting.'

She was. The silly cow had cut through the only vital word.

'Not at all, Mrs Vervain.' Cassandra Clark glared at me. 'He has absolutely nothing to offer.'

They passed like cruisers from different navies, at distance but measuring threat. Dear Mrs Vervain started on me, where was I, who the hell did I think she is, et howling cetera.

'It's no good, darling.' I looked broken-hearted. Which wasn't difficult, seeing I was screaming to do the furniture. Desdemona would be screaming for the same thing. Not to mention Luke the thief, only he doesn't scream. He stabs people. 'I can't go on.' I rose, stared soulfully into the garden. 'We have to stop seeing each other.'

'We . . . ?' She swung me round, blazing. 'Is it Del? The drunken bastard send his thugs round? I'll poison the pig—'

'Not that, dworlink. It's . . .' I scuffed the flag floor. It's what, exactly? If you let it, your brain finds lies, any shape and just right. Try to work one out, you come a cropper. 'Look about, love. Everything I own. Even that's mortgaged, borrowed, nicked.'

That should do it. The idea is to give them a start. They'll provide the rest of the lie for themselves.

Joan leapt in on cue. 'Oh, darling. You're hopeless!'

For one moment I thought she'd rumbled me. 'I know,'

I said. More soul, to hurry her. I'd never finish the work at this rate.

'Listen, darling.' She'd reached some conclusion, thank heaven. 'I've got lawyers working on a settlement. I'm not going to be palmed off with pennies . . .'

Her conclusion was appalling. She actually thought that I . . . ? I changed my inward scream to an inward groan.

'Lovejoy?' More bloody arrivals.

'Eh?' I realised I'd sounded joyous, so went sombre. 'Yes. I'm Lovejoy.'

A man and a woman stood blocking the light. The man said, 'I'm Mr Carstairs. My wife. An interview.' He looked doubtful. 'Is this the right place? Lovejoy Antiques, Inc.? The Employment Training . . .'

God. I'd forgotten. I'd applied to the Employment, saying I was an employer willing to train somebody. I didn't actually want the stupid sods to send me a real live person. I'd only registered for the money. What did the Government want, blood?

'Oh, yes. Could you wait a moment, please?' I let them retreat, said softly to Joan, 'Dwoorlink. You bowled me over. You just don't understand.'

'Yes, Lovejoy. I do.' Belief that she alone understands is a woman's credo. And nobody credoed more than Joan. She dragged me down to her mouth. We parted with a plop. 'How soon will you be finished?'

'An hour. They're . . . er, Sotheby's Educational Section.'

'I'll send the car. Love you, lover.'

We parted. I'd bought time.

Mr Carstairs wasn't the Employment Learning Opportunist. It was his missus, Luna if you please. There was an ugly little scene. I heard them arguing hotly.

'It's a dump!' Carstairs said. 'He looks off the road.'

'It's my chance, Oliver. I've made my mind up.'

A shocked gasp. 'Luna. This is a mistake—'

'Oliver. If I don't do it now, I'll never do it.'

A bird after my own heart. She knew I was the opportunity of a lifetime. A discerning bird if ever I saw one.

The lathe treadled into action, so I didn't hear the rest of the heated exchange. Later I was interrupted by a timid shout that made me jump out of my skin. I'd forgotten the silly cow.

'Lovejoy.' She was there when I came down. She looked scared, defiantly twisting her handbag strap into gangrene. Oliver was severely blocking the light. 'I'm Luna Carstairs. EOTSC.'

The what? Forty-odd, plumpish, fair, dressed by some 1950s B feature. I liked her. 'Did you bring the paper?'

'Yes.' She rummaged eagerly, gave me a letter. I tossed it aside.

'Right. Sleeves rolled up, Luna. We've work to do.'

'Now?' She unbuttoned her coat. Give me strength.

'Metaphorically, love.' I shouldn't call her a silly cow, not right off. 'You'll freeze to death out here.' I didn't want an apprentice who moaned about draughts.

'You mean I've got the job?' She was thrilled.

'Insight, Mrs Carstairs,' I said. 'I can tell worth.'

Oliver the Indignant left, in some deep-throated engined monster tethered by the gate. To Luna I explained the most important tasks in her life for the next four weeks. The first was to brew up, in my special manner.

She had enough money for us to get the town bus. She'd enough for me to buy us pasties, mushy peas and chips. Woody's is grot city, home of saturated fats and antique dealers. Noshing to repletion, I realised that a lady of Luna's restricted lifestyle brought a new dimension. She solved the local scam problem in half a sentence.

'Mahogany's beautiful material,' I was saying. She had an annoying habit of looking about. Getting on my nerves. I had to keep jerking her attention back. 'Oak was king until about 1660. Walnut came anciently from Persia. Extensively planted, Elizabethan times on. Hence, walnut furniture – *for Christ's sake pay heed!*'

'I'm sorry, Lovejoy,' she said, startled to vigilance. She was flying, blue eyes shining with excitement. I was mollified. Enthusiasm isn't far from passion. With this smart bird the lads'd see I was up-market.

'Then mahogany ruled, say 1725 on. Sauce, please.' She passed the sauce. I lashed out a pool of it. True to female tradition, Luna ate little. She actually picked up a chip on her fork and inspected the damned thing. The Employment had slipped me some extra-terrestrial. 'The main problem for the faker – er, antiques expert restorer – is that mahogany has what we call thunder shakes. An upset. Fracture across the wood, that you can't see until you've cut into it. Every time you cut mahogany your heart's in your mouth, wondering if it has one of these concealed cross-fractures – *what the frigging hell's the matter?*'

She was all thrilled-to-be-here. The lads were smiling back, taking the mickey. Was she on the run, or what?

'I'm sorry, Lovejoy. I've never been in one before.'

Woody's is a shambles of filthed tables, peeling chrome, reject lino shredded to catch the settling grease. A dozen bloated dealers were in, convincing each other they were having a hard life.

'One what?' I was baffled.

'A *dive*,' she whispered conspiratorially, head almost in my plate. I hugged my grub closer. She had her own, largely untouched. I eyed it. It would hot up pretty well.

'Dive?' I'd drawn Priscilla of the Lower Third. 'This is Woody's, love.' It is the least exotic place on Planet Earth.

Woody's barrel gut, fungating triangle of pubic hairs visible in the fumes of frying crud, adds to the authenticity.

'The *food*, Lovejoy! Hairs in the bacon!'

'Don't you like it?' I asked, hopeful.

Pause. 'It's a little wholesome, Lovejoy.'

'Don't give offence, love. I'll try to finish yours.'

'Oh, would you, Lovejoy? I really would appreciate . . .'

Where was I? 'Our problem is that tripod table, Luna. They practically never have a carved top *and* carved tripod feet. Carved table top means the feet have *got* to be plain. Tell me what I've just said.'

She repeated it faithfully, solemn eyes watching my reaction. I mopped my plate with bread, swapped it for hers.

'The second clue. If a tripod table's top is *exactly* circular, it's probably a fake. You measure its diameter. It'll have shrunk since the eighteenth century. Ours is almost five-eighths of an inch out. Repeat.'

'Oh, Lovejoy!' she cried, excited. 'To think I was actually concerned about you!' Her hand flew to her mouth. 'What's the matter? What have I said?'

I managed, 'Nothing, love. Just remembered something.'

'You've gone quite pale.' She foraged in her handbag. 'Have you got a headache? I usually find these tablets—'

'Repeat what I've told you.'

'About the table? If you're all right . . .'

To think that I was actually concerned about you . . . Was what Cassandra Clark said, almost. Joan had finished the word for her – but wrongly. Not 'considering'. *Concerned.* Which equals worried. Cassandra had come because she was worried I would chuck a spanner in her works. My transparent poverty reassured her: I clearly presented no threat. But to what? She was rich. I'd seen her at the Arcade, not long ago. When I'd sussed out Gunge Herod's/

Jeff's papal ring. She'd ignored me, of course. But now? For a brief spell, I'd had her worried.

Whatever I'd been up to – and I wasn't sure what – presented some threat. Luna had finished her recital.

'Lesson Two begins now, love.' I almost added an apology, for chucking her in the deep end.

'Here's a list of local museums, love. I'll expect you to look at the furniture in them all. Quickly.' I finished the grub, rose amid merry grins from the lads and a blessing from Psycho, our religious nut.

'Who will teach me about them, Lovejoy?'

I pinged the door open, called so-long to Woody. 'Teaching antiques? No such thing. Come on, love. We've a lady to see.'

I needed to check on Tits Alors (rhymes with doors). She'd be lurking – well, not exactly lurking; more like flaunting brazenly – on her beat about now. If Luna was going to play the antiques game she had to learn it wasn't played in a nunnery.

Chapter 7

Luna Carstairs had 'occasional use of my Oliver's motor', she told me. You get the feeling spouses communicate by memorandum. We were still on Shanks's pony when we cut past the Welcome Sailor pub. Tits Alors was at her post. Willowy, short-skirted, booted, black fishnets, enough make-up to export. Beautiful.

'See Tits Alors? Ask how near she is to a load.'

'A load?' Luna abruptly de-thrilled. I went to the Arcade, pausing to watch two Brighton blokes unload a long case clock ('grandfather', as goons like antique dealers insist on missaying). Plain case, in bur-walnut veneer on oak, done well. Fakers nark me. I mean, whoever'd faked got it perfect – then forgot these early clocks are never above six-and-a-half feet tall. And the chapter ring (its hours circle) was twelve inches, two inches too big. I hate carelessness.

Luna was blocking my path, her face flaming. 'Lovejoy! That . . . that *lady* is a . . . a . . .' She flapped her hands.

'Prostitute? So?' If you want something doing, do it yourself. I crossed over. 'Hello, Tits.'

Tits smiled through rouge, mascara, a plaster of cosmetics. 'Lovejoy! Nice to . . .' She saw Luna. 'She with you? I thought . . .'

'Sorry. Luna Carstairs, apprentice. May I present Tits Alors, antique dealeress.'

Tits smiled. 'Not dealer. Collector, Lovejoy.'

I had to laugh. 'How near are you to a load, Tits?'

'Ten days, give or take. But it's spoken for.'

'It's what?' This was unprecedented. 'Who's buying?' She wouldn't say. I said so-long, walked Luna off for a think. Except Luna was dazedly bent on interrogation.

'Lovejoy. I've actually *spoken* to a *real* one!'

Wearily I spurred my tardy cortex, to calm her.

'Look. Tits solicits. Blokes take her to some hotel. Home even, if the wife's away. She performs, takes her fee. Nicks some tom – er, steals jewellery, a small antique, anything.'

Luna gasped. 'Doesn't she get reported?'

'Never.' I quickly forestalled the obvious. 'The client would have to explain about Tits. Get it?'

She trotted alongside, baffled. 'Lovejoy. When Ti – ah, Miss Alors sells the antiques, don't the police—?'

'She sells them to *me*. Now shut up. Just listen, watch.'

That silenced her until I reached the Arcade, thank God. Gunge Herod was there like a parked troll. In his russet sheepskin he looked off the Himalayas. Luna gaped when he shuffled to meet us.

'Lovejoy. It's Connie.'

'Connie?' My innards squeezed in alarm from the way he said it. He shook his raggedy mane to allay panic.

'No. She's fine, but mad you didn't show.'

'Show?' Everybody wants me. What about me?

'You owe her a divvie. And bunce.'

I weighed possibilities. He was bigger than ever. Me and Luna together couldn't make a single sumo. 'Got wheels?'

'No. She's at the station.'

Luna paid for a taxi. We tried to balance Gunge's weight, but the taxi was practically on two wheels. Luna was thrilled. I was getting sick of her being thrilled. She said, eyes aglow, 'This is so exciting, Lovejoy!' She couldn't keep her eyes off Gunge. Never seen a Yeti before.

'Who's this, Lovejoy?'

Connie looked pretty as a picture. We made the station forecourt just as it started raining. I want one of those folding umbrellas. I had one but it got lost. My shoes reminded me they still leaked. I'd cardboarded them again only this morning. You can't depend on shoes.

'Luna Carstairs, apprentice,' I introduced. 'Miss Connie Hopkins, antique dealer of this parish.'

Luna was ecstatic again, I saw tiredly. 'Am I really your apprentice, Lovejoy?'

'No strangers, Lovejoy,' Connie said. 'Today's confidential.'

See what I mean about confidential? A lady with a ton of antiques for public sale and they're confidential. Is it just me?

'Luna's okay. She's got my firman.'

Connie eyed Luna mistrustfully. Gunge dwarfed the area. Passengers, hoping one remaining train would amble in, queued aiming vaguely for the ticket offices where clerks read newspapers.

'Lovejoy! How fortunate!'

This was one of those days. 'Hello, Miss Turner,' I said miserably. 'Er, I'm just off—'

My scruffy old genealogy-daft Yank twittered up, delved for certificates into her cavernous leather.

'I have Scots ancestors! But I didn't find—'

'—records in London?' I gave Luna the bent eye, rubbing finger and thumb. She reached for her handbag. Connie was impatient. 'English ancestors from July, 1837, General Register Offices, London. Edinburgh for Scotland, starting 1855. The General Register Office.' I said it slowly. 'Don't go to the wrong one, okay?'

'You have the address, Lovejoy?'

'It's in Edinburgh's bloody phone book.'

Luna sidled up, slipped me a note. I stuffed it into the old bat's bag. 'Only take pencil. They strip-search you for ink up there. Remember "Mac" and "Mc" are separate, or omitted, or just "M". And Peter and Patrick were inter-changeable names the further north you go—'

'*Lovejoy!*' from Connie. I told Miss Turner so-long.

Connie's impatience had decided her about letting Luna come. Much more odderer. She was frantic. I mean, what was the big deal? Miss Turner warbled a distant goodbye. I waved absently.

Connie drove us out through Polstead, towards the old airfield at Boxtenholt. The *three* of us, note. When everything was – what's the vital word, begins with C?

'Are you cold, Lovejoy?' I'd shivered, an angel on my grave. 'You should have stopped for your overcoat.'

Thank you, Luna. 'It's countryside. Nothing but scenery.'

'He's not got one,' Gunge boomed after some miles. He's not quick. Who is?

'I'm sorry. I didn't . . . Wouldn't for the world . . .' Luna apologised for the remainder of the journey.

Connie took me aside as we alighted at the disused air-field. 'Lovejoy. You're sure she's all right?' I said give over.

Boxtenholt village is in a hollow, a tributary vale. The common pasture stands higher, a windy exposed stretch of scrub with a couple of ancient trackways. During the war it was an aerodrome, American bombers. There's a derelict breeze-block building, a tumbled control tower, sheep. A wooden sign clumped mournfully against the gaping window space – had the damned thing been doing that since 1945, for God's sake? Enough to give you the creeps.

Kiddies fly kites and lovers snog on Boxtenholt Heath. There's an ancient tumulus in the centre, now rudely marked by an Ordnance Survey stone.

'This way.'

Connie's idea of deception was to park at one end of the heath, and march us to a grey guardhouse on what was the aerodrome's perimeter, down a flight of concrete steps. She had a flashlight. Me and Gunge shifted some fallen slabs blocking a metal door. Connie had a key.

'Wait, please.' I drew Luna to one side as Connie entered, Gunge close behind. We were alone. I spoke in the gloaming. 'Luna. If you say "Isn't this wonderful" once more, I'll give you a pasting. Capeesh?'

'Oh, Lovejoy! *Gangsters* say capeesh!' She scanned my face for signs that I was sharing in all this excitement.

I gathered her garments in a fist about her throat and lifted her. I can do it, with the weak. 'Do you understand? Silence. Your last chance.'

'Yes, Lovejoy.'

We followed Gunge and Connie. They had lit candles.

'Something to sit on, Gungie?' I asked. 'Pile a few blocks.'

Evidently cells, below the guardroom. Dank, now, with seepage from rain. It felt lovely, glowing with the beauty that only antiques can give. They were covered with dustsheets. Somebody had had the wit to roll an old carpet for the mound of vibrating brilliance. Concrete beams above, concrete walls around. These cells would be there in a million years. I felt queasy, told Luna, then Gunge, then Connie, to see the cellar door was propped ajar.

Divvieing is a dour, rather sickening business. Idyllic, of course. It's to do with antiques. The poor old divvie suffers every time. I've known, over the years, eight or nine of us with this gift. Some have it just for furniture, paintings, jewellery. Whatever, it's hard on the soul. Sin's easier

– you get something for that. Though aphorisms are always wrong.

For a couple of minutes before starting I have to pace, hum, walk, not look at anyone. Luna couldn't take it. In fact, Luna was an outright nuisance, especially when she gazed blankly at each of us in turn while I ambled. She finally erupted, 'Well? Shouldn't we start——?'

'Shhhh!' Gunge and Connie rounded on her.

She was startled into silence. Which interrupted my feelings, so I had to start again, strolling, jingling non-existent coins, staring at the wall, whistling. This is the trouble: antiques are human. They have feelings, doubts, hesitations just like us. I mean, you don't rush straight up to perfect strangers and grab hold, tip them up, prod, dig your fingers into them, scrape their skin, all to 'take a look'. You'd soon get your eye blacked. But nobody thinks twice about doing that to antiques. Think how the poor things must feel. And *feel* they do. Believe it. 'Taking a look' is being presented at court. A cat can look at a king. But with grace, please.

'Right,' I said. Ready.

I sat on some breeze blocks. Gunge's stack was a yard away. On it burned two candles, in a pair of dazzling silver candlesticks. Not much to look at – cast baluster, less than seven inches small, only twenty ounces put together. Simplicity ruled, when refugee silversmiths came scrambling across the Channel after the Edict of Nantes was revoked in 1685 and persecutions became the norm. Pierre Harache was a shrewd nut. He got a head start. This first immigrant silversmithing genius was already making silverware in London in 1683, his simple fashions instantly all the rage. I grinned all over my face.

'Wotcher, Pierre,' I heard my voice say. 'Can I, loves?'

They didn't mind. I touched them, simultaneous so as

not to give offence. You've only to see one, and that milky sheen streaks naked into your soul. That's the trouble with people who collect antiques: they'll go any distance to see dross, but won't 'waste time' visiting a free museum to see these breathtaking exquisite wonders.

'Thank you,' I told the lovely pair. 'Next.'

A small bowl, Egyptian Black, meaning that Wedgwood simply fired it once. Iron oxide type, mere earthenware stained with the stuff and fired at a low temperature. Made over fifty years, from 1720 on. This bowl was true unglazed basalt; it could be cut, even polished on a lathe with care. Josiah Wedgwood's supposed to have introduced the term 'black basaltes' about 1768. People suppose there were no black wares made before that. But there were. Two brothers called Elers had made them early in the century. This was Wedgwood. *Plain* bowls are very, very rare. You can touch the great man himself by touching one of these.

'Next.'

Quartetto tables, Battersea enamels – half a dozen snuffboxes if you please – one tiny wooden masterpiece shaped like a lady's high-heeled slipper with a sliding wooden lid. There was a carpet burned (actually no more than singed) to alter the colour and to age the back (rogues do it with a spirit blow-lamp). This is the only sensible fakery you get in carpets, because if you order, say, a dozen modern copies of a lovely Turkish Ghiordes prayer rug, about 1785, well, they're still all clearly handmade, though dirt cheap.

Connie had several classy items of furniture, all small. I like Victorian furniture, though I'm daunted by the immense grandeur of some sideboards. Three straight chairs had top rails which stuck out wider than the back; sure sign of 1840 or later. I explained this didn't mean they weren't class; they were. But it put paid to their having to fly under false colours. The chairs were pleased, I think.

Pewter tankards, small metal boxes for miners (they carried their chewing tobacco in these – they're dated, nineteenth century, often with colliery names on). A handful of *inro*, enough to make your mouth water: small cases on cords when wearing traditional Japanese dress; you stuck your favourite medicines in. The *netsuke*, a sort of toggle, on one end of the cord, is some of the most superb creative carving ever executed. Witty, amusing, hilarious, scary, everything you could wish. My favourite was a grazing horse, carved from a bit of stag antler, barely three inches tall. Connie had a mass of antiques, with a leavening of fakes. Good as you'd ever see.

My headaches are famous. I was some time coming to after they'd put the candles out. I went reluctantly, stumbling up the dusty steps and into the Suffolk wet. I inhaled the drizzle for size. It didn't feel too bad, so I breathed more. The pity is that rain wets your head. I went and stood under a tree, listening to the solid taps of the rain. Drizzle gets steam up by soaking leaves. Then the leaf gets fed up and sags its drop like a bird plop.

Connie and Gunge were trying to talk. Luna stayed with them, occasionally glancing across. Wearily I beckoned. She trotted across the grass, heels sinking. I walked the crumbling runway to Connie's motor, leant against the bonnet.

'Lovejoy,' she said hesitantly at last. She tried the car doors, tutting like they do as if discovering a malicious plot. 'Was that little cardboard tube really worth two of these cars?'

'Mmmmh. Don't call that masterpiece a cardboard tube. It was a genuine Campani. He made "perspective glasses", telescopes. Samuel Pepys used one for ogling pretty ladies in church, naughty old devil. That colouring and decoration is tooled leather.'

She went quiet for a bit. 'You knocked over that beautiful square knife-box, Lovejoy. Unforgivable. I have a lovely one exactly like it, Queen Anne.'

'Oh, aye. Is its herring-bone inlay veneer sunk? Or dead level, too? If so, it's a fake, like that one.' I could see she was aghast at horrifying possibilities. 'You see, love, that veneer rises in a couple of centuries. It has to, see? Changes in temperature, humidity. Only new fakes are neat and level.'

Her eyes filled with alarm. She drew breath to ask. I saved her the trouble. 'I know, I know. Why didn't I have to examine it. It felt wrong. The real antiques recognise you, and say hello. They warm me. Fakes don't. It's like . . . well, like love.'

She was still trying to remember, seeing her favourite piece in her mind's eye, when Gunge and Connie came up. We embarked without a word. I settled soggily into the back seat.

'Good, Lovejoy.' Gunge, activating a neurone.

I said nothing. Connie was driving. We came to Polstead, and she went left at the crossroads.

'Lovejoy. Do you want in?' she asked along the old Roman road. They're our only straight bits in East Anglia.

'How big, compared?' I meant how big a sample had I divvied, of the whole. My mind was going: *Connie's scam isn't Prammie Joe Godbolt's scam.* Seriously bad news. In fact highly dangerous.

'Quarter, Lovejoy.'

I hadn't a bean, let alone enough to cut in on a scam this size. I said I'd think about it. She said she'd give me until tomorrow. Lots of tomorrows lately, too.

She dropped me and Luna at the cottage. My apprentice made the yuckiest brew I'd ever had. It was horrible. I didn't know if I'd last the full month on this, and told her so. She was proud of herself, said stop complaining.

We sat drinking it, Luna saying the cottage was so cold. Daylight faded.

'Lovejoy?' Here it came, sum total of misgiving. 'Why is that Mrs Hopkins', er, scam in that disused airfield, and not in her showroom?'

'Some are stolen, love. A scam is a robber's scheme.'

'*Stolen?* Shouldn't we tell the police?'

My turn to stare. 'No, love. The less we have to do with the police, the better. We're not on the same side.'

'Not on the same side as the Law?' More mind-boggling.

'Do you know anybody who is?'

It was then that the police came clumping in. Drinkwater wanted me at the police station to see if I knew anyone called Godbolt. I told Luna to lock up, please, and count the silver after the constables had departed.

Buy *why* wasn't Connie's scam the same as Prammie Joe's? Dozy old East Anglia doesn't run to two major scams in one week. Tits Alors had already pre-sold her own load. To somebody forming up a third? Jesus. Luna, full of unasked questions, hopped from one foot to the other at the cottage door as the ploddites drove me away.

Chapter 8

Imagine a flattish area of land, pretty big and wide, with only fields, woods, rivers, farms, villages, and cities here and there (actually two). East Anglia in a nutshell. The rivers wander into estuaries that are basically sea marshes. It's truly rural. I mean, the whole Kingdom jokes about it. Like, in showbusiness they say, 'He's the best comedian in East Anglia – how *is* the other feller?' All that.

But if you know this creaking old country of ours, you'll have sussed our trick. Nothing is what it seems. Peaceful? Take care, something's going on. Tranquil? Mayhem lurks. Sleepy? Watch out, that's all. Hereward the Wake is one of our heroes. Not as well known as Robin Hood, perhaps, but at least the Normans never caught *him*. He never slept, drifted unseen through the fens, vanishing during the day to emerge more powerful than ever when the sun sank. They say he did sleep, but with one eye open. Maybe two.

'Know anybody called Godbolt, Lovejoy?' Drinkwater's clacking pot teeth asked. Twitch. Ear flick.

'No. Live around here, does he?'

'Note that, Cradhead.'

The other ploddite said right, almost as if he'd been taught to write. Really lifelike. His name is variously pronounced.

66

We drove out to the River Deben. The police motor was full of misgivings, mostly mine. There's a bridge not far from Shottisham, and a small uninhabited island. We alighted and peered at the soggy countryside. I'd had enough of the wretched stuff today. I blame the Government. What's wrong with concreting it? Mother Nature's had her chance for a quadrillion years, and failed spectacularly. Look at the damned stuff.

'Into the dinghy, Lovejoy.'

Cradhead couldn't row to save his life. Lacked co-ordination. Prerequisite for his job, I suppose. Fearing the goon would drown us all, I took the oars myself. I'm not much good, but can get by.

'Upstream, Lovejoy.' Drinkwater of the Rolling Main.

Not easy old downstream, oh no. We went about a hundred yards, Drinkwater saying 'Left a bit' and all that. I was puffed out.

'Stop here,' the nerk actually commanded.

'Reach the brakes, Drinkie, there's a pal.'

He glared. I glared back. We drifted a moment, clumping gently into the islet. That is, we would have, except we banged into something solid. I looked over into the water. Cradhead reached past, almost upsetting the boat, to grab on – to a 1713 brass chandelier, beautiful and genuine. Strapped on a semi-sunken raft.

'Comments are invited, Lovejoy.'

Here's a definite antiques tip: a brass chandelier is English or Dutch. It'll have an ugly-looking globe with waggly brass radii curving out for the candles. Travel half a day hereabouts, you can see half-a-dozen churches where they still dangle. I think they're horrible, but antique they are. Oh, and some public buildings have them, too. Minus one, Cornish Place, I guessed.

'Brass chandelier, Drinkwater. Very collectable. London

decorators are always after them from redundant churches.'
I rested on my oars. 'That it?'

We waited. I scanned the river. Something splashed with evil intent, like all countryside splashes. A little black duck with a yellow beak chugged by. I yawned. It was all happening.

'I want more comment, Lovejoy.'

'Well, these chandeliers often have a little brass dove for a finial, if it's from a church. I've never seen one with a coat-of-arms, but hear in the Midlands—'

'You dross. Why is it bobbing in the river?'

'Why ask me, you prat?' I yelled back, just as if I was really annoyed instead of frightened to death for Prammie Joe. 'There's a thousand antique dealers in East Anglia. What the hell's got into you, Drinkwater?'

'Robbery's got into me, Lovejoy.' He sat staring with his eyes just like Geronimo's. His pot teeth clacked, his ear twitched. 'This brass thing's from Cornish Place. The raft is described as one possibly belonging to Joseph Godbolt. Who finds and sells antiques.'

'Can I go home?' Biased police records, mostly false.

'The Mayor's wife'll wait, Lovejoy. I don't suppose she'll behave any different from your other tarts. Godbolt was known to be of this locality, no fixed abode.'

'Why not make the bloke who found this thing take you to this Godbolt, if he can recognise his flotsam?'

'Angler, Lovejoy. Works in a sawyer's yard near Woolverstone. He sold Godbolt this wood. It's marked.'

I drew breath, but said nothing. Woolverstone isn't even on this river. It's south, opposite bank of the Orwell, above Harwich. Where the ferries leave for the Continent.

'Clues?' I suggested idly. 'Fingerprints? You must have . . . Godbolt's down at the nick.' I nearly said Prammie.

Cradhead spoke. A cultured bloke, fair of hair and plum of voice. You just know he's got friends in Whitehall.

'Can you, ah, contribute any personal knowledge, Love-joy? Of any, ah, scam of such, ah, quantity as Cornish Place?'

Ah, no. Which troubled me too. I found myself being looked at directly by Cradhead, first time. It wasn't pleasing. Maybe he wasn't a nerk at all. I mean, a handful of idiots like him, with exactly this casual offhand manner, had run empires.

'No. Not heard a thing.'

'Shut it, Cradhead.' Drinkwater gestured for me to row us away. 'Tell the lads to bring this brass thing in.' He caught himself. I grinned. He'd almost said for question-ing. 'Lovejoy. We know you talk to that poofter on East Hill. And other dealers in that thieves' Arcade. You tell me anything you learn, hear, get hinted. Right?'

'And if you find Mr Godbolt, ask him . . .' Suddenly I wished to make no merry quips about Prammie, went quiet.

'Yes, ah, Lovejoy?' from Cradhead.

'How come you aren't doing this, Cradhead?' I said nastily, getting the oars. 'Didn't you row at Oxford?' I was narked. They'd let something terrible happen to Prammie Joe. 'That Oxford-Cambridge Boat Race is a fix, anyway. It's always—'

'—the same two teams reach the final?' he capped, smiling.

The problem was, careful watermen like Prammie Joe don't let rafts of ill-gotten plunder go drifting downriver towards the cold dark sea. Not unless . . . I backed oars, put our prow into the bank.

Cradhead knew I knew something. Nasty bloke. He was new to the district. Maybe he'd not stay long, with any luck.

They gave me a lift home, a driver who lectured the

world on the problems he was having with his bird, a pub dancer in Manningtree.

That evening, Joan Vervain cornered me, and we had a supper filled with Chinese nourishment brought in by the chauffeur. She was disappointed I had no television, electricity, gas, running water.

'You see, doowerlink,' I said with heartfelt sorrow but unyielding take-it-on-the-chin pride. 'I won't come to you as a pauper.'

'But darling,' she cooed, hands cupped beneath her chin. God, but women's tactics are unfair. And candlelight's treacherous. Everybody knows that. 'I already pay for – no. I didn't mean I *pay*. But I can't see you . . .' She licked her lips. Her eyes were huge. '. . . go *hungry*, can I?'

We managed to make smiles, though, in spite of her husband's unavoidable radio absence. I found to my horror, as I woke from that terrible moribundity of after-love, that I'd promised to leave with her the following week. We were going to Monte Carlo, to live for ever in a state of sexual ecstasy and wealthy wassailing. Our address was to be the Caribbean in midwinter, Geneva in summer, San Francisco and Florida for inbetweens. I roused blearily into panic.

'What are London and Hong Kong for?' She has ten homes.

'Shopping, you silly darling!'

She had brought blankets and some heavy coverlet that heated up when you pulled a strip thing. Breakfast was delivered by a lass in a small white van. No hairs in the bacon.

I was seeing Joan off when Luna arrived. I won't say caught us, because she didn't. Why *is* it that women always make you feel as if they've caught you red-handed?

* * *

'Your jobs are two-fold, Luna,' I was giving out as she drove us to the auction. Oliver had let her have the car.

'Isn't she well known?' Once a woman leeches on to another woman, you can't prise her off. 'I've seen her in the paper.'

I scotched this right at the outset. 'A lot of people think that. I was asked only yesterday if she was the Mayor's wife!' I chuckled merrily at the idiocy of some people.

'Impossible, Lovejoy. I'm the Mayor's wife.'

Headaches, like age and lawyers, never come alone. 'Go to this address.' I passed her the teacher's card. 'Tell him the Sotheby's agent he gave a lift to says there's no market for his coffee pot, but buy it.'

She was thrilled. 'We represent Sotheby's? Oliver will—'

'No, love. We lie. Otherwise they won't trust us.'

Adjustment took ten minutes of analysis. 'I know I said to tell him there's no market, but . . .'

Makes me wonder how folk do it. Where I come from, she'd starve.

'Second, go to the auction. I'll be there. I'll bid for a beautiful tole tray, I forget the lot number. Make sure you come in late, all casual. When you see me shake my head, there'll be only one bid left. You bid then. Okay? Make sure you get it, but look worried.'

'How will I know how much to bid, Lovejoy?'

Honestly, women amaze me. I mean, they love spending money, by all accounts. Yet send them along to spend some, and it's Prime Minister's Question Time.

'I told you. When I drop out, there'll only be one bid to go.'

'Whose, Lovejoy?' Her eyes were shining with excitement. 'Shall I make arrangements with him to—?'

'For Christ's sake!' I yelled. 'Just do it! Stupid cow!'

'It's no good getting cross, Lovejoy. What if I pay too much? And what is a tole tray? How much—?'

'Pull in. The auction's by the market. Park near the lights.'

'It's no trouble, Lovejoy. I'll take you to the door—'

'No thank you, Luna.' I struggled down to her pace. 'We pretend we don't know each other.'

Her brow unfurrowed. 'I see! Ignore each other's presence!' She blocked all the traffic. Lucky we were in dozy old East Anglia, where motor horns never parp.

'That's it. Buy the tole. Leg it to that teacher's.'

'Leg?'

'Proceed in an orderly manner. Good luck.'

She was still firing worried, but terribly thrilled, questions after me as I walked down to the auction. I don't understand some people.

The auction went like a dream. I bid for Lot 18, the lovely tole tray. One bloke made the running, your friend and mine Acker Kirwin. Just when he thought the lot was going to be knocked down to him, I did my bid. The auctioneer today was Irving, a dour Fifer with a dehydrated sepulchral voice. A tip: don't bid early. Enter late, keep your nerve. Think for a sec, and you'll guess why. It daunts the opposition. They realise that you've judged it just that wee bit better than they have.

On cue, Luna's mellifluous but shaky voice quavered, 'Yes, please.' Good girl, I thought, and left smiling to myself, but frowning in apparent distress to show others I was upset. Now all it needed was for her to get to that schoolteacher and buy his 'coffee pot' and we'd be in business. I'd owe her the money, of course, and pay her out of the profits.

Chapter 9

Something was nagging. I alighted from the lorry and called so-long to the driver – pleasant Ipswich chap, kept ferrets – and set out to walk the last two miles to Prammie Joe's hideout. I mean, those surnames. Hopkins is common, right? Clark's common. Godbolt? A bit uncommon. Maybe I'd heard them together in some pantomime, a play. Old poets, the sort you have to learn incomprehensible snatches of at school? What are the chances of any three names coming together? I was imagining things. With a moniker like Lovejoy, I have a thing about names.

The day was waning smartish. I found myself walking quietly. The path narrowed, then split off the lane proper and became an old track down to Prammie Joe's creek. You get these sudden deflections in East Anglia, usually where the Romans built a temple, like at places called Mile End, so marching legionaries could chuck votive offerings to some god for the success of their campaign. Or where Middle Ages improvers built a footbridge near an old watersplash, so making the old crossing redundant.

I walked quieter still. I've had practice, one way and another. The path – it was hard to find, nearing the undergrowth where the muddiness began – narrowed further. Occasional cows must come this way, judging from the state of the ground underfoot. The hedge was tattered, losing the battle not to become a thicket. I supposed vaguely that gravel was anciently cast into the river here, to make the bed firm enough for waggons. Our roads have always been abysmal. Forget the engravings of rollicking coaches bristling with ruddy-countenanced passengers waving bottles. When Emperor Charles VI visited Petworth, the fifty miles from London were a nightmare – Sussex stalwarts were hired to walk alongside, propping the coach upright. The Emperor was only up-ended twelve times.

There was a faint hum. Hum? Up and down, like a pub singer trying for his key before launching into his gala melody. Rasping, sort of. I cracked a twig, hissing and sucking my finger when stabbed by a hawthorn. The humming ignored me. I know little about countryside, but I do know its sounds go silent when interrupted. Except some.

I stepped through the hedge gap. Prammie had made it oblique, from cunning. Stand alongside the tangle, you've to face the way you've come even to see it. You step through, take three paces or so, and you are in this overgrown field with blackthorn and reeds. Your only way is down, towards the creek. And that constant, terrible humming sound.

From Prammie Joe's shack. I saw the shack when my feet felt suddenly cold. My shoes were water-sogged. I could see the hut door. Open? I'd never seen it open without Prammie Joe here.

'Prammie?' Nothing. The hum continued. 'It's Lovejoy.'

The humming rose and fell. Zzzzz. A sleeping giant. Always inhaling? A faint blur hung about the doorway. Dark, shifting, a feeble shadow trying to become something definite.

And an aroma. No, a smell. Not smell, even. A stench. A stench of something having . . .

'Joe? It's me. Lovejoy.'

Something came at my face. I brushed it away. It came again, troubling me. I brushed it off. A bluebottle. Flies. The hanging shadow was a cloud of buzzing blow-flies. Which breed—

'Joe!' I screamed. 'For Christ's sake, Prammie!' Maggots breed in soldiers' shot legs, in cattle wounds. I drew breath, moaning, took my jacket off, covered my head with it, ran at the hut, paused a second and stepped in, gagged, saw Joe's face one heaving mass of maggots and bluebottles that actually dripped, *dripped* on to the wood floor beside him, things squirming in his eyes sockets. I turned and ran, retching, swiping madly at the bluebottles that followed. Some were even in my jacket. I waved it round my head fifty yards up the field. My hands were shaking. I felt my eyes streaming. I was going, 'Argh, argh . . .' I tried not to, but spewed and retched and wept. I was pathetic, disgusting. I found two blowflies buzzing in my sleeve, stamped one to death like a madman, and chased the other round the universe until I collapsed, sobbing, on the marshy ground. When I'm a prat, I go for gold.

As penance, I made myself walk home, nearly getting myself killed by every night joyrider. After the pubs closed it was a nightmare. Hardly any pavements in East Anglia.

Two o'clock in the morning I reached my cottage. All night long I heard buzzing, buzzing. I didn't sleep. Fault is everybody's for everything, people say nowadays. It didn't feel like it. It felt like mine.

Came dawn, bluetits were tapping for their bloody nuts, the robin was flirting for his cheese, the hedgehog wondering what had gone into me. I shut them all out. Let them get on with it. I'd had enough Nature.

* * *

'Morning, Lovejoy.'

Luna was an atrocious call on my resources this early after a non-night night.

'Notice anything?' she asked, shy with hidden glee.

'Rain coming?' The tide turns our weather to the opposite of its dawn doings. I wondered for a ghastly moment what bluebottles do in bad weather.

'No, silly. Electricity! Water! Phone! They're coming!'

There was a van in the garden. Boiler-suited blokes were milling, unloading ladders.

'Your television licence is paid, Lovejoy.' She was especially thrilled at this, hugging herself. 'A TV set will be here soon. And radio.' Radio? Joan Vervain really would be pleased. We could shag during Hubby Del's radio show.

'Who paid?'

'Why, we did!' She drew me aside as boiler suits marched in.

A horrible feeling was growing within me.

'Where did we get the gelt, love? Money,' I explained, to smooth her forehead.

'I had the most extraordinary stroke of luck, Lovejoy!' She drew me to the divan and sat us down, breathless with delight. 'No sooner had I bought the troll tray, than a gentleman offered me a good profit. I sold it there and then!'

Carefully I didn't strangle her. 'Don't tell me. You only made one bid, and Acker – the rival bidder folded?'

'Yes! Wasn't I clever?'

'You silly bitch.'

She gasped thunderstruck. 'But that's what we *do*! Buy and sell!'

It's called the lop. Only happens at antiques auctions. When somebody does the shuff – that is, what me and Luna had planned, one partner displacing another to confuse bidders – a cunning opponent does the lop.

This means he stops bidding, allowing the shuffer to win the item. No sooner is it knocked down to her, than the Topper's colleague pants up and says, 'Missus, did you get Lot 18? Parking is such hell in Penny Lane. Will you sell? I'll give you a good . . .' Et predictable cetera. Duckeggs get lopped. I don't.

She listened, stricken. Well she might. She'd lost us a beautiful tole tray. Tole's manufacturing process is beautiful, combining art and science. The French did it wonderfully in the eighteenth century.

'Tole, not troll. You take sheet iron.' I described it from the pit of a terrible memory. 'They discovered a heat-resist varnish and paint. You put many coats of paint on your iron. Then black it by holding it in smoke from a torch dipped in pine resin. Any resin for that matter. Fakers use teak oil on pine twigs.'

'Lovejoy?' Luna said, ten miles off.

'Smooth it with brickdust. Many layers of varnish. Then you *paint* in coloured varnishes. The earlier the date, to 1740, the more beautiful. They copied Sevres. You get pots, food-warmers, a million household wares in tole.'

She blotted my face with a hankie. 'Please don't cry, Lovejoy. We'll find another one. I'll go to Sotheby's.'

'I'm not. Silly mare.' I struck her hand away. She took no notice. They never do.

'Where do these two TVs go, lady?' A bloke was standing on the porch between two large cases.

She bridled. 'I only ordered one television.'

'Two, lady. Paid outright. Is there an aerial?'

'I only ordered one . . .' And so forth.

Prammie Joe had been killed, head bashed in. Had a cord been round his throat? Some sort of wire? Country folk have wire like city folk have rubber bands, plenty and all lengths. Snares, traps, hay, fencing, those rural things.

Luna's car. In silence I went out, was unsurprised to see her keys in the ignition. She'd wisely left her motor by my hedge, where waggons used to rest when clambering uphill from the river crossing below. I got in and headed for town.

Hereabouts in Ruritania, so to speak, you can't help knowing people who live up to their umbilicus in fens, marshes, rivers. But knowing isn't quite the same as a mere nodding acquaintance. I mean, everybody on earth 'knows' antiques. But not everybody *knows* antiques. See the difference? Or we'd all own Christie's and have a British Museum in the yard.

There were quite a few possibilities for help. One was Brad, boat repairer down on the estuary, early flint-locks. Except nothing had moved much in Brad's direction since the Tower of London clearing sale. There was Fesk Dynson, on the canals. Lock-keeper. Painting is his life. He worships oils, any Victorian. Not changed much there, either. Antique furnishings I'd already learned about the hard way – or Prammie Joe had. No mega moves in silver, local furniture, collectibles, or I'd have heard from our silver man, Big Frank from Suffolk. No major scam recently, except the great clandestine smuggle to the Continent after that massive crisp job in Norfolk. In a crisp job, you fake copies of all the antiques in your decaying mansion house. You replace the genuine antiques with the fakes. You then burn the manor house to a crisp. You get insurance money for (a) the manor (b) the burnt antiques. Naturally, you also (c) sell the antiques abroad where the prying eyes of the constabulary never go. Plus, you are relieved of that massive expense, namely your poor old Queen Anne building. You buy a villa in the sun, a pool and a blonde, and live stinkingly richly happy ever after. That was six months since.

No. I'd have to explore Prammie Joe's death through the waterways of this fair kingdom, and trust to luck. There's only one true waterways man in antiques. Rye Benedict, at ye olde mill by ye stream.

He was in, working the machinery for a group of school-children, telling the three who listened how the millstones worked. The other thirty were smoking behind the river wall or groping each other on the embankments. Education, hard at the learning curve.

'Wotcher, Miss Brewer.' Therla once taught in our village school, but the kids had run her a merry dance and she'd retired in hysterics. She was fetching, desirable. Why did I never have teachers like her? I'd been taught by amorphous cylinders of black cloth called Sister Hyacinth for my first six years. They had no legs. Miss Brewer had legs, and morphology.

'Hello, Lovejoy.' Some kids paused, looked across, sniggered. My name elicits this response. 'Interested in water machinery?'

Therla Brewer is ever hopeful that somebody keen will take her next lesson.

'No, love. You?'

'The school's Outdoor Activity Interaction Expression. Two OAIE sessions a week.' She gazed about, dispiritedly trying to convince herself they were all enthused. 'Design of waterways last week. The Stour. One boy tumbled in. Saved by an ocean barge, thank heavens.'

'Amen,' I said piously, bored. 'Rye be long, will he?'

We stood listening. Rye's really quite good, giving out water heights, great sailing barges from the Thames, the current mania for petrol engines. The antiques dealer in me smiled approval. Like I keep saying, passion rules where antiques hold sway.

Therla eventually herded her brood out, after begging

Rye to come to give her children an hour's lecture on sailing vessels. The duckegg agreed. Therla has means of persuasion.

'Hello, Lovejoy.' Rye looked tired as he came back from seeing Therla's mob off. He's one of these men people call clean-shaven, as if he somehow deserves a knighthood for using a razor of a morning.

'Tell me, Rye.' I paused. Hang on. Tell what *about*?

I gaped because he'd recoiled in sudden alarm, stepped back so swiftly I had to reach, pull him away from the great millstones. You can lock the colossal discs by means of a lever. I gave him what for. 'You stupid burke, Rye!' I yelled, mad as hell. 'You nearly went into the damned things! You're always on about safety, you pillock!'

He'd gone white as a sheet. 'I thought you meant—'

'What?' The barmy conversation was concluded when he shook his head in mute denial. We walked to his office for a brew.

The walls were covered with maps, levels of water tables, canal widths, cross-sections of every river in East Anglia. This old watermill's a hobby. The Council give him a pittance to maintain the great quiet engine. Why him? Because he owns the garden centre and plant nursery on the river. His family's from Wenham, big landowners. To them that hath shall be given. Some deserving pauper like me should have Rye's job. Makes you sick, but I'm not jealous.

'I'm after advice, Rye.' I saw his guarded look disappear when I asked if he knew about some big shed, warehouse, anything new on the rivers.

'Nothing that isn't filled with container loads from the Hook of Holland, Lovejoy. It's rivalry time since the Channel Tunnel thing.'

'Any new stream? A dam? Canal being drained?

Workings reopened like they did at Dedham's Stour? You know, the ones Constable painted by that teashop?'

That gleam of caution came and went. I put it down to my fatigue over Prammie Joe. I was seeing things. And I'd selected Rye practically at random, hadn't I? Well, hadn't I? Near enough, yes. Except Rye was the only waterman as learned about tides and rivers as Prammie Joe.

We talked a while. He praised our three consecutive bad winters. Nothing improved the Eastern Hundreds' water table like snow and hard frosts. He waxed enthusiasm. I concurred, wondering what the hell I was doing there.

'Ta, Rye,' I said, bored sick. 'Think of anything, eh?'

He was too casual. 'What's the interest?'

'Oh, some old, er, canal tokens are on sale at Wittwoode's Auction. Sometimes a batch comes ahead of a rush.'

The relief on his face was a pleasure to see. He came to the car.

'Special edition motor, Lovejoy! Business booming?'

'Not bad,' I said modestly. 'Want to make an offer?'

'I'll soon have enough for something *really* special.'

I drove away, thinking there was something I'd missed. Like a fool I'd forgotten what Prammie had told me, when we were laughing about his loading up the stuff at Cornish Place.

He'd rescued a schoolboy. From a place . . . Therla said something about nearly losing a boy. From drowning? In the Stour? But her lad had been rescued by an ocean-going barge, not a small pram propelled by an old ex-convict laid horizontal in the thwarts. His last journey, had Prammie Joe told me? A week ago, had Therla said?

Luna was at the cottage, fuming with the electricity, gas, water, TV men. I beckoned, pulled her in.

'Luna, love.' I drove away immediately. Movement distracts women; any sort will do. 'I want you to—'

'What on earth?' She gaped round. 'Leaving all those men in the cottage? They could steal—'

'We've nothing to steal,' I shot cruelly. 'You gave it away.'

'There's the schoolteacher's coffee pot,' she said, stung. 'I've made the men some coffee in it.'

My headache started skull-splitting. 'You did *what?*'

'I had to pay a fortune, unfortunately, but you said—'

She was insane. I gave up. 'Ipswich, Luna. *East Anglian Daily Times*. You're a reporter from London asking about a schoolboy rescued from the River Stour last week. Okay? You're thinking of a national feature, local bravery, hazards of the eastern rivers. Tell them anything. But find out.'

'Won't they be busy with their next issue? Only, reporters are always in such a rush.'

'They won't be today, love,' I said bitterly. 'They will be tomorrow.'

Fraud rules. It rules because everybody loves deception. Who has never felt that sneaky twinge of admiration, hearing of some nerk who tricked a gullible bank out of millions? Don't let's fool ourselves. We love it. The most secret twinge of all we reserve for ourselves regret that *we* didn't dare do it. Imagine the ecstasy when, shacked up with the birds in Bahia's sunlight, you dream of old Fanshawe opening the vaults on Monday morning to find your cocky little note saying ta-ta. It's your dream, my dream, everybody's dream. No good being offended by my accusation. We all admire Robin Hood. In moral terms, he's a common thief. Legally, a rascally felon. But to us? He's superb, a riot, applauded down the centuries. *Because he got away with it!*

Come what may, fraud rules. Who leads in the Great Fraud Handicap Stakes? Well, bankers are front runners (sorry about the pun). Lawyers are contenders. Clerics closing on the bend, charity workers. Civil servants are also-rans, left standing by local government councillors. The fraud field is a cavalry charge. Politicians as fraudsters are the rule rather than the exception. Antique dealers are total. Consider them auctioneers minus respectability. For me, auctioneers are the pits. They defraud under false colours, priests who poison the chalice.

I went for the walk round the village, not to think so much as to not think. That's the way. Let learning in by osmosis. Suddenly you'll realise that you knew all the time, but didn't want to let on to yourself. Perhaps the truth reveals the treachery of a friend. Perhaps that flash of understanding proves that the ultimate nerk is none other than your very own self. I found myself watching Leone's nags.

They like me. All pets do. If I nod off in the garden hedgehogs come and kip nearby. Cats doze on my belly. Birds goof on my shoulder while I kip. I'm like Francis of Assisi. Leone's nag is Harry, a giant beast that slobbers like a baker's drain. I quite like animals. I'd like them better if they'd keep their distance. Leone's a blonde thirty. She rides up our lane from Seven Arches where her beasts fool about on the grass. She rides without a crash helmet the better to be seen. She's gorgeous.

'Hello, Lovejoy.'

'Wotcher, Leone. What's he running round in a ring for?'

'Exercise. He loves it, don't you, Harry?'

Harry looked fed up. Three littles came to hang on the fencing. Candice is their leader, aged six. I babysit for these three when their mums are desperate.

'Ooooh. Look, Lovejoy! Harry's got new feet on!'

'And skin,' added Jondie, a tiny four-year-old who steals my flowers for his rapacious guinea-pigs.

'Can't have,' I informed them loftily.

'Lovejoy's wrong,' Violet announced. She's three, can whistle through her fingers.

Then I noticed Leone had gone pink. I looked at Candice. 'New feet? What colour are his others?'

'Fluffy white. Or brown.'

'Grey sometimes,' said Jondie. 'My Dad does it.'

'Boils grass in a pan. It stinks. My Dad only plays cards.'

'Tough luck, Violet,' I commiserated. 'Hear that, Leone? Your horse Harry is fashion mad. He'll miss the point-to-point at Webberswick now, eh?'

She slowed her nag, let him crop the grass. I watched her stroll over.

'It's the usual thing, Lovejoy. That's all.' Harry was a big animal. Reputedly fast. I worked it out. Here a stain, there a stain, might help in shifting the odds. 'Does no harm, Lovejoy.' She pressed my arm, the way wheedling begins. 'It's only foreigners get bled. Not locals.'

She waxed about her fraudulent arrangements while I listened. Every so often, little Candice and her pair weighed in with small technical details. Violet's card-playing dad did a good line in false tails, it seemed. Not all poker, then.

Leone wheedled, 'Who minds if a few rich strangers lose a penny here, a penny there, Lovejoy?'

'What if I turned up and bet?'

'You never do, Lovejoy. Anyway, we'd put you right.'

Local approval justifies bleeding dry the nerks from elsewhere. Antiques in a nutshell. I'd forgotten the obvious.

Candice said disarmingly, 'Daddy gets lots of pennies.'

Leone pinked nearer red. 'Time you three got home,' she said quickly.

They left, calling so-long. Candice told the others, with the gravity of her six summers, 'Leone wants to suck mouths with Lovejoy, like she does with the vicar.'

And . . . silence. Leone blood scarlet now. The whole

village was in on it. Except me. Mind you, I'm the last person to watch nags trot, phoney feet or no phoney feet.

'It's not fraud, Lovejoy. It's usual. Good heavens, it's a saying: horse of a different colour.'

'Come here, you,' I said roughly. She came closer. I leant over and we sucked mouths. She broke away breathless.

'You won't let on, Lovejoy?'

By then I was walking quickly away, calling over my shoulder, 'Why should I? It's usual.'

And it is, truly. I'd missed it. Candice made me carry Violet piggy-back the half-mile uphill into the village. She promised not to tell the vicar that me and Leone sucked mouths. I didn't believe her. She'd blab. Females start fibs early. They made me sing 'Curlylocks', my one pathetic tactic for getting infants to kip. They listened gravely, little Vi silently mouthing the words. I felt a prat. My showstopper done, I waved the trio of wide-awakes off at my gate.

Which left me sitting on my wall. It isn't every day you discover a new universal law. But how important it was. *Small* local deceits have their own inbuilt honour. Everybody local has a right to know about them. On demand, you might say. But major ones are different. They're alien. They are the biggies, the grandies.

How many massive antique scams could I think of? A score, offhand. Leaving aside the atrocious Hammer monolith of Los Angeles, grand scams come clamouring for attention. But beware. The legitimate collection of Mona Lisa fakes covering Cartier's wall, for example, doesn't count.

Some things do. The uproar over the Dead Sea Scrolls – who should have access to study them – gave rise in 1989 to shoals of scholarly fraudsters who flitted through the groves of academe offering complete copies for 165,000 pounds sterling, in advance. Collectors fell for it. Strapped universities desperately struggled to fall for it, but couldn't raise the advance – and thereby saved their reputations. For the Scrolls are the most jealously guarded hoard in the world. Gelt in the vault. The paranoid secrecy of minders – i.e. greed – plays, as ever, into the hands of grand scammers.

If obsessional neuroses can do it, so can fame. I've seen thirty, maybe forty, valuable pieces of the Marcos silver sold in auctions never noticed by the press, when everybody knows that Christie's in New York handled the real Old Masters and silver in 1991, of course, raising a cool 10.6 million pounds. A Paul Storr silver dinner service, George III, made a fortune. Bidders wept because fame forced prices over the top. Poor them. Still, if they will go for the genuine stuff . . .

And everybody knows about war booty. If you don't, you ought. It's the commonest grand scam around. After the German Government bought some war treasure in 1991 – Quedlinburg, World War II – for, word is, a million, it became open season. You hire front men ('mouthies' in the trade) of the right educational background. You invent some treasure. Your mouthies tour museums, collectors. They whisper the terrible fact that, alas, the jewel-encrusted illuminated Gospel of 1558 is, with its ancient silver chalice, actually war loot. Good heavens! the eager buyers cry, sending the mouthies packing – only as far as the corner pub, where the secret deal is struck. Discount applies, for there's the risk that Gold Coast countries will play hell over the priceless Benin metalwork heads, or Italy over that Leonardo drawing. Inevitably, lawyers help, for where lawyers roam illegitimacy rules. Grand stammers recently offered that cache of Chesterton letters in at least three countries, though the real cache of two hundred poems, plays, prose works, now slumbers ignored in London's

British Library. And law courts everywhere rejoice over the Sevso silver treasure that the whole world will be suing over until Doomsday. The repayments newly offered to Czarist bondholders (Czar Alexander III himself pulled this majestic scam in the 1880s) has started a giddy spiral of phoney printed bonds. (Take care: the ones I've seen so far are simply Russian laundry lists, printed in Fulham.) See? Greed again.

And the world spins in its happy course. China's gigantic Orange Ape-Man. Saints' replicas (the all-time favourite grand scam). Bronze Age ferry boats discovered in river beds, the whereabouts known only to my friend here who will offer *to you alone!* this priceless genuine ancient map revealing its location for the cheap sum of . . . And the gems smuggled out from Afghanistan during the Mujahedin war, which my friend has a sack of and will offer *to you alone!* for the cheap sum of . . . Et incredible cetera.

They work. Every time. Always. Read here, they seem daft. But if somebody actually *did* come up to you Oxford, titled family, dressed to the nines, a bishop in tow – and sadly told you he was having to broker the sale of a valuable church treasure, on account of fiscal difficulties the diocese didn't want revealed, and that His Lordship the bishop here would take you round St Winston's to meet the church synod's secretary. And that the price *to you alone!* was the unbelievably low sum of . . .

Temptation? A little, maybe. And a little temptation always wins hands down. There's no recorded instance of a big temptation. Superfluous.

Now, I'm a titch in the antiques trade. We don't have grand scams hereabouts. They're for the Continent, London, Birmingham, the high levels.

My thoughts ended there. Some foods are too rich.

Chapter 10

The worst of other people's admiration is that it's deceit. I mean, even a statue of God wears a pigeon on its head, right? Feet of clay. I pulled myself together and got going.

Luna was dispatched to Ipswich – maybe she'd get the right city, of East Anglia's two. She had to get something right, for God's sake or mine. I went to the Arcade. Sandy's Dutch Treaty shop on East Hill was shut ('Catch Me If You Can,' the CLOSED notice was subtitled). No answer either at Connie's small one-room shop which stood one door uphill. I wanted to know what Drinkwater had asked him about.

Big Frank from Suffolk was in, buying silver like the maniac he is. He was especially mournful today.

'Not another, Frank?' I asked. It was my way of checking if the news of Prammie Joe was out. Big Frank has no one place, just scoots round the small coastal villages after silver.

'You wouldn't chuckle, Lovejoy.'

Indeed. Big Frank has marriage like the rest of us have blackheads. I forget how many wives he's had. He pays maintenance to a monstrous regiment. I've been to six of his weddings, plus four engagements.

'What happened? Your latest wife was bonny.'

'She accused me of having it away with the woman in the farm opposite.'

'Look, Frank.' I was disappointed, because I'd been their best man. 'These new wives. Once or twice, but isn't Dodie your eighth? Why don't I explain? After all, the woman in the farm opposite . . .'

'Her sister, mmmh. What about this, Lovejoy?'

He showed me a lovely rectangular standish, silver, with its inkwell and pounce pot absolutely unblemished. Connie Hopkins was hovering nearby: it was her inordinately extortionate price ticket. Connie uses the SUTHERLAND code I once told you about, reversing the letters every quarter day. S = 1, U = 2, and so on. Other dealers use their kiddies' names. Really truly mind-boggling clever, no? Stroll through any antique shop, you can crack their code in the time it takes to ask the price of two single antiques. Remember that they mark the price *they paid*, not the price they'll sell at. For that, nowadays, add two hundred per cent. Modern retail jewellers mark up new bangles, rings, pendants, earrings, exactly that. Test it out. Buy a new gold-and-sapphire ring, take it to a different reputable jeweller, and try to sell it. If he offers *half* the price you've paid, you've done well.

'Got the original gum?' I asked. The pounce pot was not filled with sand, as commonly believed, but with powered gum sandarac, to re-buff the paper if the old writers had to erase a mistake.

It looked right. It felt right. But sadly it made me feel as if I was sort of leaning over. Right but wrong.

'What metal?' It felt really queer, almost rippling in my hands. I stared hard at the hallmarks. 'Better Nine?'

A certain horribleness began in December, 1478. Every St Dunstan's Day, 19 May, a twenty-year cycle of letters was stamped on silver, A the first year, B the second, so on. Once King Charlie II came in 1660, the change-day became his birthday, Oak-Apple Day, 29 April. But still the letter cycle went relentlessly on. Except 1696–7, when the Britannia standard upped to 11 ounces and 10 pennyweights (95.8%, if you're a decimal crank). This means 8 pennyweights more to the Troy pound than sterling! Astonishment! New silver was worth more! (This was necessary because the naughty old public were clipping coins). And, gasp-shockhorror, the twenty-year letter cycle was interrupted! A seated woman, Britannia, showed up on the mark. There's been one other interruption to the letter cycle in 1975, but that doesn't matter, being modern.

'It's old standard, Lovejoy, looks like to me.'

'Mmmmh.' Meaning, oh, sure, but no thank you. Its matt quality disturbed me.

Lately, we'd been seeing a lot of these pieces. All desirable, all beautifully made. And all having that lovely matt look to the truly ancient (genuine) silver. I'd bet all I had – well, all I owed – that, if this piece was tested in London's Queen Mary College by flame photometry or whatever, it would be pristine medieval silver. The hallmark was a letter T on a little barrel (Ton tun, for Taunton, get it? They loved puns), and Britannia. And a maker's mark, initials, four times. The old silversmiths were past masters at dodging tax duty, and repeated their marks a few times – four's usual hoping customers would assume that one mark was the official Government-decreed one.

Well. Beautiful. But that terrible matt look. I polished the edge of the box on my sleeve. It felt ancient, bonging gently, but it felt wriggly. 'How many'd it take, Frank?' *I had him.*

'What're you talking about, Lovejoy?'

'Frank. Take a crucible filled with silver Saxon pennies. Clean them. Melt them down. Get Heppie to make you a lovely new standish like this. Stamp it with a few marks, and take it all unsuspecting to Lovejoy. He divvies it. After all, it's genuine ancient silver, right?'

These tricks make people shrink in my eyes. Big Frank looked heartbroken, but that was only the spectre of no bunce, no profit. He'd chosen the place, his audience. Now they all knew he was on the fiddle. Just to get more wealth for a new wife. Marriage has a lot to answer for. I'd thought better of him.

'You that desperate, Frank? That you'd try to con me?' On the same level as that Vienna bloke who worked the *Lucona* sinking. He claimed 18.5 million dollars insurance, after having the 11,000-ton ship blown to blazes. Fine, eh? Except for the half-dozen who went to watery graves. Horror makes you bitter, sad for us all. We only pretend civilization.

'Sorry, Lovejoy.' He sounded really down.

Everybody in the Arcade had stopped talking. Connie was studiously scanning some Christie's Impressionist catalogues. Even Acker Kirwin, apparently in to hump some old Sir Johns – chamber pots in wooden boxes, sometimes (but rarely) built up like square-topped stools – stood observing the drama.

Unpleasantness makes you feel in the springtime of senility, the dawn of decay. And Prammie Joe was no nearer seeing tomorrow's sunshine.

I drifted off. Connie didn't meet my eye. Big Frank came after me as I walked down to Woody's caff. He tried buttering me up, 'It's these payments, Lovejoy. I'm going under.' I walked on, head down, seeing only that terrible cloud buzzing in that low doorway among the reeds. Then I stopped all of sudden, by the Bugler pub near the war memorial.

'What was that, Frank?'

'Well, Lovejoy. There *is*.' He shrugged. 'It's a oncer, see? Things have been rough. I've tried a million other lines, but silver . . .' His eyes glowed with the fervour of the lunatic. 'She said I could come in, if I'd chip a tenth. Endless profits. I could buy into Continental silver, even English Huguenot . . .'

He rambled on in delirium. In the town centre, traffic swishing past and people hurrying with prams. I hadn't a clue what he was on about. But I'd never seen him like this before. I eyed him. Another huge-scale scam, for Christ's sake?

His eyes were afire. 'I'd need a year's wage, Lovejoy.' So the scam meant at least ten times that. Bridge loans in antiques cost a tenth.

'Frank. I'll try to lend you, if I can. Can you trust her, though?' With Frank, it's always a bird, sometimes even one he's married to. I was fishing.

He looked about, for ex-wives skulking among the shoppers. 'Jenny's straight as a die.' He smiled shyly. 'We're engaged.'

Par for his course. 'I'll see. Chop straight, eh?'

'Lovejoy, you're a pal. Yes, even share-out. I really appreciate you not being narked.'

'About the standish? Nar, Frank. Some punter'll happen by.'

We parted amicably. But I was now frantic, as well as baffled. Something was turning all the dealers into maniacs. I alone was sane and fair-minded, as usual.

I called in six antique shops more, and emerged triumphant. Jenny Calamy lived out near Woodbridge, and had been in Big Frank's company closer than somewhat. Calamy sounds like calamity, and Calamity Jenny's the name of her shop. J. Calamy had met Big Frank over antiques, yes, but they both attended The Great Marvella and her talking snake. For massage and conversation, the latter being three-way, four-tongued psychoanalysis. And I had an appointment with her. Had had? Some tense or other. I invented excuses as I hurried that way, in case I'd got the date wrong.

The buzzer changed to the snake's fluty voice instantly, clicked the door open. I went in slowly. One day, maybe there'd only be the snake there, fat about the middle, and no Marvella. There were two voices.

'Watch this, Cassandra,' Vell's voice said, choking laughing. 'Come in, Lovejoy. He'll dither for hours. Geronimo's gone to bed.'

Inchwise I peered round. There on the couch was Vell. And Cassandra Clark. Even lovelier. Never mind them, the snake was in its cage. It looked without hostility. I'd rather it hated me. Or loathed. That anonymity was the killer.

'Cassandra's just finished, Lovejoy.'

They smiled at each other with merriment. I didn't get the joke. Finished?

'Told a good fortune?' I said, trying jocularity. Geronimo watched. Its head moved slightly.

'Quite fair,' Cassandra said. More hidden smiles were exchanged, but women do that all the time around me. I didn't attach too much importance to it. 'Geronimo was particularly optimistic.'

'Good old Geronimo.' I didn't really want to be on speaking terms with him. I felt awkward with Cassandra here.

She's a hard lass. Looks as if butter really truly wouldn't. Cassandra Clark had quality, but her handbag was sure to be loaded. I thought about her visit to my workshop. She had a Past, the Arcade hinted. Touched antiques, examined them. Never, ever bought. Word was she used a whole shoal of buncers dealers who buy solely on commission

– sworn to secrecy, exporting to the USA. I could eat her with a spoon. Or without, though chance'd be a fine thing. She was dressed to kill, everything matching, with that casual oh-what-a-mess hairstyle that costs the earth. It needs lustrous youth, plus what Chinese dealers call Vitamin M. Money.

A man between two women doesn't have much of a chance. And knowing what they say isn't exactly the same as knowing what they mean. A man between two birds feels about four years old, and that's a fact.

'What is it, Lovejoy? Brought your problems to Geronimo?' From Cassandra, laid back, smart.

Cutting my losses, I smiled apology to Marvella. 'Look, love. About money. I wonder if you're flush. Only, I've had a few expenses and . . .'

'What do you think I am, Lovejoy?' Vell bridled. Geronimo hissed a snakely chuckle. 'Made of money?'

That sounded authentic. My begging patter sounded right, so maybe I'd convinced Cassandra I was simply here on the cadge.

'I know, love. But it's for something special.'

That seemed to stop the conversational flow. I swear there was a kind of tension in the room that hadn't been there before.

'What special?' Vell asked.

'I'm trying to escape from under,' I said apologetically, wanting out.

'A woman? You mean a woman, Lovejoy?'

'Yes.' I added lamely, 'It's a bit difficult. She wants to divorce her bloke, and marry me. I've got too much on—'

Cassandra nodded. Vell said smoothly, 'How much?'

'Grub. Today, tomorrow. A taxi to the auctions, maybe enough to deposit on something.'

Cassandra nodded again. And immediately The Great

Marvella said, 'Honestly, Lovejoy! You'll be the death of me. I thought you'd come for an ephemeris analysis.'

With that snake in the room? People are daft. Vell gave me a few notes. I said thank you so very sincerely and Cassandra smiled and Geronimo watched and Vell and Cassandra smiled and I retreated down the stairs calling thanks until I was safe among pedestrians and sweating heavily, not knowing why. Sweat trickled from my chin.

Luna picked me up from the war memorial, and I borrowed this beekeeper's gear.

Torrance is a fat geezer you wouldn't ever imagine keeps bees. He lives down on the Colne, where you wouldn't think there are many bees anyhow. He sells the honey, and brews mead and sells that. He talks to them, which all beekeepers do, as if the hives were filled with real people.

He charged me a fortune, the swine. He was desperate to know if the bees I was going after were wild bumble bees, or a cultivated stock. I told him my girlfriend's dad was mad about bees, to shut him up. The goon followed me out to the car wanting recruits for his manky beekeeping society. What a nerk. I loaded up and told Luna to drive to the cottage.

There we inspected the depredations done by the skilled artificers of the Eastern Hundreds. Mercifully, the pot was still intact. It was the first thing I looked at, but the phone shrilled. Phones are a mistake.

'He's just here. It's urgent, Lovejoy.'

'Ever known a phone call that wasn't?' I said sourly.

'Hello, Lovejoy, I'm in Edinburgh.' Miss Turner. I glared, threatened Luna with a fist. She smiled serenely back. 'It's so different! Can you tell me where I am, please?'

One day I'll escape. Then what will the world do? 'Where are you? *Exactly*? Read the name.'

Pause, clatter, a breathless hello. 'General Register House, Lovejoy. Opposite the North British Hotel. It's really quite nice.'

'You stupid old mare!' I yelled in fury while Luna tried to calm me down. I clouted her away and bawled, 'I distinctly told you not to go to the wrong place. Didn't I? *Didn't I?*'

'Please don't be angry, Lovejoy,' the old lady quavered. 'But I'm on my own and—'

Bloody fine. Loses herself, then rings me to sort her out. Typical. 'Listen, you daft old bat. Is there a big statue outside? Duke of Wellington?'

'Why, yes!' She was delighted. 'Very imposing, with—'

'You stupid mare! You're in the Scottish Record Office's place. You want the General Register Office for Scotland, silly cow. Births, marriages, deaths and census records.' I made her write it down, read it back. 'Got it, you silly old fool?'

'Got it, Lovejoy,' she cooed happily. 'Now, where exactly . . . ?'

'New Register House,' I said, broken. 'It's next door to where you're standing. Go there immediately. And never ring me again.' I slammed the receiver down on the crazy old loon. Honest to God. Where was I? Luna's pot.

Luna was quite put out. 'You haven't noticed, Lovejoy!' She indicated the cottage. Electric light, bulbs and everything. Gas, on. Water, on. Phone, on.

'The cost was too great, love. That tole tray was something we'll possibly never see ever again in a lifetime.' I smiled at her, held up the lovely stoneware nipple-spout Castleford feeding-pot. 'This makes up for it, partly. About 1795. Like it?'

What a stupid question. She smiled tentatively. 'Well, yes. But those holes in the spout. Why isn't it proper?'

Headache time. I sighed. Baby feeders are called

'hubby pots' in the trade, because Dr Hugh Smith in 1777 invented one sort and called it that. Transfer-printed ones were made by Wedgwood, or plain cream-ware. They are lovely. Specialist items, of course, but so far hardly ever faked or even copied.

'You did well,' I said. She was pleased, and we rested a bit. I asked if she'd ever heard of The Great Marvella. She said yes, several acquaintances went to her. Did I know she actually had a talking snake? I said I'd heard.

Then I had the wit to ask if she'd ever heard of Cassandra Clark. Luna said yes, she did improving social causes. In fact, Miss Clark was on the Mayor's fund-raising charity committee. Oliver knew her. She Had Money.

Dusk falls slowly at first in East Anglia, then suddenly tumbles over the edge into the pitch black. I didn't want to be on my own, not knowing what I'd have to face, so I told Luna we were going to work late and would she drive me. She was doubtful until I said it was a secret. Then she was all thrilled and shrieked of course and we went out towards the estuaries, down where the marshes meet the tides and the rivers end in low mudflats.

Chapter 11

'Lovejoy.' Luna dropped me off at the lane head. 'Why the outfit?' She meant I was getting out of hand.

I gathered it in my arms. 'You'd be surprised how much clobber you need to look at a bee.'

She looked worried. 'Lovejoy. Oliver always asks what I've done each day. What shall I say?'

'It's confidential.' Others can use the lie word, so can I.

'But this—' She gestured at the darkening countryside, the loneliness of it. 'It's nothing to *do* with antiques.'

I leaned into the car. 'Everything I do is to do with antiques, love. Remember that.'

The buzzing was fitful. I heard it from quite a distance. But I went through the hedge and donned the protective gear. I had a smoke gun to doze them, but wasn't sure how to use it. Did it make me sleepy as well? Or, worse, did it act on me but not the bees? For bees read another kind of flying object.

There was just enough daylight when I reached the little hut. Except I could hardly see a damned thing. Torrance hadn't warned me about this net mask. It blacks out your sight. No wonder beekeepers always get stung. But I made it into the hut and gagged a few times, avoiding Prammie Joe's buzzing horrible thick black teeming mess of a face

. . . I won't describe it. There was a squirming mound on the floor beneath his chair. It stank, the whole place. I tried not to stand in anything, leave footprints, but who could see? Ugh. I retched inside the mask, searched his cupboards, drawing my hands away sharply in disgust when blowflies came between my fingers. Nothing. You never do. But on the planking floor, near where he Aussie-crouched to watch the birds of an eve, was a fold of paper. I grabbed it and shot out. I'd had enough.

Gagging, I escaped, blundered, crashing, down to the water, still retching. It was some time before I had the sense to peer up and down the small tributary. I got a stick, prodded the water. A few inches. How much did a boat need?

There was an ugly moment when I found three blue-bottles were trapped inside my hood with me. I shouted, ripping off the mask and batting it on my thigh, struggled to get it back on before the rest of that hideous swarm came buzzing on my face, my eyes. I found I'd held my breath like a fool. I was almost fainting.

Which, I resumed weakly, raised the question of where the pram was. I knew about one of Prammie's rafts – safe in the hands of that Cradhead. But the other? And the pram? If hereabouts, it would be well hidden. Prammie Joe hadn't been detected by the vigilant watchers of Cornish Place. So he wouldn't be spotted by home-goers from the village pub, would he?

Twenty minutes later I'd changed, and met Luna.

Did anybody see you?' I asked, all nonchalant, Lovejoy the countryman, pally with ornithology or whatever bees are.

'No, Lovejoy.' She stared hard in the dashboard lights. It was now quite dark, our sudden fall to blackness. 'You've been sick, Lovejoy. And that clothing smells.'

Trust her, silly cow. 'Remember Ipswich?'

Half an hour's lecture on the state of Ipswich's traffic, then she told me. Zilch. Nothing. No reports in the papers, no boy falling in the water and being rescued. I'd have to suss out Therla Brewer myself.

'Luna. Ever heard of anybody called Calamy?' No. She hadn't. 'Or Godbolt?' Not that either.

But the names were worrying. Godbolt. Calamy. Hopkins. Clark? Funny, but I knew somehow there was yet another. A quite ordinary English name. I couldn't for the life of me think. I put my head back on the seat as she drove. So far, I'd heard of a scam that had vanished, lost an old pal by foul means, searched for knew-not-what, and found nowt. Now I was trying to remember something I'd maybe never heard of. God Almighty. What a pillock.

To please Luna, I told her to sell the feeding pot in Wittwoode's Auction. She'd done quite well. I had to teach her some antiquery, besides murder, or Oliver Carstairs, Mayor, might get narked.

Joan Vervain came to the cottage that night. She did her screams of abuse at her husband on his radio show while we made smiles. Wondrous, of course. That rush to paradise can't ever be anything else. But I was fed up. Her rabbiting on about Monte Carlo or Mustique narked me. I felt bought, for development. I mean, I'd ditched the bloody woman days ago, yet here she still was, more here than ever.

A pile of agents' brochures, showing Mediterranean places, was provided for me to approve. The lawyers would meet Del Vervain next Monday, and the news of the divorce would hit the world. Together, she said coyly along the pillow, with the announcement of our impending marriage. Which saw the night through, to the pale feet of morn.

*   *   *

Two things: I'd somehow see Jenny Calamy, and discover if she fitted in to Prammie Joe's scam. I had only met her once, and even then we'd had a row about a piece of Meissen. She swore the decoration was 'genuine factory'. But crossed swords marks which have a nick in them show the piece was sold 'in the white' and decorated elsewhere. It would have been better if the crossed swords had had an 'S', signifying Samson of Paris, a notable copier/faker whose work is highly sought. You can't tell some folk.

Especially you can't tell Big Frank that your visit to his next wife is entirely platonic – i.e. sexless. He's dynamite on fiancées. I'd have to think up some legitimate reason. I fed the birds – the lot of them were sulking, because I'd had a bad morning last time – then had my breakfast. Fried tomatoes pall sometimes, but there aren't many alternatives when they're what you've got. I went to do my washing. I've got one spare sheet, change it every week. The blanket rarely needs washing, but I hang it on the washing line sometimes. I forget to bring it in, and have to wear all my things to get to sleep. Night dew falls early on the coast.

There's a launderette in the village, up by the Bungalow Stores. It sells you a cup of powder, and you watch the washing going round, trying not to listen to the daft taped music. Some children came in, larking about. I watched them playing ghosts, springing out and frightening each other. One took the broom from the corner and rode it round. It wasn't All Hallows Eve yet, nowhere near. Some American horror film in town, I supposed. The dump felt empty when they were shooed out by Old Bessie.

The second thing was La Brewer. The discovery of Prammie Joe's body by the Old Bill might take a day, a week. All hell would be let loose. Why had Drinkwater been to see Sandy? Plenty of other dealers were interested in antique furnishings. In fact, you could even say that every dealer was. Maybe because Sandy and Mel were the wealthiest of our local dealers? The Cornish Place turkey job was a matter of millions, biggest scam we'd had in years. No wonder somebody killed Joe.

Had Joe wanted a share? Was that the reason?

Surely it had to be. Why else? Prammie knew what he was doing. Theft is theft, however skilled. I was the only one who knew how he'd done it, because . . . Hang on a sec. I thought about that as I counted my socks – they get eaten by Old Bessie's machines. I *couldn't* be the only one who knew, could I? I mean, whoever had commissioned Prammie Joe to turkey Cornish Place also knew, right?

Prammie had mentioned some bloke he'd met in clink. Somebody he was in gaol with. That same killer had known that Prammie Joe, elusive waterman, was the only bloke in the Eastern Hundreds who could pull it off.

Who else had been in nick lately? Answer: Acker Kirwin. Easy peasy. Acker had done Prammie in. QED? It seemed logical. Those names came into my mind, and I dozed.

'Lovejoy?' Bessie was shaking me. 'Lovejoy? You've done your washing three times. Did you mean to?'

'Mmmmh?' God, it was ten o'clock. 'Mmmh? Oh, aye, Bessie. It was, er, messy. I've been gardening.'

Bessie's an old crone who knows I don't garden. She got my stuff in silence, bagged it up for me. Wet washing's horrible stuff. Ever noticed that?

'Big Frank's his name,' I told Luna. She was waiting in the porch. She looked really attractive, pastel twin set and smart suit, the skirt well cut. Her rings were too classy for an antique dealer's apprentice. At first I'd said to dress down rather than up.

'Whose name, Lovejoy? And good morning, Luna.'

'Good morning, Luna. The dealer. Ask him if you can go and see Jenny Calamy. Her address,' I added grandly, 'will be in my new phone book. You misappropriated my money to have us connected, so use it.'

'Here, Lovejoy.' She took the washing. I followed her on to the grass while she pegged out the wet things.

She'd given me an envelope. Cheques from the gas, electricity, phone, television people. Rebates? Now, our local services don't make rebates except on the rack, not even if they owe you.

'It's money I didn't spend. The tole tray.' She had pegs in her mouth and spoke past them, the way they do. I try this, but I choke. Women's mouths are fantastic, a life of their own . . . 'Somebody else had already paid, Lovejoy. They'll repossess the spare TV set. We can leave it in our porch.'

Our? Well, she was an appentice. 'Good girl.'

'I read until very late last night, Lovejoy.' She paused, faced me. She looked lovely against the green grass, the hedgerow russets. 'I apologise. I realise now what a wonder that antique was. To me, it was simply an old tray. Seeing you do that dividing—'

'Divvieing.'

'—in the old aerodrome cellar explained a great deal.'

A But was on the way. Women have conditions; we have deceit.

'But why are you so, forgive me, poor?'

'I'm not poor,' I gave her, stung. 'It's just I have a lot of friends. And I . . .' I shrugged, looked for escape.

'You're hopeless, Lovejoy. A scatterbrain. Money, clothes. Your cottage is upside down. And . . .'

More praise? I always get this. She'd start staying late, tidying me up so I couldn't find a flaming thing.

'You are taken advantage of, get into scrapes. Incur

obligations and escape them by your love of these old things.'

'These old things, love,' I cut in, narked, 'are all that matters. I keep telling you. Frigging well listen.' I envy Americans. They have this commanding phrase, *listen up*. It means harken intently or you're for it. 'Up,' I added defiantly.

'Lovejoy. I'm worried by all these journeys you make me do.'

She hadn't enough pegs to hang the remaining wet things out. I said not to worry. They always blow about the garden anyway. I once found a pillow case with a nest in, low down among the hawthorns. I didn't know I'd lost it.

One day, I'm going to stop explaining. 'They're vital. Jenny's engaged to Big Frank. Go carefully, because of his wife. His mistress, her sister, lives in the farm opposite.'

'Lovejoy,' Luna said. 'Are we in difficulties?'

'Us?' This time I rather liked the plural. We walked back up to the cottage, my arm through hers. 'Never in a million years, love. Remember the feeding pot. Wittwoode's. Don't accept an auction number below ten, nor in the last eight.'

'Why not?'

'It's where gunge goes.'

She plugged the kettle in, cast about for cups. 'I couldn't help noticing those bee clothes. They're still sort of slimy. I'll have my maid see to them. That veil thing . . . Lovejoy?'

Quickly she stood close, taking my arm. I sat on the divan. 'We'll have some tea before we go anywhere. You look quite pale.'

'Fine,' I piped heartily. 'Take it to Torrance. Tell him ta.'

'And what do I buy from Miss Calamy?'

'You do something really sly, Luna,' I said. 'Nothing. You're just my apprentice, seeing how an average antiques shop is run. Don't go without Big Frank's permission.'

When I felt better I dialled Sandy, to get him to explain some of the nastier antique dealer tricks to my new apprentice, a lady called Luna. He was in, and garrulous.

'So you flew to me, fountain head of deceit, Lovejoy!' he shrilled. 'How perceptive!'

'You be nice to her, Sandy. Y'hear?'

'Could I fail, dear? What colours is this perfectly grotesque obese cow trying to wear?'

'Er . . .' I avoided looking. 'I'm not sure. I haven't seen her yet this morning. She's putting a piece in Wittwoode's. Guide her, will you?'

'Very well, Lovejoy. It will be a change from that *oaf* Drinkwater, though his friend Cradhead—'

Quickly sussing, I put in. 'Troubling you?'

'I mean, I don't even *know* Spoolie. He's *far* too plain!' Oscar Wilde's line. 'I shall pretend your tart's a customer.' He tittered. 'Lovejoy, I want to thank you for sending her. A perfectly *marvellous* opportunity to *shine*.'

Click, burr. 'Sandy's, er, mannered, Luna,' I said. 'Sort of eccentric. Tell me everything he says. Especially names.'

We went to the motor. I dropped her off at East Hill, then drove to The Ghool Spool.

Antiques are funny, meaning you never know where they begin and end. Some antiques are rightly seen as national treasures – like the famous Badminton Cabinet. Made in Florence in 1726, it was recently up for sale to an American heiress. Then political outrage set in, and people started bawling the usual old lines, selling our antiques is unpatriotic, all that old rubbish. It's what you mean by 'treasures' and 'antiques' that matters.

Antiques once meant only things from the Ancient world – Greece or Rome (but especially the latter, because the Romans never had any consumer-protection laws. The Greeks had). Then, modern times, antiques meant pre-1837. Gradually it crept nearer and nearer. 'Collectibles' arrived then, and 'Groupables'. Finally, 'Tomorrow's Antiques', the ultimate in fraudulence.

And the word began to spread its meaning, as well as its precisions. Anciently it meant only statuary. It then became jewellery, paintings, any artefact, and finally (fanfare, please) any marketable rubbish.

Which brings us to films, theatre ephemera. The Ghool Spool.

Of course, everybody's fascinated by the knickknacks of the famous. Bits off an emperor's gown, letters from Dickens to Harrison Ainsworth, pages of a Beethoven manuscript, anything that lends a name. They're only valuable, these googaws, because we the public make them so. Whether it's a bass guitar from the Beatles, or a Leonard Bernstein baton, age doesn't matter so much as the fame on the tag. But remember that in the shifting sands of ephemera, authenticity rules. You've got to be able to *prove* that doodle of crochets on an old omnibus ticket really was done by Delius.

Spoolie's not really called that. It's his nickname.

'Lovejoy, I've got nothing,' he said sadly as I entered under his clanging doorbell. 'Everything's less than a hundred years.'

'Just passing, Spoolie. Suppose I had a customer?'

As Spoolie launched into his spiel, I wandered round his little shop. It stands on the outskirts of Mistley, on an uphill road between two leaning pubs. I honestly can't understand the fascination of emphemera. Yet it powers mighty collectors. I know a bloke who mortgaged his house just to bid for old Ealing Studios furniture.

'That's honestly probably almost virtually nearly

positively genuine, that shoe.' Spoolie waxed eloquently. 'Carmen Miranda – remember her? She used to keep drugs in the huge heels of her dancing shoes. Did you know she danced without any knickers on?'

'Mmmmh, great, Spoolie.'

The shop was hung about with bike wheels, once ridden on by some movie cyclist. Clothes dangled from the ceiling. A rocking horse, once used on the stage. A dress, reputedly worn by Ava Gardner. (Spoolie: 'Ava said she got sold like a prize hog in that.')

'I'd love a pack of Bogart's cigarettes,' Spoolie wound on. He never sells videos, scorning secondary sources. 'I've written to the Mayor of Hollywood. I'm opening negotiations for that capital H in the Hollywood sign. You know the one? Just think, Lovejoy. Peg Entwistle chucked herself off it to her death in 1929. RKO wouldn't renew her contract. Can't you just see it? This place would become a Mecca for ephemerists.'

'Mmmmh, great, Spoolie.'

'Signatures are rare,' he told me mournfully. 'I'm down to autographs of cameramen, soundists' diaries, hankies with Orson Welles' initials. Vivien Leigh, though. I've two autographs of hers, but post-Olivier. A Marilyn Monroe cost me half a wage. Ronald Reagan's frigging *mother* signed all his postcards.'

'Mmmmh, great.'

'It's my ambition to do the Grave Rave Tour, Lovejoy. Hollywood. They finish, *Life is no rehearsal*. Pure magic!'

He had postcards, signed books, placemats and coasters, a guitar once played by youthful hopefuls long since insignificant. His shop was a hang-up trying to enter dreamscape.

'I'll kill for a photo of Mary Martin's ghost. Did you know she keeps appearing in Weatherford, Texas? Here,

Lovejoy. You're always broke. D'you think I'm doing the right thing? When I came out of nick—'

'You been inside, Spoolie?' This was why I'd come.

'Oh, a few months. I was fitted up. You know the Plod. A drainer, not even in my manor.'

A cat-burgling, outside his area. 'What got stolen?'

He shrugged. 'Money. And some letters. I thought . . . I mean,' he corrected quickly, while I affected not to notice, 'I'll bet the burglar thought they were from somebody famous. They were a professor's, to some political tart.'

I gauged him. 'Know anything about stamps, Spoolie?'

He smiled, shifty. 'So you know. Bought big into antique stamps before I went in. Left them with a dolloper.'

Valuable news. 'You jugged with anybody local?'

Spoolie's face closed. 'No. Drinkwater asked me. Some bloke called Godbolt. Never heard of him.'

'Lovely shop you got, Spoolie.' I said so-long and left, the door playing that scratchy introduction from Flash Gordon serials. Blank. Which only left me Therla the schoolteacher and her non-story of the non-drowning, and Luna's escapade with Jenny. Calamy's not a local name, but it was bothering me. I decided to look names up.

On the way I noticed that Rye Benedict's plant show-rooms were up for sale. A decent crowd queued at his mill. Maybe he was going full-time into history, and leaving Nature alone. I was all for it. A shop opposite Therla Brewer's school had a headline about a savage local murder. It made me stop until I could go on, but I didn't buy a paper.

Chapter 12

Schools dismay me. It's their air of assumption. Ever since learning that Dickens had to tone *down* the ghastly events at the real Dotheboys Hall, to achieve realism, they've given me the willies. I sense chains, cross the road even yet. I parked the car in the school, though, to avoid prying ploddite eyes. It was in this vehicle that Luna had taken me to suss out Prammie's hut. The countryside might have whispered.

Therla was in the common room being merry with a dozen somnolents. Children, all taller than children used to be, milled about the corridors, looking bored. I wish it had been boredom in my day. I can only remember worry. She came and we walked to her classroom, empty except for two snogging youngsters who marched out, the lad glaring, the girl giving Therla an impudent challenging stare. Therla sighed apology.

'I do my best, Lovejoy. You can see they're horrors.'

The girl was pretty. I could easily dislike the boy.

'That accident, love. The boy in the river.'

'Andrew? He climbed once too often. It was in the Stour. I think I said? An old man on a strange little boat fished him out. He had the oddest way of propulsion, some sort of—'

It's odd how a few words can send you really strange.

'You said he was rescued by an ocean-going barge.'

'Yes. Beside a great barge . . . What's the matter?'

'You stupid cow. You meant *nearby*?'

'Of course. I told you.' She was exasperated. Teachers are trained in it. 'It was fastened to it. For heaven's sake, Lovejoy. I don't understand how ships tie themselves to each other, do I?'

'Ta, Therl.'

'Lovejoy. Don't you think you owe me some explanation? You come here as if your life depended . . .'

It had been Prammie Joe himself. In the Stour? But Prammie's hut lies deep in the tributary marshes of the next river north, the Deben. I'd assumed wrong. I'd been mesmerised by Cornish Place.

'His dinghy was tied to the barge?'

'Yes.' Her forehead wrinkled prettily. 'Under the back, so to speak. Most odd. There were ropes, loading things on to two punts he had. Andrew was very lucky. I honestly do try, Lovejoy,' she sighed. 'Field trips are a nightmare. Next year I take forty-eight teenagers to the Urals. Can you imagine?'

No, I couldn't. 'Did the old man say anything?'

'No. In fact, he was most offensive. He hadn't the slightest intention of making Andrew feel forgiven. Just bundled him ashore – only a few yards, really.'

I said, 'Honestly, some people. What barge, Therl?'

'Therla, please. One of those slow sailing ones. They race them. It was all ready. Here.' She pointed.

A watercolour on a wall. Three Thames barges. 'Big? Like that?'

'Yes. They're quite pretty moving. Ugly just lying still.'

'D'you still teach history? Or has it died of education? There's something on my mind.'

She was pleased at my interest. 'Josh Moss.'

I kept getting these dim flashes in my mind's eye, those names. Oddly, written in an old court hand. I was sure I'd seen at least two, maybe three, on parchment somewhere.

Josh Moss was fetched from the gaiety of the common room. He seemed relieved to escape. I parted amicably from Therla. She does evening classes in poetry, keeps wanting me to enrol. I promised. I remember hardly anything of school poetry, just dim drums throbbing, and only that because we made rude rhymes of 'Lepanto'. But Therla's really pleasant. You could get to like even poetry.

'It's a silly thing, Josh,' I said. Instinctively I adopted my old tactic before the teacher, looking downcast and sorry I'm-such-trouble. 'Some names keep going through my head. I've a, er, a bet on. A mate at the pub. He says they're footballers. I think something historical.'

'Names?' He was a fresh-faced bloke, looking about fourteen. He didn't like my joining Therla's poetry class.

'Godbolt. Calamy. Clark. Hopkins. And one blurred.'

'Easy, Lovejoy,' he said, grinning. 'You're missing Fairclough.'

'That's it!' I cried. Fairclough? 'Who are they?'

'Were, Lovejoy. John Godbolt. Edmund Calamy. And last but certainly not the least, Elizabeth Clark.'

Still I waited, thick as a post. 'Yes?'

Josh sighed. 'See, Lovejoy? You too. Local history's ignored these days. It provides such useful insights. Matthew Hopkins not ring a bell? The Witch-Finder General. He was born hereabouts. Wenham, I think.'

'Wenham?' I stared. Who was from Wenham?

'A bad time. Elizabeth Clark was a witch.' He shrugged, smiling. 'So they said, the day they hanged her. It's not far. Take the main A12 from the roundabout. Be careful of the signs from—'

'Thanks, Josh. Great.'

'Lovejoy,' he called after me. 'D'you win? Your bet.'

'Er, no. But ta.'

From a street phone – one of the six was accidentally unvandalised – I reached Wittwoode's, and Luna. She seemed thrilled. I said come to the school, stat. She said she'd no motor because I had it. I told her to do as she was told. I'd had enough of being buggered about. What are apprentices for, for God's sake? I honestly think women give me lip just to annoy. I can't come because you've got my motor. Gormless.

Coincidences are coincidences, right? But four flukes in a row? Names don't mean much these days, do they? It was all possibly imagination or something.

The point was, it wasn't. Sourly I watched Luna's taxi draw up. 'What's your name?' I signalled her taxi to wait.

'Lovejoy. Whatever's the matter? You look white as—'

'Don't keep saying that. Stop frigging about.'

She stared at me, a sheaf of papers in her hand, ready for a whole Wittwoode saga. 'You *know* who I am, Lovejoy. Mrs Luna Florence Carstairs. Is it a game?'

'Before you were married, stupid.' I'd actually recoiled.

'Macintosh.' She followed along the pavement. A valeta.

My griping belly muscles relaxed. 'Prove it.'

'Prove . . . ?' She delved into her handbag, hauled out a photograph of a beautiful girl. 'That's me.'

Words on the reverse eased me more. *Everybody says Lola's 'a ringer for Luna Macintosh' when you were nineteen! Love, Dad.*

'Lola?'

'My daughter, Lovejoy. Are you ill?'

Drawing breath, I demanded her mother's name. Her mother's mother's name. Her great-granddad's . . . The family came from Fort William. I should have detected her accent. Fright had done my cortex in. I put my arms round her, bussed her in relief. She backed away, murmuring she was the Mayoress, for heaven's sake, and in public. I gave her her car keys.

'Right, pal. Ditch that motor, for good. Okay?'

'Is it making that clattering noise again? I thought they'd mended it.' She unlocked her car door. 'That garage is becoming so unreliable.'

'Meet me at the town library. Don't be late.'

I borrowed the taxi fare, and left. Talk to some birds, you might as well talk to the wall.

Chapter 13

Our town library's a non-library. A theory of a library, it's run by Scotchman, a skeletal prat whose sole function is thwarting. To him it's a good day when he's successfully obstacled the whole public from borrowing books.

'I need a book, please, Scotchy.'

'Sorry, Lovejoy, but—'

'Allow me.' I captured a young loafer. 'Look, pal. I don't know how to work the computer here . . .'

The pimply youth's eyes ignited. He shot round the desk, shoved Scotchman up and away, activated the computer. 'Wotcher want, mate?'

'Anything on Matthew Hopkins. Old timer, three hundred and fifty years since.'

Tap tap tap. I'm computer illiterate. These infants aren't. They live for them. But writing by any other name.

'Witch-Finder General?' The youth gazed admiringly at me. 'A pop group? This library's no books. There's one at Grays, Thurrock. Plenty in London.' The security guard was being fetched.

'What is it?' Miss Campbell was beside us, assistant librarian, intent on social justice for the disadvantaged.

'This lad is showing me your technologistics, communication-wise, Miss Campbell.' I said it in one breath.

She dithered, righteous anger foiled by jargon. 'Well, if—'

'Here, mate.' The computer wizard handed me a print-out. I said ta. He slouched off to be bored again.

The nearest tome on Hopkins was in St Edmundsbury. I'd no motor, so it would be bus. I made do with various dictionaries, got the names, deeds, trial details. Reference libraries have been turned into Local Studies Resource Centres. The baffled serving the baffled. Children on school projects take a folder, copy it out for teacher, and move on to their next feat of intellect. I made the bus home, but had to walk from the village outskirts because some nerk insisted on the correct fare.

Luna's origin wasn't local. Bless her. I warmed to the woman, my one trusty ally. I had a few scribbled notes on the ghoulish doings of yore. I brewed up, sat out in a cold rising wind, chucked the birds some cheese, and reflected on what I now knew.

Once upon a time, our fair land was going about its humdrum business. Good Queen Bess had faded from memory. Came James, a spectacular anti-witch nut. Thanks to him, anti-witch mania was burgeoned.

Piecemeal bits garnered in the non-library worried me worse as I began to read my scrawl. There's a lot of balderdash talked about witches nowadays. People think of them, if at all, as cranks having a bit of spare nooky in the woods at summer solstices, or encouraging Mother Earth to produce leaves.

Except there's more.

Like, seventeen people were burnt at St Osyths, near here, in 1676. As late as 1863, a poor elderly French bloke was dragged from his home in Castle Hedingham, ducked to see if he was a wizard, and died from the experience.

King George II had some sense, thank God, and repealed our ancient witchcraft laws in 1736. Isolated incidents occurred, though. Like the burning of poor Bridget Cleary at Baltyvadhen in Tipperary in 1895 by her husband and his five mates. Fine, okay, it's history. But read it, suddenly it edges close. Suddenly it's not so long ago. And suddenly the evenings draw in.

The terrible feeling comes, that the people who did those horrible frightening things were *here*, on this ground. They *lived* here. This village, that seaport. They walked our streets, maybe drank from the very bowl you see in the antique shop. Get the point? They laughed and joked *here*. Then they burnt, hanged, imprisoned, gaoled, drowned the innocent. In the name of holiness.

And nobody did this dreadfulness like the ghastly Witch-Finder General.

His dad was a Puritan minister of Wenham. Matthew Hopkins became an Ipswich lawyer, chiselling contentedly at whatever could be chiselled. It was back around the Great Civil War (Cromwell versus Charlie I, on whether Divine Right of Kingship should rule instead of Parliament. People won, making us the modern world's first ever Republic).

Lawyer Hopkins suddenly went ape. Off his own bat he decided he was gifted. His gifts lay in a particular direction.

Abruptly, he began to 'find' witches. He started with a mere handful at Manningtree, where he lived. Soon, witches were here, there, everywhere. Politicians use the same trick. You know the ploy: there's a witch/ treason/a conspiracy/plot/whatever. The cry goes up. Good heavens! All will be lost if everybody doesn't support the prosecutors! And all that jazz. Don't mock the Puritans of Salem, New England, of 1692. Or the people in Scotland who burnt thousands. James I, a loon of sorts, even prosecuted a whole assize for acquitting some poor soul. Or the witch-persecutors of Pennsylvania. Or Kalisk in Poland. You don't need to look far even today. Especially today.

Lawyer Hopkins appointed himself the Witch-Finder General. And rode out on his anti-witch crusade. He demanded twenty silver shillings a time, a whole pound. (Get it? The more witches he spotted, the richer he got.) This odious reptile rampaged through East Anglia, intoxicated with the power of life or death – and, terribly, it was always death. Exulting, the maniac invented a modification of an ancient 'test' for 'finding' witches. It went:

First identify your witch (that is, pick anybody). Bind her/him. Lob her into a pond. If she floats, why, she's guilty – for the Lord's pure water has rejected her. So she must be hanged. If she sinks, why, she's innocent. You see the problem. Either way, you're dead.

The evil spread through East Anglia like wildfire. Norfolk, Suffolk, and Essex. The horror scourged hamlets, villages, towns, cities, and finally whole counties. Bedfordshire, Huntingdon, Cambridgeshire, all suffered. Folk lived in fright. Some women, knowing their innocence, actually volunteered to come to trial to get it over with. And, Hopkins blithely reported, were hanged for their pains. The witch-hunts went on. And on. Anything was a sign of being a witch – a neighbour's roses wilting, a friend catching a cold, some skin blemish. It was wholesale utter madness. One elderly one-legged Manningtree woman was brought to trial for having a cat she called pet names. She was 'swum' – that is, tied up and ducked, Hopkins' famous test. She failed to drown. So she was hanged.

Her name was Elizabeth Clark, God rest her.

Sick and crazy, the witch-hunts stormed on, in the name of God. Even reeling from the carnage of civil war the nation was appalled by the murderous progress of the Witch-Finder. But everybody did nothing. Just like you and me would have done. Like we do today. Everybody kept quiet – and watched their innocent friends and relatives tortured, drowned, hanged. One poor old octogenarian, Reverend Lowes of Brandeston, Suffolk, was kept awake for over a week by running him about. His parishioners did nothing. The witch-seekers bound him, threw him in Framlingham Castle moat. He floated, so was condemned to be hanged. The poor old cleric begged for a burial service. The laughing Witch-Finder forbade it. The parishioners – you, me – did nothing. The old priest shakily read his own funeral service. And was hanged. His friends, neighbours, parishioners watched. And did nothing. He'd been their vicar for fifty years. Of course, the Witch-Finder was a holy Puritan who would make money from the judicial murder. Sound familiar? Piety is lucrative, properly applied.

The reason I was so distressed was something I knew, in my heart of hearts. Had I been there in 1646, I too would have stayed silent.

And did nothing. Like now. Like you.

But even crazed bloodlust ends, thank God. It came to pass that one man in the Kingdom suddenly thought, What the hell is going *on?* To John Gaule, of Great Staughton village, it seemed absurd for a so-say civilised nation to be torturing itself on the whim of a madman. *And, unbelievably, he stood up and said so!* One frightening, ghastly day, this brave cleric actually strode to the pulpit – it's still there – and preached against the Witch-Finder General himself. He even had the nerve to publish his conviction that the real witches were the witch-hunters themselves. And then walked home from his appalled congregation and waited, trembling but firm in spirit, for the heavens to cave in.

Great Staughton held its breath, stunned. All Huntingdonshire – home of Oliver Cromwell the arch-Puritan himself, remember, whose Roundheads clanked on every skyline – waited for the Witch-Finder's vengeful team to ride into town.

And waited.

They didn't come. They bottled out. Chicken.

So let's hear it for brave John Gaule of Great Staughton. Drink to his eternal memory. What makes a wimp suddenly heroic? God alone knows. I don't. Because all his life John Gaule had been wet, a drip. He'd fawned and grovelled, bowed and scraped. Until that fateful day when he became a lion. Light a candle to his courage. He deserves it.

The Witch-Finder General complained but he never came.

And suddenly everybody halted, looked at each other. The witch-finding stuttered. It was the Emperor's New Clothes. People read the vicar's rebuke, and were ashamed. Then they smarted, felt cheated. Then furious. With whom? Why, with the Witch-Finder General! They invented a legend. It goes that, on an angry day, they rushed to where he was staying, dragged him out and lobbed him into a pond in savage mimicry of his own witch-finding test. He floated, so they hanged him from the gibbet.

History is more mundane. After John Gaule's denunciation, East Anglia simply calmed down. The Witch-Finder died in his bed in 1647, of tuberculosis.

He was a local bloke. Wenham's but a stone's throw from here. On the bench alongside him sat two sombre figures, Edmund Calamy and Sergeant John Godbolt. Famous names, when you bother to remember. They had a grim sergeant, one Fairclough, to play the heavy. I'm sorry it's such a horrible tale. It's the worse for being true. Mistley-cum-Manningtree knows that. Theirs is the unenviable distinction of having the Witch-Finder General sleeping soundly – or maybe not so soundly – in their churchyard.

No names I'd managed to find in the non-library matched any of Luna's family names. I was still sitting on my half-finished wall when Luna arrived in a snarly two-tone Ford. She approached across the grass in trepidation. I watched her.

I must have been something of a tribulation. She must be at the end of her tether. She stood in front of me. A worried woman. My one ally, whose patience nearly equalled mine.

'Hiyer, pal,' I said at last. 'Friends?'

She gave a radiant smile. 'Oh, Lovejoy! You're better!'

'I haven't been poorly,' I said, narked. 'Come inside.'

She put her arm through mine. 'Antiques at last?'

'Lots, love. Lots and lots.' I meant enough to make a huge scam, the sort East Anglia doesn't have.

The answerphone, a real nuisance, had a message.

'This is Mayor Carstairs, Lovejoy. I want to know what's going on. This degree of interaction—'

There's an off switch, works a treat. 'He got nothing better to do, love?'

'It's only the motor,' she said, quite cheerfully. 'Oliver wanted me to use the one you don't like any more. I borrowed this from Oliver's cousin Emily.'

'Tell Emily ta, love. She pretty?'

'No,' she said evenly. 'Hideous, nasty.'

'Pity. We're going to need help with the forgery.' Luna turned, kettle in her hand. 'Did you say forgery?'

'Eh? No. I said copying. An antique, for a friend.'

In silence we sat and listened to the news. One Joseph

120

Godbolt had been found dead, possibly some days, in a reed-cutter's hut in a marshy area off the River Deben. His death was being investigated. The police suspected foul play, had set up an Incident Room in a local tavern.

I held up a warning finger as Luna, instantly thrilled, drew breath to exclaim at the extraordinary coincidence that Godbolt was the very name . . .

'Don't,' I said. She didn't. And I started convincing her that forgery was nearly, but not quite, the same as faking or copying or simulating. Words are great, aren't they? Prove anything, used right.

Chapter 14

'Strip off, Lovejoy, or I'll bring Geronimo.'

The threat did it. I felt a right duckegg. It must be great to take your clothes off and not feel daft. We look misshapen, a clown's joke. Women look exquisite, tailored by an expert. I didn't look at the mirror.

'Not underpants and socks, Vell?' No, maybe socks. Men's socks look the last laugh.

She tutted. 'Lovejoy, get *on*. You've paid for an hour. Prospective fortune, para-psycho analysis, massage. So far you've wasted ten minutes. I can't oil you with your clothes on.'

'Oil?' I cried, alarmed. 'What oil?'

You use oil for motor cars and painting, not for Lovejoys. Though there's one antique called an oil clock, where time is marked by the fall in an oil reservoir as a flame burns—

'Stop *talking!*' She was getting really narked. 'Oil's for the massage, Lovejoy! For heaven's *sake*.'

I'd made Vell's inner sanctum by making an appointment for The Great Marvella's services. There didn't seem any other way. A casual call meant possibly running into her clients. For once, I wanted to avoid a big seduction scene. Wondrous exalting, yes, but with death now dealt into the antiques game I needed mileage. Fortune-telling meant looking into Geronimo's terrible flat-headed gaze while he decided what the next month held for me. I also passed on the para-psychologic analysis, because Geronimo did the analysing with Vell's demented ventriloquism. That left Reconstructile Autosynthetic Massage. It sounded like a set of girders.

She started undoing my clothes. I tried to deflect her.

'This is ridiculous!' she cried, determined. 'You're like a child. Stand *still!*

Hell of a way to get an interview.

'Listen, Vell.' I struggled to keep my shirt. I'd conceded shoes in token gesture of seriously wanting her bloody massage. 'I haven't really got any aches. Maybe if I do some gardening—'

She brushed a wisp of hair away from her forehead as we grappled politely. 'I think I must be mad, Lovejoy. I've given you open invitations before now. And you've run a mile. Now you are here you're wriggling like a—

'I'm stripping! I'm stripping!'

I looked about for somewhere to put my shirt. She snatched it, exasperated, and flung it on a couch. The inner sanctum had plenty of furniture. It was a vaulted place, really surprising. Old roof beams quite chapel-like. I mean, the little street hardly seemed to have anywhere to keep a space this size. It must have been an old meeting hall, from the seventeenth century when new sects came in grace abounding.

The massage table stood grandly in the middle, ready for a Lying in State. She had heating, I suppose for her female clients. Women are always on the search for draughts, real or imagined. They'd choose a different masseuse with a different snake if it wasn't warm. She had a large expanding divan, embroidered damascus cushions and everything, and some good Edwardian upright furniture.

'Have I to get up on that?'

That left my trousers, no socks, and underpants. Clean on, as if I was going to the doctor. I'd even done my teeth a second time, just as if I was going snogging.

'Up, please. Remove *all* outer clothing before ascending the Autosynthetic Rostrum.'

These catchphrases are meaningless, aren't they. Delivered in an even, bored tone, they sound full of weighty authority. Sheepishly I lowered my trousers, folded them with defiant slowness, and dropped them on the floor. I wasn't walking the thirty or so feet to put them on the clothes mane provided, not with her looking. A bloke in underpants looks as daft as he does naked. No. Delete that. He doesn't. Couldn't.

The raised table was like in Doc Lancaster's surgery. Pillow the wrong thickness. A blanket, cream-coloured, with a red stripe. No compound light glaring down at me, thank God. If there had been, I'd have been off. I could almost hear the sound of clinking instruments and the hiss of sterilisers.

'You lie, prone. I can't do a massage with you propped up on your elbow like that.'

Prone, face down. Supine face up. Right.

'Lovejoy. The blanket over your *feet*. Let *go!*'

'In a minute—'

She ripped the blanket away. 'Lie still. Relax, please.'

Some trolley trundled near. Bottles chinked. Her hands slapped.

'Only oil.' Warm, her hands in the middle of my spine. 'It's unscented. Is this your first massage?'

'Mmmmh.' A lie, because I've been out East. I wanted to get information out of her, not put information in.

'You'll be pleasantly surprised. People have wrong ideas. They think sordid goings-on, instead of psycho-physical restorative contactile stimulus.'

'Quite honestly, I think we do,' I agreed. 'Er, forget the psycho-restoration, er, thing.' I wanted to butter her up, get her to talk. 'Do you have plenty of sufferers?'

Her hand smacked me smartly. 'Clients, Lovejoy. I don't inflict suffering.'

'I meant clients. Honest.' I thought only lawyers and prostitutes had clients.

'Business picked up about a year ago.' She was working. 'Even among your cynical profession.' Profession was a laugh. Antique dealers call rich antique-buying smoothies professionoils (oily professionals, get it?). Sotheby's and Christie's are full of them. And TV nowadays, those road-show people with antique shops syndicated on the side.

'Vell, I came on condition you don't tell.'

She laughed. 'Men all want confidentiality. Not the women. And Sandy, of course. But he doesn't count. As if it mattered! Massage is therapy, not something to be embarrassed about.'

'I know, I know.' Smooth, smooth. I think I meant that I was being smooth, not that her hands were moving so pleasingly. I began to feel sleepy. I could see how folk got to like this sort of thing. 'It was Connie suggested I came. I've been very, er . . . .' Why did people come, anyway? 'Er, fed up, lately.'

'I heard Tinker's away. And your little fat cow. Doing quite well for yourself. Selling wood, isn't she?'

'My apprentice? Mmmmh.' Vell hated Lydia. My erstwhile apprentice had given her the sailor's elbow once in the Arcade. Lydia's very beautiful, but if Vell wanted to bitch Lydia up, fine by me. Lydia was seconded to an august antique furniture showroom off Bond Street for a year. 'Selling wood', as Vell sweetly described it.

'Arms extended. Over the end of the reclination.'

Reclination? I noticed there was a blemish in the door, like for a cat flap. The infilling wood was wrong. The door itself was lovely ancient English oak.

'Had a flood?' We were on an upper floor.

She looked, laughed. 'Oh, you know. Clients like to hear tales. Geronimo—'

I shot up, shoving her away. 'He comes in here?'

Vell shoved me down. 'No, silly. He stays in his cage.'

Calmed, I felt myself slipping into a quiet bliss. Vell was really good at rubbing. I made myself come to.

'How do you advertise, Vell? I don't see your postcards.'

They're still called sixpenny cards, from thirty years ago. You write out your advert on a postcard and a shop-keeper sticks it in his window.

'Honestly! What do you think I'm running, Lovejoy? I advertise, when need be, in expensive magazines. Not in alleys.'

'Course not. Big stuff, eh?' I was there at last. 'I know. Cassandra Almighty Clark.'

Vell gave one of those half-embarrassed laughs that make you wonder. 'Cassandra and I are friends. Sort of. Except she went to a different school.'

A little bitterness there? I could imagine, though. Cassandra Clark filthy rich, Vell peddling ventriloquism.

'Nice you've met up.' Time for a shot in the dark. 'I'm hoping to sell Cassandra some good stuff soon. But she's not bought much since she arrived in the area.' Meaning never. Not a piceworth. Yet I couldn't remember an auction Cassandra Clark hadn't been at. How odd. A dealer groupie?

'You are?' Very guarded, all of a sudden. Had the hands stilled a fraction before smoothing onward?

'I can lay my hands on a mountain of superb stuff.'

She trilled an unconvincing laugh. 'Cassandra might not like them, Lovejoy. She's very discriminating.'

'She will. I'm looking for a really wealthy, er, client.'

'Over, please.' I could have sworn she was so sad. I'd thought she was jolly. 'Lovejoy. Stay in your own league. I know it's none of my business, but—'

'Antiques are my league, love.' I smiled up at her. 'The others aren't on the scale I want. Hey, Vell. You're making me nod off. Is there a surcharge if I do? I'll have to owe.'

She was smiling in a queer way. 'Thought as much, Lovejoy. Wait.' She went to the outer room. I heard her bleep some message service. 'No calls until further notice.'

She returned, and got on with her work. Refreshing.

It was three o'clock before I rose from her divan, bathed, found all my clothes. She lay on the damascus cushion watching me go. It felt odd, like farewell. Yet in one sense we'd only just met. But with women you can't ever quite work out exactly what you should be exactly working out, if you follow. I've often found that.

Time I went down the estuaries. But not with Luna in her snarly two-tone. I didn't want Drinkwater wondering what sorts of motors Mayor Carstairs and his wife possessed, in case he lucked on to some report of her near Prammie Joe's place. I should have thought of that beforehand, but you're sometimes too scared to go to some places on your own. I've often found that, as well.

'Lovejoy, dear. Old scrubber Luna is positively *charming!* I told her *everything* about your dreadful past!'

'Hello, Sandy.'

He came gushing to welcome us. 'Oh, here she very *is*, Lovejoy! Woolworth's, dear, your wig? A bargain seconds?'

'Sandy,' I warned, uncomfortable. Luna didn't seem to mind.

'We got on very well, Lovejoy. Didn't we, Sandy?'

'Like my outfit?' He drew Luna inside. He looked loony. A long eastern caftan, a decorated print blouse, pearls, and mirrors on each fingernail. 'Wait!'

He snapped his fingers. The fireplace rotated. A bar, complete with stools, pivoted out. 'You worship? Admire?'

'I'd rather have the fireplace.' It wasn't anything special, but Carrara marble and nineteenth century is something you don't see every day of the week. It made me think of pricey house furnishings. Cornish Place would make some dealer a prince.

Sandy fluttered his eyelashes at Luna. 'Isn't he the one? *Nothing* but antiques. He must adore *you*, Luna! Are those still your own teeth?'

'Now behave.' Luna was smiling. Women always seem so well adjusted to, well, Sandys.

We hadn't had time to do much. I'd been preoccupied. Luna was relieved we were moving into antiques. I'd given her a session on jewellery. Costume next. Riches to rags.

'Sandy told me that antique dealers use delaying tactics for payment, Lovejoy.'

'He did?' I said, while Sandy did his eyes in another ton of mascara. The lashes were like bat's wings, stuck out a mile. 'Let's hope he pays The Great Marvella on the nail. She has a snake for a debt-collector.'

'Isn't Geronimo perfectly *sweet*?' Sandy crooned, pouring a vodka and vermouth in a glass with a five-foot stem. It stood on the floor alongside him. 'So erotic! Visual! Drinkie-poos?'

Luna asked for orange juice. I had nothing.

'Question One!' he announced. 'Who used a wine glass

exactly like this in a film?' He tapped Luna playfully. 'You ought to guess this, dear. He too wore a blonde wig!'

'Dirk Bogarde. I loved the Mediterranean terrace!'

Sandy's smile vanished. *'Aren't* we a clever cow, then?'

'Sandy has a pal,' I explained to Luna. 'Spoolie. He's show-biz ephemera. The Ghool Spool. He's not long out of gaol.'

Sandy eyed me. 'That doesn't make him a bad person.'

Luna frowned. 'Rod Steiger? Played a multiple murderer?'

I yelled, 'Shut up, Luna!' She thought Sandy was playing his famous film quotes game. 'Which gaol, Sandy? Parkhurst?'

'Not the same,' Sandy said quickly. Which meant he'd already been on the phone to Spoolie, discussing Prammie Joe's demise. The rotated fireplace was one I'd seen auctioned some time since, so nothing suggestive there.

'That's good,' I said. 'See, I want a place burgled.'

Quietness supervened. Sandy's face set to mutiny. I looked at a breakfront bookcase. It was a really pleasant fake. I'd done it myself out of an elderly wardrobe.

'Luna. Come and look. Remember I was telling you about fakes?'

'Fake?' Sandy shrieked so loud I reeled, but kept doggedly on. Time to stop mucking about. I wanted help, not tantrums.

'There was an old furniture man in antiques called Crawley. He published a number of maxims. He had records of fifty-three thousand pieces of furniture he'd worked on over twenty years. Either altered, or complete fakes. That shows the size of the market.'

'I think it's lovely.'

'Thank you, love. I made it. Of course it's lovely.'

'You?' Sandy shrieked. *'You?'* He burst into tears, to Luna's consternation. She rummaged for a hankie. I wearily made her desist and listen.

'A million pointers give it away, love. Look on the inside of the doors. Usually there are graze marks, because the tray-shelves slid. Some housemaids didn't push the shelves all the way back in, see?' I opened the doors and showed her the marks. 'Proves it was an old wardrobe. I cut these glass windows from old framed prints – dealers are always chucking the glass away. You can find marks – the glass can never quite be cleaned free of them.'

'But it looks original, Lovejoy.'

'Don't talk. Listen. The smaller a breakfront bookcase, the more expensive. The easiest test is this: lower the writing flap, and sit as if you're going to write a letter. Measure its height from the carpet. It should be two feet seven inches, give or take. If it's not, then some faker has miscalculated.' I shrugged modestly. 'This is two foot seven, dead on.'

Sandy was bleating, but still holding out.

I looked about the shop. 'See this little Pembroke table? Oval's more costly than serpentine or rectanglar. Here, you see, the faker—'

'Delia,' Sandy said murderously, giving in. 'Delia's the burglar you want. I'll ring for you. But don't think I'm your friend any more, Lovejoy. This is *war*. You made me *cry*.'

'Oh, now, Sandy,' from Luna, all worried.

Sandy squared off, narrowing his eyes, trying to jut his chin.

'This – is – no – easy – assignment – men!' He smiled, confident. 'Right, trolls! Who? Have to hurry you, gargoyles!'

'John Wayne?' Luna spoke before I could tip her the wink to guess wrong. 'I never like those war films, do you?'

Sandy glared malevolently. It was hopeless. I started to leave. '*What* a clever little whore our *dear* mare-ess is turning out to be, Lovejoy! Isn't it time you went back to

Jessica? Or Lydia? Connie, perhaps? Or that Berlin bomb-shell who positively *begged* to be thrashed, and collected Georgian silver stirrup cups? Or Dolly? Why *didn't* you marry Dolly? The poor bitch was on *heat* every single *hour*, I mean practically *wet* trailing you round the market with her hubby, I mean *sobbing*—'

'Sorry about that, love.' I spoke over the door's farewell tone 'Marching Through Georgia'. We emerged into East Hill's cool wet air. 'Sandy likes to be clever. Forgot to tell you.'

'But I love the cinema, Lovejoy.' We walked towards the museum. 'What was the joke about the burglar?'

'Shhh,' I said. I waved cheerily to a friend across the road. 'Hiyer, Jeff. Eleanor okay, is she?'

'Fine.' he called across cars. 'Get my message? Gungie wants you. It's important.'

'Ta, Jeff. Love to Eleanor.'

We went to see if any of the graves at St Mary-at-the-Walls was dry enough to sit on. When we were perched in comfort, I began. 'Luna, love. We want a robbery carried out. I need to know which antique dealers go to a particular fortune-telling masseuse. I can't ask Marvella directly. So we want somebody to do a drainer – er, burgle her establishment, by climbing down her drainpipe – and delve in her records.'

'We do?' She was wide-eyed.

'Exactly. I'd go myself,' I lied candidly. 'But I have scruples.'

'Oh, scruples are *right*, Lovejoy!'

Sometimes I'm lucky. Luna might become an ideal partner.

'Let's get to Woody's and have a bite.' I'd never used a female burglar before, but Sandy knew his business. If he said Delia, Delia it had to be. 'Tell me about Jenny Calamy.'

The rain came down in torrents as we left for Woody's caff. Luna had forgotten her umbrella, the stupid cow. I sometimes think I draw the short straw. Apprentices get my goat. Why are they never efficient? I'd have got wet through if I hadn't sent her off for a taxi from outside Marks and Sparks while I sheltered in the church porch. Women basically have no organisation.

Chapter 15

We tore back to the cottage with some shopping, at Luna's insistence, the motor full of plastic bags. I deplore shopping. You can't just pop in, can you? You take ten hours instead of three minutes. It gets me wild.

The answerphone wanted attention. That winking eye riles me. Worse than a bird asking where you've been, and who with.

'Lovejoy,' Joan's voice said, all tense. 'We have to talk. Del's not going to take this lying down. I'll call.'

Why? She'd already been, left two vases of flowers and three envelopes, one containing money, the other two various instructions about lawyers and where we were to meet every hour from now to Doomsday. And a couple of air tickets to Monte Carlo. Luna, distributing the shopping, paused at the sight of the airline logos.

She gauged me candidly. 'You have no intention of going, Lovejoy. Have you?'

'Eh?' I'd not given elopement much thought.

There was a nervy message from Connie. 'Urgent. Please find me, Lovejoy. Arcade, Woody's, Dennison's Auction till five. White Hart thereafter. Gunge's looking out for you.'

I smiled weakly at Luna. 'Everything's always urgent.

Ever noticed?' We were leaving, but Luna had to delay us by answering the phone.

'I'm out,' I hissed frantically, but she passed me Miss Turner, smiling. 'What now?'

'Hello, Lovejoy. Have I had *success!*' Might as well talk to the wall. 'But I'm at a dead end. Though I did find—'

Take the shortest way. 'What religion were your Scotch ancestors? Nonconformist? Protestant?'

'Of course, Lovejoy! Though . . .' The old bat's voice lowered to guilt. 'Some English ancestry was . . . Catholic.'

I did a pretend gasp, bored out of my skull. 'Have a go at the Census Records. They might get you to 1841. Then go to the Scottish Record Office. Look there for your Protestant people. For God's sake don't miss out the congregation number. They get ratty.'

'Oh! I simply didn't *think!* How very clever, Lovejoy—'

'Chiseller.' I hung up, rounded on Luna. 'There's books galore on finding your ancestors. Tell the old boot I've emigrated next time.'

She was smiling. 'You're so sweet, Lovejoy.'

We drove down the estuary then, and finished up standing on the banks of the River Deben. Along its course it has a small islet or two, but essentially is a straight, uninteresting river. For me its importance lay in its end, in the North Sea. A mile south along the coast lies the port of Felixstowe. Sail down a couple more miles for the Orwell Basin. It doesn't sound much, but it's the conflux of two other rivers, the Orwell, and the Stour – John Constable's river. You can take your pick of any number of estuaries, tributaries, moorings, marinas, small islands, lowly sea marshes, and come gliding in of a dark night—

'Lovejoy?' Luna was shaking me.

'I'm just thinking of the water.'

The river looked innocuous, really ordinary. From

Ramsholt to Hemley where we were standing was barely more than a mile, the river between. There's a promontory on the south side where we were, with a couple of creeks joining the main river from the marshes.

Luna was thrilled by the onshore wind and the sea birds. 'Lovejoy. Isn't this near where . . . ?

Fine like now, with the air dry, no more rain this afternoon so far, the wind whistling across the sedge and a wherry or two gliding serenely down to the sea. Fine, too, in sun, with children playing and a few small boats enjoying themselves. But bleed the sky's light, and it becomes very, very different. The pitch night has a solidity that chills your soul. Then, the wind's brisk whistle loses its flute quality. It becomes a sombre moan. The breeze drains warmth, tugs fretfully. Your feet slide in the mud. Rain slashes at your eyes, vicious. The very night air can shove you over, send you down slithering into the water, where the river has gone mad—

Luna said brightly. 'Time to go! We're going mental!'

'Right, right.'

We drove off, me telling Luna to go via Rye Benedict's.

It could be done. A waterman born and bred could easily scull a shallow pram from those creeks. He'd have to choose his nights, of course, and know the tides. Then it'd be easy to reach the sea. All right, so I couldn't decide how Prammie Joe had got along the coast from the Deben to the Orwell Basin. But once there he could paddle upriver to Cornish Place.

Yes, that was how he'd done it all right. But where had he taken the stuff? Stripping a mansion of its furnishings is a major task, cubed. The fireplaces alone would weigh tons, taken together. Consider doors – not the least valuable items. They'd have to be wrapped up against getting wet, or they'd spoil. So Prammie didn't carry the blinking things once he'd got them on to his rafts, but it was still a mighty feat. I mean, there you are in your cosy little hut, with the wind howling, rain slashing, onshore gales, you'd naturally want to read, listen to some music. But no. Up gets old Prammie, and night after night sculls off down the river . . . Down the *same* river? Wait a minute. Or somewhere else?

'Is she the friend?' Luna was asking as we reached Rye's mill. I saw the garden centre's notice had a red *Sold* poster diagonally across it.

'Who?'

Luna pointed. 'Connie. You said, helping a friend. Faking. I mean, copying,' she amended neatly as I drew breath.

Connie was speaking with Rye. I didn't realise they were friends, not 'calling friends', as country folk say. But here was Connie, fetchingly attired in beige, speaking intently with Rye on the forecourt. The mill was motionless, the millrace burbling into white froth below. We'd had enough rain lately. No school mobs, thank goodness. The mill shop was closed. I realised with a faint smile I'd never seen it open. Some businessman. But he'd seemed hooked on some massive investment last time I came by. At least, that was how I remembered it. And here he was, chatting – no, conversing intently with the lovely Connie.

Luna drew in, parked. I waited. Their deep talk went on. Not at all animose, but certainly profound.

'Do I interrupt, love?'

'I should. Or they might think . . .' She pinked. Women are strong on not prying, because they can do it sly.

I alighted, making din enough to wake the dead. Connie and Rye moved apart. I was unobservant. Luna came with diffidence.

'I see you've sold your garden centre across the river, Rye. Into history full-time, then?'

It honestly was an innocent remark. Hang it all, there was the notice for all to see, nine feet tall. But he looked positively shifty, which is definitely not Rye Benedict.

'Not really, Lovejoy.' And he put a big envelope under his arm, shoving photographs back inside it. I pretended disinterest.

'With all that profit, you can buy your own mill,' I chuckled, until I noticed I was chuckling on my own. Connie looked strained, Rye nervous as a kitten.

'What a lovely old place!' Luna enthused, womanlike, wanting to blot up the silence. 'And how beautifully kept!'

Rye unbent slightly, but licking his lips nervously. 'Yes. Thank you. I run it for the Council.' He looked at it wistfully. 'I wish it were.' He waved across at the nursery garden. 'That seemed more profitable to my family. Everything was steam, electricity, coal. Now, we're beginning to realise. Old-fashioned mills were clean.'

He spoke almost bitterly, as if he resented the mill some way. Weird. I saw Connie looking at me.

'Don't knock the great inventors, Rye,' I said. 'I love the Victorians.'

He unbent with an enthusiast's instant fervour. 'Oh, you can say that again, Lovejoy! They really were the greats. Think of them – James Watt. Telford. Brunel.'

'Rye—'

He wouldn't let Connie interrupt. I didn't want him to, either. 'Lovejoy. I really believe there should be an order, sort of sainthood, for people like Brunel. They are the true immortals! More than any popes or politicians.'

His eyes were shining, hot, almost afire. Another acquaintance gone ape.

'Brunel your hero, Rye? Pity he never worked locally—'

'Oh, but—'

Then Connie really did interrupt, with a firmness that made Luna take a step back. 'Look. This is all very well. But Lovejoy, I wanted to—'

'Connie,' Rye said. It came out vehement. He caught himself and smiled. It wore him out, but he managed. A lot of past argument went into that negative.

'I have a proposition, Lovejoy. About my antiques.' Connie said it with some kind of sadness I couldn't fathom, looking at Rye as she spoke. Luna was pinker than normal, I saw with surprise. I thought, God, more eyebrow play than a melodrama.

'All right, love. Meet at the Treble Tile?'

'Give me a lift?'

I asked Rye for a table of tides. He said he's send me one, because his shop was shut – as if the door had just slammed accidentally and him with with no key. I had to laugh: a non-shop.

Connie sat in the back. Luna drove us. Connie sussed Luna out first, though she already knew Luna was my apprentice. A typical woman, judging how far things had gone between me and the Lady Mayoress of the Hundred.

'My antiques, Lovejoy. Can you fuff them?'

'To what?'

'Double what you divvied?'

That made me swallow hard. The fuff is a con trick. You pad out a number of genuine antiques to make a larger number by adding some more. Except there's one small detail: the additional 'antiques' are fakes, lookalikes, sham. Now, don't get all indignant. Prestigious auction houses the world over do this. Of course, they catalogue the fakes, replicas, the false, in eloquent vagueness that makes the bidders think they too are genuine. The auctioneers, who can't ever be trusted, may even point out that there's been 'controversy' over this 'interesting' item . . . Read the words carefully, and you'll realise the auctioneers are being their own glib selves, pulling a con.

Luna listened to my explanation, trying hard not to be so appalled she could hardly keep the motor on the road.

Connie kindly added her pennyworth. 'It means buying or creating fakes, Luna. Or multiplying them somehow. Lovejoy's the expert.'

'But you already have so many, Connie . . .'

'Why us?' I put in. 'Because buyers, on this sort of scale, will believe the lot if I authenticate a few.'

Luna coloured even more when I'd said 'us', pleased. 'And you'd do that, Lovejoy?'

'No. I'll fuff, all right. But passing them all off as genuine antiques is the buyer's responsibility. Correct, Connie?'

'Yes.' She wanted me to say I'd do it all, but I wouldn't. Too many things were going on in this drab old countryside for me to start carrying the pots and pans. I'd already decided before she asked. That didn't mean I'd carry out the whole sale. Fair's fair.

Another thing. Until I knew exactly what was going on, I was a swinging compass, no direction.

'Any particular antiques you want?' I asked casually.

'Anything, Lovejoy. Furniture, silver, jewellery, clocks, weapons, furnishings, treen, instruments, microscopes, household, dolls, ephemera . . .' Onward, ever onward.

The list pleased me. It included household furnishings. So she wasn't in on Prammie Joe's scam after all. Her voice hadn't even wavered. So she was going it alone. I could tell she was a very worried bird. As worried as Rye Benedict. Had she been trying to borrow money off Rye, knowing he had the profits from the sale of his market-garden estate? That didn't quite ring true, somehow. She'd asked my help 'urgently' by phone, sending Gunge looking.

'How soon?' That's the only problem with a fuff job. Dealers want it done yesterday.

'As possible, Lovejoy. On the drip feed.'

When they become available. 'Local, or abroad?'

'Oh, overseas.' Easier still. Local fakes sell afar, as far fakes sell near. It's a saying. The point being that real antiques sell anywhere.

We dropped her in the old station yard, where nobody waits for buses any more. 'To seem unassociated,' I explained to Luna.

We went among heavy traffic – two buses and a brewer's dray – towards the village. Coming off the station round-about a tall, precisely dressed gentleman – you couldn't simply call him a bloke – stepped out into the road, bowler hat raised politely. Luna felt obliged to stop.

'Good afternoon,' he said in the window, smiling. Military tash, Old Etonian tie. Pin stripes, patent leather, a symphony of upper-crust wealth. 'Have I the honour of addressing one Lovejoy?'

'And one Luna,' I said, smiling in spite of myself. His sort usually narks me. I was surprised. 'Whom does one have the honour of addressing one?' That old Etonian tie was no sham, I bet myself. 'Osbert Sitwell said he'd been educated entirely in his holidays from Eton.'

He chuckled. 'Sandy said you would be odd, Lovejoy. How d'you do?' Odd from Sandy was rich. He got in with swift grace. Which was really strange, because I distinctly remembered locking the rear door. He'd slid in as if it was wide open.

I looked at him in the rearview mirror. 'Delia?'

'Pleased to make your acquaintance.'

Luna opened her mouth to say something, but I gave her the bent eye, and all was well.

Chapter 16

'Thanks, Delia. Sure you can get a lift?'

'No,' he chortled, straight from those children's comics where everybody always chortled. 'Better to walk. Opportunities.'

'Well, do my drainers first, eh?'

'Willco, old bean.'

And off he strode. I shut the door, and we sat and looked at each other. Luna was sitting on the divan, her head on one side.

'You told him to burgle The Great Marvella. And to watch out for the snake?' It'd take too long to explain, my sigh told her. '*And* Mr Benedict's watermill shop, Lovejoy?'

'Look. If you're going to pick on every little thing—'

She became heated. 'Every little *thing*? For heaven's sake, Lovejoy! I'd no idea it would be criminal! I mean, I've even started lying to Oliver! I'm never deceitful!'

'No? What about when . . . ?' I saw her eyes widen in apprehension, then calm down as she got the joke. She smiled a bit.

'Be serious, Lovejoy. Oliver's not only the Mayor. He's a lawyer. Secretary of the local Bar Association and everything.' She flapped her hands helplessly. 'And now I'm an accessory. I'm *embroiled*. Burglary. On commission. I don't mind the money.'

I'd had to borrow a bit from her, to pay Delia his earnest penny. Uncomfortably I totted up what Luna had paid for lately, and gulped. I always cut corners adding up what I owe.

'I'm sorry, Luna.' I was so sincere. If I'd not had to flog my phono I'd have put on hearts-and-flowers. 'I honestly am. I'm not usually like this.'

'That's not *it*, Lovejoy.' Then why mention money? To lead into obligations, that's why. 'I just don't know where I stand.'

And miraculously the door thumped. I leapt, joyously reprieved, to welcome Big Frank. He entered, darkening the world for miles. Luna gaped, never having seen his like before in her august circles. First Gunge, our gungey giant. Now a clean one. Thank God he was smiling. I introduced them.

'Oh, you're the gentleman on the phone!' Luna was so pleased. 'Miss Jenny was lovely. We had such a lovely chat. I'm so glad you and she . . .' She halted, stricken. She wasn't supposed to be glad about Big Frank's impending marriage, because he was still wed to Mrs Big Frank.

'Thanks, missus. Silver, Lovejoy?'

'None, Frank.' He sat on the divan, so he could adjust his head to the vertical. Normally he stoops anywhere within twenty feet of any doorway.

'Lovejoy. I want you to help Jenny.'

'What with, Frank?' More help? From me again?

Abruptly I too wanted to sit on the divan of a sudden, but there was no room. Already Luna was tilted high in the air from Big Frank's weight compressing the universe.

'She's got something really big on. I mean, really

142

ginormous. Bigger than anything in the Eastern Hundreds, Lovejoy.'

Another? My cottage was headache city. I've already explained that East Anglia isn't given to mega blitzes, nor scams of international proportions. We're more your actual one-offs. I cast about for the kettle, finally gestured for Luna to brew up. She smiled happily, as Big Frank gave it out.

'Lovejoy, she won't even tell me.'

'She won't tell *you*? But you're going to be . . . husband and wife.' The great goon's face melted into soppy fondness. If I hadn't been his best man so often, my own face would have melted too. 'But she's right, Lovejoy. The sums are fantastic.'

'Fantastic?' Now I really did slide down the wall and sit on the bare flagged floor. 'Look, Frank . . .'

The best dance of all, the exit shuffle. If it had been one silver chalice, fine. Big Frank could at least recognise some makers' marks, and knew to assay silver content. But that had taken him thirty years to learn, from birth. The silly loon was so infatuated with his Jenny that he was willing to step outside silver to serve her whim.

'No, Lovejoy. Straight up. She only needs a few more days, and it'll be England.' He beamed at the image. 'Then we can spend for ever on antique Georgian silver.'

His eyes glazed at the very thought of unimagined paradise. 'England' is antique dealers' slang for perfection, the triumph of profit. Comes from the sailors' cry when leaving foreign ports on the journey homeward: 'England, home, and beauty!' Meanwhile, my mind had gone dreamy too, wondering what on earth was possessing us all. Scams so huge, with money so vast, that the National Debt would shrink if the Chancellor could get his hands on the wadge? Barmy.

Luna brewed up while Big Frank and I thought our mutually excluding thoughts. I was helping Connie, from past love. I was also helping Prammie Joe, if you can call it that, from sorrow. I had the feeling somehow that I should be helping Rye Benedict – correction, please. Delete that. I ought to be helping myself. It was me that was broke, not this load of deadlegs.

'Help how, exactly, Frank?' As if I didn't know.

'Lovejoy. How many divvies are there?'

'Me,' I said miserably. 'I did hear there's an old dear near Saxmundham for porcelain—'

'One, Lovejoy.' Frank's voice is so deep you sometimes have to actively listen out for it, like the deepest bell. 'You. I want you to be there when Jenny accepts the antiques.'

Plural. Plenty, again? 'Frank. I'm pushed at the minute. How about a dollop broker? I've heard there's a really superb one around these days.'

'Yes, she's great. Jenny'll be using her.'

She again. Same one. Sooner or later I was going to have to think about this mysterious person, and tell Luna what a dollop broker actually is.

'If your Jenny's working up a dollop, and you know a dollop broker, then where's your problem, Frank?'

He stared at me sadly. 'Tracing the seller, once the money's been handed over. That's the problem, Lovejoy.'

So the vendor was foreign? Crikey. Jenny, soon to be his wife, wouldn't even tell him who was going to sell her all these valuable antiques? For a brief instant, as Luna dished out tea and biscuits, something occurred to me. Something wrong, but notably right, if you follow. I tried to hang on to it, but it was gone.

'It's sensible, Lovejoy.' I stood, to look out of the window and think a bit. Frank rumbled on. 'I mean, who tells anybody?'

Except a fiancée wasn't just anybody, if she was going to be his eighth – ninth? – wife. Maybe that feeling I'd nearly had was the dawning realisation that I was in greater demand than I'd ever been.

'About the old soldi, Lovejoy. I'll see you get a fee.'

'You will?' Big Frank is quite a good payer. But never up front.

'Up front,' he promised. Queererer and queererer.

'Right, Frank. I'll go and see her. If it's okay?'

'Any time, Lovejoy.' He looked down into his tea and didn't grimace, 'Your bird here will show you the way.'

He left, politely thanking Luna for the hospitality. Which would have left me food for thought, if I hadn't been thinking what it was I'd almost been thinking about.

'A dollop broker?'

We were going to nosh in a restaurant, to celebrate Luna's first ever sale of an antique at auction. She'd got word from Wittwoode's that she'd made a week's wage on the bubby pot. Of course I threatened fire and slaughter if the lads dared to ring it. They'd thoughtfully stayed out of the bidding. I didn't tell Luna that I'd asked Jeff to bid it up. I didn't want Luna disappointed, first time out.

'Is it an antique dealer, Lovejoy?'

That was a laugh. 'No, love. All they do is hide stuff for you.'

'Hide? Not sell?'

'It works like this, love. If you're going to gaol, or having to do a runner – that is, leave the country for any reason – you use a dollop broker.'

It was dark. We were under the station bridge, queueing at the traffic lights so commuters could come staggering off the train in droves.

'There are none in the phone book.' So she'd looked.

145

'They aren't legal, love. They store stolen antiques, any quantity, for you to recover when it's safe for you to come home. Or out of clink. Or when the Statute of Limitations has expended – in Japan it's only a short time. Give you an example: you pinch paintings, say, from France, anywhere. You give your dollop of stolen paintings to a dollop broker. He guards them until you come for them, maybe years hence, and gives you them back, against a fee. You take your stolen paintings, whatever, to Japan. And sell them.'

'Why don't you hoard them yourself, where it's safe?'

I stared. Why can't people see the obvious?

'Well,' I explained as we started to move on the green. 'Just think. You're inside gaol, ten years for robbery, right? You have dolloped up – that is, given into the hands of a dollop broker – your loot, your valuable sculptures nicked from the British Museum. If you'd hidden them in Friday Wood, you'd have to wait until you got out. You'd be old, right? But with the loot in the hands of a dollop broker, why, you can sell the loot. To any other crook you wish to name. Bill of sale and everything. The loot is described somewhat differently than if they were coming up, say, at Christie's – in some code you've previously agreed with the dollop broker.'

She drew breath as we started up North Hill. 'Don't,' I said quickly to forestall her saying but that was illegal. 'It's done everywhere. All you need is to identify yourself to the dollop broker, and he'll surrender your goods—'

'Your *stolen* goods, Lovejoy,' she reprimanded primly.

'Until they get to Japan, or some other country where the Statute of Limitations is short. Then it's all legit. Out come your stolen Monets, Rembrandts, and you invest in Switzerland's holier-than-thou banking system, with the other mafiosi.'

'I've never heard the like.'

'You did it yourself, love,' I pointed out quietly. 'Today. You bought a hubby pot, a very valuable item, from an unsuspecting teacher, for a fifth of the value it realised at auction.'

'But that was legal, and *fair*, Lovejoy.' She gave the woman's too-patient smile.

She was proud of that, but somebody had to tell her. Will you send him the balance?'

'Of course not!' she cried indignantly, swerving in the traffic at the fork. 'You're talking of hiding, well, *stolen* goods! Crime's ill-gotten gains!'

'If you say so.'

Truce time. We arrived at the restaurant in the friendly silence armistice brings. But to me there's not all that much difference. I mean, on the one hand a bloke thieves some precious work of art and stashes it away in a dollop broker's shed or wherever, maybe gets caught, does his time. He then comes out and shifts it overseas and sells on the open market, possibly even at a famous multinational auctioneer's. And retires to blondes and a casino. On the other, you give a person a pittance, hoof it with his antique and keep the profit. The only difference is that one defrauds you of *all* the antique's value, and the other denies *most* of it. It's the sort of scandal everybody dreams of, you and me, kings and presidents. Oh, and antique dealers.

We dined, had a lovely candle-lit supper, becoming friendly and apologetic as the hours turned quiet and the town edged into slumber. She dropped me off at the cottage, and I went in to find my own brand of hell waiting.

At first I thought there was only one man waiting for me.

He was sitting on my chair. Bulky shadows behind the door told me he was well gooned.

Del Vervain's show is a scatty prattle-and-tune radio

thing. Really boring, but so popular for so long that everybody knows his voice. It's interviews with the flighty and mighty. He does a written-out patter of mind-bendingly dull boyish wit. Every so often he ushers a new guest on, who grovels to set up Del's next punch-line. He occasionally slips into the vernacular, you-and-me friendly, changes accents admirably. The standing joke is that Del's jokes are utter dross, lines deliberately wrong. Del tops them with infantile slickness. The audience is milked of every handclap. You've probably heard it. It's really crud.

'Lovejoy. Sit down.' That magic accent.

I didn't, hoping a run was on the cards. In the corner of my eye a shadow stepped a yard. I stayed where I was.

'You recognise me, I'm sure.' Del Vervain seemed about to make a quirky remark, then remembered I was the only audience. Odd to see him real, so familiar from the tabloid supplements. But threatening.

'Yes.' I cleared my throat, tried it without falsetto. 'Yes. You're on the wireless. Heaven With Vervain.'

'Bright, bright.' Somebody snickered behind me. 'You know my wife Joan.'

Flat statement, denial out of the question. 'Yes.'

'You've been fucking her ragged, Lovejoy.'

Put that bluntly, my breath went away. 'Well, I, er—'

'She's going to take you away from . . . all this.' A casual look brought a roomful of snickers, snuff-snuff-snuff.

'Nothing definite's been arranged. Honest.'

'No air tickets? No grand Rolls booked in Monaco? No marriage ceremony? No media notified? The banks?'

'She's *talked* of a, er, flight. But the rest is news to me.'

'Honest?' He leant forward, smiling eyes questing over my face as if in wonderment. 'Do you mean honest, Lovejoy?' Snuff-snuff-snuff. Two goons? Three?

'Well, yes.' My squeaky throat had gone again.

'Honest is a word you seem to use rather a lot, Lovejoy.' He clicked on a hand recorder. It whittered and a snatch of my conversation came on, scratchy, but definitely me. I seemed to say honest every second word. It was me in Woody's, fixing up a chop on an item in Wittwoode's Auction.

'I'm an honest bloke.'

He smiled then, with relish. Sickeningly I knew what was going to happen. He reached some letters off the table. They'd been opened.

'Here,' I said indignantly. 'Those are my . . .'

'Air tickets, Lovejoy. New lease, apartment in Monte Carlo. Bank accounts in your name. One account in joint names, you and . . . guess who?'

I groaned. The stupid, stupid cow had jumped the gun. Monte Carlo? I live here, for God's sake.

'I was going to talk her out of it,' I whimpered. 'Honest.'

'There you go again, Lovejoy. All honesty, no reality. I gather you're famous for it.'

'It's a mistake. I wasn't ever going away with her. Honest – er, truly.'

He stuffed the letters into a pocket, dropped an embossed envelope on the table. Two nerks came into the light where I could see how very big they were. Their noses were crushed, their foreheads corrugated iron. Vervain went out as they started on me. First time he's left anywhere without an exit line, I bet.

They belted me silly.

Some time later the phone rang. I dragged myself to it. Joan's voice came on, breathless with secrecy and urgency and, I daresay, confidentiality.

'Lovejoy? Darling? I want to warn you. Del is absolutely *furious*. We must go tonight. Be at Stansted Airport in three hours . . .'

I went to soak my face. Little bruising on the features, though my ribs creaked and my skin was sore as hell. They must have punched me unconscious, because somebody had stolen four hours from the clock. I could hardly move my right thigh, swollen to a tree trunk. It stung every time I moved. The fancy envelope contained an invitation from Mr and Mrs T. E. Vervain to nosh, days hence. My mind was in its ? mode. It required no reasons.

Another hour later, the answerphone bleeped to tell the county it was recording. A man's voice, old and querulous. 'Is there a Lovejoy there, please? I have need to dispose of my son's antiques business. I wish to obtain guidance – for a fee, of course. Please ring Mr Fairclough, South Corn Mart, Norwich, any time between—'

Fairclough?

I reached for my one glowing neurone, and flicked it to snore.

Chapter 17

There's something wrily humorous about being beaten up – when you see it on that inert cinema screen. When it's real, well, no. It hurts like hell. Quite as bad, the shame makes you vomit and shiver even when you're over the worst. In fact, you're never sure which is the worst. Bruises mend, after all. Skin heals over. But the degradation lingers, festers, a core of hatred that never ever leaves. Like foxhunting must seem like poetry in motion – to the hunters. To the fox it's less than a giggle. I'll bet foxes never forget.

That morning I didn't answer the phone. I ignored sustained knocking. My curtains stayed drawn. Ignored the post girl's shower of catchpenny missives. Hermit Lovejoy. It was all of noon before I surfaced. I must say, superficially I looked pretty good. Not a mark, just a faint graze or two on the knuckles. I left the cottage – at a careful strolling pace, definitely not wincing at each step – as some bloody airport phoned, frantic about flight reservations. The messages could have a nice uninterrupted chat amongst themselves.

Delia welcomed me at St Peter's Church at the top of North Hill. That is, he was waiting to cross at the traffic lights near the linen shop and ignored me. People like

Delia have this strange skill of directional non-greeting, to call attention to one specific person even in a crowd. Before I'd realised, I was strolling slo-o-o-wly, thigh hurting like hell, up the alley to the theatre coffee shop. The military figure in smart Savile Row clobber marched briskly ahead. Nobody goes there for midday nosh so there are crannies for people to meet.

'Bad, old bean?'

Delia hadn't glanced at me, but he knew all right. There must be something in Eton that tunes pupils in to the plights of others. Maybe so they can mostly ignore them, I shouldn't wonder.

'Wish I'd gone to Eton. Like Captain Hook.' I rummaged in my useless labyrinthine memory. 'Were you a contemporary of James Bond? Tarzan?'

Delia smiled. A waiter brought him coffee, none for me. He unfolded his *Financial Times* and absently started to read.

'Is it true you bounders literally used Shelley as a football?' Eton has this peculiar Wall Game. Nobody's scored since 1912.

The counter was vacated before he spoke. He hadn't risen to my jibes about Eton. 'Rum friends you have, Lovejoy. You might have warned me about the snake.'

Burglars have to take their chances, but I was ashamed.

'I did hint, Delia.'

'Put the fear of God in me, old boy.' He looked unruffled. I wondered if he wore his bowler hat on a job. 'When I depart, Lovejoy, you'll find a folder under the table by the door. Only imitation leather, I'm afraid, these days.'

'Oh, aye.' His faint headshake made me refrain from looking. Had he accomplices, then? 'What impressions?'

He read on a minute, tutting at some Share Index perfidy. 'Rum thing, all those tiresome underwater photographs,

Lovejoy. Some old boat. Amazing hobbies, people, what? He's taking too low a price on his market garden. By a mile.' Tut tut tut.

He must mean Rye. 'And TGM?'

'You've got the lot, old fruit. Scan your folder.' Photocopies of all Vell's clients' records? I gulped at the price Delia'd charge. Class tells, on an invoice.

'Money, Delia.'

He told the bill. I would have gulped again, but I couldn't. Delia's sort are deceptively casual. Default would leave me permanently damaged, with plenty of reproach that I lacked principles. No anger, though. A sigh or two, then on to the next job. Delia knew I knew this.

'Right,' I said heartily. 'Ta, Delia. I'll leave the money with Sandy in two hours. That okay?'

'Fine. If he's closed, drop it through his letter box.'

'But what . . . ?' If you can't get in, I was going to say, like an idiot. I rose with a whimper, having to push myself up with fists on the table.

'Er, Delia. I'm sorry I was narked about Eton. Jealousy.'

'Don't give it another thought, old boy.' He smiled in reminiscence. 'We play a Wall Game, sort of rugby. I scored a hat-trick. I was pretty famous.'

'Great. Wish I'd been there. Cheers.'

'Chin chin, Lovejoy. I advertise in the Personals, if you need anything.'

Honour indeed. 'Ta, Delia.'

The folder was under the table. I collected it and left, feeling ashamed. Delia was class. So what, he pretended he'd been to Eton. I'll bet Eton wished he had.

'Mayor Carstairs?' I phoned from the bus station among throngs. Everybody seemed to be noshing enormous flat hamburgers. The place stank of fried onions. What did you call a Mayor, for God's sake? 'Lovejoy. Er, I need to contact Mrs Carstairs urgently—'

'You need to contact *me* urgently, Lovejoy.' In the permafrost, another angry bloke. I sighed. What is everybody always so narked about? I mean, have they nothing else to do? 'We have to discuss the degree of interaction which you and Mrs Carstairs have established—'

Well, once an administrator. 'I'll call, sir,' I intoned gravely, trying to disentangle my legs from some corgi yapping in pursuit of its minder, a little girl of six laughing her head off. 'I too see the necessity for analytical interim negotiation—'

'Are you being frivolous, Lovejoy?'

The frigging hound was back, barking deliriously. 'Her next antiques lesson is vital. Starts in half an hour.'

'Very well. I'll motor phone her. Where is this lecture?'

'I've arranged transport, sir. So if Mrs Carstairs could be at the post office in twenty minutes . . .' Et phoney cetera.

She came in a tearing hurry, eagerly hoping she wasn't late. I warmed, then quelled the feeling. I'd been as good as warned off Luna, and we hadn't yet made a single smile.

'I had to stop off for a notebook, Lovejoy! You should have *said!* I tried to catch you at the cottage, but you'd gone!' That explained all that knocking. 'I'm so looking forward to the lecture, Lovejoy. Should I have brought a lens thing? Only, the chemist's shuts for lunch and—' A bus came. I drew her out of earshot.

'Luna. Take this folder. I had it stolen. Don't lose it, or we're sunk. I need a load of money. Now, to pay him.'

'You . . . ?' She gaped, except her sort doesn't really gape. They raise eyebrows, look round vaguely then back to stare some more. But it does pretty well, as gapes go.

'There's no lecture, love. We're going to produce a load of antiques. Very speedily.'

'We are?' She did the gape. 'No lecture? We *are*?'

'Once you get the money to pay Delia, yes. To save somebody from being murdered.'

'Like that poor old—?'

'Very similar, love. Ouch.' She'd put her hand on my arm. 'Watch it, Lune. I, er, fell.'

She stepped back to appraise me, slowly nodded. 'Are you being blackmailed, Lovejoy?'

'No,' I said impatiently. 'Silly cow. You need a reputation to be blackmailed.' I would have glanced at the post office clock but there's only this red-glow digital kidding that the world is permanently fixed at 09:37 am and 68 celsius. 'The bank, love.'

'Have you had anything to eat, Lovejoy?'

'We had such a big supper last night.'

She went and got the gelt. She drove us down East Hill and I shoved it through Sandy's letter box in good time, so relieved I almost stopped groaning. Sitting in a motor when you've been kicked silly's even more painful than a bus ride.

'Are you all right, Lovejoy?'

'Fine, ta. Take us somewhere we can read Delia's loot, eh? Then the swimming baths. Then Calamity Jenny's.'

'Should you be going swimming if you're so stiff? Only—'

'Lune,' I said wearily. 'Just drive.'

She was frightened, or she'd have told me off. She hated being called Lune, but that was her fault, not mine.

We'd almost started to pull away from the kerb when a police car slowed, blocking us in. Cradhead got out, and approached at funeral pace.

I smiled and waved. He leant down, quite affable.

'Sorry I can't stop, Chief Superintendent. But I've a valuation for our Lady Mayoress. Perhaps some other time, eh?'

'Now, Lovejoy. You know I'm only a corporal.' He opened the door. 'Forgive me, Mrs Carstairs.'

He stayed there, holding the door wide. Cars crawled past, faces peering, the swine. I could be being kidnapped for all the action they took. They wear the same expression when having a nice drive out to ogle some shambles of a motorway accident.

'Very well, Commissioner.' I got out, unable to suppress a groan. 'Please don't think this happens every day, Mrs Carstairs. I do assure you. I am the most respected antiques expert in the Eastern Hundreds, for valuations, estimates, repairs—'

He coaxed me away, which is being dragged with your heels trailing. I saw Luna's stricken face, mutely urging her to get the hell out of it, seeing we'd just paid off Delia for stolen materials now on her back seat.

She called, 'Shall I follow, Lovejoy? Your folder—'

God Almighty. *Wave it around, you silly bitch* I tried to radar, but she dithered on the pavement.

'We'll go over your list later, Mrs Carstairs.'

'My list?' she asked, baffled.

My grin felt it weighed a ton. 'Of your antiques. And thank Oliver. I'll call him, soon as I've done with Superintendent Cradhead.'

That did it. Her expression wiped clean. 'Oh. I *see*, Lovejoy!' she said brightly. 'I'm to take the folder until you come for it!'

Put it in neon lights, love, I raged. I'd throttle her. We went to the police car and I got in, grunting.

'Gardening aches,' I said quickly. My ribs must be busted.

'Sitting comfortably, Lovejoy? Then read on.'

'A telephone number?' I looked on the reverse. Blank.

'It's yours.'

The other bloke in the motor chuckled, shaking his head. 'He's a one-off, right enough.'

'Mine? Fancy that.' I gave it back, waited. My heart was sneaking down nervously to my boots.

'Written in the shaky old hand of one Godfrey S. Fairclough. He'd not long phoned you, Lovejoy. Left you a message.'

The other nerk snickered. All ears and nicotine teeth.

'Here,' I said, narked. 'You had no right to break in and listen to my messages. It's against the law.'

Cradhead said, 'Lovejoy. One Godfrey S. Fairclough was injured by intruders. Fortunately, the assailants were disturbed by a door-to-door charity collector.'

'Why didn't you catch them?'

'How do you know we didn't?'

'You wouldn't be working up to your daft question.' He opened a palm, inviting it. 'Where was I on the night of the fifty-first? And did I do him?'

'And?'

'Daft, like I said.' I stared back at the other ploddite, who was trying to give me the bent eye. A laugh, really. Witnesses all around. A couple of kids were staring in, noses pressed to the windows. Drinkwater might be a nerk, but this Cradhead seemed to possess a rudimentary cortex.

'The collector almost caught a glimpse, but the foliage . . .' He hesitated. 'You know this Fairclough?'

He must be seriously injured, poor old bloke, or they'd be asking him instead of having to take my word for it. I shrugged.

'Parker. Go for a walk, will you?'

'You what?' Parker said, amazed. But he went.

'One of your brightest?' I said.

Cradhead sighed. 'It's these frigging courses, Lovejoy. They're never on the job. Sociology.'

I warmed to him. Somebody who hates sociologists can't be all bad.

'I don't know much, Craddie.' I thought I'd better get in first. 'Except that old bloke Godbolt who got topped was involved in some antiques thing. I've not heard for sure, but word is some shipment out to the US is on, through the Midlands. It seems a bigger shipment of antiques than we're used to.'

'Is it out, Lovejoy? Or in?'

In? This startled me, because it hadn't occurred to me. I decided I was wrong to warm to Cradhead. In fact, I wanted him on the next sociology course, preferably in Aberdeen.

'In?' I would have shrugged, if I could have done it without a screech. 'We don't import antiques much, Craddie. Don't you know the local scene? We export them, for coin of the realm.'

'Just a thought.' He patted my shoulder, harder than he needed. 'That was some gardening you did, Lovejoy. No hard climbing, no clobbering old gentlemen?'

'Del Vervain.' I had to admit it, or he'd turn as nasty as his gaffer. 'He got some thugs to do me over last night.'

He took the news calmly. 'Not going to Monte Carlo then?' He let me go, smiling and shaking his head. 'Time you settled down, Lovejoy. Oh, Drinkwater wants to see you. About a whole series of burglaries.'

'Series?' I said like a fool, startled.

'Sorry. Only two, weren't there? Ta-ta, Lovejoy.'

Delia's break-ins had been sussed, which was fine by me. Good old Delia, in the clear. I wished I was.

By the time I found Luna again, I'd almost worked out how much I owed her. It made me pale around the gills. No wonder hubby Oliver was having doubts about his wife's behaviour. But could I help it if she liked antiques? One thing: if Drinkwater wanted to see me, why did Cradhead let me go?

Poor old Fairclough.

Chapter 18

The swimming bath was heaving like a tin of maggots. Children of all ages screamed, plunged, had water fights. The echoing racket was deafening. Plasher was vigilant, never taking his eyes off the turmoil. He's the lifeguard, always in swimming trunks, never looks at you. He has a voice like thunder.

'Wotcher, Plasher.'

'Wotcher, Lovejoy.'

A score of children ran past, leapt howling on to the seething mass in the water.

Plasher bellowed, 'Less of that!' And unbelievably for a second the pandemonium faltered slightly before redoubling. I wish I could do that.

Luna was all admiring, thrilled at the spectacle of a zillion infants wriggling in water.

'Plasher, I want your brother to suss out some shipments. Big. Anywhere. Recent, within say a month. Back or front.'

'Okay.' And in his foghorn voice, a yell, 'Smithson *out!*'

'Ta, Plasher.' I gave him the note with my phone number on and we left, almost deaf.

'What a marvellous man!' Luna said through a

cotton-wool tunnel, thrilled. 'Controlling all those children! What did Mr Cradhead want?'

We drove out of town to Calamity Jenny's antique shop.
I explained the way antiques were distributed by night
lorrymen. 'They accept illicit loads, from laybys. You pay
on mileage, plus extra for each switch, one lorry to another.'

'And that back or front business?'

'We want to know what big shipments were made last
month, or are booked by night lorries next month.'

'Aren't they ever caught, Lovejoy?'

'The drivers? Their bosses know. If they stopped it, the
drivers would walk out. So they condone.'

She drove without speaking until we were parked outside Jenny's. Here it comes, I thought. The big morality
blip.

'Lovejoy.' She switched off. 'Why should I continue?
Your apprentice, everything.'

'Eh?' It wasn't at all what I'd expected. But then nothing
ever is. Even retrospect usually lets me down.

'It costs me a fortune. You don't pay me the money the
National Employment pays for me. You don't tell me what
we're doing. You are bad-tempered. Then you do *that*.'

'Do what?' Women can't be stopped when they're gab-
bing like this. It's like verbal sweat, has to come out. Then
you can get on.

'You tell that hulk Plasher to do something, he agrees
without question. You look so murderous sometimes.
Then you picked up that little girl when she'd grazed her
knee and was crying.'

See what I mean? There'd been this titchie girl with a
leg that needed blotting. She'd shaken my trouser leg, so
I'd sucked her knee pale to stop it blooding. Because I was
nearest, you silly cow, I thought in exasperation. So?

A girl – no more than nineteen – was peering out of the

shop and beckoning. Jenny? Big Frank's wives were getting younger every single marriage.

'There's Jenny!' I exclaimed, and escaped out.

The welcomes over, I had a quick look about Calamity Jenny's place. Very affluent, very splendid buying. Not all true stuff, of course, but it surpassed Luna's feeble description of 'Really quite nice, Lovejoy'. And Jenny herself? 'R.q.n, Lovejoy'. That had been the sum of Luna's earlier exploration.

She was beautiful. Pretty with that wicked winsomeness any man'd go for. I could see why Big Frank had placed her top of his next electoral roll, so to speak. Luna overdid the merry prattle, until I told her to nark it and come and look. She tried telling me she'd already seen most of Jenny's antiques. A laugh. She might have been in their presence, but hadn't *seen* one.

Big Frank had succumbed to Jenny's beauty, yes. Another reason was that she had a ton of silver, some fake, some Belgian and north French and not hallmarked. And (watch out for this) plenty of the new silver they've been turning out like Ford cars in Lebanon and Egypt. The trick is to take a genuine piece of antique silver abroad on your holidays, complete with Customs and Excise stamps, all that 'snow', as necessary documentation is called. Then in Alexandria, Cairo, Calcutta, you have the piece copied by their silversmiths of prodigious skills. Reimport them into Great Britain's frantic antiques silver markets, and sell them as genuine antiques. If you're going to try this, go only for 'clean-line' styles. That means the earlier the better. In fact, I'd even say fake all silver before 1730.

'Any of these Indian, love?'

Luna smiled, clapped her hands. 'I've *checked* the hallmarks of those sugar tongs, Lovejoy! They're Paul de Lamerie's marks, 1728.' She was being all thrilled again. 'You see, Lovejoy? I did what you said. *I looked them up!*'

'The marks are fake, love,' I explained as Jenny blushed fetchingly. 'They're not sharp. If a silver mark looks sort of soft, blurred a bit, it's probably fake.'

'Fake?' Luna rummaged for a little paperback which listed silversmith marks. I'd come across her reading it. 'But—'

'Fakers are greedy, love. They think in shillings, pennies. And they're slovens, usually. They know they're duff workers. They make fake dies out of soft metal, see? Brass, copper, even tin. Not the hard metal required.'

'You mean . . . ?' Luna coloured up, looked at Jenny, who was still being winsome. 'Shouldn't we tell the . . . ?'

God Almighty. Still thinking like a member of the public, and her an apprentice antique dealer.

'Jenny had them made, Luna,' I laboured. Luna was proving heavy load. 'She wasn't tricked into buying them. And they aren't sugar tongs. That's a tongue scraper.'

'For . . . ?' Luna felt at the sprung silver's spatulate ends.

'A tongue scraper. For – forget it.' I flapped my hands. I was talking a private language, no means of contact.

'It's no good getting ratty, Lovejoy.' Luna was now unthrilled. Deo gratias. 'I'm doing my best. You never tell me what we're *doing*. You were cross yesterday because I couldn't remember how to tell a real chastity belt from a modern—'

Et reproachful cetera. I'd told the silly cow ten times. Let her get on with it. I ignored her. 'They Indian, Jenny?'

'The silvers?' She reached into a small decorative inglenook taken from an old cast-iron industrial fireplace range. 'These were done in the Isle of Man. What d'you think?'

The punches weren't too bad, but soft metal again.

Possession is illegal. I interrupted Luna's deplorings to tell her this small fact. She silenced, stared in amaze at Jenny.

'The silver-mounted meerschaum pipe bowls are Cairo,' Jenny said proudly.

She had a collection of pipes, all eroticas – mouths doing wonderful things, frank anatomical organs, and figures of couples busy, er, coupling. Very valuable now, if genuine mid-Victorian.

Luna said, 'I thought those looked almost . . .' She paled. They looked almost because they were.

'Erotica's in, love. Especially tobacciana, which is a dying thing. Forgive the pun.'

Luna gave up, settled for wonder. As soon as we were driving away she'd tell me sternly that Jenny wanted a good smacking for being so, well, absolutely *bold* . . .

'Meerschaum means sea foam, Lune,' I relented. 'It's a sort of natural porous mineral, silicate of magnesium. You can carve it, work it even with a small file. Chosen because it keeps the tobacco smoke cool, see? Insmoked and new, it isn't that meerschaum amber colour. That's only the nicotine. But fakes—' I smiled fondly at Jenny. 'Fakes come ready stained.'

'They're *horrible*, Lovejoy. They're people *doing*, well, *things*.' Luna was so distressed, poor lass.

'Any one'd buy a car, love. If really Viennese.' Austria made them a national art in the nineteenth century.

Yes, silver was one of Jenny's things. Her collection was incoherent, in spite of this. She must have vacuumed all that Big Frank had missed. And she'd imported fakes enough to sink a ship. Ship? Time I looked at the photographs and papers Delia had burgled for me. He'd mentioned some sunken vessel. But erotica was distracting, making me think of Jenny. Big Frank's Jenny. Not mine.

'Jenny. Big Frank wanted me to call.'

'Yes, Lovejoy.' She glanced at Luna, still being mesmerised by the meerschaums, and raised her eyebrows faintly. She was making the oldest offer. I brightened, then sombred. Big Frank was going to wed this lissom lass. Minimally I shook my head. Jenny gave a rueful smile, shrugged.

'I want some things divvied. Imported. High class. Soon.'

'Where?'

'Hawkshead.'

'Okay.' I smiled, but with an effort. 'Fix time with Luna.' I bussed her. She moved her mouth more than is customary. I was still gulping when I waved at her shop window. Big Frank was in for multo hallelujah choruses, once he'd got rid of his wife and got wed.

And in the motor it happened. Luna suddenly proved her worth. We were hardly on to the Lavenham road.

'That young lady's up to no good,' she said reprovingly. 'She should still be at school. I mean, all those holidays to Cyprus! If she were my daughter I'd censure her.'

We'd gone miles before the penny dropped. *What* was that?

'Pull in, love.'

'I can't just yet. That little tractor has right of way—'

I yelled, 'Pull in for Christ's sake can't you do a frigging single thing I tell you just for once instead of giving me frigging lip back everything I say?' Hardly the English of Milton. She pulled in, to a merry cacophony of motor horns and one bawled obscenity. Ignition off, and furious reproach.

'Lovejoy! I will not be spoken to—'

'Cyprus? What about Cyprus?'

'Cyprus?' Her brow unwrinkled. 'Miss Calamy goes a lot to Cyprus. I told you, Lovejoy.'

I leaned away to look at her. 'What did you tell me?'

'Of all the . . .' She saw my raised finger, drew a calming breath. 'If you *must*, Lovejoy. She said she only went once, to Paphos. But she was fibbing. She goes to the eastern side. And far too often. She's a child. My daughter Lola's age!'

'More than once?' Jenny saying she holidayed once when she went plenty was a very, very significant lie. Not without serious implications for life and death.

'Several times. I only discovered it accidentally.' Her mouth set sternly. 'This is confidential, Lovejoy. You promise?'

'Hand on my heart.' Some folk never leave Planet Mongo.

'I was in her shop, first visit. She was on the phone. Some stupid airline clerk. Though I know how she felt, Lovejoy. Sometimes they are hopeless. Once, Oliver took me to—'

'Cyprus?' I cued desperately.

'Yes.' Luna was Mrs Surprise. 'You don't even have to go via Geneva at all. Jenny said she *always* went that way. There's an excellent direct service from Heathrow, though the arrival time—'

I swear I'm the most patient bloke on earth. I can prove it. I didn't even thump her. She tutted at being restrained from criticising a pretty younger bird, but clinched it.

'Jenny told the stupid booking agent she'd been seven times lately and *always* caught the same flight. To meet her friend.' Luna shook her lovely hair in admonition. I suddenly saw how very gorgeous she looked. 'I should have gone straight to the managing director—'

My mind pretended to hear her out. 'Turkish Cyprus, then?'

'Yes. I'm not exactly sure where she goes, but—'

But I did. Clear as day, sure as taxes.

'Come here, Lune.' I dragged her head close, sucked her

luscious mouth longer than mere approval allowed. She came up gasping, pink-faced, looking round in embarrassment in case gawpers lurked nearby. A passing lorry driver bipped in cheery salutation, earning a serious tut.

'No more of *that*, Lovejoy! What on earth would Oliver think? No wonder he—'

'You're beautiful, Lune,' I said. She was radiant. All women have allure. But some really reach in. 'I could eat you.' She was doing her stare. 'Drive us home, love. Sharp.' I honestly don't know how I managed to keep my hands off her.

She drove, looking at me from time to time.

In the end, she compromised. Which to a bird is doing exactly what she wants. She dropped me at the cottage and drove away in a racing start.

A pity. In the end it didn't matter much. Using my new water-cooled phone I got Hilda – receptionist in Knowles Travel – to come by on her way home.

Hilda's a constant and smiley long-time-no-see but what're-we-doing sort. A friend, I suppose I'm saying. I chucked her brochures away as soon as she'd gone. Then I caught the bus into town, hired a car from Ogden's on Luna's credit. Then lit out north. I reached Hawkshead at eleven o'clock.

Hawkshead. Roar up the motorway through Lincolnshire, after a couple of hundred miles you come to a service station. Loos, nosh bar, restaurant, slot machines, and inevitably one of those widespread yellow-lit shops filled with things you'll never need in a million years – London policemen dolls, toffee moulded into gruesome creatures, plastic bugles. Outside, roaring traffic, and acres of vehicles pausing to buy chocolate dwarfs.

Until night, when suddenly you notice how lonely the place actually is. An oasis of light in a dark and louring hilly landscape. It's then that it happens.

The place becomes an antiques market. Vans arrive, and park far from the lights. While the motorway below roars with night traffic, dealing begins. A score of pantechnicons drop their tailboards and reveal interiors crammed with antique furniture, porcelain, flintlocks, paintings. It's joked that you can buy back your precious bow-front corner cupboard, stolen in the morning, at ten o'clock the same night in Hawkshead.

Some very heavy goons lurk there. Like a nerk I'd left my pencil torch behind. I depended on the dealers' rigged battery lights. I wandered, had sweet tea and a pasty – good pasties at Hawkshead – and sussed out the place. It felt like home.

The people to avoid are the bloggers. Tonight they were here aplenty. These hoodlums follow you home, and burgle/rob/mug, stealing the antiques you've just bought. They're in collusion with the antique dealers themselves, who get their – read *your* – lovely antique back an hour after they've sold it. They sell it again tomorrow and tomorrow and tomorrow. Recycling at its best. I was tempted, but desisted. There were a couple of baluster pewters – waists, a handle, a lid with a knob. Tip: go for hammerhead knobs, ball knobs, or bud-shaped ones. Of course, they'll be expensive. Pewter is definitely in. Find a King James vessel taller than seventeen and three-quarter inches, you can spit in your boss's eye and retire for life.

This far north I didn't know too many faces. I was glad. It gave me the chance to talk to Nuala (you've to say Noola) from Belfast. She's a pretty lass with Celtic colouring – blue eyes, hair jet. She runs a ferry line with her dad. This doesn't mean they steer ships, only that they operate two businesses – Belfast and Liverpool – as one, using the ferry. Nuala is heap big business, and she's only twenty.

'Hello, love. How's Sean?'

'Lovejoy! Nice to see you. Dad's fine, thanks.'

You don't buss Ulster folk as greeting, only in serious snogging. Meekly I kept my distance. 'He doing anything?'

'He'll be down East Anglia, soon. He'll call.'

'And be welcome.' News indeed. Four blokes suddenly were standing close. Nuala travels mob-handed. I prattled inanities until they drifted off, disappointed at not having to club me insensible. 'Here, Nool. Sean interested in a Snettisham?'

Nuala raised a beckoning finger. A couple of wiry Liverpudlians stepped from a pantechnicon and took over her pitch. We climbed into the driver's cab. She lit up the longest cigarette I'd ever seen. 'You serious, Lovejoy?'

'Not for me, Nool.' I shrugged, looking down. These cabins are high off the blinking ground. Like flying. 'Too rich. You'd need a dollop broker in your pocket. And who's got one of those?'

'Dad, Lovejoy.' She's a cool girl, is Nool. I wish I had one like her. In fact, she herself'd do at a pinch. Except she's married to a Manchester racecourse grifter. You leave those alone. Sean, her dad, had done time for a series of church robberies. He'd made a fortune selling the antiques when he got released. Which meant he'd used a dollop broker.

'That your stained glass on the blanket, love?'

Antiques placed casually on a blanket at these fly-by-night gatherings claim to be genuine. Fakes stand on the tarmac.

'Interested? Genuine, Lovejoy. I had Donk lift a piece of calme to show the glass's edge—'

'Tch. Silly cow, Nool.'

She laughed. 'Sorry, Lovejoy. I forgot you'd know.'

Medieval glaziers had no steel-wheels or diamond knives, so they nibbled the glass's edges with a notched thing called a grozing iron. Moth-eaten margins under the lead calmer mean genuine ancient stained glass. I've never known this test lie.

'Scotch, is it?'

She laughed again, getting the joke. There is no surviving medieval Scotch stained glass.

'A dollop broker's too big for me, Nool. You have to deposit, what, ten per cent? Jesus!'

'That'd be my problem, Lovejoy. Whose Snettisham?'

'Promise you'll use an East Anglian?' I glanced about, all suspicion, worrying I was overdoing it. 'Reason is, we've a local lady dolloper. Once did me a favour. Okay?'

Nuala's frown vanished. She grinned. 'Miss R is the one Da used! She's marvellous. Deal?'

'Deal, Nool.' I chuckled. 'Miss R's great.'

'Da was annoyed she wasn't willing at first. He had to take *me* along! I was only fourteen! The year she started broking.' Oh, how we laughed.

I chanced an arrow. 'Same with me. My sister.'

'Once a teacher, always.'

My mind went: Miss R. Teacher. East Anglian antiques dollop broker six years. *Deals only with females!* I haven't got a sister.

I quickly invented, 'The finder's one of three Beccles treasure-seekers. They've shown me a torc. Genuine. There's the usual gamekeeper trouble. The gold is being sussed by a tame museum scientist. Okay?'

We mused possibilities, then shook hands on it. I lowered myself to resume my earthly wanderings.

A Snettisham is a major treasure-trove find. Called after the mega one at Ken Hill in Snettisham, Norfolk. There, over thirty-eight precious torcs – neckbands of Ancient

British tribal kings – were found, with two dozen bronze torcs, coins, bangles, ingots. The decent old gent whose gadget bleeped them into King's Lynn Coroner's Court was a sterling character. He was unbelievably honest. Actually had asked the landowner's permission to treasure-hunt. And reported his stupendous discovery to archaeologists and the British Museum. Knowing he might not get a penny (our daft Law of Treasure Trove dates from 1195 AD, believe it or not), still this gentleman behaved with absolute propriety. It's true.

Other treasure-hunters are not so loyal or honest. Our loony law states that treasure originally *hidden* goes to the Crown – i. e. national museums. Treasure originally *lost* is the finder's. (Get it? It's the very opposite of finders keepers. Finders = losers). Since we're talking 70 BC, out-guessing some pre-Roman warrior chieftain means you'll probably get zilch from your mind-boggling discovery of, what, 30 million pounds sterling.

Is it any wonder treasure-seekers, 'moonspenders', 'moonies', as they're called, mostly sell their loot secretly and say nothing? Rotten laws make rotters.

A couple of hours more I strolled, noshed. Saw antiques come and go. There was only one fake I'd made myself, a lovely 1852 painting by C. J. Lewis of two ladies with dogs on punts. Chocolate-box sort, of course, but now all the rage. I was pleased to see it go in exchange for a trio of 'traveller's pieces'. People think these tiny pieces of furniture were salesmen's or apprentices' samples. They're not. They were simply for doll's houses, children's toys. Highly sought these days. They show us the authentic furniture of the time.

Smug, I drove homeward at two in the morning. Miss R was the dollop broker for Jenny Calamy's importing trips to Cyprus.

That lovely island is split into two chunks. Turkish, Greek. I'm not knocking any one political system, honest I'm not. And people conquer people, don't they, bend them to their will. We of these islands know this. I merely report that, with Cyprus split, a mighty change came about in Ancient World antiques. All of a sudden, great shipments happened. Geneva's the centre, Munich the residence, of the modern loot bootleggers. The fact that the antiques are plundered from the churches, houses, schools of Cyprus is ignored. Buyers have plenty of money for the genuine thing. The Greek Government has been forced into being a serious buyer, to recover Greek art from the looters' middlemen. It's not new, in this terrible world. In 1258, when Baghdad was sacked by Hulegu the Mongol, the Tigris ran black with the ink of the city's priceless manuscripts dumped in the river. We're the predators.

It would be somewhere not far from Lythrankomi, where Jenny went so often, via Geneva. Had to be. The buyer would probably be from Munich. The loot would be priceless mosaics, ikons, paintings, church furnishings, religious jewellery. The shipment would be large – and for large read *large*. Everything would be unbelievably genuine. Jenny'd gone to a deal of trouble and expense to acquire Big Frank's marriage proposal. Birds do this sort of thing. I once knew a Southminster girl who pretended she loved cricket – went to matches all through one long wet summer, finally married the opening bowler. Never seen another match since. Fiancée fans, you might call them. Love-stricken as Jenny purported to be, she'd all but offered me the family vault when I'd hesitated. So she was more than a little desperate to have me divvieing. She'd needed Big Frank, so she'd acquired some silver, as a lure. It's the one thing he could never resist. She'd persuaded Big Frank to ask my help, to divvie her imported loot. Big

Frank for protection, Lovejoy for authenticity. She was going to import a huge Cypriot shipment, via Hawkshead, direct to the mysterious Miss R, dollop broker.

Good old Luna. I'd catch it tomorrow – today – from her, of course. I retired smiling at the thought of her eyes, staring wide and astonished into mine.

Chapter 19

It was the day of the nosh party at Del Vervain's. No chance of ducking it, of course.

I was tying my tie the new American way. There used to be two ways: the old over-over knot, and the Windsor. Both slip. It took umpteen centuries until a 92-year-old Yank invented Method Three. Start seam out, wide end under wrap wide end over and again under the short bit. Tighten. Cross wide bit to your right then under, shove it through down. Voila! Right way out, and non-slip! Good old Yanks. Mind you, a cravat'd be the thing. James II's coronation cravat, lace of course, cost thirty-six pounds ten shillings. You can buy genuine ancient lace cravats for less than that even today. If only I knew which lace cravat was King James' . . .

'Think what we've done, so far, love,' I told Luna the instant she arrived. Different motor, I saw with admiration. A low sleek job, shape of a sucked toffee, electric blue. I set her cooking my fried bread and tomatoes while I thought. 'We've got facts, but no solutions. And antiques.'

'You ought to explain, Lovejoy.' She looked good enough to chew. Style, high heels and smart, better than a New Year sale. No mention of my earlier gratitude. 'I'm confused.'

Explain what? I didn't know myself. But the Lunas of this world expect omniscience from adjacent males.

'I'm almost sure what's going on, love,' I lied easily. 'I'll sum it up tomorrow.' For me too. 'Say what you *think* we've done. I'll say if you're close.'

'Well,' she began doubtfully, slicing tomatoes. 'Poor Mr Godbolt died. The police still think foul play.'

'Right!' I praised. Actually, the Plod would be at the boozer, until Prammie Joe faded from memory. 'Anything else?'

'Connie asked you—' I raised a finger. She smiled shyly. 'Connie asked *us* to divvie her antiques at the disused aerodrome. And to fuff them out for a major sale.'

'Excellent!' I started on the bread and tea. My technique is mop-and-nosh, unaided by cutlery.

She coloured up slightly, attended to the stove. 'Miss Alors, the, ah, street lady has diverted a load of handies, small stolen antiques, to another buyer instead of yourself. Jenny Calamy wants you to assist the sale of her antiques.' She deftly stepped back as the next load of sliced tomatoes slid into the hot margarine. 'I don't care for that young lady, Lovejoy.'

'Mmmh. Very forward.'

'She's had everything. Splendid school background . . .'

Hang on. I paused, slice of sopping bread halfway across the plate. What had Vell said? Some marvellous school? She was from one not so posh, something like that? Of Cassandra Clark.

'. . . especially Big Frank, all those wives. Of course, I blame the woman. I mean, a man's obviously swayed by anything flighty . . .' Woman blame woman. But interesting. Schoolmates?

'We've burgled Rye Benedict's mill shop that's never open. And Marvella's flat at the old Meeting House. We went to the River Deben. You asked Miss Brewer about the little boy falling into the water. We've asked Plasher at the swimming baths for a great many fake antiques . . .

'What's up?' She was slow with the next plate, silly cow, staring into space with rapture. 'I'm starving.'

She turned, thrilled times ten. 'Did you *hear* me, Lovejoy? I've talked with prostitutes, fakers, thieves, rogues!' She spoke the word with relish. '*Gaolbirds!* Can you believe it?'

'I will, if I survive.'

'Oh, sorry.' She hurried with the grub.

'Which leaves us with quite an interesting day. You'll meet Tinny today. Object: to come gathering nuts in May, Lune.'

'Luna, please, Lovejoy. And you gather—'

I held up a soaked slice. 'It's a saying, Lune. You *can't* gather nuts in May, see? Soon as you've fried the next lot, get out the stuff Delia stole for me.'

'Us, Lovejoy. Us.'

That gave me pause for a second. I agreed, 'Us, love.'

The folder held two sections. One was Vell's records of her clients. I was surprised at the diversity of people who went. Luna raised her eyebrows at my name there, but I explained I'd been trying to get the list, legit means first.

A score of antique dealers were in. Connie, Tits Alors. And, making Luna go quiet, one Oliver J. Carstairs, Mayor. Regularly, once a fortnight. More women than men. Now, some things are really certain. It's that women go to dentists, health classes, all those sort of things, more than men. They're more practical. We hide; they don't. But I'd seen Cassandra Clark chatting in Vell's after a massage-and-horoscope session. And Cassandra Clark wasn't in the records at all.

'Odd,' I mused. Delia was the ultimate pro. He'd not have missed a card. How the heck had he photocopied this lot?

Which left Rye Benedict's dull stuff. I told Luna to get on with sussing those while I finished dressing and saw to the birds' nuts. She was sitting staring at them – just a series of rather blotchy photographs and a few maps – when I said I was ready.

'Lovejoy. Why do people go to The Great Marvella?'

'Eh? Why . . .' Then I thought, yes. Why? To do what? Massage? Then horoscope? Talk with Geronimo about the future? I suddenly realised I honestly didn't know.

Luna clearly suspected Hubby Oliver went there to make smiles, thinly disguised. Maybe Vell was a posh kind of . . . well, a Tits Alors with a meeting house of a special kind.

'Dunno, love. Honest.' I'd told her about the snake, the fortune-telling act, the ventriloquism, how daft it all was. I didn't tell Lune that Vell feeds Geronimo on live mice. I looked over her shoulder at Rye's secret photographs.

An underwater boat? That shape, anyway. I found myself tracing its outlines with a finger while I explained to Lune about how a man with work stress would need a massage.

'Oliver maybe has to go, for Council reasons.' I expounded a new theory of commercial development of Priory Street and the old ruins. She looked disbelieving.

'He's never mentioned it, Lovejoy.'

'No, of course he couldn't!' I cried, mechanically shuffling Rye's photocopies while I tried to invent an alibi for her bloody husband. More than Oliver'd do for me. 'It's confidential! All Council work is. Look, love. If people knew there was some development going on, why, the

Council would lose a fortune! Everybody would snap up those small shops . . .'

Boat. Sunk, but definitely a boat. With a huge arc projecting from the mud. A paddle-wheel? The photograph looked murky. A fish faced the camera, thunderstruck at light where there should be none. The maps were charts. Sandbanks. Submerged wrecks, marked with symbols. Photos of a wreck? Maps of submerged sands? Surely Rye wasn't falling for the old I've-got-a-sunken-galleon con? Then I thought. I actually recognised one particular map. The coast between the Colne and Deben estuaries. Weakly, I faced what I knew I'd been shunning, and drew out of a drawer the folded paper from Prammie's. One was a tracing of the other, done by a slow patient hand. A pencilled note: *Only place X, if less than 40'*.

I leafed through the photos as Luna explained her deep trust in her Oliver. And found it. One picture was jubilantly overwritten, massive initials in ballpoint: *IKB!!!* with half-inch marks along it. Somebody's scale, of a sunken paddle-boat? Isambard Kingdom Brunel, IKB. Who never worked on the east coast. His was the *Great Eastern*, the mightiest iron ship of all. Rye Benedict's hero.

'Eh?' Lune was still on about her frigging Oliver.

'Do you suppose Oliver has had a premonition? He has a bad back—'

'Sod Oliver. Get your knickers on, Lune. We're off.'

That quietened her down, otherwise we'd be there yet. Some people simply ask for it.

'Tinny, Luna. My apprentice.'

Tinny's a container bloke from Felixstowe. He's always ready to do a deal, any antiques, any size of order. He was admiring a painting, *The Falls on the Caravogue* by Jack B. Yeats, the Irish painter. In fact, so was I. I'd painted it about a year since. I love it. Sold it to Suki Sharland for love, one terrible lonely night. She happens to be the most beautiful bird in this land. Tell you about her some time.

'Tiny? How d'you do?' from Luna. She'd worried all the way about Oliver's possible need for Marvella's massage. Her powerful prowly motor turned out to be a Jaguar, one of the sort you have to call by letters, XKX and that. My face felt three miles back.

The yard of Tinny's small firm looks like a builder's supply merchant. Bricks, pipes, paving flags, sheds, timber. It's a front. He gets really narked if genuine customers come, wanting nails and suchlike. It's a staging post for containers shipped to and from Belgium, which are filled with renegade antiques.

'Tinny,' I corrected. 'When was it, Tinny?'

He smiled modestly. 'Three years gone, Lovejoy.'

'Tinny had himself shipped inside a container. Room size. Filled with antiques. Takes his job seriously, does Tinny.'

'Ever since, they've called me Tinny. Tin Can, see?' He smiled with pride, a wizened little bloke with an oddly protruberant belly, waistcoat, watch-chain and all. He looks a dehydrated bookie, but is all there.

'It was that fire in Norfolk. The great house at—'

'Pentlesham Major?' Luna cried. 'I remember it! Seventeen paintings, all burned!' Her thrilled mode again. She was getting the hang of the antiques game. Not before time.

'And?' I prompted, with mute apology to Tinny.

'And . . .' She worked it out, after apologising to Tinny. 'And Mr Tinny took the paintings to the Continent to sell, because . . . *they hadn't been burned at all?*'

'Bravo, lady!' Tinny patted her hand while Luna blushed. I liked that. She fluffed out like a preening bird.

'We want at least a can, Tinny.'

'Christ, Lovejoy. You don't ask much, do you?'

A customer drove in, parked, got out and looked around at the fence-posts.

'How much, mate? There's no prices marked.'

'Get stuffed,' Tinny called over.

'You *what?* You'll never make any sales with that attitude!' The customer drove off in high dudgeon, shouting that he'd go to Blakeson's at Nine Ash Green, serve everybody right.

'Get on my nerves,' Tinny grumbled.

Luna stayed silent. Like I said, learning. A couple of days back she'd have given him a lecture on business charm.

'Right, Lovejoy. Two weeks?' It was very reluctant.

'Sooner, Tinny. Four days?'

'I'll do what I can.'

Luna asked what had we asked for. I told her Tinny would get us a container shipment of antiques four days from now. Tinny never lets me down. Except I'd caught his worried frown. It was old time's sake doing me the favour, not Tinny.

So others, probably instant payers, wanted the same. And just as fast. I told Lune. She was indignant, said the very idea and what cheek it was for others to want what we wanted.

'Now,' I said. 'Station, please. Got enough for the train?'

'Can't we go by car?'

'No. It's their London flat, not their local shed.' Also, I didn't know if I was going to get beaten up again. Del Vervain's mobsters might abstain if they knew I had Luna along. She wouldn't go over big with Joan. True love never does run smooth.

The Vervains occupied one of those flats that seem divorced from reality. In darkest crammed London, they stand aloof, away from it all behind tall iron railings. The gate was surmounted by lions. Paving, mostly, with a few jardinières but no Sevres porcelain. That would be a real find. I told Luna I live in hopes.

'What are we here for, Lovejoy?'

'Eh? Oh, this invitation.'

She looked with horror. 'You mean you—?' She would have clawed my eyes except the door opened.

'I thought you'd be pleased,' I grumbled. There's no pleasing women. Here I was, taking her to the lovely London home of a famous radio personality, and she flies off the handle.

'I'll kill you, Lovejoy,' she said through a fixed grin as Joan and Del Vervain advanced to welcome her. Luna started apologising, for not having known, that she hadn't had time to go and change, the whole grovel.

'So you're Lovejoy!'

Vervain announced this. He meant, pretend we haven't met before, Lovejoy, or else. It felt like being given gracious permission to hereafter call myself my own name. He was definitely tubby. He was living up to his reputation, already well-soaked. Irish whiskey, by all accounts.

I shook his hand, a flabby dough-filled glove of a thing, made the feeblest stab at bussing Joan. I'd have been clouted as a little lad for such a half-hearted calling kiss. Her eyes startled me. She looked lovely, cocktail frock in a rich royal blue. Real pearls, a double choker, and a pearl bangle. Mid-Victorian, and suffering, but that's what pearls go through. I could have throttled the stupid bitch for the slow murder she was inflicting on such lovely jewellery. Pearls must *never* be worn against a skin sprayed with perfume. Yet the silly cow had—

'Eh? Oh, may I present Mrs Lune Caterer, Mayoress of—'

'Luna Carstairs. I've met Mrs Vervain. At your work-shop, Lovejoy.' Luna raised her game, smiling, admiring the lovely hallway, but I could tell by the red dots on her cheeks that she really would murder me when she got me somewhere safe.

'Come in. What's your poison?'

'Orange juice, please.' Luna bravely faced the flak of Joan's interrogative gaze. I said and me. We were taken by the hail-fellow-well-met sweaty Vervain into the company.

Three other guests, all seemingly stamped out by some machine round the corner. Girls, lank of hair and drab of garb, skeletally thin and smoking with edginess bordering on the frantic. All were well into their poteen. One quite stoned.

'This is Lovejoy. Count all available rings!' Vervain held the shot for some imaginary applause. Pause, two three, then a quick capper, 'I mean jewellery, nothing anatomi-cal!' Chuck-chuck-chuck and move on. The girls tittered, looked at me with hard appraisal.

Christ, I thought. The bloke's a cipher, a print-out.

'Catch my show, Lovejoy?' asked His Heartiness.

'A few times.' I was going to say only the start, but caught Joan's sharp reminding glance and went, 'It was quite good.'

He'd actually started to preen when the words hit him.

'*Quite* . . .' He managed the word. It hung alone in the vast room. I waited, looking out into the lovely walled garden. I bet myself those bricks were truly William IV. It was about then that red brick became imperative for gar-dens. '. . . *Good?*'

He sounded choking, ready for a duel. What had I said? I thought I'd given him a compliment. Amiably I looked about.

'Hey, Lovejoy,' one slightly staggering lass said. 'You in

the presence of thee repeat twice thee Mister Personality of ever-ee radio band in the wide countree, y'know it?'

'Yes, we have met.'

Once before, I met some broadcasters. They frightened me to death. Like now. But none of them scared me like the look in Joan's eyes. My view kept finding her bright, brilliant eyes somehow even if I wasn't looking. They looked wrong. And women don't as a rule have wrong eyes, do they? I'm hooked on faces. I can't help it. Sometimes I'm caught staring at a face just for nothing, and create the wrong impression. But faces are great, aren't they? Except when they're wrong. The eyes are something people forget. Babies and little children know the truth about faces and eyes. They can spot a dud miles off. I think that's why they always grin at me straight away, knowing an easy touch.

'He for ree-yull, team?' The staggery one flopped, beckoning for more sustaining fluid.

'Exactly my question!' Del Vervain cried. He affected a suit that looked cut by some trainee tailor with the wrong scissors. Image again.

I hadn't a clue what they were on about. Luckily Luna took up the gauntlet.

'Oh, Mr Vervain! My husband and I think your show is absolutely marvellous! Why don't you do it on Sundays too? It's lovely. The way you say that . . .' The three lankies from Alpha Centauri nodded, flicking ash, sipping, murmuring.

Del grinned modestly. 'All er-rightee too-nightee!' he intoned. The girls beamed, 'Great-great-*great*!'

And Luna, to my embarrassment, almost fainted with delight, exclaiming, '*Yes!* Oh, Mr Vervain! We think it's the best thing!'

That was what I'd done wrong. I'd forgotten to worship his ego. He was addicted to worshippers, fawners, acolytes.

Without them he would vanish. In fact, as I turned to That Look in Joan's eyes, I actually saw him become a different person. Genuinely twinkly, humorous, jokey and welcoming. To Lune, that is. Me, I was written out of his script of existence. It gave me a chance to talk quietly to Joan.

'I'm sorry, love,' I told her. 'I couldn't escape the invitation. His blokes beat me up. Is there somewhere we could meet?'

The best I could do to stay in her good books. It gave me the chance of a look at her eyes.

They were a-glitter, expectant, almost as thrilled as Luna's. I'd expected anger, calm shielding her inner distress. But she looked like some bird about to go to a boxing match. You know, that deep intensity which women show at savagery. Mystically charmed, by the prospect of violence. She smiled a confined smile, wetting her lips, and drifted me aside.

'Shhh, Lovejoy. Careful.' A roar of laughter from Del's admirers gave cover. 'Go along with what Del suggests. It's the best thing ever. For us, darling. I'll come soon.'

'Come?' I said in dismay. Tried again, brighter. 'Come?'

'Your cottage. He's starting a new contract. I've missed you, darling.'

'I've missed you, Joan.' Not with those eyes I hadn't. I'd rather have her old eyes, brittle with anger, delirious with—

'Hey, Lovejoy. Do your divvie trick, hey?'

Sod it. Party time. 'If you want, Mr Vervain.'

'Del, if you pull-lease.'

Another riot. Admiration's great in a way, but in excess becomes worrying. Like the chanting mania you see on television sometimes, with a uniformed general sitting in some council chamber acknowledging his voteless subjects' plaudits. You think, Christ, isn't somebody in that crowd simply bored witless?

'They're here. Props!'

The three girls fell about, stroked Del Vervain, did the subtle-monger's near-accidental touch. Open day here at Betelguese House. I wondered which he'd had, if not all.

A maid brought six plates. Four fakes, two authentic.

'These, Del?' First-name terms with the great.

'Don't break—' he caught himself theatrically, twinkled, 'the ones that *cost*. Break the BBC canteen crockery!'

Oh, the merriment. I nodded gravely. Luna was being super-thrilled, laughing at every non-witticism. Marvellous what fame does for sham. Like in the antiques game, really.

'Take your time, Lovejoy. What special effects, sounds . . . ?'

The rioting stopped. I'd taken four of the plates and dropped them on to the carpet. Two crashed and broke.

'Bristol delft,' I said over Luna's faint scream. 'Don't worry, Lune. They're modern fakes. Junk.'

Her face looked imploring. 'What if they're not, Lovejoy?'

The question didn't arise. But I politely stepped aside to give her room. She lifted the two unbroken plates and put them reverently on the table.

'I'm so sorry,' she was telling everybody.

'Gunge is best broken, love.' One of my maxims. I never do it, except for effect.

They were looking at me in silence. Luna was trying to say we'd get replacements, but Del shut her up with a slowly-growing smile, his first sincere response.

'Oh, yes,' he said softly. 'He's the one. Definitely.'

'I knew it,' Joan Bright-Eyes said.

'You didn't even look, Lovejoy.' Del was still smiling. And his eyes looked the same as Joan's.

'There'll be a faint bluish tint to the white glaze,' I said, 'if you held them up in daylight. There'll be three little uneven marks beneath where the plates were put on

Jonathan Gash

stands for the kiln firing. That indigo decoration isn't quite the proof of Bristol delfware it's cracked up to be, but—'

'But nothing, Lovejoy. You're the one.'

I'm still not sure if it was Del's forceful personality that moved us across to the buffet, or whether he actually shoved us. Power is as power does. Joan's eyes glittered as brittle as her husband's. I realised I didn't know her at all.

The buffet was some of the best grub I'd ever had. Luna ate sparingly. The Martians only picked, but drank with the solemnity of purpose. Joan also picked. Del noshed with vigour, raising his plate for minions to leap and replenish. Twice he sent the maid back. She'd guessed wrong. The usual display of moronic power.

Fifteen minutes after we'd started – I'd hardly got going – two people arrived. One was a rotund misery, the other a febrile nervy woman chained to a briefcase. Both denied hunger, both smoked, both cried for vodka. They were producers, I learned. They accepted Del Vervain's pronouncement that I was The One, and got down to business. One of the girls tried to chat me up, but I was starving. I mean, it had been a hell of a journey.

Joan watched. Her eyes said I was being fattened.

'Glad you're on the show, Lovejoy,' she said. 'It'll be the all-time winner.'

It wouldn't, because I wasn't on any show. I'd once done an *Antiques TV Showtime*. It was pathetic, a real fraud.

'Glad to hear it,' I said. 'Any more flan, please?'

'I'm afraid it's finished, ma'am,' the maid told Joan, but smiling properly at me. 'We have several quiches, sir. And salmon. The fish pie is—'

'Ta very much, love.' I accepted with elegance, in spite of Lune signalling me to refuse. It's all right for women. They can go for days on the smell of a grape. But the maid was pleased, and we settled down to a supply and demand.

186

The three thin birds gawped, Lune smouldered, knees together but smiling tightly. Joan circulated. Del and the producers guffawed mirthlessly. And me? I noshed and agreed with everything. I was to go on Del Vervain's show. He was to milk laughs by pretending to drop a priceless Ming vase. I would 'react'. The script would make the best impression – as if broadcasters could do such a thing.

The grub was great. We left about four o'clock. I'd quite taken to the maid. The *Del Vervain Show* script would be ready the following Tuesday. He waved us off with, 'All er-rightee too-nightee!' Lune reeled in ecstasy.

Quite honestly, I was glad to get on the train. Lune wasn't speaking. I wasn't sorry. I thought about telling her why Bristol delftware's properly before 1800, that the name applies now to seven or so factories as far apart as Wincanton and Bristol itself. Of the master painters' different designs – who'd slyly nicked their styles from China and Japan. But one look at her face and I sat thinking about Rye Benedict's underwater photographs of the great Brunel's non-existent paddle-steamer. And Joan's eyes.

Then things started to look down, because Lune's gorgeous Jaguar XKX whatnot motor had been stolen. I sighed. I'd had a lot of days lately. We got into the car, Lune fuming. She turned the ignition key, and started to pull out of the station car park.

'Turn right, love,' I said. 'Head for Drackenford.'

'I'm sorry, Lovejoy, but no.' She said it coldly. 'I for one need to know where you and I actually *stand*. Your conduct—'

Enough. I reached across, switched off the ignition, and took the key. She screeched and struggled with the locked wheel. The motor glided to a stop, nudging the kerb.

'Lovejoy! If that isn't the most irresponsible thing—'

'She started to get out. I restrained her. She might be madder than me, but I was tireder.

'For fuck's sake listen. You've had a robbery.'

She gaped. 'I've . . . ?' She tried to speak, looked at a housewife who was pushing a pram on the pavement. '*I've* . . . ?'

'You've,' I confirmed gravely. 'Your home has been entered, broken into by thieves five hours ago. Your very own antiques have been stolen. By a master thief. Taken away. To Drackenford.'

'My home?' Tears welled up in her eyes. I honestly felt sorry for her. Well, I would have, if she hadn't made me so mad. '*My home*, Lovejoy? How do you know?'

I put my fingers against her cheek. 'Drackenford. Then we'll make up, eh?'

Chapter 20

Drackenford's one of those wood-and-plaster hamlets. Nothing much to its name except plenty of black-and-white architecture, leaning cottages, leaded windows, and pavements so narrow you always have to look behind in case some cart's going to run you down. Four shops, a school the size of a kennel. A river, one bridge, a church filled with ancient alabaster saints, tombstones frittering away into yews and copses. And a war memorial, five names. That's your average East Anglian hamlet. You could guess about six hundred souls on a lusty night.

'Left.'

'There's no road, Lovejoy. It definitely says.'

'Ignore the signs. Right, at the end.'

She braked, turned, at a rocketing two miles an hour. 'It's a farm, Lovejoy.'

'Straight on.'

One mile an hour. We crawled past the farmhouse, down past ornamental gardens and an oxbow river bend. Two small pools large enough to swing a cat. I smiled, squeezed Luna's hand.

'That gravel drive, love.'

'What are you smiling at, Lovejoy? This is private property. I shall get a summons for trespass—'

'And Oliver will be narked,' I finished for her. 'Stop saying that. Pull in by the taller of the two barns.'

I was out before she'd got the brake on. I cupped my mouth and yelled to the sky, 'Same-Same! It's me! Lovejoy!'

Rooks rose, cawing and creating at having their idleness disturbed. Well, I was hard at it. Time they did a bit. 'Lovejoy.' Good old Lune with yet more reproach, buttoning her coat against the rising wind. I was heartily sick of her. 'Couldn't we go over to the small barn and simply knock? This place is . . .' She shuddered, pulling her lapels tight.

And indeed this place was . . . I scanned it. Big, dark, no life. No tyre marks. Broken windows stuffed with old rags. Sacks trailing from fractured glass. Sealed and shuttered and barred.

'Plug your ears, dwoorlink.' I cupped my hands and bellowed, 'Half a minute, Same-Same. Then I'll damage your shed.'

Luna was pacing, distraught. 'This is *positively* absurd, Lovejoy. Shouting at a disused barn is ridiculous. There's a farmhouse back there to make enquiries—'

'Fifteen seconds, Same-Same,' I howled. The birds did their annoyance thing.

Then a faint noise came from inside the great barn.

'Step aside, Lune.' I drew her back a few paces. A part of the old barn's side began to swing in, making a humming sound. Lights, the clink of metal on metal. Somebody whistling. A voice called casually for turpentine. And out stepped Same-Same.

'Wotcher, Samie.' I'd forgotten how tall Same-Same was. Gangly, with that deceptive ease lanky folk possess. 'Notice anything?'

He waited until the panel whirred back into position. He walked round Luna's motor. 'Nice job. How much?'

'Not for sale, Samie. It's Luna's here. My apprentice.'

He'd been kicking the wheels until then, the way buyers do. Now he stopped, looked at Lune, at me, and groaned.

''Cking hell, Lovejoy.' He was disgusted.

'Sorry, Samie,' I said.

'Sorry?' he yelled, apoplectic. I'd been trying to let him down lightly, but he gave me stick. 'It's all very well saying sorry, mate. But I've worked all 'cking afternoon on bits of 'cking rubbish.' He glared at Luna. 'If you'd pay for one of those touch-locks, missus, you'd have saved me a 'cking deal of time.'

'Well, I'm sorry, Mr Same,' from Luna. 'But they're far too expensive. My friend Betty put one on her motor and it went off in the night, and she lives near the hospital and the police—'

'Lovejoy?' Same-Same gestured to me, and walked off shaking his head. 'Do I honestly believe this?'

Luna came to stand beside me. 'I don't understand, Lovejoy.'

'Samie's just gone for your antiques. Unlock your boot.'

'Mr Same's *got* them? *My* antiques?'

'Aye. He used your car to nick them from your house while we were away at Del Vervain's.'

It was all too much for her. I explained the 'samer' con. You go to the railway station car park. You ignore commuters, who're likely to leave wife, children, grandads at home. You wait for the mid-morning crowd. The man-and-wife off to London for a jaunt, who take luggage out of the boot. That means they're off for the day, at least.

'Pinch the car. Nobody's surprised to see the car in its own drive. The more expensive the motor, the more likely is the house to be posh, with tall hedges. The milkman and post girls have all done by noon.'

'Same-Same does that?'

'He's famous for it, among dealers. He never pinches big antiques. Always small, that can fit in . . .' I shrugged apologetically. 'Open your car doors, love. Wide.'

Same-Same came carrying her antiques. I nodded approval as she gasped, recognising each one.

An Austrian bronze, only Edwardian, that made her glance guiltily in my direction. A desk object, really. A bronze rock on a bronze pool. Luna knew, but did not say, that the rock would open at a touch to reveal a naked nymph in a singularly naughty pose. These items are highly collectible, especially if the nymph looks as brilliantly golden as the first day she performed her erotic perversion hidden in her bronze rock. A painting or two, Victorian sentimental – the sort you couldn't give away twenty years ago but now can't buy for love nor money. Then the two things that made me gasp.

Globes. One terrestrial, the other celestial. Mounted, so as to stand on the carpet of some master's study. The surfaces are printed, if they're right, done about the end of the Napoleonic Wars. Printed amendations were issued, to be stuck on the surface as more lands were discovered and new seas charted. I glimpsed one patch with 1828 on it, quite like an ordinary printed addendum label in a book. The surround is usually boxwood, like a girdle. Three beech legs stained to pretend they're rosewood. It doesn't mean fake; it means fashion of the times. They would stand about three feet tall. Lovely, Lovely. I heard myself moaning. They can be dry-stripped of their old yellow varnish and made like new. New, in their instance, being 1816 or so.

'That it, Samie?'

'Mmmmh.' He was disgruntled. Everything my fault.

'Going to the Kensington Antiques Fayre this year?'

'No.' He smiled a cold smile. 'Sending stuff, though.'

'I'll look out for it,' I joked, though I was really far from merriment.

'See you, Lovejoy.'

We left. I looked at the garden ornaments in the farmhouse's lovely ornate garden. Tudor design. The river was charming, only shallow but with a pair of swans gliding serenely along.

'D'you know swans mate for life, Lune?'

'Don't call me . . .' She bit back the rebuke. 'Oh, really?' she said, all casual. 'That's lovely.'

A mile further on I told her to draw in by the Drum Major, a pub. I told her to wait, in the scree of a low hedge.

'Parking light off, love.'

We waited for almost thirty minutes, but nothing came past except a tired tractor and few cows urged on by a cowherd.

'Home, love.'

Some days I'm really thick. I got Luna to phone from a roadside phone box, to tell Oliver not to call the Plod in when he arrived home and found his belongings thinned.

'He rather disbelieved me, Lovejoy.' She sounded miffed. 'He thinks I borrowed the antiques for your purposes.'

Well, that's what the Olivers of this world tend to believe, thinking themselves treble shrewd. Once a prat, and all that.

We drew up at their substantial house. No palace, but certainly the inhabitants weren't going hungry just yet. It's times like this I wish I had a watch. You can look at it, go tut-tut, and scarper.

'Look, love,' I said uneasily. 'Could you give me a lift to the Volunteer? Only, Sandy might have some news—'

'Us, Lovejoy.'

'Er, us, Lune.'

She was already out. Oliver emerged instantly. He marched down, shot glances into the car, turned on me.

'What's all this, Lovejoy? Not content with purloining my wife, embroiling her in goings-on, you have the effrontery—'

'Sorry, but—'

'Oliver. Please.' It was a humble request.

Oliver gave way, but only because I was a potential vote. He didn't know it, but I was now of an opposing political persuasion. They withdrew. I waited for the verdict.

Luna came back, Oliver in self-righteous attendance. 'Lovejoy. Could you please tell Oliver how . . . ?'

'I notice the place you'd parked, love. There was a crack in the tarmac. My side of the car, just below the door. When we left for London, that is. When we came back the motor was a good foot to one side of the same crack.' I waited. It was now quite dark. I should be in the White Hart trying to chat Connie up. 'While we were on the train, your car had been used, then returned to the station car park.' I looked from her to Oliver. 'That your question?'

'Yes.' She turned to her husband. 'See, Oliver?'

I'd threatened her not to disclose Same-Same's scam. I'd drilled her to say it was some lunatic chancer, and we'd managed to catch sight of him off-loading the antiques from the bridge over the by-pass. Best I could invent at such short notice.

'Well, thanks,' I said into silence. 'Is there a bus?'

The police came just then, and I was borrowed from the Mayor's parlour to receive the intentions of one Drinkwater.

Police stations have a curious pong of dried sweat. I suppose they import it wholesale. Drinkwater didn't let me sit. He paced, ear twitching, pot teeth clacking.

'Fairclough, Lovejoy.'

'How is the poor chap?'

'Convalescing. Remembers nil. His son's a fitter on a North Sea oil rig.' Clack clack. 'Had an antiques business. Went bust in a bad patch. The old man decided to sell. Somebody gave him your name.'

'Who?'

'A tart on the by-pass. Tits Alors.'

'Her recommendation was, ignore Sotheby's, and ring me?' Well, an old geezer's entitled to his perks n' jerks, as they say. 'Good stuff, is it?'

'Stolen. All of it. Neighbours saw a van loading up. Very usual at the Faircloughs'.'

Not too convincing, but as it was Drinkwater's tale it'd have to do.

I looked at a map on the wall, seeing we were both strolling about each other like sparring partners wondering whether to have a go. Same-Same's river was a tributary of the Orwell. And 'room to swing a cat' is supposed to be from swinging the cat o' nine tails, naval punishment in confined deck spaces. Except river people hereabouts say it of shallow rivers. Because a cat's a sort of boat. Several different sorts, in fact, from sailing colliers of the mid-nineteenth century to fifty-oared galleys. I'd noticed that Same-Same's little oxbow river had two pools with room enough to swing a cat boat round and start it back down the Orwell for another load.

And Same-Same now had several workers, all busy in his massive sound-proofed barn. People who whistled while they worked and called for the frigging turpentine and look sharp about it. I hadn't seen a thing, but I'd heard enough. Samie used to work alone.

'. . . be inadvisable, Lovejoy.'

'What would?' I came back.

'Going it alone. This thing's worth more than the county.'

'I don't understand.' This the first recorded case of Plod benevolence?

He leant close to me. God, his breath stank. 'You understand all right, Lovejoy. Give me a share. I'll see you right.'

A bribe? 'I wish I could, Drinkwater. But I've heard nothing. Honest.'

He let me go then. It was as clumsy a bribery act as any I've yet come across. He was as bent as a ruler, just trying me out. You can tell a bent ploddite on a foggy Alp. Drinkwater hated me too much to forgo the pleasure of clanging me up. I sighed, taking my leave. And ran into Sandy, yoo-hooing away outside. I tried to duck into the night, but he drove alongside, parping his horn and waving. He had Mel with him. As if I hadn't enough trouble, I'd now got allies and, worse, they'd obviously come to help. Friends plus allies plus help meant utter total immediate disaster.

Resigned, I went towards their motor, hoping the populace was early abed tonight.

Chapter 21

The White Hart was thronged, thick with smoke. Dealers were crammed in, all pretending (a) they'd just pulled off the biggest sale on earth, and (b) a group of Americans were coming tomorrow to buy even more. For human grandeur there's nothing so moving as the sight of antique dealers on the make.

I wanted to creep in last, after Mel and Sandy had Entered (note that capital). But Sandy insisted I go first.

'Swell the audience, Lovejoy,' he trilled, roguish with eyelashes.

Mel said nothing. He doesn't talk much, just glowers. Sandy's the verb, Mel the pronoun, so to speak. He told me to admire the various aspects of their main motor, an old Rover the size of a tram. It's never the same twice.

'Admire the silk curtains, Lovejoy.'

'Great, er, great.' If you like bamboo, strings of rock crystal and strips of purple sacking twined with orange shot silk. I was worried for non-artistic reasons. Didn't Highway Code have rules like car windows you could see through?

'Admire the fringes, Lovejoy.'

'Er, yes, Sandy. Great.'

He went through a litany, once sharply pulling to the kerb to admonish my lack of enthusiasm.

The Rover was probably a good motor underneath the crud. I'm sure it was decoratively brilliant. But it always reminds me of those fashion shows where clothes look straight off a tat-monger's street barrow. Talk about rags and bone.

The thing was ribbed on the outside with small wind-mills, perhaps a hundred or more, flashing the whole colour spectrum. The windows were back-lit, Sandy at the wheel. Fluorescent strips ran round the car's outlines, reds, orange, opalescent plum and a creamy green that almost made me puke. Each headlight wore enormous eyelashes, the rear lights golden. A large red kid-leather tongue trailed panting from the boot. The bonnet's grid was shaped into an enormous chrome pout. The steering wheel wore pro-jecting digits like spokes of a nautical wheel.

You have to accept a lift from this pair, partly because they never let up and partly because they're clever rich antique dealers. I needed to know who was being cleverest.

'Great, great,' the umpteenth time.

I went in, to a welcoming chorus of abuse. Sheepishly I gave Ted the shrug that told him to get ready for Sandy's Entrance. This entailed banging a gong, and balancing a tall glass of crème de menthe on a kneeling plaster cherub on the bar. The outside lights came on over the pub fore-court. Everybody crowded to the windows for a look. Sandy's Entrances are famous.

'It's Sandy! How this time, d'you think?'

'I hope it's the steps,' from Liz Sandwell. She's admired Sandy ever since he poisoned a Birmingham bloke who was giving her a hard time. 'I *love* the steps.'

'It'll be the trolley,' from Flavour John, a rugby-playing gorilla dealing in porcelain and musical instruments.

Somebody wouldn't have that. 'They did the trolley Entrance last Monday. Bet, four to one against, Flavour?'

Wagers were struck. Some dealers crowded out to see. I hung back, tried to get served. I think the whole thing's stupid. I can't honestly see the point.

A military band struck up from the Rover in noisy intro, blaring. God knows what the country ducks thought. 'The Entry of the Gladiators' stunned us from the radiator grille's chrome mouth. You can't help watching.

The roof slowly opened as the music reached its crescendo. Mel was standing beside the car swinging a thurible, the cloying incense wafted on the evening air. To murmurs of appreciation, Sandy slowly rose through the unfolding car roof, as the Statue of Liberty without the torch. He was swathed in her robe. A corona of stars circled his head.

'It's like them pictures!' somebody cried. 'United Artists? I know it's somebody—'

'Two to one against the steps from now—'

I wondered vaguely where the motor got the energy.

'It's the waterfall! The waterfall!'

Amid a shimmering spray of golden fireworks, Sandy was carried down on a small escalator that protruded from the motor. The music pounded. He held his pose, smiling nobly into the distance. Mel's thurible chinked, incense drifting into the taproom. God, but it was a sight. Flavour John came to join me.

'Lost my week's takings. Bloody poofter.'

'So why bet, Flavour?' He'd bet on the trolley Entrance.

'I thought I'd win,' he said. The inveterate gambler's logic. Sometimes the dark thought comes that maybe they hope they'll actually lose.

Sandy was gliding forward to applause from the pub crowd. Flavour John gave a hopeful glance, but no trolley. So far I'd wasted almost an hour, including Drinkwater's hamfisted bribery act. Which only went to show that Drinkwater was worried as me. Cradhead was an unknown. I started asking Flavour if he'd done much at Wittwoode's Auction Temple lately.

Meanwhile, back in showbusiness, Sandy was being showered with rose petals from a gilded bucket.

'Take that fire risk out of here, Mel.'

Ted had lately been prosecuted for letting Mel carry in six candelabras, one an exploding variant. The thurible was bundled out. Sandy smiled and waved. I saw his gaze rake the assembled company, and wisely applauded the nerk with the rest.

Flavour was complaining. 'Been shunted off some flavour porcelain this week. Frigging criminal.'

'Tough luck, Flavour.' Everything he admires is flavoursome. But I've no sympathy. Rugby four days a week and antiques three – when it could be seven days of antiques? No wonder dealers like Flavour John are never satisfied.

'Tough luck?' he said scathingly. Sandy opened his mouth. Mel stood on a stool to pour the crème de menthe in his gob. 'Where's the frigging *luck*, Lovejoy? Acker warned me off, the swine.'

My ears tingled. 'Look, Flavour,' I said, steaming him to further revelations. 'There's not a dealer here won't chop a deal.'

'Go shares?' He laughed hollowly. 'Think I didn't try? I'd have bought the bugger off if I'd had the gelt.'

Flavour owed me. Recently I'd warned him off a mathematical treatise dated 1491 AD. The faker, a real pillock, had filled it with the = equal sign. And that was invented by Robert Recorde, much later.

I said, still steaming, 'Maybe the stuff wasn't good—'

'Good?' He said it so loud people turned round. 'Good, Lovejoy? Nantgarw porcelain four plates. No, straight up. So translucent you could almost read through it. That's *flavour*.'

This sounded the real business. When Bill Billingsley set up the Nantgarw (rhymes with shoe, sort of) porcelain factory in 1813, his factory crashed – his plates were warped, full of firing cracks. So clever old Bill and his son-in-law Sam Walker worked in Swansea for three years. And learned superior technology. Their new super porcelain became craved by wallet-wielding tycoons everywhere, because Bill Billingsley in his second go managed to make porcelain whiter than white, yet somehow so translucent that we say, 'Is it Nantgarw clear?' meaning so translucent when you hold it up to the light that you can imagine it's oil-soaked paper. The trade nickname is sodden-snow translucency, believe it or not. I moaned inwardly. My life was becoming a saga of antiques missed. The stuff was everywhere, but just gone.

Then I remembered that Nicole Frères musical box. I mentioned it. Flavour snorted a sardonic snort.

'That should have been mine too, Lovejoy. And them old cameras – you know Acker Kirwin's a photography nut. Very flavour, them. They've gone too.' He'd have won my sympathy vote, except he was an antique dealer. 'I'm leaving the Eastern Hundreds, Lovejoy, going up Smoke. No flavour left here.'

'London? Where, though?'

'The Belly. You know Wheatstone? Invented the concertina, made thirty-five thousand of them. They're always around, right? Not now, Lovejoy. I saw six last month. None, this.' He was a broken man. 'Even Salvation Army are scarce.'

'The old black bellows issue?' I was frightened.

'Can you credit it, Lovejoy? No, it's the Smoke for me.'

Well, rather him. Portobello Road has broken stauncher hearts than mine. 'Well, Sandy'll be giving up his shop now him and Mel are back.'

'Haven't you heard, Lovejoy?' Flavour tried to beckon for another pint. 'He's already sold up. This is the celebration.'

'I don't believe it, Flavour.' And I didn't, yet I did.

'True. Don't know who to. Mel's sold up too.'

What the frig was going *on?* It was getting beyond me. Just when I thought I'd sussed out the main buyer of Prammie Joe's turkey stripping of Cornish Place – Acker – and so learned who'd done for him – ditto – the pattern crumpled again. I was sick of the whole thing. I'd never known antiques move about like this before. Antiques go in dribs and drabs. I mean, when the Countess in Long Melford does a tin can for the States, it's cork-popping time in the local taverns. Yet now we were drained of antiques. And in dollop numbers. Beyond belief.

As Sandy did his parade – Mel goes before, strewing rose petals while people clap and have a laugh, Sandy waving with queenly magnanimity – and Flavour John groused in my ear, I started to watch faces. I've told you how much they matter. And there was something not quite right. People were laughing, oh, sure. As usual, blokes were mock-whistling and the women admiring. But there was the occasional glimpse of tautness. Nobody, but nobody was doing a deal. Margaret Dainty was talking to the exotic Jessica who lives down the estuaries in sordid circumstances. They should have been talking antiques, but instead seemed to be commiserating. Margaret raised her glass, inviting me to come and join them. I smilingly declined. She's an older woman, friend for years, with class in spite of her limp.

There was Dyllis Washburne, sitting alone. She has a friend who isn't in the trade but helps her out. They go on holidays together, but he's loyal to his wife who's got hard religion and wants to bomb non-conformists. Now, Dyllis is very gregarious, mostly dressing furniture and

pen-work japanned furniture. Dyllis alone and palely loitering? Impossible.

And Big Frank, talking to Mel, saying right, right, with
many nods. He caught my eye, waved, mouthed 'Ta', presumably for my having visited his red-hot mini-mamma
Jenny Calamy. I must do something about that promise, if
I could remember what the hell I'd worked out to do about
whatever promise it was.

'Cooo-eeee!' Sandy, pausing to do his Queen Empress
wave. He wore elbow-length white lace gloves with jew-
elled glove-bands, very seventeenth century. One thing,
Sandy gets it right. 'Admiration?'

'Sandy. You didn't say you'd sold up to Big Frank.'

'Don't spoil my moment, Lovejoy. There's a dear. Sell to
Big Frank? Have you seen his *nails*?'

Connie came in, with Rye Benedict. I waved, but she
moved on Mel with smiley determination. Big Frank
shrugged the shrug of the loser. Mel allowed Connie to
buy him a drink without quite looking at her. She began
talking animatedly. He sniffed and kept his distance, but
they were dealing.

'Reckon Connie bought Sandy-Mel out?' I asked Flavour.

'It's some bird right enough.' He didn't look round.
'Frothy Lane was saying that yob who runs that poxy old
mill's sending the vans. Word is the dollop broker's flitting
around. Who knows?'

Some days everything goes wrong. I realised now why
Sandy and Mel had insisted on giving me a lift. Sandy
knew I was worried about the big antiques shifts round the
area. He wanted to tell me he and Mel were contributing
to it. Maybe he lost courage on the way over. Or maybe he
didn't want anything to spoil his Entrance, the night of the
big reunion between him and Mel. Whatever. I'd come for
solutions, and everything was more tangled than ever. The

dollop broker was coming nearer. I said so-long to Flavour John and left.

Some days everything only *seems* to go wrong because deep down something is chancing its arm and going right for once.

As I walked down the lane to my cottage between the hedgerows I saw a light in my window. I thought, oh, hell fire. Another duffing up from Del Vervain's mob? Or Drinkwater brewing up looking for the sugar, waiting to arrest me?

'Hello, Lovejoy.'

It was only Luna. Supper was ready, a delectably sinful meal of all the things you've got to leave alone or Doc Lancaster'll get you. The place was depressingly tidy, honed to brilliance.

'Don't worry,' she said, a little breathlessly. 'I had Elsie and Madge here. They do for me at home.'

'Er, look, Lune.' I didn't go in. Just stood there looking round. 'I'm in enough trouble without Oliver—'

'He's had to go to Manchester. Finance meeting.'

Manchester? Quite a way. It was late. No means of getting home for some time, I should suppose. I didn't say this.

'Manchester's quite a way,' Luna said, checking the stove was still doing its stuff, the quick suspicious way they do. 'He probably won't be home tonight, I shouldn't suppose.'

'Really?' I cleared my throat. She looked up, tutting.

'Well? Are you going to stand at the door all night?'

Obeying women is in a man's nature, really, in spite of the party line preaching the opposite. I thought of Oliver's powerful position as Mayor. But a man never really leaves a woman. We can't. We haven't the power. We can only go if we're shoved. A woman can leave a bloke, though, and often does. I decided I'd better find out which version was in operation, and stepped inside.

By the time I'd reached this conclusion, Luna had shelled me from my jacket, close and warm. She wore a lovely woollen dress, pale green. I like those. They fall round shapes.

'Coming,' I said. There isn't much you can do when a woman extends an invitation. Choice is a luxury for others. Not me.

Chapter 22

'I didn't intend this, Lovejoy.'

'I'm glad, love.' We spoke along the pillow.

'I want you to know I don't . . . I *don't*.' She looked away. 'This is the first time I've ever . . . apart from Oliver.'

'Shhh.' I think God got emotions wrong. We've too many. Remorse heads my list of redundancies.

'What do I do about Oliver?'

Why ask me? I sighed inwardly. These questions are irrelevant. Who's got answers? We'd had a short session during the night, after we had made our first smile. I'd been desperate to fast fade, but she'd clung on, interrogating until I thought I'd never slide out of the minor death. It makes me wonder sometimes if women ever understand. I mean, all they need do is stay quiet a minute, give your soul time to climb back in. But no. Rabbit, rabbit, rabbit. One day, maybe some bird'll have the sense. She'll be my goddess. I'll follow her for nowt.

It was early morning. We'd made our morning smile. Luna was a willing rider, too anxious to rush us to orgasm, thinking that right. It's basically too much rote in love-making that creates this misunderstanding. It's better slower. She found time to rejoice, to her utter astonishment. She questioned her being flabbergasted, daring to rollick in lust.

'Is he back early?'

'About noon.'

'We've time to go to Rye Benedict's. I must see him.'

'The pictures you were looking at? Delia's?'

'Mmmh. The charts, but they're beyond me.' A sub-merged I.K. Brunel miniature paddle-steamer would be priceless. If available. But I didn't believe in its existence, let alone the other factors. I think Rye Benedict was being had, his market garden's sale profits the reason. I mean, is anything easier to fake than a photograph? Flavour'd said Acker Kirwin was a photographer. Oho, I thought. But found I'd baffled myself again. Oho *what*?

Daybreak comes too early when a woman is around. I've found that. Bluetits woke us about five-thirty, greedy little sods. Never leave you alone.

'Lovejoy?' Pause. 'I had no intention of . . . of sleeping here. I just thought you deserved a good supper. Getting my things back off Same-Same.'

'Least I could do. Still mad about the Vervains?'

'No. Though you could have warned me.'

'You might not have come, with a scruff like me.' She leant over me, propped on one elbow, smiling as her breast touched my face and produced the inevitable.

'You're always wrong, Lovejoy.' She frowned. 'Was there ever anything between Mrs Vervain and you?'

I never betray confidences, so I hummed and ha'd, finally told her to mind her own business when she pressed. That led to a struggle, then a protracted smile that made us late, with a rushed breakfast and her nearly burning the blinking tomatoes and too little margarine on the fry-up. I can't drink hot tea, so I had to do that business of pouring it into a bowl and blowing. We made the town road by about half-ten. I grumbled as we left the cottage. Rye's mill would be heaving with infants. I wanted a quiet conversation with the bloke. Luna tried mentioning Oliver, but I wasn't having any. I'd just escaped being married to Joan Vervain. I didn't want another divorce impending, just yet. Though in fact Del and Joan now seemed accomplices. Maybe my influence worked equally well both ways, for reconciliation as well as division? I'd have been a great marriage counsellor.

'What was that, Lovejoy?'

'Eh? Nothing.' I'd been talking to myself.

'There's that Connie you wanted to speak to. Quick!'

I held on while the car slowed and juddered to a halt. Other motors parped. She tutted at their impatience. Connie was coming from the station forecourt. At this hour? I told Luna to wait and nipped through the traffic, calling out. She paused, more of a hesitation, before hurrying on. I raced, caught up.

'Hey, Connie! It's me, for heaven's sake.'

'Hello, Lovejoy.' She smiled, with effort, didn't stop to chat. 'I'm in rather a hurry. Sorry about last night.'

I remembered. I'd beckoned, she'd declined. 'Okay, love. You did the deal everybody's talking about, eh?' That stopped her. 'Everybody's *what*? But it's . . .'

So there was a deal. 'Sandy and Mel. You bought them out.'

'Oh, Lovejoy. Yes!' It was wrung from her. She seemed distraught, beside herself. Where the heck had she been so soon? And why hadn't she gone in her car? Or was it somewhere overnight? 'Yes! On commission. You'd only find out.'

That terrible word's enough to cause most dealers I know to keel over into the custard. To sell on commission's only one step from going on the knocker, which is virtually begging from door to door. Sell on commission means you starve until you sell – then the dealer for whom you're selling takes the whole price except a measly ten per cent.

'What favours did you do Sandy and Mel, love? I thought I was the one fuffing your stuff out.'

She twisted, right there in the weak morning sunshine. As if I had her entangled in a net.

'You are, Lovejoy! Don't think I don't still need your load.'

'Thank heavens for that.'

'I must go, Lovejoy. I—'

'Where'll I leave it, Connie?' I had to ask the question, exactly as if I believed her. And explained, when she looked blank, 'Your load I'm assembling.'

'Oh.' She thought quickly of this problem, possibly for the very first time. 'At Boxtenholt aerodrome. See Gunge. Okay?'

'Right, love.'

We bussed, she sprinted. No night ticket on her windscreen, so it had been this morning that she'd hurtled off down the bright silver road. She made a Le Mans start, her face tense and staring.

I walked back to Luna's motor. Luna also did a racing start, but talking, asking, informing.

'Shut up a sec, love.' Thinking's bad for you, some say. Let her do some. 'Luna. Who of all the people you've met is untrustworthy?'

'Among the dealers?' She thought. 'Calamity Jenny. I didn't like her one bit.' Which wasn't quite my question. 'She's too saucy for her own good, that one.'

'And who is trustworthy?'

'Sandy,' she said immediately. I pressed her for more names. 'Big Frank, though he's hopeless. Quite different from that Mr Kirwin.'

Hang on. How come she knew Acker Kirwin? 'You've met?'

'Yes. He bought ever such a lot at Wittwoode's auction. You remember? You sent me.'

'So I did.' I made her describe the scene in detail.

It was the collar job. He'd worked it on unsuspecting punters as the crowds had dwindled. It's not done much nowadays. It's quite simple, puts the average public bidder, the 'women', off bidding. Thus:

You wait to bid, at an auction, say, for a small carriage clock for your mantelpiece. Say Lot 200, about teatime. Happily you wait. You stand quite near it. You don't want to be startled into bidding for the wrong thing, so you've pencilled a ring in your catalogue round the number, Lot 200. All clear. Then something very worrying happens.

A suited gentleman, smart, dour, unsmiling, shoves his way towards you. He looks at the carriage clock, Lot 200, and compares it with a photograph he pulls from his pocket. He murmurs a curse, checks a list of items on a clipboard. It bears the police insignia. He quietly asks, 'This item yours, madam?' in sepulchral tones. 'No, no!' you gasp, by now convinced something sinister is going on. He peers at the marks in your catalogue. 'It's just that I was thinking of bidding for it,' you bleat in terror. 'For my Auntie. A present . . .'

He whispers gruffly that he's police. Would you please bid for it? And bring it to court, present it as evidence? It would only mean a few days at the Old Bailey, appearing as witness, you see, ma'am. The clock was stolen, you see . . .

'No, no!' you exclaim. And depart.

Leaving Acker – for that's who the 'inspector' will be, or some pal – to buy the carriage clock cheap, having got rid of the one serious bidder.

'I knew he wasn't a police inspector,' Luna told me.

'How?' She was shrewder than I'd thought.

'I know the inspectors,' she said blithely. 'We were

guests of honour at their annual dinner.' Silly me. 'I told the gentlemen attendants. They only laughed.' She bridled in annoyance. 'No sense of vocation. It's not good enough.'

Whizzers, the scene shifters at auctioneers, are always on the take. Asking them for morality is whistling wind.

'Terrible, isn't it,' I sympathised. And it's then that I think I looked at Luna for the very first time.

Oh, I'd had a gander, shufti'd her in passing, so to speak. But actually looking . . . ? No. I'd missed the sureness, her quiet cleverness. She couldn't exactly be the humdrum duckegg I'd assumed. Maybe because she'd gone along with most of what I'd decreed, I'd assumed she was a mundane housewife tremulously peering at the great world beyond her front door. And maybe I despised such, thinking why the hell hadn't they already got on with life instead of whinging about being oppressed, that 'jargoneering', as Florence Nightingale called it.

There were other attributes. She drove sedately, but better than me. She was composed, attentive when I spoke about antiques. She didn't believe me on anything else. Rightly, I suppose. She did things off her own bat, sometimes got them right. She was smart enough to notice people, suss out their character. Gulp. Might she actually be more astute than I am? I'd already awarded her a secret medal, for she had made love hesitantly at first but eventually very, very well. Luna Carstairs had pleased me more than any woman I could remember. I looked away. She'd caught my glance, coloured up.

'What, Lovejoy? Did you say something?'

'No.' I was gruff, dismissive.

'And Rye,' she added. 'We can trust him. Not like Mr Vervain.'

'Not at all . . . ? But you were all over Del.'

'I was nothing of the kind, Lovejoy! I was merely . . . attentive. He's a famous broadcaster. But shifty. And so scared of the producer people—'

'Wrong, Lune. *They* were scared of *him*. He's the star.'

'Lovejoy. You have it the wrong way about. He *is* frightened. He was frantic lest you didn't show.'

'Really?' I remembered that strange glint in their eyes, the hot expectation. And Joan's rather sinister glitter. What were they planning? I remembered the rumours, Del's links with the rough toughs of Whitechapel. I felt suddenly cold and told her to put the heating on. She did so, looked at me, said nothing.

'Gawd Almighty, love.' The mill grounds were heaving with school-children. 'You made us late—'

'I?' she blazed, pulling in at the far end of the car park. 'Lovejoy?'

Therla Brewer was somewhere in the maelstrom. Josh Whatnot was trying to make four lads come off the waterwheel. It was locked static, thank goodness, but two of them were wet through. Why didn't they take this mob to the pictures instead? The thought of a hundred screaming ikes in the tumult of a dark cinema made me delete the question unanswered.

'I want five minutes of Rye's time, that's all.'

'He's lecturing. Look.'

And there he was, the trustworthy Rye Benedict, leaning out of a hoist window, hanging on to the dangling rope of the hoist's pulley with one hand, speaking through a megaphone with the other. His feet were on the window ledge.

'Good heavens. I hope he's safe, Lovejoy.'

'Course he is, love. As houses.'

'Knee, Lovejoy.' Red-cheeked, she angrily pulled her

212

skirt over her knees. 'Not here. This is a *public place!* With school-children everywhere.'

'Sorry.' My hand had accidentally fallen on her knee, but the space in front car seats is always cramped.

'He's winching the rope thing. What's it for?'

We watched. 'They unloaded the grain from waggons on the ground. Winched the sacks to the top of that pulley. Then swing it in.'

A horseless waggon stood beneath the hoist. We watched desultorily. The children gathered below watched desultorily. The teachers expounded, pleased at Rye's activity. Three or four sacks were arranged on the waggon. Rye was leaning out, speaking down to the children, indicating something up above the hoist, probably some control rope to stay the pulley's speed.

'That way,' I said on, cursing my luck for being late. I could have been at a viewing day in Norwich. 'That way, all the grain's on the mill's top floor, see? Fewer rats, as well as being able to chute the grain down into the mill-wheels when required.'

Rye was calling for somebody to hook the pulley rope into a sack on the waggon. Josh sprang on the waggon to do it, amid jeering applause. He took it in good part, leaping spectacularly off when he'd done and bowing to the mob of children. Rye reached inside. The pulley started moving. The sack rose.

'See? Simple. The old folk knew a thing or two. Used the waterwheel power to lift the grain.'

'The waterwheel's stopped.'

'Probably got an electric motor inside, make it easier to demonstrate to children. Principle's the same, though.'

We watched idly, Luna saying how marvellous that people like Rye took interest in these old things like water-mills. He'd tried to buy it from Oliver's Town Council, offered substantial money, she was saying quite casually, but the Council weren't allowed to sell. It was a trust.

The pulley slowed, stopped. Rye disappeared inside to check something. Emerged, smiling, feet on the space ledge, looking down at the children some eighty feet below, the waggon with its sacks. And at the sack being winched higher and higher to the hoist window. Him stretched out, steadying himself. I couldn't hear what he was saying, with the car windows almost closed and the children making a din.

'Benedict offered for the mill again quite recently. He has the river rights, on account of the market garden . . .'

Rye reached, failed to find the rope for some reason. He turned as if to look behind into the dark interior of the mill. And started to move outwards.

I thought, what is he doing? Quite idly, my thoughts went. He's going to fall, isn't he? Looks quite like it.

Luna shrieked. The children screamed. Rye was in the air, reaching, still with one hand outstretched. Still with that smile on his face as if to say, This is what shouldn't happen, children, so you will be careful, won't you? and suchlike.

The screams rose as he tumbled over. Once. Twice. And a half. And smashed into the edge of the waggon beneath. Blood spurted upwards, oddly, moving outwards in a graceful arc.

Luna was clutching my arm, weeping madly, crying out my name. I only sat staring. The children began to run in every direction.

Somebody knocked on the window, opened the door. Josh looked in, shouting had we a car phone for Christ's sake couldn't somebody call the ambulance or something because a man had fallen from the mill hoist.

I got out then, walked to the office, and smashed the

window, got to the phone and asked for ambulance, and police. I said to send Cradhead. I got Luna's car blanket from her boot, went and covered the body while children and people shrieked and wept.

Chapter 23

Rye Benedict's fall drew the short straw. Drinkwater established a Star Chamber in the mill, ground floor, to waste everybody's time. Police surged. Ambulance people tore up, had a fag, ogled the schoolgirls while the police photographer flashed and ogled the schoolgirls. We were questioned.

'It wasn't me, Drinkwater,' I told him in case he got ideas. 'Four million witnesses'll tell you.'

'That's enough from you, Lovejoy.'

'Here.' I gave him a list of registration numbers on a card.

Luna had started keeping ruled cards in the glove compartment. As soon as we'd come down to earth (sorry) I made her list all the car registrations. There were maybe a dozen parked motors.

Drinkwater read. 'What's this, Lovejoy?'

'Car numbers, Drinkwater. Shall we check?'

He flung the card back. 'Pathetic. Get gone, Lovejoy.'

'I'm a valuable witness, you burke. I was actually here—'

'You were actually groping the Mayoress, Lovejoy.' He gestured me away. 'I know you. About your level.'

Luna was with the children. Astonishingly, she had been out helping the teachers to round up the screaming children and line them up by the river, looking across to the market garden. She had the bloodstained ones go down to the little landing stage and rinse the ghastly splashes off. It was a brisk, businesslike act, and I admired her for thinking of it. In fact, the teachers started coming to her for orders. I was proud of her.

'He's chucking us out,' I told her. 'Come on.'

A reluctant ploddite tried delaying us at the gate, hurt that we were being allowed to go about our lawful business. I enjoyed myself, walking over to tell Drinkwater his orders had been countermanded by beat feet. We drove away in silence. I made to chuck her card out of the window, and paused.

'Hang on, Lune. What's this line?'

'The other car park, Lovejoy. You said list *all* the cars. Twelve at the mill. Three more across the river, Lovejoy, in the market garden.'

'Pull in.' Near somebody's gateway, I counted. The river, though small, was too wide to leap. There was some sort of footbridge round the river bend, beyond hedges, trees.

'How could you see into the other car park?'

She tutted. 'The footbridge, Lovejoy. I knew you'd get cross if I forgot some cars.'

Me? I'm hardly ever cross. In any case, it was only an incidental, right? But the world's made up of atoms.

'I'll walk on, love. You drive round to the market garden. Ask whose cars they are.'

She caught me up ten minutes later. I was walking along the approach road to the dual carriageway by then. I was narked as she drew up.

'Where the hell have you been?'

'Talking with the old lady who does the bedding plants. They were all down in the potting sheds, on the far side. They'd only just been told. She was most upset about Mr Benedict. Of course it's bound to've been a shock—'

'Was one motor his?'

'Yes. The estate car's the sales lady's. She's done the job since the father's time. There are five locals, four girls and a gardener for the outdoor work.'

'Whose is the third motor? Customer?'

'No. When they move the potting plants for public parks, like today, they admit no one. It had gone.' She almost smirked when I grabbed the card. 'Yes, I *did*, Lovejoy.'

And she had. Two numbers below the line were ticked. She'd drawn a ring carefully round the third.

'Did you say anything about the third motor? Ask them or anything?'

'No.' She drove meticulously as yet another police car tore past, shrieking its important way to the next pub. 'I wasn't sure if I should.'

And another, following an ambulance. No lights and sirens this time, more sedate, without haste. Luna pulled in to let the cortege pass, then drove after towards town. It was starting to rain. To wash Rye Benedict's blood off the waggon.

'The garden has a second entrance. It stands ajar on potting days. A notice on it says so.'

I found myself looking at the car number, said casually, 'Anybody could have just dropped in. Fuschia for their Dad's birthday, eh? Sort of thing anybody'd do. Easter cactus.'

'Benedict's is terribly expensive,' Luna said. 'Cheaper at Bellows and Calder's nursery. Except for bulbs. Their shrubs are better value, because Oliver—'

The sky falling, Tinkerbell dying, the ticking crocodile rising from the swamp, and Luna goes ape on the price of daffodils. I slumped in my seat, and said to drive to Cambridge. She complained she hadn't left a note for Oliver. I said he'd be too busy planting cheap shrubs to notice. She flared up at that, and played merry hell. Lulled me to sleep in seconds.

It had to be Cambridge University. Not Oxford – I can't forgive Balliol College for rubbling its lovely medieval chapel and replacing it with a pre-Walt Disney clone. And for mangling the exquisite medieval stained-glass windows when they reset them. Incompetent sods. Dr Dymond was the bloke they dredged up for me. He arrived in his office, swirling his cloak and dropping things. Some student followed him in, languidly arguing for exemption from something. The little bald-headed don was equal to the challenge. He shoved the student out, patting him like a ball player.

'*Omnium rerum principia parva sunt.* Cicero, Tomlinson.' He entered, rubbing his hands.

Half of what these dons do is an act, I'm sure. Music halls did the damage, making all professors absentminded and all clowns heartbroken. If I hadn't been there, Dr Dymond would have let Tomlinson off his next essay or whatever.

He sat in a swivel chair – modern crud – and placed his feet on his piled desk. He was untidy. If I'd not sent Luna out snooping antiques, she'd have had the vacuum out.

'*All things begin small.* Sort of.' He twinkled at some declension. 'Local history, eh?'

'Only societies, if you could, please.' I told him of my colleague's growing interest in the events of the 1640 decade. 'Not proper research, Dr Dymond. Just a hobby.' I smiled. I didn't want to be banished with a Latin tag like Tomlinson. 'He's quite elderly, so I had to come for him.'

'Local history societies are often least help, Lovejoy.' Dr Dymond opened his palms, started one of his diatribes. 'But I'll list the most active ones for you.' He did, but I knew them all. I'd looked them up. 'I suppose your friend has tried those? Particularly . . . ?'

'It's some trial thing, I think.' I chuckled in embarrassment. 'The mid-1640s. St Edmundsbury. We're waste metal dealers. Our own lorries and everything,' I said proudly. 'Course, old Fred doesn't do as much as he used to. Getting on.'

Hell fire. I was getting carried away, waxing lyrical about my imaginary old pal. It was me wanted to know, not old Fred, interfering swine.

'One trial was held in the house old Fred lives in. It used to belong to . . .' I wrinkled my forehead in perplexity, let it clear '. . . Calamy Somebody. I'm almost sure—'

'Doubtful, Lovejoy. Edmund Calamy – did you know there were several of that name? – didn't actually *own* a house there. In fact, I'm practically sure he lived in Holborn, London. Very famous family.' He sighed, genuine regret. 'You can't trust the *Dictionary of National Biography*. Most history societies are frivolous. Like the Sealed Knot, who enact Great Civil War Battles. Plenty of interest, little academic focus.'

'Have you a section dealing with it?'

'That period, Lovejoy? Heaven help us, no! It's as much as we can do to keep the colleges solvent these days.'

Blank. He took my name and address, in case he dug something up. He told me a great deal about the hideous Witch-Finders, recommended a million texts, wrote them all out. I said thanks, and went down through the college grounds to meet Luna.

Cambridge's antiques were disappointing. Too dear and too new. That didn't mean they weren't desirable. I needed tons of antiques, even if some were fakes, but I didn't want a third fraudulent mortgage on my cottage. She'd tried hard, though. In fact, her eyes were thrilled. Just like she'd always been before poor Rye Benedict was topped. I mean, just before poor Rye Benedict fell accidentally.

'I think we've had enough, Luna, love.'

'Home now, darling?'

'Home, er, right.'

I didn't maul her knee once. I made her phone home as we left Cambridgeshire, to check Oliver would be there. I asked her could I come and say hello. She was pleased, but became quiet as we turned into her lane.

'I don't know if I have a cake for tea, Lovejoy.'

'I don't mind, love.'

'One thing. Please.' She pulled to a stop in the drive, made a prolonging fuss with her seatbelt. 'Perhaps you should stop calling me that. In Oliver's presence, I mean.'

'You mean "love"?' I was amazed. Where I come from you get a thick ear for rudeness to a lady. 'Is it feminism?'

'It's . . . it's relatively unusual in these parts, Lovejoy. Oliver might see it as . . .'

'Oh, well,' I said, cheerily alighting. '*Omnium rerum principia parva sum.* Seneca.'

'*Operae pretium est!*' she riposted merrily. Then halted, stricken. I thought she'd suddenly remembered something terrible about Rye's fall at the mill.

'What is it?' I whispered, frantic, my heart pounding.

'Seneca? Wasn't it Cicero?'

I could have throttled her. 'You stupid *bitch!* I thought—'

'Hello, darling!' she cooed, quickly edging me aside. Oliver was standing there, glowering. Well, bitch isn't love, is it? 'Oliver, Lovejoy wants to . . .' She paused, her smile frozen. I hadn't told her what I wanted to.

'To ask you something, Oliver. A proposition.'

'Oh? I regret I haven't all that much time.'

As near a no as I'd ever get before asking.

* * *

'No, Lovejoy. It's out of the question.'

Oliver was one of those who pose before fireplaces, staring solemnly ahead as if at infantry.

'I haven't explained yet.' I did my ingratiating smile, trying to copy Dr Dymond's open-palm gesture. It had really added to the don's eloquence.

'Your explanations, Lovejoy?' He breathed a stoic breath. Ready. Take aim. 'It smells of one of your antiques machination situations.'

I forgave him his language. A Mayor is a politician. Probably called sleeping with his wife an intercourse opportunity situation. I cancelled the thought instantly. Him and Luna.

'Good heavens, no!' I exclaimed. 'It's honest, quite legal. And profitable. I don't mean for me! I mean Mrs Carstairs here!' My joviality was just this side of hysteria.

You can always see a politician's mind whirring because the cogs are on the outside. His went: profit = money; and money = votes!!

'But I understand, Oliver,' I said, all kindly. 'You wouldn't *want* profit. In case your opponents accused you of amassing money.'

'You said it's confidential, Lovejoy.' From Luna, bless her little heart. On cue. I'd not even told her to say it.

'Of course it is!' I said stoutly. 'Well, was. I'd best be wending—'

'A moment.' Oliver paced, even steps. 'Do no harm to hear you out, eh?'

'If you promise not to divulge a single word.' I drew up a chair. 'It goes like this. You embark on a fund-raising, for some deserving charity.'

His disappointed frown washed itself away when I continued, 'You purchase a load of antiques. And sell them at a considerable profit. Everybody gains – you, the charity. Your wife gains the commission.'

'How do I gain?' asked this philanthropic politician. Not how does the poor children's charity gain, note. Nor even how much commission Luna'd get.

'Oh, you gain the sum equal to your investment, Oliver.'

'Spend fifty to make fifty? That's nothing, Lovejoy.'

'No, Oliver. You *gain* one hundred per cent.'

'Gain?' He glanced sharply at Luna, rocked on his heels, came to rest. 'You mean profit?'

'Gain.' I smiled, knowing he was hooked. 'Antique dealers call it profit, alas. Anybody can do it, Oliver. Luna. You. I'll be the front man. But there's one thing. You'll be open to accusations.'

'What accusations?' He paled at the thought.

'The worst of all, Oliver.' I parted my hands to show honesty. Nothing concealed here. 'Your opponents will accuse you of electioneering. Making political capital out of charity.' As if a politician ever lost votes by giving to an orphanage. He'd be Prime Minister within a week, play his cards right.

'Oh.' He nearly said, Is that all? He smiled, bravely. 'Facing false accusation's my bread and butter, Lovejoy.'

Indeed. A thought crossed his brow, possibly an innovation. 'If anybody can do it, Lovejoy, why don't you? You're poor as a church mouse.'

'Oliver!' cried Luna, scandalised.

'Me?' I was so beatific. 'I do it all the time, Oliver! How do you know I haven't got millions stashed away?'

'Then why do you need me?'

Shrewdness is a pest. Bloody politico. 'Because I'm known. Not that I'm a real antique dealer. I have a brain and everything.'

'He is good, Oliver. Honestly. I know,' Luna caught the double meaning and rose suddenly to hide her confusion. 'I'll make some tea while you talk, shall I?'

'Please.' We both said it together.

Chapter 24

Sleeping the sleep of the just that night, I imagined all sorts, dozing in snatches. I kept seeing Rye Benedict's accident. Over and over he did his fall, taking me with him so I shot upright crying aloud as I tumbled. I sweat like a pig – always do. But this night was worse. I slumbered in damp sheets, my hair drenched and glued to my face, tormented, dripping wet.

He fell again. But that smile, as if . . . Always he turned in before starting his fall. One hand outstretched to the pulley rope. One hand outstretched behind, into the interior of the hoist space, as if expecting to take hold of something. Feet on the hoist's sill, rope dangling in front, free hand outstretched. And his other hand holding on to something. Then suddenly it wasn't, and he began his stately descent, smiling the smile that became tinged with horror as . . . I woke, whining and breathless, soaked. Had Rye's mouth moved? Was he saying something just before he started to fall? *To someone standing there behind him?*

By five o'clock I was up, checking for dawn, hearing the first birds hesitant about cheeping. I have a pint of skimmed each day. Koala delivers it about half-past five in good time for the bluetits. The little sods drill a hole through the foil cap and somehow suck the milk out. Like

Jonathan Gash

a fool I pay through the nose for peanuts. They have a wooden holder I fill each day, Michaelmas to Candlemas. Koala's an Aussie artist who paints triangles. He swaps jobs with his cousin, our local milkman, six months in Sydney. Koala pulls my leg about the birds. I'm sure he whistles them down.

'I'm going to have to do some night milking, Koala, prices you charge.'

'Send your cat, like the witches did.' He reached up and pulled the pear tree branch down to take the nut-holder. He's lanky, and I'm not.

'Ta.'

Koala hooked the string over a twig and let the branch go. It sprang up into place. He left, laughing. Like witches did? Anciently, villagers stole out to milk other folks' cows on the sly. A punishable theft in country areas. Herds whose milk failed were called bewitched. And culprits had to be sought, of course. Witches sent cats to do their thieving for them. All stupidity, folk fable nonsense.

For a minute I stood in the cold morning air, watching dawn. I looked at the pear tree. Koala had reached up, held the branch with one hand, took the nut-box with the other . . . Had Rye's hand slipped? I was going barmy. I went inside for my breakfast. Fried tomatoes in margarine again, fried bread, tea with one sugar. I'd have eggs and bacon except you have to handle them raw. Anyway, nowadays you've to starve yourself to live healthy.

Odd, but even sillier thoughts kept coming back. I should have been thinking about money. Oliver had guardedly agreed to give half the wadge I needed. Once an accountant, always blinkered. He heard me out, said it seemed cast iron, then offered half. In vain I'd pointed out that his profit would be reduced. He'd smiled the glacial grin of accountants everywhere, and said, 'Circumstances preclude totality.' Beyond belief. It's a question of the scam being a biggie – 'grandy' in the trade – or a titch.

Tip: In antiques, major scams, the grandies, begin about ten times the average wage. Now, some scams have no *material* theft. Lincoln Cathedral's goings-on over its Magna Carta Exhibition would be an example; what was it, quarter of a million? Others depend on stolen reality. Say for the sake of instance you live in a country where 20,000 dollars is your national annual income. Then ten times that is where grand antiques scams begin. Nor need they not be stolen stuff, like a fifth of all antiques sold these days. It could be one single precious painting stolen from the Prado in Madrid. On the other hand you can amass a hundred legit pieces of crummy old near-derelicts, and the whole lot might not qualify as a grand scam. Anything less, therefore, than $20,000 x 10 would be regarded as ordinary. Of course, among the lower orders of antique dealers – and there are plenty down there, here – even a few quid profit is cause for rejoicing.

Then again, there's the sword of Simon Bolivar – or Simón Bolívar if you insist on accents. This hero of 1824 had a sword. In February of 1991, Colombian rebels returned it to a Bogota museum. This kind of fanfare gift is a godsend to the world's fakers, who instantly turn out a trillion fakes, sell them, whispering the fatal words, '*This* is the original, mate. You don't *really* believe anyone in his right mind'd *give away* the real one, do you . . . ?'

Why am I telling you all this? Because I needed, vitally importantly urgently desperately needed, to move out of the titch class and into the grand, at speed. Sod Oliver. I found myself out looking at the pear tree for the millionth time. Koala had reached out with one hand—

'Aaaargh!'

'Good morning, Lovejoy. Did I startle you?'

'You silly old bitch!' I'd have clocked the stupid hag if I hadn't been in a state of collapse. 'Why can't you knock first, frightening me out of my skin? First thing in the frigging morning. I'm hardly out of my pit, you ignorant old . . .'

'Do forgive me, Lovejoy. But I can't knock if you're out in the garden, can I?' She smiled up at me. 'We've rather reached a dilemma.'

'We have, have we?' Beware birds using plurals. It means they've elected you to do their next job. Plurals and confidentiality, my bane.

She looked more dilapidated than ever. Reluctantly I reheated my tomatoes, and shared them with the old biddie. I gave her my other chipped mug.

'We've reached the end of our resources.'

'Oh, aye. Datewise? Geltwise? Genealogicalwise?'

She examined the tomatoes doubtfully, cheeky old sod. Had the nerve to prod the fried bread. It was a beautiful breakfast. One day cure myself of charity. Then scroungers had better watch out.

'Eat it,' I ordered. 'I'm not going to have you fainting on me.' Tomatoes are a Yank invention anyway.

'Thank you, Lovejoy.' She looked around, steeled herself, and noshed along. 'The information you gave me was most helpful.'

'Giving you the address of the building you were in?' I was narked. I'd hoped she wouldn't eat, but she trenchered away like a guardsman.

She reached over, eyes misty, touched my hand. 'I've written to my friend in New York commending you.'

Jesus, she was importing more spongers. Time to get rid. 'What now?'

She smiled. I looked away. These crones get to you by having lovely old eyes. Well, I'm up to their game. I'd cut and run as soon as I was dressed. The social security could have a riot with this poverty-stricken New Yorker.

'It's 1837, Lovejoy.' She accepted more tea, the mare. I had to brew up again. 'And 1855, in Wales.'

She rambled on while I got my jam. It's local, the usual half-pound jars you get at bring-and-buys in any village in the kingdom. Oddly, she was enraptured, asking how I'd made it. I said I'd write out the recipe. She said blueberry must be some sort of relative of our whinberry, because—

'In Scotland,' I told her firmly. I'd never get shut. She was whittling through a loaf, and reaching for my last bit of quince jelly, I saw with rage. I snatched it away with a second to spare, thieving old bitch. I ought to put a lock on my kitchen alcove. I will, when I get a minute from genealogy. 'In Scotland, they've the Register of Sasines. Land's feudal, held ultimately of the Crown. A good system. Only one channel for ownership, see? Their Register of Sasines is from 1617. If your Scotch ancestors had land. Some's in Latin.'

She cried through a mouthful of my bramble jelly, 'My great-great-great grandfather had a croft in Fife!'

I caught her reaching for my fried bread, got it back with a polite wrestle. 'Deeds start about 1554 contracts, selling something important. If your ancestor died without heirs, search the Ultimus Haeres records, Scottish Record Office. The Crown, the final heir, took charge.' I looked for the fortune-hunter's gleam but saw only unbridled enthusiasm. So she was simply what she seemed, a loony coot hoping Grampa was Henry V.

Wearily I sided up while she rabbited on and I rabbited back. Yes, for Wales go to Chancery Lane hatchings, matchings and dispatchings in non-conformist registers from 1700 to 1858. 'Court of Great Sessions in Cardiff,' I told her, snatching her plate in case she wolfed crockery too. Christ, she'd scoffed more than me. I was astonished she could still move. 'And St Cat's House, of course.'

'*Wales*, Lovejoy,' she said patiently. Like I'd never heard of it.

'Best combined records of all, has Wales. The one thing Wales lacks is surnames.' I paused, suddenly hopeful. 'Philips? Morgan? Evans?'

'All those!' she cried, clapping her gnarled old hands. 'How *did* you guess! And Jones!'

I brightened. Once she started excavating that lot, she'd vanish into some dusty file and never be found. Genealogy searchers make a surcharge for Welsh ancestors. Not quite fair, because combine PRO and GRO files and you're back to 1837 in an afternoon. I was so happy that I handed her a note as we finally left. I marched her up the lane.

'Sorry, love. I'd have liked a longer chat. Don't forget about Regimental Registers of Births, for ancestors born into regiments from 1761 – abroad from 1790. Okay? Your US-born Britons are harder – the PRO's earliest are Texas, I think. They're only 1838.'

I made the top of the lane by the chapel, and heard the bus coming. Farewells are quite pleasant, sometimes. She was trying to scribble everything down.

'I think the bloody Government should let you see family wills free. I mean, whose wills were they, for God's sake? Your own Grampa's. The Record Office charges, stingy swine.'

I would have gone on – it's one of my grouses – but the bus hove up and I had to run. Which meant cunning old Lovejoy escaped, old biddies being a mite slow.

'No, Percy,' I said. 'She's only out for a walk.'

'Thought she was waving, Lovejoy,' the driver said.

An odd thing. As I'd paid, a bonny girl was alighting. She changed her mind, came round and got on again.

Percy charged her another fare, mean sod. Maybe he'd worked for the PRO in some earlier incarnation. He pulled us away. We left Miss Turner wheezing.

'Lovejoy?' The girl came and sat by me. She was brilliant with youth, loveliness. 'Laura. My only name. All surnames are remnants of feudalistic paternalisms.'

Dilemma time. Should I have exchanged Miss Turner for this? 'Lovejoy,' I admitted. But it only takes ten minutes to town, then I'd be shut of her, 'It's all I have.'

She toyed with the idea, found it gratifying. 'You're against pseudo-religious degeneracies.'

Time to change my seat. I couldn't stand one minute of this, let alone ten. Is there any ism worth a thought? We were the only passengers on the lower deck. Plenty of space.

'Excuse me, love, but I—'

'Money, Lovejoy. To invest. No strings.'

She smiled. I froze. I'd admired her comeliness, her pure adorable style, of course. But now I looked deeper, I saw the mystic loveliness in her, the brilliantly dazzling glory of her nature. I'd been a fool.

My voice wouldn't get going for a second. 'How wise, er, Laura. And I agree about, er, names. They really are degeneracy things.'

She told me the sum she had in mind. It was enough to lift a small country firm called Lovejoy Antiques, Inc. from a titch to a biggie. I listened admiringly to her lecture on totalitarianisms all the way into town. I agreed totally, every word.

We went to a bank. I wrote out a receipt, specifying how the spoils would be divided. Laura fell about at this. I grinned amiably along. I quite like mirth at these moments – not that I've had many such. Signed, sealed, and, most important, delivered. The manager wrung my hand. He gave me a chequebook, pen, briefcase and a set of stationery. He'd have blessed me, if he'd known how.

'One point, Lovejoy.' She waited by the bank door, looking into the busy thoroughfare.

My heart sank. 'Yes?' Too good to be true?

'I insist on absolute confidentiality. Understand?'

Only ethics. Phew. 'Confidentiality's my other name!' I was so jolly with this delectable angel. 'What if I run short, Laura?'

Then she really took my breath away. 'I'll give you more, Lovejoy.'

She swung off into Head Street, leaving me standing. I wondered if she was unmarried, and would take a bloke like me. I'd get my hair cut, maybe even buy a new jacket. Yet I'd done all right with Lovely Laura as I was. Never change a winning team. A faint superstition nudged my mind: maybe my heartfelt charity to old Miss Turner brought me luck. You know, the leprechaun gambit? I was rich. Bulging. Loaded. Word would get around. And I would fly into a heaven of antiques, antiques.

For the first time I felt I was winning. I tore round by the post office in search of Luna. I was exhilarated. The chequebook felt the size of a ledger.

I was going to spend, spend, as in splurge. My heart was filled almost to bursting, with true happiness, that only money can buy.

Chapter 25

We drifted into Woody's caff like thistledown, me and Luna. Tip: if you've money – I mean serious gelt, not your piggy bank raped by a nail file – don't advertise. Not in antiques. Because antiques are different. Luna didn't understand.

'It stands to reason, Lovejoy.' She grimaced delicately, swiftly controlled, and put aside her chipped mug. Woody's tea was in fine fettle, a slimy sea of liquid grot. 'With money—'

'Shhhhh!'

She bent to whisper. The dealers leaned in, ears on the wag. 'Why not simply tell everybody? Then they will come to *us*. Think of the petrol we'll save!'

I managed not to groan. Women are better money managers than us. Where they fall down's on little things. I once knew a lovely middle-aged bird, Doris, who missed buying that Rembrandt nicked from Dulwich because she paused to have a row with a shop girl about the price of envelopes. Honest to God.

'They'll up their prices, love.'

Her expression changed. 'They would do *that*, Lovejoy?' She glared round Woody's caff through the blue fog of fat fumes. The lads looked away. 'But they're your friends! It's scandalous!' There was more of this. I pinched her tea, sucking through the film of scummy leaves, waited for her storm to blow over.

'Lovejoy.' Eyes downcast now. Still, a little guilt does a woman good. 'I tried with Oliver. He's had second thoughts. I'm so sorry.'

My heart dived. 'He's backing out?' It really had been too good to be true.

'No. But he's cut his offer.'

'It was already inadequate.' I thought I'd explained all that. 'A scam's titch or grand, love. To go upmarket—'

'I'll make up the difference, Lovejoy.' She misinterpreted my gape, and said quickly, 'His quarter, I mean. So we only need the other half.'

Oliver a quarter, Luna a quarter. *And Laura half!* I didn't tell Luna about Laura. She'd get the wrong idea. I just had enough money. The point being, that only one great dollop of antiques would leap to the dollop broker. Logic.

'Here, Woody. A couple of pasties.'

Woody's rotund belly shook with mirth. The cholesterol king is the only spherical bloke I know. His clothes gave up years ago, and now split majestically. Modesty was satisfied by an apron stiff with decades of solid grease.

'Come into money, Lovejoy?'

The world stilled in reverence at the mention of the great god M, the way congregations stop coughing at the Consecration.

'Aye. I've found Mark Twain's *Huckleberry Finn* manuscript.' There was a general laugh of relief-regret. Another version of this find had lately hit the antiquarian scene. It happens in America once a year, give or take. 'On the slate, Woody. Hang the expense.'

The world relaxed, Lovejoy still the indigent quirk.

'Can you afford it, Luna?'

Worried, I gazed at the lovely woman opposite. Luna had been more on my mind this past couple of days than she had a right. I mean, what did my old Gran say about women? 'A rag, a bone, and a hank of hair.' Affection doesn't come alone. It brings obligations. And who has time for those? But a bonny bird bringing money is a goddess of unsurprising beauty. I ought really to tell her the risks. I mean, if you own a favourite Royal Doulton piece, then you're at risk from roaming dolts, burglers, dealers on the knock, plumbers coming to mend your bathtaps, visiting priests, Aunt Jessie. But that's simply opportunistic theft, done on the spur. Titch antique, titchy risk.

But there's something else. Something far more serious. Big league. It's the ominous death-dealing malevolence that lurks in the world of the grand scam. It's dollop broker country. There's only a dozen genuine dollop brokers in the entire kingdom – I mean those operating well outside the law. All honest, God-fearing hoods and crooks in the known universe keep shtum about them. For the dollop broker is sacrosanct, the Machiavellian figure behind the biggest of the grand scams. Local, national, and international.

There are a million stories, mostly true. Of the English noble who did a humble Italian to doom for failing to deliver his promised tomb-robbings in Tuscany. And to whom is attributed the appalling statement, 'A promise paid for, is marriage; infidelity justifies fatality.' Needless to say, the antiques trade thinks this the height of logic, and praises the nobleman's propriety. And of the Yorkshire blokes, dealers all, who sank their three friends' boat in the North Sea by simply cutting it in half with a larger vessel one dark and stormy night, having transferred the smuggled antiques. (It saved having to pay, a tiresome chore.) Word is that a Dutchman survived, and broods vengeance. He's expected in Newcastle later this year. I'll let you know what happens, if I hear. And of the Turkish lady whose very special girlfriend took this Egyptian antique dealer under her wing. She caught them in flagrante, but was very good about it, and said never mind these things happen don't they. And then framed them for the attempted robbery of a French museum and murder of a Levantine security bloke doing a job for that Munich-Swiss combine—

'Lovejoy.' Luna took my hand. I withdrew it sharply. The dealers were sniggering, nudging. 'Please accept.'

'Eh?' Who'd refuse an offer like this? The pasties were gone. I hoped I'd had hers as well. 'If you insist, Lune.'

She went misty, smiled. 'Thank you, Lovejoy.'

The favours I was doing! Laura's thanks, Luna's gratitude. I felt peeved about Oliver. I was trying to do the selfish pillock a favour, and not a bleep of gratitude.

'Think nothing of it, Lune,' I said magnanimously.

We left then, after a sordid verbal skirmish with Woody over when I'd settle his wretched slate. Luna had a fit of conscience on the pavement, wanting to discuss the problem of world debt. I simply walked on, round to the auction rooms by the Beehive tavern. I mean, Woody had a thriving business, right? So why continually try to exploit travellers like me? It's just not fair.

'That's the wrong way of looking at it, Lovejoy,' Luna countered, trotting alongside. 'We *should* pay. It was the same with that registration. The girl proved most impertinent. I had to speak very firmly to the manager, I can tell you.'

'Love,' I said wearily, halting. She bumped into me. 'I'm crazy about you. Making love was the peak of ecstasy. But for Christ's sake button your frigging mouth. We're bidding this afternoon. Sod ethics.'

'You're . . . ?' She searched my eyes. A woman's gaze is never still, is it. Switches side to side, thousand times a minute. Even baby girls do it. Boy babes simply look, steady and level. Sometimes I wonder why.

But not for long. Priorities established, we zoomed to Wittwoode's Auction Temple. Viewing ten to one o'clock, auction at two precisely.

A viewing is such a wonderful experience it's no good trying to describe the sensation. You must see for yourself. And I promise. You'll fall in love with antiques. Oh, I know every viewing day's disappointing when you glimpse the load of tat, crud, dross. But your job is to go in *knowing* that bliss awaits. The bliss is antiques. And every antique is worth any amount of money. Why? Because money's machine-spun paper. And antiques are legacies from the hand of Man, the gifts of angels. Never mind that money is the modern religion. Only idiots preach that money counts. Business barons know that they're duckeggs. Sooner or later, they come to their senses. They frantically start buying like maniacs – and they buy antiques. They are trying to capture Time, encapsulate it as if Time is theirs to re-use. Is there a mighty dictator who fails to stuff his presidential palace with antiques? Trade tycoons raise unedifying edifices – museum, art gallery, foundation – to their self-glory, and thereby prove themselves prats. The megalomaniacs who carry on this way expect knighthoods for caressing their own egos. Quite barmy. When you're that far gone, remorse should be silent grief. Building bizarre cathedrals simply embarrasses the rest of us. (Of course, we're green with envy, which is why we scorn their 'achievements'. Like I'm doing, I suppose. It must be great to be well-adjusted.)

Wittwoode's Auction Temple.

* * *

'Drift. Don't look. Don't seek or search.'

Luna was puzzled. 'But you said—'

'I've told you before, Lune.' I pulled her roughly behind the stack of chairs and occasional tables the whizzers chuck together near the long wall. Nobody was close. 'The antiques will pull you. They're here somewhere. They'll shout, call, maybe just touch your mind as you walk by. But they're here.'

'They'll . . .' She looked at the chair legs sticking out at all angles from the mound. 'Are they here now?'

'Yes. And when you find one,' I begged, pleading, 'don't shriek and wave your handbag. Just tell it hello, then tip me the wink.' I shook my head. Give me strength. 'Not *really* a wink, Lune. Metaphorically. Direct my attention.'

'How?'

'Lune. You directed my attention the other night—'

'Shh!' She pulled away, prim. 'Twice you've mentioned that episode. Lovejoy. Don't think I don't deplore my . . .'

'Shhhh,' I said. 'Please, Lune. We're in public.'

'Yes, well.'

'Here.' I stopped as we emerged. Something she'd said. 'What registration? The impertinent lass?'

'Registration? Oh. The motor car.' She lowered her voice. I bent, anxious. 'Do you think I ought to complain? Officially, I mean? The girl's rudeness—'

'No, love.' I was broken. She'd worn me down. 'Don't complain. She might have trouble at home. But what car?'

'At the garden centre. Poor Mr Benedict's. Don't you remember? It belonged to a Mr G. F. Cooley, Waylance Street, Weston Hammer. It's quite a nice village, in Staffordshire I think . . .'

Hopefully, sanity lived. Somewhere. I left her, and drifted.

* * *

It happened in the first pass. I called Luna over. She came eyeing the dealers, mistrustful. I held up the bottle-shaped carafe to the light, smiling.

'See the medallion on the side? Enamel. Trying to be German eighteenth century.'

'I think it's rather nice.'

Loud with merriment, I chuckled and wagged my head. 'Sorry, love. Fake. Look through the other side. The glass is quite clear. Somebody's ground out depressions, enamel pastes in and fired it anew. It seems true enamelling. Authentic enamelled glass has no sign of grinding. The grinding wheel's marks show up as a slight prismatic effect. See them?'

'Well, no.'

There weren't any to see, so I was glad she said no. I replaced the lovely antique carafe among the job lot of pressed glass jugs and butter dishes, mentally apologising to it. It stood there, regal.

'That's inexperience, love,' I said airily. 'It'll come.'

There was a small collection of decoy ducks in a wicker basket. They're collectors' items, but take care. Most aren't genuine, because wandering fairgrounds have started selling new ones, suitably aged, on the now-fashionable 'country antiques' stalls among their sideshows. I make some myself when I'm desperate. As ever, antiques bring surprises. Some collectors'll pay a year's average wage for some rarities. I think they're horrible, but A. Elmer Crowell's Black Duck Preening – East Harwich in the USA – or Black-Bellied Plover are current favourites. I mean, who wants a wood duck? Once you've seen one, and all that.

I called loudly to Betty O'Connors – lives down on the wharf postal-selling thimbles and stitchery by subscriber catalogue – to bid for a porcelain firemark for me.

'Bid yourself,' Betty called back.

'Misery,' I grumbled. 'I can't stand this heap of dross. Just bid, eh? I'll owe.'

Dealers snorted, but sidled across to inspect the firemark.

'All right, Lovejoy,' Betty relented.

'Ta, love.' I waved a piece of paper between my fingers, and left it with Alf, a whizzer famous for having lost a leg in the service of antiques corruption. He fell through a wardrobe one night. He'd been bribed to swap the decorated surrounds of two pieces of furniture before the following day's auction. It's a common practice (swapping, not falling through wardrobes). Alf was trapped. His leg went bad, and he was discovered by a charlady who had hysterics. He's a blabbermouth. We call him Radio Alf. I'd chosen carefully. The price I'd pay – a month's wage – was about right, for an Atheneum Fire Office porcelain firemark. They're rare, especially mint.

'People had them on their houses,' I explained to Luna. 'The fire insurance firm would reward the firefighters.' I didn't explain the fertile grounds for corruption and extortion that fire insurance provided in early days, as now. Luna would find some reason not to believe me.

'Now, love,' I said, having sussed the entire place. We were outside, strolling down a riverside walk by some cottages. I quite like trees now and again, even in towns, as long as they don't gang up and threaten to start their own countryside among our harmless streets. 'Your first job.'

'I've *done* several, Lovejoy.' Her lip was quivering. What the hell now?

'This one's your own. Pick seven or eight pieces of furniture. Any. Buy them, changing your mind, hesitating. Now and then start bidding, then drop out. Look . . .' I searched for a word that described her to a tee. 'Incoherent.'

'What if I guess wrong?'

I smiled. I was going to turn them into antiques anyway. 'You can't. You won't. Believe me, love. I know.'

Her eyes filled. 'Oh, Lovejoy. You *do* trust me!'

'Eh?'

She sniffed, did the hankie bit. 'You wanted Betty O'Connors to bid for you, when I'm perfectly—'

Well, I rolled in the aisles. 'Betty? She won't.'

'But she said she would, Lovejoy.'

'Of course she did – so I'd say how much I'd pay. I wrote it down. She'll buy it for herself.'

Luna instantly went nuclear. 'But that's . . . *dishonest*, Lovejoy! Actually to *resort* to such—'

I heard her out, shaking my head sadly at the perfidy of an unkind world. 'Go in this afternoon. Bid for the German carafe, the one shaped like a retail sherry bottle. And that job lot of decoy ducks.'

'But you said they were fakes, Lovejoy.' Wide eyes and all.

'Er, did I?' I'd just deplored Betty O'Connors' lies. 'Er, yes. But the vendor's been in hospital, and wants to move near his daughter's. To, er, Bognor.'

She looked about for lurking observers, decided and gave my arm a surreptitious squeeze. 'You're sweet, Lovejoy.'

'Lune. A little kindness to an old soldier . . .' I welled up at my fictitious old git, controlled myself manfully.

'Should I bid higher than necessary, Lovejoy?' She was thrilled again. 'I mean, the old gentleman would appreciate a little extra. Is his daughter married? Just think how happy he'll—'

Luna got out of hand fast. 'No, love,' I said firmly. 'He's very proud. He would hate charity. Some of these old folk . . .'

'You're so *wise*, Lovejoy! I had a great-aunt once—'

'Look. I'd better go. Remember what I've told you.'

241

'Yes,' she said solemnly. We walked to the road by the bridge. 'That horrid Mr Cooley was looking at the carafe after we looked at it. Did you notice?'

'Cooley?' I didn't know any Cooley.

'Who owns the motor you wanted to know about.'

Cooley? I halted. Who had been in, milling around among the women non-dealers? Acker Kirwin, Betty, Marjorie, Olive Bremner from Stirling, a few of the Brighton circus, Big Frank, Jeff for ten seconds, Chris who collects hammered silver, Mannie the maniac clock-faker in his caftan and cowbells, Connie Hopkins, Deg the parchment forger, Lonnie Marklin who makes model coaches. Who else? Stan Tell who's furniture. Liz Sandwell, today unfortunately guarded by her jealous rugby-playing monster lover. A scattering of lesser dealers. One I like particularly is Rhea Cousins. She's Georgian furniture – pays in very personal services administered in the privacy of her own home. Her husband Willis is her accomplice. They're very, very rich. I ran down this list, checked myself. I was speaking aloud. Luna's eyes were like saucers, the list making her weak at the knees.

'Cooley?'

'The one I told you about at the other auction, Lovejoy.'

'Acker Kirwin?' I described him.

'Yes. He's not very nice, Lovejoy. Shifty. He's the same one who . . . conned us before. I *told* you.'

'Give us a lift to the mill, love?' It wouldn't take long. A breath of country air would do us no harm.

Chapter 26

The watermill was on a flow from the river. Artificial, of course, meaning manmade. A small fishing lake lay above, fed from a little tributary that came from a valley a mile or so off. The influx passed through the mill. Undershot, they call it, the water flowing beneath. You don't get as much power as from an overshot wheel, but that's just hard luck. If you have hills, like in Lancashire, you get significant power from big overshots.

Luna went in the car for the key from the garden centre office. It's quite tall as watermills go. Red brick, with a warehouse for sacks, and a loading bay where Suffolk horses clomped in with their waggons. Gingerly I looked, but the rain had washed the flint cobbles clean of crime, except for moss. Did I think *crime*? Wrong. Everybody saw it was an accident. Witnesses can't be wrong. The victim – sorry, the poor unfortunate – was in full view. Well, nearly full view. One hand was reaching in, out of sight. Taking hold of something, keeping him safe. Dead safe.

The surrounding countryside was quiet. Somebody was whistling across the river, in the market garden I shouldn't wonder. A motor started up. A dog barked, was ballocked crossly for not coming when he was told, the whole family was late now, bad dog. Slam. Rev, and off. Two anglers walked the riverside path, turning in to seek the lake. More gear than spacemen, camouflage jackets, rods, wicker baskets. Bet they only lived a hundred yards away. A laugh.

Somebody had shut the hoist door. A notice said *Council Property Keep Out*. The mill was closed until further notice; trespassers would be prosecuted. I felt indignant. We common folk owned the frigging place – but once a robber baron, always a robber baron. Calling it politics fools only the perpetrators.

The mill doors were locked, and the windows on the second floor wore wire mesh. You'd have to be Delia, at least, to get inside. That set me thinking. Had Delia himself found something in the offices, and come back later to kill Rye? But why? Delia came highly recommended. And asked for more jobs, any time. That's not the chat of a secret murderer, not round here. Also, he seemed as ignorant of antiques as any antique dealer, which is ignorance of a pretty stupendous degree. Here came Luna with the keys.

'I want to see the hoist, Lune.'

Oliver's Council hadn't the sense to use the original ancient locks, still functional. They'd spoiled the great doors by adding enormous metal bars, with modern padlocks. Typical.

The mill inside felt lovely, cool and spacious. The millstones were not turning, which was fine by me. Stairs you could ride a horse up led to open floors, substantial beams across each ceiling to carry almost any weight. 'Jolly' millers were hated down the centuries – think of the extortion they could perpetrate, controlling the only means of processing grain. And their ancient technology is beautiful to behold. Normally I would have been smiling but today I wasn't. We climbed higher.

'This is it, Lovejoy. The hoist.'

It was closed, that great wide window through which the sacks were pulled in. I'd expected a gap, like a fool.

'Why are we here? Do you think Mr Benedict left a clue?'

'How the hell should I know?' And why were we whispering?

I cleared my throat noisily and clumped with giant footfalls down the length of the room. Skylights, walls red brick, patches rimed to white. Only a single sack. One, by the hoist. I'd seen Rye reach out, swing it in. The selfsame sack? Or had Drinkwater taken it away in his extensive investigations of the tragedy? They'd lasted all of ten minutes. Really thorough.

'Luna,' I asked her. 'What happened? You were watching.'

'You saw, Lovejoy.' She gestured helplessly at the hoist window. 'Poor Mr Benedict leaned out. And fell. It was awful.'

'We saw him do it before. Why didn't he fall then?'

She thought, trying. 'Because he had hold of something?'

'What?' I nodded, go and show.

'That line of sticks, perhaps. There's nothing else. This hand.' She spun, aligning her hands. A pretty sight. I'd have reached for her, except this was where Rye was murdered.

Into a long oaken beam, fixed to the wall, was a line of wooden rods. Belaying-pin fashion, the sort you get on old sailing ships. Basically a simple wooden rod, tapered, thick at the top so it won't fall through. Purpose? To tie a rope on. Several pins. Simple.

Except?

Except, take hold of a pin at the top, and move about vigorously, as when pulling in a heavy sack through a hoist window, you might just waggle the stick enough to pull the damn thing out. And down you go. But Rye had no belaying pin in his hand when he fell. Even Drinkwater might have seen one.

'Hold the bottom of the belaying pin, love. And lean away from the wall.'

She took it carefully. 'Like this?'

'Keep your feet together, close to the wall. Now lean away.'

Suddenly I pulled the pin up and out, and she fell away, just regaining her balance.

'Lovejoy! That was a perfectly silly thing to do! I could have got splinters in my hand!'

'No, love. You couldn't.' The pin was worn smooth as silk.

Rye always used that first pin to hold on to. By its projecting *base*. Waggle it as you may, it couldn't come out. Unless somebody unseen in the mill, exactly where we were standing, perhaps chatting amiably as Rye had conducted his demonstration for the children below, had quickly lifted the belaying pin from its hole, leaving Rye's hand grasping nothing.

Acker Kirwin, alias Cooley, whose motor was waiting in the market garden across the river footbridge for him to escape. In the confusion, we'd all been too busy being shocked, running about phoning ambulances, controlling children. A good time to slip away. And it was clearly an accident, no? We'd all seen him miss his footing.

A man starting to fall to his death might well scrabble with his feet when the world is taken away from under for the first time. And last.

'Lovejoy?' Her voice seemed miles away. I was sitting on the floor. 'Lovejoy?' Her arms were round me. She was scented peach, some blossomy thing. 'Don't take on, darling. He went quickly, I'm so sorry. Please don't.'

Roughly I got up and shoved her away. 'Don't what, you silly cow?' I rounded on her, narked, pointing a finger into her face. 'You stop giving me orders. I won't have it, y'hear?'

'Yes, darling.'

'Just get that straight, all right?'

'Certainly, darling.'

Which having been decided, we descended and locked up, and she drove back to the Wittwoode Auction Temple to do her – read my – bidding. And I went to prepare my workshop for the labour that lay ahead. Serious, from now on. I was working for Prammie and Rye Benedict. And, who knows, some old bloke called Fairclough.

On the way, I caught a bus. More on a whim than with anything serious in mind. An advert had caught my eye. The sailing barges were gathering. Fifteen minutes later, in the estuary, I stood among a scatter of old salts, children, and the odd housewife, to watch the boats.

'They loaded up, all ready for the race?' I asked one elderly nautical. A spherical whiskered gnome, smoking a foul pipe. I stood to windward.

He snorted. 'Loaded? You're thick, booy. Don't load for a race. She'm travellin' loight.'

These Thames barges, few left now, are massive great things. Two-masted, with a heavy spritsail. They stain the sails with red ochre and oil. A real mess.

'Why're they so low in the water then?'

He spat past his pipe stem, the grottle donging a well-spattered bollard quite ten yards away. I admired that. I knew I'd be trying it myself, soon as I got home. I'd fail.

'Thames barge is flat-bottomed, son.' He scathed me with a look. 'These coasts, see? Leeboards instead of keels. Let her move to leeward in shoal water, stay upright if a-grounded. Her mast's lutchet-stepped, so she can go under bridges.'

He told me a lot, the way of coastal folk yapping about boats. I stared at the three great sailing barges. So they sail up even shallow rivers, these things? And race the Blackwater Race cargo empty? So the use of one as a depot for tons of stolen antiques would be purely temporary, while it was moored. Decoys are temporary. So Prammie's heavy stuff from Cornish Place was still ashore.

'Ta, Dad,' I said to the old seaman. And went to work.

It isn't much of a place. A converted garage with a home-made furnace and bellows. Toolracks. A window for north light, when painting fakes. A folding bench hinged to the brickwork. Saws, planes, nails in screw-top marmalade jars – they keep moisture out. Paints in a cyclist's plastic expanding box (buy Italian-made boxes; they're cheapest and best). Brushes in earthenware pots (cover them with plastic freezer bags, with a rubber band). Containers of turpentine, various painting oils. Linseed oil I try hardening in sunshine, like the old sixteenth-century painters did. But rushing out with the jar the instant our watery sunshine creeps over the garden has seriously weakened me over the years. Canvas, wood-stretchers, glues, ancient nails nicked from various things. It's a mess. Perfect.

It took me a good two hours to get going. I carried out some precious pieces I'd been harbouring.

Clearing up is one of those postponable jobs that, when they're done, makes you feel surprisingly holy. I'd been saying I'd get the workshop ready for two months, but I hadn't. Now there it all was, pristine. Ready for action. Pleased, I went inside and brewed up.

Plan: with a massive number of antiques, fulled out by fakes, I would be in a good position to demand from Connie Hopkins, my partner, access to the dollop broker. Maybe even meet her. Ex-teacher, Miss R. Find out from her who owned the Cornish Place dollop she was guarding, and goodnight, nurse. Proof for all my suspicions.

'Two lumps, Lovejoy.' Joan Vervain, in the porch, smiling.

'Still not reached Monte Carlo?' Gorgeous as ever.

She strolled in, spread herself on the divan. 'You're quite tidy.' She gave me a firm stare I didn't like. The new sort. 'Had any assistance in that line?'

'Women find it difficult here, love.'

'The Lady Mayoress been busying her little self in your service, Lovejoy?'

I wish I could do that, give words twice their meaning.

I made tea, gave her some. She tasted it, grimaced. 'She hasn't taught you any domestic skills, Lovejoy.'

'Don't drink it then.'

She smiled, lay back, kicked off her shoes. 'Discontent, darling? You always were impatient.' She was doing the woman's laugh that isn't a laugh at all. I was the butt.

Something amiss in that smile. Still lovey-dovey, but with a secret joy. Del Vervain had shared it, when last seen.

'I'm delighted, love.' I came and embraced her, to get her over with. She embraced me back. We were so pally.

'Did you hear him last night?' She traced my features with a finger. 'Del announced your coming . . . appearance.'

'Soon at this theatre?' I quipped, but unhappy. I've no illusions about broadcasters. They march to a distant drum, out of sync. Del and she were planning something. To my detriment, if not destruction. Were the other producers, who came and read sheafs of documents at the Vervain's party, in on the giggle? 'One of those producers asked me to give her a call—'

'No, darling. Don't do that.' Too quick. '*I've* been asked to take care of you. Those stinking girls bother one so.'

Answer: the producers weren't in on the giggle. And in Joan's phrases lurked a concealed joke. I felt it.

'I'm a bit unhappy, love, I mean, me and micro-phones . . .'

'Darling.' Her gentle hands were everywhere, urgent and moving. I felt my shirt come undone. When Luna might come thrilling in with waggonloads of antiques? 'Darling. Trust me. This setback with Del is only temporary. We'll be away soon. I promise.'

'If you say so.' There isn't anything a man can do when a woman comes on like this. Her breasts, her shape, phys-iology, take command and it's yippee and waves on the seashore and passion blinding you to the entire galaxy.

So it happened. Mercifully, Luna was elsewhere, and occupied.

As I came round and Joan's cigarette smoke curled to the ceiling, her satisfied smile revealed she'd ditched me. No Monte Carlo. No escape to happiness to violins. No stealth to wealth for Lovejoy. I was to be sacrificed in some noble cause, namely and to wit, Joan and Del Vervain. Lovejoy would be down in their lion-infested arena with a chocolate sword. I used to watch the faces of women at cockfights when a tiny lad. As the poor feathered creatures slaughtered each other, the woman's faces wore identical uglinesses that I could not then name.

Now I know it well. It's passion. There are other words. Rut. Ecstasy. Orgasm. But none does half as well as that word from the darkness of Man's uncharted past. Joan had been bought back by Del, by the promise of a passion she had never yet experienced. What woman could resist? I was glad. I'd started all this when deciding to ditch her.

She went after an hour. We promised to meet tomor-row somewhere I forgot instantly. I spent a few troubled minutes on the telephone, and got through to an agency, pretending I was the *Bolton Journal & Guardian*. I was the Arts and Entertainment Correspondent: I wanted the ratings for Del Vervain's talk show.

'You've heard, eh?' the chap said, laughing. 'Jesus! The north got pigeons listening to the wire services? It's down the chute, mate. Word is they're going to pull the plug. I mean, four million's goodbye country. Two months'll see it off.'

'Ta,' I said gutturally, and Luna arrived.

Babbling, she hurried in, showing me notes, chits from Wittwoode's, catalogue photographs, ticks on lists. Her face was almost delirious with delight.

But not ugly. I put my arm round her. She stopped talking, possibly an all-time first, and asked what was the matter.

'Nothing,' I said. I bussed her. She pulled away, breathless.

'Lovejoy. This is no time for that. The vans are coming. The . . . whiffler said so.'

She noticed the divan. I hadn't straightened it.

'Did you have a doze?' She rounded on me. 'Lovejoy. You distinctly promised you'd tidy the workshop. Now we'll be hours behind. Get started *this instant!*'

'I love you, Lune.' I'd said it before, differently.

She drew back. The words seemed outside her experience. 'You . . . ?'

No good asking me. I was as astonished as she. Hesitatingly she made to come towards me. But three whizzers from Wittwoode's were suddenly bawling and clattering in the garden, and the waves on the seashore would have to wait. Luna must have power beyond Man's knowing. They'd never been on time before.

Chapter 27

'You didn't do so badly, Lune.' I scanned the stuff.

She blushed with pleasure. 'I had to pay highly for the carafe, but it helps your old soldier friend.'

'My who?'

'The elderly gentleman, moving to his daughter's in Bognor. The German enamelled bottle—'

'Ah. *That* old friend.' I'd forgotten. 'Bidding rough?'

'No. That Acker Kirwin tried, but I outwitted him. I pretended to give up, then re-entered. He became discouraged.'

Well, well. I warmed to her. 'Acted like a veteran.'

She was primly disapproving. 'Some of the dealers' practices I find reprehensible.' She swung on me because I wasn't taking notice. 'Especially your friends, Lovejoy.'

'No!' I said, aghast. 'Acting dishonestly?'

'It's true, Lovejoy.' She shook her lovely hair, deploring all crime. Here was me eager to turn this junk into priceless antiques, and she was giving me bleeding-heart morality. 'I saw Sandy swop lot numbers' tickets.'

'Are you sure?' I asked weakly. I don't know anybody who doesn't do this elementary trick. I should have asked Luna if she was real, never mind sure.

'And I saw that . . . that lady. She *propositioned* a Brighton gentleman.' Her face was flaming. 'Her husband made the arrangements! Exchanging sexual favours, for a small oaken Canterbury.'

'Rhea Cousins?' Payment in kind's routine in the antiques trade. Like in every other, I might add, except not quite so obvious. Rhea's husband Willis keeps records on a home computer. Rhea's pretty, but worn out in the service of antiques. Luna must mean Lot 146, mid-Victorian but nice. Good old Rhea. 'I told you.'

'Yes, Lovejoy. Arranged *out loud! I mean.*' She was stunned, thrilled. Sweet Mary among trolls.

'Listen, love. It's normal. It's life. It's antiques.'

'But the first auction wasn't like that, Lovejoy.'

'It's just that you were new. Now, you're learning.'

'But . . .' She flapped her hand, sat on the divan beside me. 'But even Mrs Dainty, who's so . . . well, *proper.* I saw her move a battered old painted chair from one job lot to another. She was most put out when I explained her mistake.'

Margaret Dainty would be. I suppressed a grin. The trade calls it 'waltzing'. You examine some item, forget-fully put it back in the wrong lot. That way, you steal the item from whoever buys the first job lot, and give it free to whoever buys the second job lot (and that'll be you, of course). Waltzes are so prevalent that auctioneers started taking photographs, but gave up. The law says sale hap-pens on the fall of the hammer – is it your fault if whifflers have misplaced the stuff, for heaven's sake . . . ?

Luna was staggered. 'Surely Mr Wittwoode supplies lists—'

'Come on, love. No chatter in work-time.' There's no tell-ing the Lunas of this world. I pulled her up and we went to haul the furniture. 'Mrs Dainty pays the whifflers to turn Nelson's eye.' Like the rest of us, I could have added, but didn't.

'She actually *paid?*' Etc, etc.

Luna had got twenty-one pieces. I got my trolley – pram-wheels and a plank – to lug them round to the workshop. She had done very, very well. I told her so because women like approval. I don't know why. They're strange. I couldn't care less whether people approve or not.

'One. This dumb-waiter.' Small pieces first. 'It's a small single-pillar table, right? It should have three circular mahogany trays with raised margins – dishtops, we call them. It's only got two, right?'

'Yes.' She was looking about, downcast.

'Pay heed. That tips you off that the tripod feet and the top tray have been taken away, married up, and sold as a tripod table. Remember the one I was working on?'

'Is it no good? I shall take it straight back—'

'No, love.' Luna was serious effort, for all that she looked lovely in her smart suit and high heels. Dressy. I like that. 'We'll make it *look* antique and original, see? All we'll need is some flat-matched mahogany to replace its third tray. The previous faker couldn't be bothered. Well, we can.'

'Is that honest, Lovejoy?'

Untruth called. I looked her straight in the eye. 'Of course. We'll describe it accurately.' I did my injured expression. I wasn't going to stomach her woebegone dolour every blinking time I faked a veneer. Best fight the battle now, and have done. 'Lune,' I said quietly. 'If you doubt my moral standards—'

'No, Lovejoy! Of course I don't!'

'Please let me finish, Lune.' I closed my eyes, opened them, clearly seeking strength to go on. 'You harbour suspicions. It's too . . . too distressing to even think of.'

'I *know*, Lovejoy. I'm sorry I even *spoke*—'

God, the emotional turmoil. 'I won't conceal the truth, Lune. I've developed an . . . an attachment for you that's deeper than, well, I . . . I'd almost reached the shaky lip. 'I want you to feel sure.'

'I do, Lovejoy! I was wrong to even *think*—'

I looked into her eyes. 'We stay within the law. Every item.'

Her eyes were brimming. 'I'm for you every inch of the way.'

'Very well,' I said quietly, smiling nobly through anguish. 'Then I forgive you. Load that dumb-waiter. Shove it round to the workshop.'

She was looking down at her lovely stylish clothes. 'I can't. I mean, are we actually going to . . . well, *work*?'

'Of course, you silly bitch,' I yelled. 'Get frigging started!'

'My suit will be ruined.'

She was worried about her high heels. Can you believe women?

'In the cottage you'll find trousers, wellingtons. There's an old shirt.' I bawled after her, 'And wear your own knickers. Them underpants are my even-dates pair, d'you hear?'

She trotted in. I started on the furniture. My spirits rose.

Three Victorian work-tables she'd bought were pedestal supported. I up-ended them. Easiest and commonest job in the world, to remove the pedestal (carefully keeping it to make another fake) and plug the four (sometimes six) screwholes underneath. Add four lovely tapered legs. That would add a good seventy-eighty years to each table.

'Beg pardon, Lovejoy?' from Luna. I'd been muttering.

'Remind me to order three sets of legs from Channie in Long Melford. I've got some veneer to cover the traces of the screw holes.' I straightened, beamed. 'We'll have created three new fake antiques – er, restorations, I mean – by six this evening. Channie fakes – that is,' I corrected carefully, 'he's a master woodworker specialising in supplies to the antiques restoration trade . . . Hellfire, Lune!'

Luna was blushing, shifting from foot to foot. Where was the elegant, edible woman? She was shapeless. She rattled about in enormous wellington boots that seemed to reach into her. My old trousers hung on her like twin sacks. A tee shirt – surely mine could never be that gross? I'm dead average – was draped over her. A marquee after a storm.

'Am I all right?' she asked anxiously. 'For helping?'

'Yes, love,' I said gravely. 'You look really, er. Wheel the tables in. We've a lot to do.'

We found a table with four round legs. Only a crude Victorian wash-table, and battered almost to dereliction.

'We'll make this eighteenth century,' I explained. 'You simply take off each leg, and lathe it down to about three-fifths of its diameter. I'll show you how. Thick veneer from Herman the Gerbil at Eccles, and taper each leg on its inner face. Hey presto! It'll look eighteenth-century London!' And be as phoney as St Peter's bones in the Vatican.

'Me? The lathe?' Luna was really into it. 'Properly?'

'Of course, Lune. I trust you.'

'Oh, you.' But she was pleased, and set to willingly.

'The problem is that the legs will finish different, as they say. From a distance they'll seem a strange colour. So we'll dress the top to match. Then distress it a little, knock it about a bit.' I smiled at her sudden consternation. 'Customers expect it.'

'If you're sure, Lovejoy.' Her brow swept itself free of doubt, as always when a bird has a man in her pocket. Women are a great invention. No wonder sex caught on.

We set to.

It was bliss. Don't knock what we were doing, incidentally. I mean, if you knew how to change your old (or even new) chair into something antique and highly valuable, wouldn't you give it a go? And emulating the great masters of Georgian London, unexcelled for artistry before or since, gives a thrill of utter delight.

We had a tallboy – a stack of drawers, the bottom three wider than the top set. Hepplewhite was the tallboy king; though this was a feeble Edwardian copy, nicely aged. You separate the two sets. The top set consists of three single drawers plus the top level of two matching smaller drawers. We had a table top spare – the Wittwoode vannies had used it to offload the smaller items Luna had bought. We would cut it, then use it as a top for the lower stack of drawers, making a luscious early Victorian chest-of-drawers. The surface finish would be a problem, but that's always so with a faker. We'd get round that somehow.

Showing her how to use the spindle lathe, I was astonished at her proficiency. In half an hour she'd learned to keep the foot-treadle going while balancing herself to keep the pressure even on the chuck.

'Do you know prices have gone up two hundred per cent this year?' I groused, measuring a derelict piece to see if it could be turned into a bachelor chest. It was nice walnut, the right wood, but the bachelor is usually shallow – not more than ten inches, back to front, and only two feet nine inches wide. So a crumbling old bureau has to be savagely reduced. There's a giveaway: when you pull out a bachelor-chest drawer, it's 'tit-heavy', meaning tending to fall forwards—

'Luna!' The voice made me jump. 'What on earth?'

Oliver, marching in and nearly falling over the peg bath I'd set up yonks ago.

'Hello, Oliver.' Luna was being thrilled on the lathe. Not bad, either, turning her wood slowly, tongue out (Luna, not the spindle). Tousled but accurate. I liked her. 'Lovejoy's taught me! I'm thinning it, so—'

'Look at you!' Mayoress, he almost said.

'I hadn't time to come home. Lovejoy said I'm doing superbly.'

'Lovejoy!' Oliver's whiplash command was one I'd have instinctively disobeyed, but Luna was there so I followed him out. 'Lovejoy. I will not have my wife consorting with the district roguery! And where did she change? Dressed as a scruff!'

'Oliver.' I'm noted for my patience, but this was too much.

'No, Lovejoy. I've had a call from Del Vervain urging me to attend a rehearsal, with the Council, in our Moot Hall, of his radio show. How do you think this will make me look? I demand—'

'In, Oliver.' I pushed him into the workshop. This was an Oliver *vs* Luna conflict, nowt to do with me. 'Sort it out.'

Which made me think. I searched for pieces of cock-beading round drawers among the pile. This is moulding, semi-circular in section, that sticks out round the edges of drawers. Classically pre-1800, mahogany or walnut. Too much to hope for original post-1720 cock-beading, but plenty of Early Victorian lookalikes would do. The mistake fakers make nowadays is to fix them with minute pin-nails. The originals were glued. So to a criminal faker (I mean an honest restorer, like me) an authentic length of cock-beading is worth its weight in gold. I kid not.

'Look at you, Lovejoy.' Oliver was out, lip curled in scorn. 'Junk. To think I sent my wife to work with you.'

Oliver was a wart, but I heard him out. I've been slagged off by champs. I needed Luna. I'd no other loyalty. And, I thought indignantly, I was paying her, wasn't I? Well, nearly. I had that girl Laura's gelt, and Luna's. And possibly still Oliver's. Maybe I should pay her? A cheque had come this morning from the Employment Office. To me, not her.

Transferring it seemed an unnecessary labour. I needed to cut down my administrative costs. Also, Luna was rich.

'I'm withdrawing my finance, Lovejoy. Completely.'

'Maybe I'll withdraw from Vervain's show in the Moot Hall.'

'You can't.' He was smiling. What else did he know?

'I can do anything I want, Ollie.'

'Don't call me Ollie,' he fumed. 'Attend. Or you'll suffer harassment every hour, on the hour.'

'Threats, eh?'

'Yes.' He said it simply enough for me to believe. 'See that Mrs Carstairs is home never later than five.'

'Yes, b'wana.'

But I'd found two small lengths of glued cock-beading, not a nail-mark on them. I went inside happily, but wondering what deal Oliver had struck with Del Vervain.

'All right, Lovejoy?' Luna asked, worriedly watching me.

'Don't stop,' I told her. 'It's difficult enough to get you women started.' She tutted, smiling, returning to her task. I added laconically, 'The circus is coming to town.'

Chapter 28

Those working days made Luna realise that antiques are, if not everything, so nearly everything as to make no difference. News spread that Lovejoy Antiques, Inc. had money. We became a mecca. Dealers beat a path to our door. They came singly, of course, which is always a problem, because you don't know who's done a deal with whom. That matters, because you can force prices up or down with that knowledge. Without, it's free fall.

Luna showed amazing aptitude, especially for somebody with no experience. She learned to lathe table legs, to plane even. She could use a routing plane almost better than me within three days. And she was neat, so neat I had to ballock her and say for God's sake stop putting the chisels in order of size, and to leave the solvents alone instead of arranging them with the darkest shades near the window. Can drive you mad.

She liked seeing who would come next. Of course, she had likes and dislikes. She hated that evil swine Acker.

That week spent itself in buying from dealers, and making stuff. We didn't allow dealers into the workshop, of course. And every day as the light faded Gunge arrived in borrowed vans. We stopped for tea about then, and he'd load up while we discussed the evening plans. Luna had contrived an arrangement with Oliver so that she went home to change afterwards, while I made myself some grub. Then we'd meet in the White Hart and buy, buy, buy bandies from dealers in the saloon bar. Mostly jewellery, miniatures, portable antiques like porcelain, small statues, glass, silverware, chatelaines, a few books – though I hate booksellers too much to buy on the hoof. Some stuff was memorable – a velocipede, early nineteenth century. And a collection of mustard pots brought in by Bullrush, a tramp with an eye for a window catch. Don't laugh at mustard pots, incidentally. Odd but large mid-Victorian silver gilt ones are even more valuable than small genuine sterling silver ones. Supposedly on account of their usefulness as marmalade pots, but I doubt that. Look for one with a monkey approaching a barrel. Chances are it's a John Bridge, 1825-ish, and costly as a small car. Mostly they're only a week's wages.

Luna had something of an eye for jewellery, I discovered to my delight. I'd taught her to fake amber, of course, using various resins (copal's the faker's standby) and incorporating dead insects or chips of dried bark or pine cones shredded in a food-mixer. The usual. (Don't overdo it, if you try this. I had to admonish her for stuffing the fake ambers with everything but the kitchen sink. One insect wing's fine, a zoo's a giveaway.) By Friday, I wore strings of her fake ambers under my shirt to get the right shine. I'd carved a few into small religious scenes from an invented saint's life. Future archaeologists will write theses on them in years to come.

Another curious thing: Luna was red-hot on modern stuff – 'tomorrow's antiques' – the oldest of frauds. I mean, she bought a watercolour sketch by Leon Bakst (never heard of him). Costume, like nothing on earth. She was ecstatic, hugged me afterwards in the car park. It was from *La Boutique Fantasque*, 1918, apparently, worth a new motor. Can you believe it? I shrugged. Not antique at all. I liked the hug. I'd taught her erotic tobacciana at Jenny Calamy's. She snapped up, on description alone, a score of cigarette cases – some cheapish Birmingham Edwardian enamels, others French Art Deco 1920s, others German Edwardian in debased silver. They all had sexy scenes: 'risque' if you're posh, naughty if you're not. Ladies up to no good, in various postures. The rule is, the more erotic the more pricey. She bought from a wandering shuffler, the sort of bloke no respectable dealer will look at twice. Luna paid him on the nail. He vanished for an hour. Just when I was getting uneasy, in he shuffled, stinking and bleary, carting this old sack of tobacciana. I was proud of her.

Yet she missed others. I can't understand it. There's a pretty famous bronze called *Tiger Devouring a Gavial*. It's gruesomely explicit. In 1831, Bayle the Frenchman exhibited this bronze – they're faked a-plenty by now, of course – and created a sensation. Within milliseconds, all Paris was churning out little animal bronzes. Tigers devouring elephants, lions chewing serpents, even innocents like rabbits and kipping cows. Bronzes vary from Viennese cold-painted cheapos to stallions being boring (a month's wage). Bronze-workers are called animaliers, in the antiques trade, but the posh pronounce it through the nose, prefixing it with 'les'. This enables you to charge double, if the buyer's a nerk. Luna missed a 1585 bronze she-wolf, probably Padua, when it was worth all the rest put together. I told her to stick to modern.

There's a limit to what you can buy in a night pub. You have to travel for the bigger-priced antiques, furniture, paintings, collections of porcelains.

I developed a strategy.

* * *

'See, Luna,' I told her after we'd unloaded that night. 'We're vulnerable.'

'But Mr Gunge takes it away safely, Lovejoy.' She instantly checked the latch. 'Don't we trust him? We should.'

Luna's sound instincts: trust Gunge. 'Look about, love.'

She did. The place was crammed with antiques, fake antiques, going-to-be antiques. I'd given IOUs like confetti. Later tonight, when she'd gone home to Grolly Ollie, I'd do my late-night ritual reckoning, how close I was to the thin red line. I must be skating on the very edge. Money really gets me down, the way it spends itself.

'I've taken options on some paintings. And church woods – old pews, lecterns, vestry wall panels. No. It's all right, Lune. The Church Commissioners have approved their sale.' I smiled disarmingly. The Church Commissioners would have hysterics, if ever they heard about the transactions.

'So we have to travel?'

Divvieing antiques is prodigious emotional effort. It's not like the January sales. It's draining. And recovering's like a shattering re-entry from space. It was a long time since I'd done something straightforward and pleasant, like making a fifteenth-century manorial table out of redundant chapel pews. The profit on these is fabulous. Cost: about five or six quid, going to press as they say. London selling price, two months' wages. On the Continent, about six months' wages. All for enjoying yourself, a day's light handiwork.

'We can't, until after next week's meeting, Lovejoy.'

'Can't? Meeting?' I'd promised myself this re-energising therapy. I wasn't going to be baulked. We'd set up about thirty meetings, pubs, auctions, an oyster fishery even. 'You do the meetings, love. You're a natural dealer.'

She coloured, smiling. 'Silly. Mr Vervain. It's tomorrow.'

'What?' I didn't remember any meeting.

'The answerphone. You agreed to attend. The Moot Hall.'

I would have collapsed on the divan, but it was covered with mounds of Dux porcelains wrapped in tissue paper. Scantily-clad nymphets draped about mirrors and marine shells are the vogue. There are plenty about, from 1860 on. Think of unglazed surfaces in pastel colours, and you'll make a fortune.

'I can't,' I said, narked. Just when I'd got my own scam going. God, I was nearly within reach of Miss R, the mighty dollop broker, where all would be revealed. And now this media mouthie was—

'Oliver has gone to inordinate lengths for Mr Vervain, Lovejoy.' Reproach time. Luna looked soulful, but the divan was inaccessible. 'Think of the benefit for our town! Such an important personality . . .' She wasn't a Mayoress for nothing. Oliver must have worked on her. Why did he want *me* there?

'Can't I postpone it?' It was more than worrying.

Sod his ratings. Vervain's tactics were as transparent as Oliver's. Politicians and broadcasters are in the same game: grabbing acclaim. The slightest wilt means lying awake night after night as the fear burns into the brain that you aren't loved out there. They'll stop at nothing. And Oliver had as good as admitted that he and Vervain were fellows in a common cause.

'No, Lovejoy. You've given an undertaking.' I couldn't remember this conversation. But she was honest and true, right? She said firmly, 'You can't shirk it.'

One word I'd ban if I were king for a day is shirk. It's always used *at* me. As if the word itself aims blame. People missile the bloody word at whatever I want to do. I hate it, my cross since Day One.

'What have I to do?' my traitorous reflex asked dejectedly.

'Come to the Moot Hall to examine the Borough Regalia. A crowd of dignitaries, headed by Oliver, will be present. Del Vervain will make a speech about the community in local broadcasting, and declare it open.'

'Declare . . . ?' My headaches wait until I run out of aspirin. You'd think doctors would get off their fat bums for once and find a cure. And chemists these days only sell batteries.

'The fund. To launch the Borough Broadcasting Station.' She smiled fondly. 'It's my idea. I mentioned it to the Vervains. Oliver won Council approval.'

'What's this got to do with me?'

She spoke at length on community bondings, whatever they are, Oliver's need of revenue enhancement . . . Once a Mayoress, always political.

After she'd gone, with much hesitation tonight, I did my sums, reaching a sorry conclusion. Money spends fast, earns slow. I tend to re-learn old truths every day, with surprise.

I came into this through Drinkwater's mistake. Him thinking I'd done the Cornish Place robbery. Then Prammie Joe's death drew me deeper – police now guessed some wandering psychopath. Then came the inexplicable clustering of antiques into grand-scam patterns. So unlike East Anglia, home of the titch scam. And they multiplied: Tits Alors the prostitute, Connie, anybody with money, plus dealers without, Big Frank's next fiancée Calamity Jenny . . . Mostly clients of Marvella. Then Rye's fall to death.

Which was frightening. Unprecedented, as politicians say when they've ballsed up the economy yet again.

Money. Luna's wadge and Laura's formed quite a sum, but I needed more, thanks to Oliver's defection. I had

Laura's number, to ring at ten-thirty each evening. She'd made me swear in blood never to ring at any other time.

'Hello? Lovejoy. Laura?'

'Wait.' Clatter, mutter. To another phone? 'Yes, Lovejoy?'

'I'm running out of groats, love.'

'Hasn't a certain politico's spouse funnelled you enough?'

Birds have this knack of inferring you're sleeping with another woman even when they're only asking you to pass the toast. Narked, I said, 'Look. There's nothing between Mrs Carstairs and me—'

'No? Why is *she* supplying your wants, Lovejoy?'

See what I mean? Ten meanings, one set of words. 'Investment,' I snapped. 'And if you can't talk about money without bringing—'

She purred, 'Don't take on, Lovejoy. I'm on my way.'

On her way? I hadn't asked her to come. It took four goes to replace the receiver.

She arrived in less than half an hour. We sat and talked. I got a cheque for another quarter. With that, I'd be well in. We talked for a short while. Not long enough. I tried sussing what she was playing at, her funding a shoddy like me.

'You're an investment, Lovejoy,' she told me several times. 'Don't look a gift horse in the mouth.'

'Investments aren't a gift.'

'No. They have strings attached, called profit.' I found some sherry. She was amused. 'The last time I was offered leftover Christmas Tio Pepe I was fourteen, Lovejoy. Is this how you seduce Mrs Carstairs?'

'Mind your own business. It's all I've got.'

She did that slow-waggle stroll, touching the antiques, feeling the divan. I'd cleared part of it, for sleep.

'Is this where you . . . what's the term you people use, Lovejoy? Shag?' She smiled, cocky, watching my face. 'Lay? Bonk? Hump? . . . our esteemed Mayoress, Lovejoy?'

'Listen, you.' I was getting hot under the collar. She was gorgeous, agreed. But she had no right to come hard. 'I don't disclose confidences about birds. It's my way. If you think your gelt buys you confidences, you can take it and shove off.'

No good. It only fuelled her interest. Her eyes were shining. 'You love antiques so much, yet you'd abandon them? Just to preserve . . . ?' She came close. I was having hell of a time getting the sherry cork out. Rusted in, probably. 'She must bed really fantab.'

'That does it. Out.'

I slammed the bottle down and pushed her. She fell back, on to the divan. I just managed to rescue two Royal Dux pieces before she hit.

'You silly cow!' I blazed, gathering them safe from this marauder. 'These damage easy! Don't you know the effort that went into making—?'

'Best you've ever had, Lovejoy, was she?'

'Any one of these is worth two of you, you dozy bitch.'

'Better than you think I could be, Lovejoy?' She was swinging her foot, her shoe almost off the upturned toes. Her legs were slender, beautiful. Might as well talk to the wall. I surrendered.

'What is it, Laura?' Wearily I put the Dux pieces on a harmonium keyboard out of her way. 'After a bit of rough scruff? Between college romeos? Mrs Carstairs beat you at tennis? Doing down Daddy's hand-picked fiancé? What?'

'All nine, Lovejoy.' She moved the rest of the porcelains to the harmonium. 'I hope these are new sheets, Lovejoy.' She stood, shivered elegantly. She was beautiful. 'Turn the heating on. I'll catch my death.'

'Heat spoils polishes.' My voice had thickened.

She laughed, dropped her clothes, slipped into bed. 'My teeth are *chattering*. In, for Christ's sake. Get me warm.'

'Look,' I tried weakly. What's the use? Women can do what they like. We pretend for our self-respect that we're making decisions. We're not. It's a woman's world. The proverbs lie.

Next morning she was gone by seven o'clock. She stared astonished while I made us both breakfast, followed me about saying how on earth, all that kind of woman's incomprehension. She dressed after I'd had both our breakfasts. She wasn't hungry. She smiled, paused in the porch to ask who said thank you and to whom.

'Etiquette doesn't cover this, does it, Lovejoy?'

'What's etiquette?' I said, making her laugh. She seemed so familiar, her face filled with life. Almost as if I'd known her in a previous incarnation. Lovely.

'Verdict, Lovejoy?' I had to work that one out. Was she better sex than arch enemy Mrs Carstairs.

'That's confidential.' I was narked. 'I have no relationship with that lady.' Who keeps score, making love? Love is yippee, hundred per cent of itself. Believing there are grades of totality is a woman's myth. I didn't tell Laura this. They never believe me.

She left in her colossal motor without a wave. It howled off up the lane, round at the chapel, then silence.

Reliable old Gunge, the dealer who could be trusted, came about thirty minutes later, to make his usual daily collection. He was in distress. Connie Hopkins had gone missing. Gunge asked did I know where she'd gone. He'd searched high and low. No sign of her in her shop. He seemed to have a key. Interesting, this. I didn't know he and Connie had got that far. I went through the daft rigmarole that telly series have taught us: where did you see her last, have you phoned her parents. Quite lunatic. Lost is lost. The only person who'd know about Connie was sitting on the divan, head in his hands, stuttering, in a state of collapse.

Luna arrived, bright of eye and bushy-tailed. Within seconds she was contributing stupidity.

'You should have put an advert in the newspaper, Mr Gunge!' she said cheerfully. Then wrinkled her nose. 'Is that perfume?'

Another of those days. I took her outside by the elbow. 'Luna, love. Just for today, stay mum unless I say. Understand?'

'It's a perfectly sensible suggestion, Lovejoy. Newspapers are a sound medium—'

'Gunge can't frigging well read, you silly cow.' I waited until it sank in, saw her face discard thrill for horror. 'Haven't you noticed that I mutter the catalogue descriptions out loud when he's close by?'

Her eyes filled. 'Oh, Lovejoy. I never dreamt—'

'It's all right. He's used to stupidity.' I tried to look thrilled, Luna-style. 'I'm quite looking forward to the, eh, Moot Hall.'

Chapter 29

'The antiques, Lovejoy. Do we keep adding?'

'You've our lists, Gunge?' He keeps me a handwritten tally somewhere in his massive bearish presence. Doesn't need any, of course. Illiterates have a fantastically accurate visual memory. I've seen him spot a dud Wellington chest from a reflection in a window across the road, because its veneer had changed since it was auctioned a year before. Hawkeyes.

'Aye, Lovejoy.' To my dismay great tears began to roll down into his beard. I looked at the floor. 'I don't want anything to happen to Connie, Lovejoy. She's scared. Even before Rye died.'

I'm really useless at times like this. 'Look, Gunge. Who else did Connie confide in?'

'Nobody. Not even you. She wondered, but said you're unreliable about women.'

Bloody nerve. Typical womentalk. What do they know?

'What was she frightened of, Gunge?' Luna, ears wafting in the breeze. I glared at her coldly. This was supposed to be a private conversation.

'Of being killed. She talked a lot about spells.'

Spells? Was Connie going off her trolley? I'd met her that day off the train. She'd been edgy, definitely spooked about something.

'By whom? Why didn't she go to the police? Was it an antique dealer? I think we should—'

My bent eye made Luna peter out, sulking.

'Right, Gunge.' Leaving the antiques in the old Boxtenholt aerodrome would be asking for trouble. 'What help've you got?'

'Just me. Connie didn't want it any other way.'

'Then we're in business,' I said. I felt as near to a smile as I'd been for many a day. Or night. 'Find Sandy, Luna. Tell him and Mel I want to contact the dollop broker. Today.'

She inhaled a gale, only said, 'Will he know how?'

'Not himself, no.' But telling Radio Sandy is our equivalent of BBC One. 'Gunge. You and me will gather everything I've got, ordered, can find, before nightfall. Okay?'

'Will it help us to find Connie?'

'I don't know, Gunge. But we'll try, eh?'

'Thanks, Lovejoy.' He heaved his enormous mass upright and shambled off to start the loading. This morning he had a pale-blue three-tonner. You never see him twice in the same vehicle. I wondered if he simply nicked them.

He'd been gone an hour, with me and Luna finishing frantically in the workshop, when Drinkwater visited to say that one Miss Connie Hopkins had gone missing, and did I know anything about her, I said no, how terrible, and had he checked her parents. He issued warnings, and left with his teeth clacking and ear all a-twitch.

Cradhead appeared in the workshop doorway about eleven, stood watching a while, wandered in, careful not to waft off slices of walnut veneer, and pausing to observe Luna putting the finishing touches to a prunt. These are small glass medallions, very rare alone. They were incorporated into antique roemers, actually only stuck on to the wide hollow stem. I honestly don't know why the German Rhineland liked these great spherical-bowled drinking glasses with the trailing-decorated foot (think of a thread of glass wound round and round), but they did. You have to admire style. These prunts, especially knobbly-surface ones dealers call 'raspberries', are highly sought after in their own right now. God knows why.

'Only ordinary soda glass, Craddy,' I admitted before he asked. 'I borrowed glass tubing from Therla Brewer's school. Lower temperature, see?'

'The Lady Mayoress is very adept, Lovejoy.'

Cradhead shouldn't have such a quiet posh voice. Makes you think he's thinking. Only disguise, him being a peeler.

'Thank you, Inspector!' from Luna, so pleased at yet more praise that she paused to discuss her prowess. 'I'm—'

'Get on with it!' I yelled. Then smiled weakly at Cradhead's raised eyebrows. 'Er, Luna my dear. Please don't let it get cold.'

'Deadline to meet, Lovejoy?' He wandered. My back prickled. I wished he'd sod off so I could get on.

'No. Only, the Employment want a report on Mrs Carstairs' progress.'

'Connie Hopkins, Lovejoy.' Cradhead bent to sniff at the surface of a medieval apothecary's measure. Nice, simply two pewter cones joined at the apex. One cone was a half-ounce measure, the other one-ounce. Very pricey. I'd made it myself today. I didn't like Cradhead sniffing it – you can tell a new fake; the lead smells for quite five days after it has been made. Was this fascist swine cleverer than he seemed? 'Absent,' he went on. 'She was collecting antiques fast as . . . well, as Big Frank's new wife. And her studying astrophysics at university!' So he'd checked there too.

'Maybe she's gone off with a boyfriend.'

'Gunge Herod's her boyfriend, Lovejoy. You see him about. Six feet eight, giant, runs a dealer's barrow without a street licence. Can't read—'

'At least he admits it, Craphead! Unlike you frigging peelers . . .' I petered out, swallowed, resumed my varnishing.

Cradhead's eyes lit up at my response. The nerk had goaded me and I'd fallen for it.

'You're worried too, eh? Like us frigging peelers. Apologies, Mrs Carstairs.' He drifted to the door. 'What's on tonight, Lovejoy? Council meeting in the Moot Hall. Schoolchildren. Women's Institutes. Local history societies. Del Vervain. And . . .' He smiled a sleet-shaped smile. 'And you, Lovejoy.'

'Some promotion thing. Charity.' I was off-hand.

'Seven o'clock, Mr Cradhead.' Luna interrupted her glass-making. I'd throttle her. 'Would you like a ticket? I could speak to Mayor Carstairs.'

'Unnecessary, Mrs Carstairs.' Cradhead found his trilby. 'I'll be there. Duty calls, you see.'

'Goodbye,' my silly bitch trilled. 'Good luck finding Miss Hopkins!'

Chintzy chintzy cheeriness. I snarled at her. She bent quickly to her labours. A woman's job is never done, because they can't be bothered. From then on we really moved.

We did seven places, bought some paintings of the oiland-slush Victorian sentimental schools. Tip: dealers are consters, the lot of them. They still preach there's no demand for sentimental paintings of the Pax Britannica heyday. So they offer you about one-fiftieth of the going price for that lovely stag painting on your parlour wall. And I mean one-fiftieth. Not even a twentieth. Two per cent. Well, thirty years ago that was true. But now? The pendulum's swung. Heartrending paintings of little girls waving doggies goodbye from nursery windows, children building sandcastles while Fond Father Dotes, are pure gold. Tear-jerking's in. Just learn your fifty-times table, that's all.

Speed was the essence. I'd bought wisely and fast with Laura's extra gelt. Luna was hard put to keep track, thank God. Payment on the nail for instant delivery. I'd had five bike couriers tearing up the tarmac for days. Every five hours we returned to the cottage, Gunge loaded up like a stoker raising steam. I rejected some fake furniture and a few porcelains, but mostly the dealers, braying after instant coin, played fair – as always, when all else fails. Luna wanted a serious chat about where the extra money had come from, simply quelled.

The answerphone went odd. Its number promised several messages, but only gave bleeps, to Luna's annoyance.

We discovered the reason about three o'clock. The phone rang. I answered, from the strangest of premonitions. I knew it was the dollop broker before the gruff voice spoke.

'Lovejoy? Who d'you know?'

'Sandy. Mel, Nuala. A load of locals collecting antiques.'

'Who for?'

'Some dollop broker.' I waited. 'Who do you know, then?'

'Everybody. Except your sister, Lovejoy.' The voice waited for me to fill in. I said nothing. She'd heard about Hawkshead. 'Your problem's not lessening with time, is it?'

'No.' This was the one all right. 'What's the arrangement? I've never dealt this big before.'

'Be outside your cottage in ten minutes.'

I was going to protest, but old gravel-throat had gone. I felt scared. Who climbs highest does so by a winding stair. Gulp. I told Luna I had to go out.

'Get Gunge to collect what we've got. Now.'

She was worried, refering to lists, ticking things off. 'I've run out of wrapping paper, Lovejoy. And those Royal Doultons are . . . What's the matter?'

'No more, love. It's all done. Anything you can box, parcel, shove into Gunge's next vanload, do so.'

'Done, Lovejoy! But some are still to be faked up.'

Faked up, if you please. I had to smile. Two weeks ago she'd have fainted at the thought. I embraced her. She tried to pull away, looking through the window in case some arriving vanny jumped to conclusions.

'It's come, love.'

'What's come?'

'Gawd knows. But it's here.'

Chapter 30

Luna went up the lane to wait for Gunge. I was nervous as a kitten, now I'd actually made it to the big league. I'd never dreamt I'd actually do it – me, meet a dollop broker! Mega trade.

The car sent for me was a common station taxi. It dropped me at the local hospital. I was collected again by a hire car. The driver knew nothing, took me to Toll Gate shopping mall. Among scores of people loading their wheelies I was collected by a third car, driven miles to a countryside crossroads. By a lonely bus stop, I was met by a saloon car with heavily tinted windows.

The last two drivers were women. Neither spoke. I was in the rear seat. The penultimate motor was replaced after a couple of miles by another. My head was spinning. Why not a chat in Woody's instead of all this motor mix? I thought I saw a blonde driving a car following, but couldn't be sure. In a pub yard I was swapped one last time. One with black windows, no vision at all. Coward to the last, I tried the handles. Locked. The driver was a thin lank-haired girl wearing reflector sun specs, the sort that puts mirrors where eyes should be. I'd only seen her when embarking. For thirty minutes I sat looking at the car's interior.

Ten miles, twenty? I was dropped in some estate. The motor cruised away. I was alone.

From where I stood, at a mansion house door, I could see ornamental gardens. Tallish chimneys, Tudor in style. But fake. A smallish red-brick dwelling stood visible through the trees. An old tennis court, now overgrown. A hockey-size field was newly planted into rosebeds. Trees everywhere. No rivers. It wore an institutional air. A phoney coat-of-arms, modernish stained glass, adorned the main door. I was left to knock.

Silence. I turned slowly on the top step. Balustrade, lawns neatly cut. Tidy flowerbeds. No wheelbarrows, rakes or mowers left lying about. I could see a greenhouse roof. It felt weird, almost quite alien. Home for retired gentlewomen? Too many steps, no wheelchairs. No car park. Ancient family seat, Lord Lieutenant of the County? No serfs.

And the door opened.

Thin women I can take. Medium to plump, fine. Old, young, superb. But voluminous? So obese you can't see the edges? Every step a waddle, a susurrus of rasping clothes? Each breath was an orchestra of squeaks. Chin to knees formed one long convexity. Contours were definitely not this lady's thing. I found her eyes, fixed on them like a pointer dog in case I lost them.

'Lovejoy,' I told her.

'I suppose you'll have to come in.'

Spoken with disgust. I followed. Her incredible jeans moved ahead like heaving stratocumulus. The corridor passed between rooms stacked high with food, crates of tuna fish, sacks of beans, cereal packs, bottles of sauce. Other rooms we passed were rimmed with hanging dresses. Folded jumpers and woollens filled shelves to the ceilings.

'Expecting war, missus?'

'Exploiters don't dun me, Lovejoy. I stock up.'

'Antiques too?'

'Be funny and I'll bin you.'

Funny? Antiques? 'Love isn't funny, missus.'

'Phoney philosophy's what I don't stock, Lovejoy.'

She reached the end room and sat, back to me, on an old garden bench before a television set, some game show with constant applause. She overflowed the seat, lapping in pendulous sags nearly to the floor. A plastic bucket half-filled with salted peanuts was handy, to suppress lurking anorexia. She slumped into the viewer's sprawl, feeding her face handfuls. A crate of cola tins gave fluid support. I was left standing. Was this the famous Miss R, Super Planner herself? Scam Superba? Or merely another intermediary lackey?

The screech frightened me out of my skin.

'It's beheaded, you stupid fucking mare!' she howled at the television screen. 'Anne Boleyn and Catherine Howard were beheaded!'

Roars of dismay from the TV as the contestant was banished back to Hartlepool. 'Just bad luck,' the idiot presenter bawled.

The dolloper was a rage-filled blimp. 'It's fucking ignorance for fuck's fucking sake!' she screamed.

I covered my ears until the din subsided. 'Missus, I'm a delicate flower.'

'Where was she educated, the unlettered bitch?'

There was more. Invective's dull, so I won't summarise the next hour. The fat lady blasted the game show, the news, a fashion parade, a scene with dog-handlers.

'Just watch!' she thundered, immense mass quivering. 'Parading like stuffed cattle! Cruft must be spinning in his grave, the way they're handling those dogs!'

'Cruft wouldn't care, love.' I was fed up. 'Charles Cruft of Cruft's International Dog Show fame kept cats. Never owned a dog.'

The world swivelled, looked at me. The screen clicked off. 'You're in difficulties, Lovejoy. You've taken over Connie Hopkins' stuff, brought it to the right level.'

I drew breath, but it didn't have anything to say.

'My preference is to broker for females. As you now have female partners and backers, you'll do. These are my terms—'

'Here. Just a minute—'

'Silence! I don't accept people wanting hideouts. Nor immigrants. Drugs are acceptable, but only those not requiring special storage conditions. I store any type of criminal deposits, as long as the dollop's owners are clearly identified. I specialise in caches left for the duration of a prison sentence, and for Statutes of Limitations of specified countries. Understand?'

Uttered with the feeling of a copper's caution.

'Fine.'

'Terms: build-up from three perc, one perc weekly to max of ten to a fifth one year and over, inflation adjusted. Take or leave.'

Queen of précis. She'd summed up the usual dolloper's arrangement. Three per cent of our antique's total, rising to ten per cent. She'd conceal the antiques for ever, but charge us a tenth when they were finally sold, even if we were imprisoned.

'Final charge?'

'Two perc after the second year. Flat removal fee, plus mileage.'

I didn't smile. Flat-fee mileage meant you couldn't guess how far your stuff had travelled. That implied her storage space was here. Except I didn't know where here was.

'Okay.'

She picked up a control slab. A woman's voice came on.

'Yes for Lovejoy,' said Miss R. 'Go now.'

'Herod's van is south of Lavenham,' a loudspeaker said. 'I'll let it do its drop in the cran before evacuating. Willco.'

The broker huffed to her feet. 'Settle any arguments between you and Connie before final audit.'

'Right, right.' I felt like in school. You wouldn't want to cross this formidable lady and her slick team of women.

A bleep sounded. She listened to earphones, barked, 'South American bonds, after *that* escapade? The answer is no.'

'They offer to bank through Georgia, USA,' the control panel persuaded.

'Still no. Unless they bank via Washington, DC.'

I felt slim and willowy following her bulk out to the front door. No visible telephones with giveaway numbers. No local scenes. The place was stacked for a siege. Crates of apples rose in a serene curve, upstairs to the landing. Sacks of lentils and dried peas filled the hallway. Yet the place was spick and span.

'Pay one per cent today, Lovejoy.'

'Who to?'

'Whom, cretin. A courier.'

'How do I know I'll work one per cent out right?'

'Correctly,' she corrected, in reflex. 'I shall judge.'

Aye, I thought sardonically as the door shut firmly on me. I'd better get the money right. She would have my antiques. I stared about a moment or two, looking for clues. I'd found the right dollop broker all right, but learned nothing. No chance to bring up Cornish Place. I was dying to know which dealers had been here. I couldn't quite see Sandy or Big Frank making much of a mark with this formidable lady. Calamity Jenny, now, seemed somehow to be right for the place. Or Cassandra Clark? Not Vell, though. Connie? Maybe. Plum-in-the-mouth country.

The black-glass motor came. I got in. It drove away. I tried the door and windows. No views, for the likes of me.

We did the car switches in reverse, and I learned nothing.

Gunge told me he'd called at the old aerodrome in Boxtenholt to drop off three Victorian desks and a case of Edwardian jewellery, final afterthoughts Luna couldn't resist, but the place was cleaned out. He'd had to bring the afterthoughts back.

'Fine, Gunge. Just leave them here.'

I sent Luna to unload them, and sat on my unfinished wall to feed the birds and think. Miss R had spoken in tones so precise it made me think of school. And a massive mansion like that. Big rooms – never mind the clothes and grub stacked everywhere. Obviously she was a nutter. Well, a dollop broker had to be, harbouring stolen antiques until such time as the robbers served their prison sentences and came back to spend their ill-gotten gains. She was class, despite her appearance. Worked out foreign bond percentages without conscious thought. Able to hold together a band of women. (*All* women?) Forceful, authority unquestioned. Shrewd as all dollop brokers. The word trick again, though. A dollop broker doesn't broker anything. Just stores stuff, safe from police, law, other gangsters, insurance companies.

What did I know about her? Only the scams she'd catered for. I guessed she was the dollop broker who'd handled the German medieval treasures until Greck got sprung from gaol. Who'd handled the marijuana from Holland after that Spalding bulb fiasco (the lorries got caught on the bypass from Felixstowe). Who'd handled the French paintings, and brokered their return when the museums and galleries bought them back on the sly. So, a genius. Who could organise a cool lift of three hundred and eighty antiques from a disused aerodrome, while watching TV and eating a bucket of nuts. Not bad, seeing I'd not said where the antiques were.

But that place. The tennis court, traces still visible but now given over to bushes and lawn. A pitch, now flowerbeds. Grass always grows thickest by corner flags. I remember my cousin Glenice playing hockey when she was a little girl, the pitch smaller than the football pitches I'm used to.

School? A girls' school. The big house, gatehouse of red brick. The scrupulous neatness. Her private cursing, public propriety. Her exasperation at the clueless woman contestant who'd not known some elementary history about Henry VIII's wives. Calamity Jenny, she of the august social background, belonged there, and Cassandra Clark. Connie. But not me, not Big Frank. An ex-girls' school, now engaged in a different sort of activity.

What was it somebody had said? I called across for Luna to brew up. It was Vell. She'd said something about Cassandra Clark, being from a different school. With bitterness.

Connie Hopkins? Cassandra Clark? This was the first time I felt something true. Had they been together at school? Yet I'd never seen them as much as swap a greeting. Avoiding each other? Or was I jumping to conclusions, as usual?

Luna emerged. Gunge sat with us on the wall. He could dwarf Miss R, just about.

'Lune,' I said eventually. 'Where did you go to school?'

'Me? Stirling. Quite nice, really, though games was the thing they . . .'

I didn't listen after that. Libraries list schools. They were open tonight until eight o'clock, plenty of time before the Moot Hall gathering. I had Luna try to reach Cassandra Clark, but she could get no answer. Still ruminating, I told her to check the phonebook. It said E. C. Clark.

'E for what?' I asked.

'It doesn't say.' Luna sat primly beside me, finally hunting. 'Why are you interested in Cassandra Clark?'

Dunno.' I asked Gunge where Connie went to school, but he didn't know. 'We'll find Connie soon, Gunge,' I said, wondering how.

We sat glumly, three monkeys, each with our thoughts. I honestly did feel I might be edging close. Honestly. Gunge sat in silent misery. He saw me as his one last hope. Pathetic. She could be anywhere. I felt she was somewhere not far. Miss R's school? That was the most likely. All I lacked was reason, logic, and a load of troops to storm the place. If I could find it again. With caches of criminal loot littering the grounds, there'd be aggressive security. Not just a fat lady with sacks of beans.

An hour later I came to, and told Gunge to ask around around after Connie. 'Miss out nowhere, Gunge,' I ordered. 'Everywhere. Strangers, even. But especially the Arcade. Antique dealers. And call in at the cop shop.'

'Peelers, Lovejoy?' He stopped, already halfway to his van.

'No time to be proud, Gunge. Find me at six. I'll look round Connie's place.'

'Me, Lovejoy,' Luna asked. 'What have I to do?'

It was late afternoon. The day waning, birds having a last scour about the garden. She usually went home about this time, after Oliver's tantrum.

'I want you inside, love.'

She took my arm. 'Don't sound so sad, Lovejoy. What is it? You're so soft-hearted. I mean, so upset because poor

Gunge's ladyfriend has gone away for a few days. She's having a day or two away. That's all.'

'Yes.' We started inside. 'Draw the curtains, love.'

She already had. And the window fastenings were locked. She was slipping off her shoes even as I reached the divan. Like I say, women are miles ahead of us. Still, I don't like women who are mean. Surely everything's not too much to ask? The cottage felt coldish without so many antiques around. It warmed.

Chapter 31

Gunge showed me Connie's miniature shop. Tiny, sparse. Modern chair, trestle table, kettle and enough to brew tea. Nothing else. I wrestled the town library for facts, scoring best of three pinfalls. The immortal I. K. Brunel's *Great Eastern* paddle-steamer, wonder of the nineteenth century, 18,915 gross tons, launched in 1858 at Millwall. She was marked by disaster.

Not her fault. She was just eerie. During her building, accidents multiplied. Workmen died, were maimed. Brunel himself had a stroke as she readied for sea trials. An explosion in September, 1859, killed six seamen. Brunel relapsed, died. It was a grim paddle-steamer that finally hit the long wet road.

Long before, even her launch was doomladen. She simply stuck for years, the 1 in 12 hopeless. Legend says Isambard built a secret model with his own superb hands, tried it out somewhere. Five funnels, six masts, side-paddles. Like the pictures Delia nicked from Rye. Those features were on the murky photographs. Was it here that Brunel came? Was his model brooding the river serving Rye's watermill? The part of the river Rye'd sold his birthright to try to buy from Oliver's Council, as Luna said? Or was it a con? A photo of a cloudy underwater model would be easy to fake. Any photographer, blindfold.

The unhappy question came. Connie seemed keen on Rye – as long as he funded her drive into the big antiques league. When he'd offered for the mill and its river instead, she'd turned to me. I was a replacement. Frigging cheek.

Nothing for it. We had to find her. She'd gone missing some hours. No bird on earth assembles a wealth of antiques, then strolls away leaving them for others, does she? I made the Moot Hall in good time.

Every town has an ancient meeting place. The Moot Hall is typical – meaning the Borough Council has let it crumble, and now whines for handouts to restore it. You can see it's been patched by cowboy builders hired for a pittance.

'Oliver's so proud, Lovejoy,' Luna whispered as I walked into the hallway. 'This is the biggest event of his mayoral year!'

Some year. Luna had to go. She looked smashing: dress midnight-blue velvet, genuine pearls, four-carat diamond ring. A brooch would have been too much, but her Edwardian pearl-drop earrings were just right. She was thrilled to bits, of course. I wished her luck.

The Hall was once splendid. Now, it's virtually derelict, faded walls hung about with a few oil paintings in a sickeningly bad state. They depict our ancient councillors avariciously welcoming Huguenot refugees yet more immigrants to exploit – and two unarmed Royalist knights being gunned down (another form of East Anglian greeting) and the like. The place of honour's reserved for Queen Boadicea, who razed the town in Roman days and rewarded local developers by crucifying everybody, Dealers keep wondering whether to nick these paintings

(Big Frank's offered them to a Swiss dealer in Rotterdam. I'll keep you posted).

The place was filling. It smelled musty. The stage was hollow, every footfall rolling thunder. Dust, the Council's hallmark, lay everywhere. Housewives drifted in, excited about the great radio hero Del Vervain. Commercial fawners were filing in to the front rows, so they could be seen to be worshipping those in high places. A few old winos drifted in.

'Wotch, Lovejoy.' An old soak hawked up phlegm and swallowed with relish. 'Reckon they'll have nosh?'

'Wotcher, Forage.' He used to run errands for me once, but finally couldn't leave the pub long enough. 'Doubt it, for the likes of us.' The ante-room, the only one properly restored, had busy waitresses laying an enormous buffet.

'Bastards,' he croaked, settling in one of the rear seats. 'Junketing on our taxes.'

His mates muttered agreement. Marmalade Emma's the second of Forage's trio. She's mostly in black, with a black lacquered wicker hat and two bobbing cherries. The *My Fair Lady* prototype. Grimes is her bloke. Stays stout on booze, God knows how. I've never yet seen him awake. Moving about, yes, but that's not the same thing.

'Forage? Sit at the front,' I suggested. 'It's warmer.'

'They can chuck us out easier from here, Lovejoy,' Forage said. 'The door guard is Grimes' cousin's lad Andy.'

'Oh. Right.' They'd embarrass him all right.

I sat down with them. Marmalade Emma was reminiscing. She makes me wistful. I don't know why. She sings outside pubs – inside, wherever she's allowed – and does a shuffling clownish dance that makes people laugh. They throw pennies to make the drunken old lady show her tattered soiled knickers. You can imagine what an admirable and merry scene it is, in this rural corner of Merrie

England. Our village social club hires her to do her dance. They pay her in booze. And critics say wit is a dying art.

'There used to be big chandeliers up there, Lovejoy. See?'

'I don't remember them, Emma.' I looked.

'Ooooh, yes. Very grand. People say they wuz real gold. You're too young.' She quavered a few bars of a waltz. I lalled along. My Auntie Alice was a great laller. She could turn any melody, Handel's *Messiah* down, into lal-lal-lal.

'Did you dance here, Emma?'

She demanded indignantly, cherries bobbing, 'Did I dance here? Lord, Lovejoy!' She nudged Grimes, who chuckled in his sleep and said Lord too. 'Lord above! I danced to dawn, in this very hall! With the Mayor! Old Alderman Adamson. Very grand.' Slyly she checked that Grimes was kipping. You could have heard her whisper in Harwich. 'He kissed me. After a polka. Under the painting of the two girls with lanterns. My favourite.' Her rheumy old eyes searched the walls to point it out. There was no painting there. I thought, odd.

'Lovejoy.' Forage nudged me. 'They're calling you. What you done, son?'

A red-coated Master of Ceremonies was bawling for attention. People were still filing in. 'Nothing. Yet.'

'Lovejoy.' A custodian tried to prise me up but I wouldn't go. 'On the stage. The Mayor said.'

'Tell him no thanks.' Andy, embarrassed after all.

A number of dignitaries were slowly filling the chairs on the podium. Oliver and Luna weren't yet in, nor Del, Joan. Arriving audiences always create a hubbub.

'He won't like it, Lovejoy.'

Emma cackled. 'Lovejoy'll worry chronic, Andy.'

It was quarter of an hour before the proceedings showed signs of starting. Emma talked nonstop, tales of ancient goings-on amongst the nobs of yesteryear. She must have been quite prominent in her day. Grimes hadn't been prominent at all.

'Here, son,' Emma asked as folk hushed and had a last cough. 'It true you're shafting the Lady Mayoress, is it?'

'Mind your own business.'

She fell about at that, Grimes laughing along in his slumber. Forage looked frosty. He disapproves of immoral talk.

'Lovejoy, we loikes you, bony. Even not local. But shafting carriage trade makes for bad blood.'

Other people didn't like me, I noticed wrily. The four of us were in an island of space. A school of children was in the body of the seating. Shoppers gossiped in the back row. The hall was about two-thirds full. Blokes adjusted microphones. I was disappointed. You'd think radio would need spectacular wiring, tons of transmitters. There'd been just one radio van outside. That was it. Television's better value. No wonder Del Vervain was worried sick about ratings if this was radio's only technology.

People quietened, the children enjoying making shushing noises, making such a racket they had to be silenced separately. I was glad Therla Brewer was in. She and Josh were sitting closer than teachers ought. I sighed. That's life.

'Ladies and gentlemen. The Mayor and Mayoress of the Borough!'

Recorded fanfare, barely making it. People stood, some applauding. The line of dignitaries beamed. Oliver and Luna entered. He wore his chain of office; she was merely beautiful. Lights held them as they took their places. People sat, scraping the floor. Why do people *do* that? There's no need. You just sit down, for God's sake. But have you ever heard an audience sit quietly? I never have. It's a queer world.

'Pray silence for His Worship Mayor Carstairs!'

Oliver rose, to feeble clapping. Councillors and front-row fawners were ecstatic. Luna's eyes were shining as she clapped longest of all. I wondered if remembering how differently those hands had behaved at my cottage was jealousy or something, but gave over and listened to Oliver, resplendent in his regalia.

'Councillors! Members of the Social Promotions Committee! Broadcasting fraternity! Last but not least ladies and gentlemen of the Borough!'

This drew a roar of laughter from ingrates. Housewives tittered, with that anxiety women always show on posh occasions, hoping all will go right and nobody will be ashamed.

'He always was a smarmy bleeder,' Emma whispered shrilly.

People looked round. Oliver pressed on, delighted with the sound of his own voice and a multitude.

'A famous local radio personality and his lady are gracing our ancient town tonight. Even as I speak, this event is being broadcast *live* on Radio Camelod!'

Thinner applause. Oliver raised his hands, quelling a riot of adoration.

'His dad was a ram,' Emma confided. 'All fingers, he was. His wife left him. No bleedin' wonder.' She plucked my sleeve. I bent close, though I'd have heard her if I'd been out sailing. 'His father shagged half his wife's pupils.' She cackled. She had about three teeth left. I wondered vaguely why she didn't have a good false set. 'Headmistress, at Colney Varr.' She gathered herself for a joke. 'Wish I'd gone there, Lovejoy!' Colney Varr was a posh girl's academy somewhere, once famous.

'Silence, please!' Some uniformed guardian on tiptoe.

'Sorry, mate,' I said. God, but Emma ponged. I began to wish I'd sat further forward after all. Grimes snored and

twitched. He always does. In solemnity Forage now wore
his spectacles, one lens a cracked bifocal, the other missing. I wondered vaguely why *he* didn't have proper glasses.

Our Mayor was waxing lyrical. 'This evening is a
Council initiative, to raise funds for the restoration of
Council buildings such as this noble edifice in which we
currently speak. We are displaying Council regalia and
. . .' he twinkled, signifying impending wit '. . . baubles,
ha ha ha!'

A few grovellers tried to get applause going, failed.

'All the Borough wealth – portable variety only! – is out
for inspection. Under guard, of course!'

He was sweating heavily. Forage nudged Grimes, for
snoring. Emma was on about some soldier she'd known. I
felt myself nod from the warmth, came to when the celeb-
rity of the evening was announced.

'. . . Del *Vervain!*'

In he strode, laughing, shaking hands all the way down
the hall. Bouncing on to the stage and grabbing a hand
microphone. He was made up. Astonishing: He looked
about twenty years younger.

'Here we are! Radio Camelod, in the oldest Moot Hall
in the known world!' He roared with laughter. Everybody
roared with laughter. The Mayor and the councillors roared
with laughter. I looked about. What gets into people?

'Here, Emma,' I asked. It was narking me. 'Why have
you no proper teeth? Or Forage specs?'

'Shhhh, son. I like old Del. Used to be a pub singer.'

Del Vervain was babbling, striding. 'Folks, this is your
opportunity! You'll hear the dulcet tones of my gorgeous
wife Joan! Come own a-here, honey!'

Applause. Oliver went forward gallantly, escorted Joan.
Del was being poisonously jocular. God, having to do that
for a living? Broadcasters think imitation New York accents

entitle them to instant fame. Lunatic. You'd spend your life wondering why people do what they do, if there was hope of an answer. I was getting narkeder and narkeder.

Joan said hello and how marvellous and everything. Excited, brilliantly dressed in lime green, flouncy skirts a little youngish but delectable. Del displaced her in two sentences.

'We're here, listeners, by popular request. Our first outside broadcast! No phone-ins this time. So save your pennies, ha ha ha ha!'

A bloke seated at the rear of the stage signalled. Del grabbed Oliver and grinned at us with aggressive confidentiality. The show was on. One measly microphone.

'My first guest is His Worship Mayor Carstairs. Oliver, how does it feel, Mayor of this ancient Borough?'

Snoozetime. Oliver intoned his feelings. Del quipped hearty quips. Excruciating. Emma occasionally whispered bits of slander, Oliver's randy Dad and fading family fortunes after Oliver's Mum slipped the traces.

Between gossip and guests, I really did nod off. They were electric. An octogenarian who'd once known the Prime Minister. A historian with theories about Normans. Somebody else – the coast was eroding, we'd all get wet. Yawn city. Del Vervain made me wonder how boring blokes like him get to be broadcasters in the first place. He was hopeless. He'd need a miracle to revive his fortunes, not a pathetic outside broadcast in a dingy old hall. People had come because anybody on the air is still a wonder to behold. But radio doesn't have the appeal of television. Not half so degrading.

People started to drift out, fed up. I was almost on the point of joining them, when Del Vervain struck.

'Now a special treat, listeners! A famous antique dealer. Lovejoy by name. And, by nature, ha ha ha!'

To my alarm here he came, actually walking down the aisle at me, grinning, his microphone a staff of office before him, our modern totem. The prick. I wondered what to say.

'Er,' I managed. My mouth was dry.

He posed, winking at the audience. He was drenched in sweat. No wonder, if this was the best he could do. He ought to leave this sort of thing to the BBC. They've been doing it for years. Better. 'Isn't it true that you have the gift of . . . divvieing antiques?'

'Er, well. Sort of.'

'No?' More winks. He was leaning confidentially on the seat in front of me, grinning round. Smarmy sod. Just how deep my dislike went I only just then discovered. Maybe I disliked Joan too. Why didn't he *look* at me, for God's sake? Maybe broadcasters are trained not to. 'This divvieing. What is it, actually?' Twinkle twinkle midget star. Somebody sniggered. He spun towards the sound grinning hopefully. 'Do I have to slip you a fiver to find out? Ha ha ha!'

'Well,' I said, looking nervously round. 'Well, you touch an antique. And it lets you know if it's genuine.'

'Is that it?' He strode about the aisle. 'Hey, folks! Challenge time! Trial by antique! What say, hey?'

He paced threateningly, chatted up elderly shoppers, got an indistinct ripple of applause.

'Bring out those baubles!' Del commanded. He addressed the microphone. 'By kind permission of Mayor Carstairs – my good friend Oliver! Hi, Mayor! Okay up there? Ha ha ha ha! – we can test the regalia of this great and ancient town!'

His voice had sunk to a sepulchral hollowness, clearly deeply-felt reverence. He grabbed my arm. I shook him off. He tried to pull me up. I wouldn't go.

'Bring the Great Mace, please!'

Sweating heavier. I thought, what's the big deal? Okay, I admire it – huge, gold and silver, a John Flaxman design. Paul Storr, one of the greatest precious-metalsmiths, made it about 1838. Not long, as antiques go, but weighing heavy, adorned with gems. Too ornate, but that only makes it more praiseworthy. How can you fail to admire . . . ? I watched the macebearer come. A stout old military bloke, decorated from a million battles.

He stood at attention in his grand livery, the Great Mace on his shoulder. There's a proper way of holding them.

'Here it is, Lovejoy.' Del Vervain, his awed gravedigger's voice. 'Listeners. Honestly most sincerely! You should see the majesty of this great emblem of authority, nay local civic pride!' His voice caught. 'Most sincerely. The atmosphere is electric. Lovejoy, the, ah, divvie man will prove that the stupendous array of silver plate, jewellery and golden, ah, emblems, which we so admire, nay, applaud, are truly genuine repositories of this ancient Borough!'

'Er, Del,' I said. He was talking codswallop.

'One moment, Lovejoy.' He was milking this. As on edge as any bloke I'd ever seen. Too sweaty, in fact. 'This, listeners, is a moment to savour. Lovejoy is one of those special people – I mean that most sincerely – will enter a mystic trance—'

'Er, no, Del,' I tried. He raised a restraining hand.

'Lovejoy. Take your *time!* Listeners. You should see Lovejoy's intense gaze as he enters that zone of ineffable mystery, where the spirits roam in search of the splendours of antiquity . . .'

Emma was chuckling. Grimes was snoring. Forage was nodding behind his spectacle with episcopalian gravity. Del Vervain was going on and on, however I tried to interrupt. Pillock.

He posed, frowning. 'I'm sure some might think Lovejoy is pretending. After all, they say antique dealers try confidence tricks, even robbery. But here in this ancient building we are privileged to see a trial of the truth . . .

The bearer was holding the Great Mace. I looked at it again, but only for show.

These things are usually precious, often silver gilt, emblems made to signify authority, whether royal, parliamentary, whatever. Essentially a posh stick. Each town has one. No use, of course. Symbols. Which really raises the question of what a genuine symbol is trying to be.

'. . . Lovejoy seems ready, folks! Finally willing his mind into that great abyss where the answers to life and death lie hidden. He will now, at this moment in time, touch the Great Mace, live! And will know whether this vital, nay holy, emblem of this great town's historic past, is genuine.'

'Well, yes, Del. Except the . . .'

'Ladies and gentlemen, listeners! The atmosphere is breathtaking.'

It wasn't. Grimes was snoring so loudly Marmalade Emma had to nudge him quiet. Forage looked grave. I saw a flea leap from his clothes on to Emma. I edged away another inch, touched the Great Mace. I nodded.

'What?' Del Vervain asked. He looked aghast. A couple of security people from the back were standing beside the mace-bearer, blocking the aisle. Everybody was looking. A security bloke in every aisle. By every doorway.

'Yes, Del. Lovely.'

'What?' he asked again. He looked round. Oliver was looking down, tense. Joan was on her feet, stepping forward. I could see Luna glancing in wonderment at Joan, at me. 'Fine?' He was thunderstruck. 'Fine?' he asked as if the word was new.

'Sure.' I paused, helpful. 'Want me to tell you a bit about

the silversmith? Actually, I think he sometimes went over the top in design. You see, silver has this terrific high refectivity . . .'

He went to pieces, tried to start an interview with the town crier, but it was no good. The show disintegrated. It was pathetic to see him trying to speak the sort of coherent gibberish he'd made famous, but failing worse with every bleat.

People began to drift. While the proceedings were still limping on, I nudged Marmalade Emma. The four of us made the ante-room, after a decoying exit through the main doors, and waded in to the grand nosh provided for the councillors. The buffet waitresses didn't say a word, just backed away from us at their clean and aseptic tables.

Well, I thought indignantly as Grimes woke and swigged the first bottle he could grab. Serves them right for rigging their crummy broadcast with a dummy Great Mace. They'd assumed I'd blurt out the astonishing truth, that it was a fake. Skilfully made, but still dud. Then presumably there'd have been consternation. Maybe an arrest? And a swift rise for Del's ratings. Pathetic.

'Here, Grimes. That wine properly chilled?'

'Not bad.' He dropped the empty, got another. Emma cackled. 'Here, son. We in trouble for nicking their victuals?'

'No, Emma,' I said, offering Forage a florentine. I can't resist them, though they're too small. 'They'll let us leave untrammelled.'

'Why?' Forage was stuffing his face, going down the line of filled glasses like a conjuror.

'I just feel it, Forage.' I could have asked why they'd brought me along to recognise the Great Mace for the fake it undoubtedly was. I'd seen it on display not less than eight months since. It had been genuine then. So what had happened in the meantime? Oliver had been Mayor almost a year. I said nothing.

Lovejoy's friends had grown too big, that's what. And I'd fallen among thieves. And listened too often to the lies of fair ladies.

We finished our repast, and departed with dignity.

Chapter 32

'Lovejoy!' the old lady across the road trilled. 'I've been waiting for you!'

Miss Turner. Just when I thought it was safe to go back into civilisation. She trotted over among the traffic, said good evening.

'They wouldn't let me in, dear.' She giggled. 'Three policemen stopped me. Aren't your policemen wonderful?'

That old one. Drinkwater hovered in the brightly-lit doorway of the Moot Hall. Cradhead stood with him, observing life's rich pageant. All roads led here tonight. Which raised the question why. Three and two make five. Eleven Borough security guards. Sixteen? For a radio broadcast? Whose arrest did they have in mind?

'Miss Turner, may I present Marmalade Emma . . .' I did the honours. Miss Turner said she was charmed. My lot said how do.

'Lovejoy has been most helpful,' she told them. 'My line-age goes back three centuries. In East Anglia! Delightful!' She fluttered her lovely old eyes. 'We might be related.'

Great. 'Not me, love. I'm not from—'

'I need more help, Lovejoy. Some of my English ances-tors were soldiers, but—'

'Ah, well. If your regiment's after 1660, you're quids in

298

– lucky. After the Restoration, we began a standing army. The PRO has some War Office soldier's records. And the Imperial War Museum, the National Army Museum, regimental museums dotted about. Regiments often started up in taverns and inns, so . . .'

Suddenly I thought, what am I *doing*? I was lecturing to three derelict alkies and a nut, on the rainy pavement, splashed by passing motors, glared at by a cluster of peelers. I must be out of my skull.

'Interesting point, Lovejoy,' Forage interposed, removing his spectacle. 'St Cat's House *does* have Army births and weddings from 1761, but I'm a critic of their records. Madam, you must devise a plan . . .'

With sinking heart I recognised Forage's papal grandeur. It can go on for days. 'Look, folks,' I said quickly. 'Here's a couple of notes. Go to Woody's caff. Nosh up.' I threatened Emma with a fist. '*Before* you swill yourselves stupid in the four-ale bar. Okay?'

Emma fell about laughing. This is typical. Whenever I try to assert myself, women and babes roll in the aisles. They can always spot a dud.

'Lovejoy.' Luna was suddenly there, blazing. 'I want words with you.'

'Hello, Lune. Marmalade Emma and Miss Turner, may I present the Lady Mayoress—'

'*Lovejoy!*' Lune stepped away a pace. '*If* you please.'

And suddenly I'd had enough. Her and Oliver up to their political tricks. Del Vervain up to his, Joan to hers. Connie Hopkins vanished. Rye Benedict dead, murdered by somebody who'd stood chatting all pally. Prammie Joe battered, left for maggots in a marsh. And me summoned like a dog. I'd been introducing her to my friends, for Christ's sake.

'Forage,' I said. 'Your specs. Why're they duff?'

'Ah, Lovejoy. Thereby hangs a tale. I'm *persona non grata* at the eye clinic. No fixed abode, you see.'

'Same as Emma's teeth?' I glared at Luna. 'No health provision for folk without an address?'

'Lovejoy.' Lune was out of her depth, but still apoplectic.

'I'll see you right,' I told them. 'Miss Turner, Grimes. Tell Emma if you've secret bunions. Meet you later.'

Dispiritedly I watched them go. From one sponger I'd worked my way up to four. At least I'm consistent. Pathetic.

'Lovejoy!' Lune exploded. 'You deliberately wrecked—'

'Meaning I didn't do as I was told?' I'd have clouted her, except ploddites skulked in the Moot Hall doorway. 'Lune, I'm done with doing what everybody else expects.'

'You never do what anyone expects, Lovejoy.'

'Never?' I said bitterly. 'Or just hardly ever?'

'You realise what this means, Lovejoy,' Luna rasped, keeping her voice down. 'I withdraw, forthwith. Return every penny by nine o'clock tomorrow morning. Or I'll have every stitch off your back, every antique in that load impounded. And you arrested for fraud.'

Her hand was trembling as I reached out and shook it. 'A deal, lady. Now sod off. Leave me alone.'

She stormed away, her heels clicking on my eardrums. I called up the steps of the Moot Hall, 'Cheers, Drinkwater.' Don't know if he heard.

Hurrying now and uneasy, I went to the Ship Inn to see if there was any word of Connie. Nothing. I phoned Margaret Dainty, then seven other dealers. Nil. I tried Sandy's number, then remembered where he'd be. Music was coming from Sir Isaac's Walk. I took a short cut, so I'd guessed right.

Sandy and Mel were doing their dance in the precinct square. It has a covered way, glass roof and ball lights.

I don't think Mel likes these lunatic events, but Sandy claims his public demands. Tonight they'd hired a harpsichord girl from the music school. She wasn't bad, but her instrument was made from a kit. I can't think of anything more ridiculous than a prefabricated harpsichord – except maybe two blokes dancing a gavotte watched by two tramps and a dog. I waited for the end.

'Didn't you *exult* at my minuet, Lovejoy?' He wore a glittering lametta sheath dress, a cavalier hat with genuine ostrich feathers. Mel was dressed as a Spaniard, all black and high-heel boots. I just can't understand two people spending a fortune to look barmy. It's beyond me.

'Great, Sandy.' You've got to go along or he weeps himself into a tantrum. 'Where's Connie?'

'The trouble is, Lovejoy,' he said, adjusting his hat in a mirror. 'This mall's lighting is absolutely *criminal*. Don't you agree?'

'Absolutely, Sandy. Bad lighting. Seen Connie?'

He smiled with malice. 'You've been positively *rummaging* in the Lady Mayoress for *weeks*, Lovejoy—'

Mel groaned in horror. '*Don't*. I've not had my tablet.'

'Perhaps you could . . .' Sandy tittered wickedly '. . . persuade her to wheedle better illumination.'

'Maybe, Sandy. Seen anything of Connie Hopkins?' The bad feeling about her had started out a mere foreboding. Now, I was scared, my hands wet.

'Promise you'll *stir* Lusty Luna into *passionate* action?'

Mel shrieked, hid behind the harpsichord. Good veneer, correct for 1750. Repro people take a lot of trouble.

'Promise,' I said. 'More lights. Incidentally, heard anything about Connie Hopkins, Sandy?'

He came closer, fluttered his eyelashes roguishly. The musician girl turned a page, oblivious. She was nodding slightly to some inner rhythm as she read the notes, warming up for the next gavotte. She had a small torch for better light.

'You're third in the queue, Lovejoy. *Naughty* Connie! Dear Gunge, Acker Kirwin. Now you! *Do* ask the bitch where she gets her perfume. She had a terrible row with her ladyfriend. Yesterday.' He whispered, 'Was it jealousy? Connie's ladyfriend's been seeing a lot of Big Frank's Jenny.'

'*Sandy!*' Mel screamed in a temper. And that was it. Sandy rushed back. The harpsichord started up again as I headed for the Priory ruins. The whole town centre is only a mile square, for Roman reasons. Not far to go.

I was startled to find Cradhead jogging alongside me. On his own.

'Thought Keystone Kops went in groups,' I said.

'Any idea, Lovejoy?' He wasn't breathless. 'Connie Hopkins.'

That slowed me to a quick walk. I looked at him sideways in the occasional street lamps.

'Not much. You?'

The old aerodrome was out. Not after sussing Oliver's scam at the Moot Hall. I had enough trouble, without getting help from the Plod. The Priory was too frequented, what with the amateur drama people being Othello in every nook and cranny most nights. The dollop broker's school? That was the likeliest place. The Mayor's grounds? Too dangerous, seeing that Luna knew nil. But it was Oliver. Takes a thief to know one.

Too long replying. 'I'm not sure, Craddy.'

'You're off to find Gunge?'

'Yes,' I lied. 'At the Priory ruins.' No lag then. I was proud of my swiftness in deception.

'Don't lie, Lovejoy. I believe Connie Hopkins is being confined against her will. By whom, I don't know. For why, I don't know. But hereabouts, in the Eastern Hundreds.'

The old mill? No – Luna and I earned our squeaky clean alibis there, hadn't we?

'Go your own way, Lovejoy, eh?' These peelers kill me. I'm never anything, except alone. 'Which ladyfriend did Sandy mean?'

'Ask him, Big Ears.' Cassandra Clark, Marvella?

My final shot. I offed through the narrow town lanes like a rabbit. I'd wasted too much time on negatives. I shot down Eld Lane, past the corner pub – still heaving behind its smoke-frosted windows – and by the old almshouses, the steep lantern-lit steps through the Roman wall. And to the Priory.

Visitors are astonished to find spectacular remains of a great priory, somehow secluded in the very heart of a town. There's a new priory – gruesome mustard-coloured Victorian replica – in the grounds. I suppose it sounds like a scenic garden, all laid out really posh. It isn't. It's as close to waste as land can get. The ruins are behind a low wall, set among scrubby trees and gravestones. Occasional winos swill and murmur, desperate lovers gasp deep among weeds and bits of old bicycles. The perimeter consists of small shops that face out on to the street, a semi-derelict railway siding, and that little thoroughfare I mentioned, where The Great Marvella and Geronimo live. It's an ancient part of town. Not spooky, not really.

Except tonight the Priory was empty. No rehearsals. Just a clink of a bottle somewhere among the gravestones. Smoke from clean wood. Jake must be in. He's a hitch-hiker, Norwich to Bradwell eleven times a year. Got to do this barmy pilgrimage four hundred times before he dies. He's thirty-one, done over a hundred so far. Work it out.

'Jake?' I blundered forward. The ruins are set low. The ancient monks had fish there.

'That you, Lovejoy?'

He's too cunning to let firelight show, in case a bobby comes a-strolling. He might be near the old ruin's looming gateway. How come ruins always have gateways standing, when their roofs and walls are tumbled? Odd, that.

'You scared me, Lovejoy.' Filth conveys status. Nothing so convincing as a tramp's dignity. 'Thought you was the Plod.'

'Oh, aye.' There's never anywhere to sit. 'How many, Jake?'

'Eight. Three to go this year. I'm on schedule.'

He had a fire, packing cases. I warmed my hands.

'I'm searching for Connie Hopkins, Jake.' I described her, antique dealer who worked the Arcade, empty shop on East Hill. 'Just wondered if you'd clapped eyes, Jake, you working the Ship tavern a few doors up.'

'Blonde tart? Didn't you have your feet under her table?'

'That's private.'

He chuckled. 'Saw her when I woke yesterday.' He nodded towards the top road, over the little wall. 'With that snake tart.'

'Vell?' There was no light from Vell's sparsely furnished parlour. I could see. 'She went in?'

'Went off in a motor. Some tits on that Vell tart, eh?'

'Mmmmh.' Jake wakes at teatime, then retires sloshed out of his mind at two in the morning. So, five o'clock, give or take. 'Hear anything, Jake?'

'No. Just them two birds rowing. Couldn't hear what.'

Sandy said, having words with her ladyfriend. Connie, a special friend of Vell's? I'd assumed somebody else.

'Ta, Jake. If you hear, eh?' I went off through the trees and regained the narrow side street, pausing under the lamps.

Behind, Jake's overgrown grounds of the ancient Priory. Here, the shops and town proper began. Through there, the busy town bus station through the Roman wall. To the right a Congregational church hall of antique red brick. Facing, the pawnbroker's, florist's, the stairs up to Vell's barn. As unmysterious as you can get. This was once consecrated ground in old times.

'Hello?' I buzzed Vell's door, shouted like a pillock when nobody answered. 'Hello? Vell?'

Nothing visible through the letterbox. Just the oblique shaft of light from the streetlamps showing the stairs, the door ajar at the top. Nothing. Except Vell had no real friends that I knew in the district. And where was Vell? My head throbbed. There was an aroma, oddly offensive, as I looked through the post-flap. Couldn't place it, put it out of my mind.

One of the nine public phones in the precinct was still working when I got there. Sandy and Mel had gone. Only the dog remained, forlorn under the glass canopy. I rang everybody I could think of, including Vell's number. Answerphones, nothing. Then I had a stroke of genius, and rang my own number. They give you one of those bleep things, comes with the set. There were three messages. A dealer from Bedfordshire offering an Act of Parliament timekeeper. (A five-shilling tax was slapped on clocks in 1797; taverners hung these wall clocks in taprooms. They're highly sought-after with their big wood face and thin body. They don't strike or chime, so count as 'timepieces' proper.) He'd missed my boat, but had timed and dated his message. A pal.

Second was The Great Marvella, saying she was going away and would I miss her. She'd call in a couple of weeks. She gave an address in Stourbridge, Worcester. Some snake farm, I shouldn't wonder. I'd almost hung up, having got the important negative I wanted, when I heard another voice. Luna, whispering. She shouldn't have said those horrid things. She would come to the cottage as soon as, etc, etc. Nothing from Connie. I set off through the rain to find Gunge, and ran him to earth in the Welcome Sailor about an hour before closing time.

The Welcome Sailor is a traditional East Anglian pub. That is, it's been on its last legs for nine centuries. You couldn't insure it to save your life. The joke being it'll outlive Lloyd's of London. Creaking doors hang longest.

The regulars were relieved I'd arrived. As well they might. Gunge's idea of tactful interrogation is to lift you up into his bearded face and stutter, 'S-S-Seen Connie?' We leant on the taproom bar, safe from ears. He'd had no success, I could tell from the slow tear that rolled down into his vast beard. I'm quick at clues.

'Listen, Gunge. We're going to take a risk.' I waited respectfully while he wiped his eyes with an arm like a hairy log. 'I have an idea where – Gunge. Put me down.' He lowered me and undid his fist so I could move. 'Where we might *look*.'

'Let's go now, Lovejoy.'

'We need a mob, Gunge. Not just you and me.'

He stared, the astonishment of the giant. People his size simply can't understand. They've never been pushed around.

'I have an idea she's in an old school. Eastern Hundreds. Trouble is, it's a dollop broker's.'

'Where? How many we need?'

More giant think. Notice he didn't doubt his ability to storm Dollop Towers? I was shaking in my shoes.

'Within thirty miles. Famous, now closed. Luna knows. But we'll have to be mob-handed. Twenty, thirty. An army.' I felt weary.

'We ring the fire brigade, Lovejoy,' he rumbled. 'That gets us past the door, see?'

I nearly fell into my ale. 'Fire brigade?' I went all casual. Gunge having an idea was a shock. 'Right. I know a torcher—'

'No, Lovejoy,' his bass vibrated. 'A fire might hurt Connie. We only *say* there's a fire.'

Typical giant idiocy. 'Gunge,' I reasoned. 'We need the hoses, the shambles of it. Otherwise the gatemen will—'

'No, Lovejoy.' I was tired of No, Lovejoy. 'We're firemen, see?'

Narked, I drew breath to correct this hulk's tardy thought processes, then exhaled without a word. I felt redundant.

Chapter 33

'Sure it's the right place, Lune?'

'Don't keep *on*, Lovejoy.' Luna was getting snappier by the minute. 'The eighth *time*.'

The van was stiflingly hot. I was soaked inside the fireman's suit. The helmet alone weighed a ton. Mine was yellow, Gunge's white. Was one of us a pleb, the other a boss? I'd begun to lose heart as I recognised the faint outline of the red-brick gatehouse in the headlights. The tiny van had no space for anyone except Gunge in the front. Me and Luna rattled around like peas in a tin all the way. Now, we were concealed in a layby about a mile off. Apart from a couple of disappointed snoggers who'd left when we disturbed their tryste-spot, we went unnoticed.

One in the morning. Sandy had kitted us out. He always knew somebody, this time a theatrical widow who catered for local thespians at mind-boggling prices. He'd enjoyed himself, asking could he be the first to light Gunge's fire, or be the damsel on the burning balcony, all that. He wears you out just listening.

'I mean,' I pleaded, 'what if it's a real school. See what I mean?' It had been such a great idea in the Welcome Sailor.

'It's the right place.' Luna had her woman's voice on. 'The school Jenny Calamy went to, Cassandra Clark,

Connie Hopkins. Credit me with sense, Lovejoy. It's quite bad enough to be a *scandal*. The excuses I had to make! A trace of scandal is enough to—'

'Silent, please,' Gunge rumbled.

Quiet descended. Not even Luna would argue with Gunge. I fidgeted, played I Spy with myself – only you can't cheat when you're your opponent. I tried to remember 'The Green Eye of the Little Yellow God', but couldn't do the first stanza. I hummed 'She went and married a lawyer,' until Gunge swivelled to look back, whereon I shut it. It seemed hours before he spoke.

'Ten past. Phone.'

'You, Lovejoy.' Luna passed me a handphone. Women are skilled shirkers. Nine nine nine, and the nasal twang saying emergency fire ambulance or police.

The fire office sounded itching to go. I made myself breathless.

'The school – you know the old Sampney Young Ladies Academy? It's all afire. Come quick. There's . . .' I gasped, cried out, made a crackling noise, getting really worked up until Luna furiously snatched the phone, tapped it to mute.

'You're simply ridiculous!' she cried. 'I've never *known* . . . Overdoing every single thing.'

'Shush.' Gunge wound the van window down.

We listened. The countryside was silent as only East Anglia's rural quiet can be. You could hear worms crawl. I heard a crinkly leaf skitter along the road. Grass gave faint groans. It would have made me sweat, except I was already pouring with the stuff.

Then in the distance a thin wahwah, instantly deafened out as Gunge turned the ignition and we roared off. I'd have had a pee from nervousness but for Luna. We careered between the tall hedgerows. Gunge took from his vast paunch a light, reached a hand out. I heard it clunk on to our roof as we zoomed along. An intermittent cobalt-coloured glow revealed that he'd nicked a Plod light. We were now a copmobile.

'There!'

Luna saw them cross the flyover, lights a-flash and sirens wailing. Gunge slowed to let the fire engines go, then accelerated so swiftly my face shifted on its bones. We tore along the lanes after them.

The school gates were already ajar. Gunge rolled us inside. Two security uniforms were there. The fire vehicles were already at the front door. Lights switched on. Somebody was looking out from a second-floor window, immensely blocking the light, shouting instructions, demands. A security uniform trotted alongside us. Gunge did an expert curve into the foliage.

'What the hell?' A bloke, young, cool enough to be armed.

'Keep clear, sir,' Gunge said, braking. 'Where's the fire?'

'What frigging fire?'

'Fifth-degree blaze, major casualties.'

I alighted, listening with admiration. God, Gunge was a better liar than me. I heard a scrabbling inside the van, saw the security man turn, and yelled, 'Do I signal for more help, sir?'

'Ascertain status first, Schuller,' Gunge rumbled.

'Very good, sir.' Schuller? 'This the way?' I demanded.

The security man was distracted by uproar from the house.

'Inspect residential perimeter, Schuller.' Gunge, curt.

Schuller. 'Yes, sir. How many resident?'

'Fourteen,' the man said. Reply by reflex.

The real firemen were calling, hoses unwinding. Christ, a searchlight. I swore. Who'd think? Like Bonfire Night. I'd no idea. Did every blaze get this? Fantastic.

'All residents mobile?' I barked. 'Lame? Wheelchairs?'

'No.' Instant again, therefore true.

'Schuller,' Gunge boomed. 'Keep that drive clear. More vehicles coming. How many entrances?'

Schuller, I muttered darkly, hurrying off. I'd give him Schuller. Made me sound like a Transylvanian cobbler from a Disney cartoon, I fiddled with my pathetic little Woolworth hand torch, stumbled off among rose bushes while the guard followed Gunge to the action.

A couple of minutes among the bushes watching the consternation develop, and I returned, knocked on the van's side, three long, one short.

'I'm ready, Lovejoy.' Luna slid into the driver's seat. She was in a policewoman's uniform, so fetching it made me wonder for a second about fetishes, uniforms, leather buckles.

'You look terrific, Lune. I'm off, then. Got my bag?'

She passed it. My ordinary clothes. 'Lovejoy. Be careful.'

But I was already eeling through the black night, falling over. Why didn't roots grow down, for God's sake? Roots are supposed to.

The side of the mansion seemed a mile long. A security bloke came round the far end as I reached there. I talked into a bleeper, like I imagined firemen do, and barked a question about how many entrances. He hesitated, told me five. I told him to open the kitchen door, not let anyone else in.

'Understand?' I shouted, professional in a hurry.

'Right.' He unlocked the door. 'What the hell's going on?'

'Any signs of the oil fire?' I rasped, wishing I could go octaves down like Gunge. 'Straight ahead to the main hallway?'

'Oil? Er, I think so. Fire? There's no—'

'No lights. Fire risks, lights. Close it after me.'

I snapped an order, meet the senior officer at the front, and was inside and free. So he'd never even been inside, this security man. I trotted after my torch-beam.

Kitchens revolt me. I mean, they say even a cabbage screams. This one shone, chrome and steel on black. Marble floor. I stepped round the inner door, switched my lamp off, listened. The suspicious sod was hesitating out there. I could hear him, shuffling on the gravel. A torch-light shone in, roamed about a bit. Then he moved off. His sort gets on your nerves. I could feel the blighter thinking he should have demanded my pass.

Boots are problems. Socks are almost as difficult. Slippy on wood floors, fine on carpets. Outside came the distant hullabaloo of order, counter-order, disorder. Inside, somebody came downstairs, a woman's light tread.

'What is it?' a woman's voice called. Nobody I knew.

'The fire station.' Another, distant. 'Is there a fire?'

By the kitchen door was a wall cupboard, the sort you keep brooms in. I pulled the door, lifting it for possible squeaks, and stepped inside. But what excuse can a hidden fireman offer? I was soaked, enough sweat to put the bloody fire out without hose pipes.

Then the stentorian voice I knew. My favourite dollop broker. She must be a vision in curlers. 'Who heard a fire alarm?'

Five or six female voices denied hearing a thing. A man's boots clumped. A fire officer shouting, who was in authority?

A general search, I was done for. A walk-in freezer at the far end of the kitchen? No, ta. I'd seen too many mafia films to hide there. I could always nip out into the garden. What if the suspicious security man was lurking among the hydrangeas, the swine? I'd have to brazen it out, join the real firemen – except had Sandy's widow got the garb right? One wrong epaulette and I'd be exposed as a fraudster.

'You check, lady.' The fire officer was disappointed the entire place wasn't going up in flames. 'I'll run smoke tests.'

'Is that necessary? You can see quite clearly—'

'Regulations.' He wanted tea with a dash of Glenfiddich.

'I run the test, chief?' some hopeful bloke asked, concealed lust in his voice. I imagined a bevy of beauties on the staircase in fetching disarray, and swallowed. At least he could see them. I was stuck in a cupboard.

'I'll do it, Polkinghorn. Outside. Check the roof.'

Mutters of reluctant obedience, the low thunder of boots.

The voices receded. I risked opening the door slightly. Light fell obliquely in from the corridor. Silence. I wavered, put my boots on. I should have asked Gunge where they did smoke tests. Upstairs? Stairwells? I realised with a shock that I was silhouetted in the doorway, tiptoed out of the kitchen. Three steps up, I was in the hall, where I'd first met the dollop broker, among the stacked lentils and jerseys.

Dejection set in. Sweating, cursing, quivering, I stood like a lemon. The plan seemed so simple: get in, wait until quiet night sanded everybody's eyes, then find Connie. But with fourteen birds wafting about could they possibly keep a fifteenth imprisoned?

The question I hated: Was Connie still alive? Voices returned. I ducked under the stairs, a small cupboard with meters, gas, electricity. Wires everywhere. A couple of metal boxes hummed steadily. I kept well away, scrunged into a ball, switched my torch off, prayed.

'. . . country vandals ought to be tackled by the Goverment.' The grumbling fire officer.

'I agree,' gravelled Miss R. 'Flogging too good for them. None of my girls ever . . .'

'We'll check again in the morning . . .'

'I blame the parents . . .'

Talk, farewells, doors slamming, men distantly calling, engines starting. I prayed Gunge and Luna had got away, that Luna had done her rehearsed little act with the gateman. I was just congratulating myself when shock struck.

The women's voices approached. Lights in the hallway clicked on. More voices. Sets of feet slapped by slippers. The kitchen lights. Somebody filled a kettle, women talking. If I hadn't moved to under the stairs I'd have been caught. I almost fainted. Killed by a dozen birds in their private mansion.

'Right. Post mortem.'

The dollop broker clapped hands. Somebody said Mary and Eliza weren't here yet. There were shouted for, somebody finally going to fetch them. Cup clinked, saucers rattled. Midnight feast in the dorm.

'Versions, everybody.'

'I think I heard the sirens first, Miss Reynolds,' a voice offered. 'I called Maria.'

'I answered the security gateman's phone, Miss Reynolds. Fire engines had already entered the drive, and a police van. They ignored his signals to halt.'

'Norma. You're D site supervisor tonight. Any action?'

'None.' Norma was crisp. I imagined her in jodhpurs, riding crop and waisted tan jacket. Mustn't get the wrong side of old Norma.

'Carol.' Saying Carol's name was the nearest Miss Reynolds would ever come to cooing. 'You checked the electronics?'

'Nil for person activity, Miss Reynolds.'

The signal for relief all round. Except the mention of

electronics was worrying. I didn't want anybody probing my nook. Talk began, a few mild quips about the firemen's expressions, vandals who thought it funny to phone the fire brigade.

'We'll double Norma's watch. Patricia's next on call.'

Patricia groaned, but accepted her duty. They moved out, Miss Reynolds calling for two to come back this instant and clear away. She scolded them all upstairs just because they were a business partnership didn't mean the Sampney Ladies Academy encouraged slatternly behaviour . . . Sounds diminished, leaving me solitude.

D sites. D for dollop sites? Where constant nocturnal supervision was required? Very likely. Electronic surveillance, rotas of vigilants from within the mansion, not mere security hirelings. The gatehouse could be left to men, never part of the dollop broker syndicate.

It was simple. Headmistress, her school going into liquidation, has a ready-made team. Maybe their adoring daddies brought in the first dollops. Educated, socially elegant. And eminently trainable. Who would suspect a schoolhouse of being involved in international roguery? Playing host to the revenue of great robberies, storage of antiques filched from museums and country houses. Poor old Prammie Joe had died because he realised the Cornish Place stuff wasn't going abroad on the Thames barges, but somewhere inland. Here, in fact. But whose dollop was it? The killer's, that's who.

Which left the problem of Connie. She'd presumably been to this school. Wasn't that what Luna'd said, back in the van? And so had some other birds who were now into antiques. But some must be nurses, teachers, politicians. So?

Barefoot time. I got my socks off, edged out of the cubby hole, bumping my head with a blasphemy as I stood erect too quickly. Gloaming coming from the distant front door's side panels, but not enough to move by. A door slammed upstairs, some bird calling sorry. Silence.

Houses are queer places. Not only that. This was female, a nest of those unattainables. One on her lone's pretty formidable. But fourteen? Benign, the house seemed to be smiling, we ladies are caring, sweet. You have nothing to fear, Lovejoy. Oh, aye, I thought sardonically. That chestnut. Then why was I trembling, sweat maddening me down every sloping surface I possessed? I stood a second, moved across the spacious cold floor. Stairs curving up, me giving the bottom step a wide berth. I'm clumsy at the best of times. A door at the far side, shown by a single click of my torch. The damned thing blinded me. I got there, turned the handle. My boots were hung round my neck, instinct bringing them the safest way. I halted – what the hell had I done with the bag, my mufti clothes? Christ. I'd left it outside in the bushes somewhere. Or inside the broom closet? I heard a faint sound that scared me witless. It was me moaning in alarm.

Then I sussed myself. Typical. Four whole minutes I'd been standing in the semi-dark, hand on the door knob of this mystery room, about to go in and discover . . . what? Connie hanging, dead? Thoughts are only deceits, ways of avoiding doing. I stepped inside quickly. Not a sound. Closed the door after me. Darkness, wholesale. No windows, no light. Not even a wash of nightglow from a curtain edge. I fumbled the torch in my hand, and felt a faint reverberation. The place was vast, panelled. Only spacious cathedrals and banqueting halls do that. I switched it on.

Vast was right. For a country mansion, that is. Width, distance, length, a roof of lovely rafters. The panelled walls receded. It could have been an assembly hall, a decorated gymnasium. I guessed it once doubled as the dining room as well, in the way of private schools.

But it felt cold. Parquet flooring, polished. Round the dark oak-panelled walls were photographs. I moved forward, careful not to crash on my bum to bring the bevy down on me. The wall photographs showed schoolgirls by the dozen, the score, the hundred. Coloured, then black and white, then sepias. I inspected one – a daguerreotype, I could swear. The place was a mausoleum, the record of the Sampney Young Ladies Academy over the years. I shivered, cold. Nothing to cause a draught in the silent place. But it felt . . . tomblike. A shrine. Nothing living, except a vase of flowers on a central table – by Ince, I felt, smiling. It deserved better. A luscious mahogany dining table like that should have been living with people, not stuck here in this sepulture.

Now, you can't trust pictures – whether paintings, photos, or engravings. I mean, in 1644 our first-ever illustrated newspaper, the *Mercurius Civicus*, publishing engravings of Prince Rupert and his sworn enemy Sir Thomas Fairfax – different issues, same portrait. It turned up later as Prince Maurice, et al. No, pictures aren't trustworthy.

How old would Connie be? From her deception about that barmy astrophysics, I worked out a possible date, started along the lines of photographs. Maharajah's daughters were among the fresh faces, African nobility. It was weird, seeing the dress styles evolve through the decades, right from 1840 – something. Hockey matches, cumbersome skirts for tennis, punting in impossible but lovely high-neck, long-sleeved blouses properly covering every inch of forearm. Straw hats. One sad Indian girl wearing a black armband on Speech Day, bravely trying to smile, learning the Stiff Upper Lip first go, God help the poor little lass. Except she was long passed on.

The faces came closer. Now war-time, a group of girls

laughing fit to burst in Women's Land Army uniforms. One rolling up her sleeves, about to blow up a barrage balloon. Girls falling about as a mistress tried to stay sternly in control as shy soldiers manned their antiaircraft gun, crocodiles of Sampney Young Ladies filing past. VE Day, clownish celebrations. Long trestled tables on lawns, this mansion in the background, strolling dignitaries taking tea and cake.

Years moved nearer. I inched down the panels, flashing and peering. Brighter photographs, hints of variation in dress. A scarf here, a watch there. School plays, tableaux of improbable history. Scenes from Empire eased into Commonwealth. Faster changes as educational theories tumbled, to balls learning up into the current shambles. Lines of girls depressed at computers. Nervy teachers trying to look jocular at Last Day celebrations. Diploma lists.

My breathing felt funny. I was getting close. I knew it. The girls were modern now, dates recent. Bicycles, a motor cycle even. Sleeker motors parked by this mansion, now captioned Big School House. Foundation ceremonies, blokes in chains of office, improbable gleaming spades and sham trowels, breaking the sod, laying foundation stones.

Plays, even dances, standards tumbling as the years rattled numbers. One long school photograph, Miss Reynolds the headmistress looking moronic in a mortar-board and gown. Democracy wasn't going to raise its head at *her* Young Ladies Academy. Then the shortening. The school dwindled, few from overseas. The school uniform looked archaic. Biology laboratory's closure, Miss Reynolds smiling defiance at the camera. The last sixth-form physics class. Chemistry no more, as costly subjects bit the dust. One bright spot as the Academy launched a Grand Joint

Venture with somewhere else – a stiffly segregated arrangement of imitation smiles as two groups of school governors learnt the cruelties of double-entry accounting. Then the end game, desperate Sampney Goes It Alone photographs. One sad spurt of hope as a new boathouse was donated by a new up-and-coming local politician. Good old Oliver Carstairs! Luna not with him – before they were married? Hardly. She'd mentioned some troublesome daughter, wouldn't work or go to college.

The This Year's Intake pictures ended. The Academy dwindled, down to the last pained photograph. Jennifer Calamy, happy to be the smallest. It hurt – not that I loved my school; I hated the damned place. But these lasses and their teachers didn't seem to. Are all school photographs frauds? Dated some six years previous: Miss Reynolds, chin raised, among her charges. I could tell she'd determined to punish society for the degradation suffered by her beloved Academy. Her expression was no longer defiance. It was cold, aimed. Aimed out there, at the horrid world that had shredded her dream-time. At us. And us was anyone.

That final year was something. Parties, merriment, a veritable Waterloo Ball of devil-may-careness. And the ending, motors arriving, girls tearful on steps, parents shaking hands. A final cheque-donation ceremony but this time amid piles of packing cases, stacks of books, desks balanced. The hallway. A vigorous local politician, electioneering even as the crew ejected. Ubiquitous old Oliver.

The photographs ended in Favourite Memories. The last of the girls. Girls looking up from desks in bright sunlight, so lovelily young they pulled at your heart. The last team match, hockey, lacrosse. A dash of craziness at tiddleywinks, an illicit dorm party with – gasp at madcap naughtiness! – two bottles of beer and a bra on show, girls rolling in the aisles with laughter. Then one photograph I stared at closer.

A fancy dress party, with faces I knew. Connie Hopkins, close to tears, in a witch's cloak, pointed hat, astride a broomstick. Cassandra Clark, more mature, in a tricorn hat and gentleman's frockcoat, white flat cravat on black. Cromwellian, a Puritan? And a tiny girl, an executioner with an axe. In that get-up, was it Jenny Calamy? I peered at the names below the picture. Difficult with a torch, small lettering. E. C. Clark must be Cassandra. C. A. Hopkins the witch. Yes, J. E. F. Calamy.

How long I stood there I don't know. But now there wasn't any point in staying. Nor even, I realised, in keeping quiet. I only needed to know one thing now. And I could go. Time Cradhead and Drinkwater earned their cost-of-living adjusted monies. I walked away, switched the lights on. The place shrank, became sadder, unthreatening in the harsh glim.

Across the hallway, me putting the lights on as I went. God, but the lunacy of storing all those dated schoolbooks, desks, struck me more than ever as I made the kitchen and found more switches. What did Miss R hope to do, reopen the Academy with her ill-gotten gains? My bag wasn't in the broom cupboard. Sod it. I must have left it outside. You can't depend on things.

And, I noted bitterly, the bloody tea they'd brewed was cleared away. The biscuit barrels were sealed inside a glass-fronted press. I was really narked. Typical selfish women. No thought of an intruder happening by during the owl hours and feeling hungry. Oh no. I clattered the kettle, got it going, but the bloody tea was locked, and I can't make coffee to save my life. But there was a radio, and a smoke alarm. A smouldering hankie takes only seconds to do. Wake up, idlers.

They came at me mob-handed. By then I was sitting on one of their crummy stools, whistling along with the golden oldies. The fire alarm was shrilling its intermittent bat-squeaks. It set off others through the building.

'Anybody got the key to the grub?' I asked them while they stared. Miss Reynolds shoved through.

I was right. She *was* a fantastic sight. A nightgown big enough for four. No curlers, but perfection shouldn't be ruined. The girls were gorgeous, but threatening. Being a barefooted fireman saved me.

'Wait, please.' I counted them.

One or two had rounders bats, I saw uncomfortably. Twelve, thirteen, fourteen. I'd reached the total. Still no Cassandra Clark. No Connie, because she was being tortured, chained to a chair elsewhere. No Jenny Calamy. And of course no Vell – too poor to have shared in their exalted upbringing.

No more theories.

'Thank you, ladies,' I said. 'Could you call the police, Maria?' I didn't know which one she was, but I sounded as if I did. 'And waken those idlers at the gatehouse, will you, love?'

The kettle shrilled piercingly, adding to the din from the wireless and the smoke alarms. I'd be glad to get home.

Chapter 34

They gave me more than tea and a wad, as it happened.

It was like being in a beautiful assembly – it *was* being. The police still hadn't been called. Maria quelled the vigilantees outside by a terse call. No fire brigade. No blue lamps blinked on the lawns. It was three in the morning. Four sorts of cake on a silver gadrooned tray. I felt a hobo gone royal.

Miss Reynolds was holding forth in her private drawing room. She looked wrapped in a linen shroud. 'You see, Lovejoy, we give an essential service.'

The girls murmured, nodding. I liked Maria. She could nod to me any time she liked.

'Yes, I see that,' I said, to general relief.

'We're looking after a dollop of yours, for heaven's sake!'

'And I'm glad, Miss Reynolds. After seeing your organisation. Cast iron. I'm very pleased.'

More satisfied smiles. Only one lass yawned, and she'd tried not to. Infected, I yawned as well.

'The point is, Lovejoy, we manage well. On our own.' The silence hung. Heads moved, paused in mid-nod. 'We don't need partners.'

No dollop broker ever starves. They take virtually no risks. Company fronts, banks in Jersey or the Isle of Man, and they live the life of Riley. People with stolen goods have simply nowhere else to go. If a thief wants to be safe from arrest, he has to use a dolloper. Or take the staggering chance of burying the loot under his pal's shed. And we all know what happens to loot stashed with friends, right? It vanishes, along with the friends.

Something in my expression must have showed, because there was a faint stir. Any other time I would have sat mesmerised to watch so many birds stir, but I hadn't long. Forty hours since Connie went missing. I, no, Connie – had few hours left.

'We know how you antique dealers see us, Lovejoy.' Miss Reynolds was all prim. 'But somebody has to maintain standards. Morality is preserved here at Sampney Academy. We're proud to—'

'I need a phone,' I interrupted, to show whose side I was on.

Miss Reynolds nodded. I was given one from a wall compartment.

'Gunge? You there?' I went even redder, because he'd just answered. I'm hopeless on phones. Only Italians and Yanks have telephone skills. Genetics, I daresay.

'Found Connie?' the receiver rumbled. My hand vibrated.

'I think I know where she is, Gunge. The place near the Priory ruins. Upstairs. In the massage—'

'Marvella's? Where are you?' I heard Luna demanding, let me speak to him this instant and all that.

'Where you left me.' I fixed Miss Reynolds. 'Connie Hopkins isn't here. I've not searched, but—'

'What if she is?' Deep voices have more threat, haven't they.

'Then I'm wrong.' Blood drained from my face. All very well for me to be wrong. Connie would die. 'Am I, Miss Reynolds?'

Her face looked genuine. The girls' responses seemed so. One or two were asking each other questions, tilting their heads like they do when confidential.

'Connie Hopkins? No, Lovejoy. Is she why you're here?' She interrogated her lasses with sharp glances. They all looked back, shaking heads, wanting to ask what was going on.

'Everybody says no, Gunge.' Just me, trying to spread the responsibility. 'Go now.'

The phone burred. I looked about. I was sick of my fireman's uniform. I'd taken my helmet off. I didn't know whether to wait for Gunge to rescue Connie, or to get going myself. If this lot was having me on—

The doorbell went, one long peal. Again. Miss Reynolds gave an imperious flick of a finger. A lass scampered off, nightdress billowing about her form, making me swallow.

'Listen,' I told her. 'I need a lift. Can I have a motor?'

'To what purpose?' Miss Reynolds was a bargainer.

To the purpose of stopping one of your illustrious young ladies horribly murdering another of your IYL. I thought it, but could not say.

'Evening all.' Cradhead entered briskly, doing the thick copper joke. 'Bit much even for you, Lovejoy.'

He meant so many birds. I was up, beaming. 'Can you drive fast, Craddie? We've a way to go.'

'Fast as I like. Evening, ladies.'

Miss Reynolds came after, her bulk darkening the hall-way. 'Lovejoy. You will keep us informed, won't you? This establishment always had prided itself on the welfare of its young ladies. We shouldn't want anything untoward—'

My hate suddenly broke. I turned, thrust my face at hers. She recoiled, actually lifted her arm to ward off a blow. I never swung it.

'I just don't believe you never saw the plight of little

Connie Hopkins in your rotten school,' I heard myself say. 'Or realised the horror Cassandra Clark was planning. Keep your fucking standards, Headmistress. Find out what happens any way you can.'

Cradhead was alone, I saw. An unmarked motor car. He set a siren going somehow, me saying left, head for town.

'Anything to tell me, Lovejoy?' he asked conversationally as he roared and braked, battling the narrow lanes with swift gear changes. 'Seeing you've told the whole school.'

We were on the trunk road before I recovered enough to think. 'Do us a favour. Tell them not to nick Gunge's van for speeding.'

He called on a squawk box. 'Description?'

Whoops. I cleared my throat, looked at the speeding night. 'Sort of Bill box, actually. Blue light.'

He inhaled, gathered himself. 'It's a phoney police van, lads. Let it through. Follow—' He glanced at me for confirmation. 'Do not detain.'

I asked if this frigging wheelbarrow couldn't go any faster. He set his mouth in a thin line, and drove on, grimmer than before.

The town seemed derelict, empty. But that was only night's hand, cold over everything. The traffic lights, changing for no traffic to obey, always gives me the spooks. And that part of town, one of the oldest, never was Piccadilly. Like I said, it's got old buildings antedating the Tudors.

No light in the upper storey where Marvella held her rejuvenation clinics, or what, while her pal's snake eyes stared.

'She has a snake,' I told Cradhead. 'Watch out.'

'Snake snake, old chap?' he asked.

'Real. It's enormous. In a cage.'

Gunge had barely arrived. He was trying the door. Two

Old Bill cars were winking blue fractiousness, five or six uniformed bobbies milling uncertainly. They hadn't been told what brain cells to use – always assuming, of course. They're taught to surge to no effect in basic training. They stared at me, a barefooted fireman in part of a uniform.

'Break it, lads,' Craddie said.

Neurones chugged into life on command: break it.

They leapt and crushed the door in, stood back with pride as me and Cradhead bounded up the stairs after Gunge's massive bulk ripped on and through. He was so worked up he didn't put the lights on. I did, knowing where the switches were. Cradhead noticed that, said nothing. The constabulary came thundering after.

'Phew. Christ.'

The stench was appalling. Nothing in the sparse outer room. Nothing really in the massage room, the long upper storey with its beams and plain ancient walls. I was struck by the curious resemblance to the chapel-like form of the place.

'That's where she held her.'

One chair, plain wood, still with its auction number on it. Ordure, excrement, urine stained the poor old thing. Quite good, just mid-seventeenth century, when chair-making became a craft separate from village joinery. Basically a chair in medieval joinery style, panel back with a carved crest, flat seat, plain front legs neatly turned. Its arm supports were missing. I saw those, crudely sawn off and chucked against the wall. Chain links trailed to new iron rings set in the wall. Sampney taught its young ladies all manner of skills. Maybe she'd practised, I thought queasily. On what? On whom?

'Lovejoy?' Cradhead asked, wondering.

'She kept Connie here, chained. Forty-eight hours was her goal. I knocked some time since, no answer.'

'Search the place, lads,' Cradhead called. The uniforms plodded downstairs, meeting another load coming up. He exclaimed in exasperation. 'Well, Lovejoy?'

Consecrated. This place was not a church exactly, but a Meeting House. I was looking at it. A prerequisite. The Witch-Finder General used holiness like a net. Was this the selfsame holy place where the witch trials were held? I didn't know enough to be certain. But the door to this upstairs hall was original. And that horrible chunk anciently cut out of it, like a cat flap, clumsily repaired with wrong beechwood by some nerk. For the familiar, the gremlin spirit that accompanies a witch. That's why Vell had gone, maybe knowing something evil was about to happen. Maybe her message to me was a kind of warning.

'The Priory, Craddie.' The one place left. 'She's there.'

'Why?'

Because Connie would be too ill, after over forty hours chained to a chair in her own filth, maybe maimed or battered, to walk anywhere. Had her kidnapper helpers? Like, say, Acker Kirwin, who'd killed Connie's business partner Rye at the mill? I wasn't sure. I was already clattering downstairs, thrashing my way through the useless Plod in Gunge's wake. I said nothing. Forty-four hours. Four left. It would be dawn when Connie died.

'Jake!' I yelled, tearing across the narrow street into the ruins. 'Jake! It's me, Lovejoy!'

Like an idiot I'd forgotten my torch. I realised I was still barefoot when the churchyard path started hacking my feet. I've a brain like lightning. Gunge crashed ahead. Somebody running with me among the old overgrown gravestones shone a lamp. Others took up the cue. Somebody with sense rushed along the street to the main Priory gate, and now shone torches into the steep ruins from there. Cromwell's men, Fairfax and his lot, had crunched this religious foundation in the Great Civil War. It had stayed crunched.

'Go right, Gunge,' I called, still yelling for Jake.

But the fire was out, cold some time. No Jake, presumably wanting a quiet night, or starting off early to notch another trudge to Norwich.

'Lovejoy?' Gunge, tears a-trickle, looking at me. 'What've they done with her?'

'Wait.'

A plodmobile, its driver brighter than the rest, drove in from the street below. Its beam heads shone through the elder and birch. Surreal. Browns, creams, russets, of the gaunt ruins stretched into the night sky. Scrubby little shrubs clung to the mortar, hung over the toothy remains of arches. Pillars always stay last, don't they. Eighteenth-century gravestones, several dozen. Connie could be in any one. Or not. Could we search them all, underground vaults, in, what, three hours? It had been an enormous Priory, supporting scores of religions. They'd had fish-pools for Fridays, two wells . . .

Wells. I looked up, astonished to discover rain teeming on my upturned face, oblique light catching the drops as they came at me out of the night sky. Wells. I wish I'd asked Therla's friend Josh more, fought the library harder for a book about the Witch-Finder. I'd had time, once. No time now.

In the old days, they'd caught the poor old crones, the so-say witches. Strapped them to a chair. Tortured, as a matter of course. Kept them awake. Extracted confessions. Then, forty-eight hours later, they'd 'swum' them. Float equalled guilt. Drown, innocence. Water. You needed water.

'She's here, Gunge. In a well. Or in the fishpools.'

'Fishpools are dry here, sir. The wells aren't.'

I stared at the tall constable. Cradhead asking him details,

'I come painting here, sir,' the constable said, embarrassed. 'The fishpools dry four or five times a year. Like now.'

'Lovejoy. What wells?'

'The abbots had wells. The Colne's half a mile off, downhill.'

Cradhead started calling orders. Uniforms rushed off. More cars came, more lights. Somebody rigged up spotlights – in the wrong places, of course. Gunge was like a mad thing, tearing aside the great gravestones, anything that possibly might be a well-covering, blubbering in panic that infected us all. The tall constable came with me.

We wasted an hour. They'd put out a call for Elizabeth Cassandra Clark, but that only warns miscreants to get the hell out. Some hopes. Wet through, worn out, I found myself at Jake's cold fire.

And finally began to think. Jake usually seemed to camp hereabouts. Never up slope. Never down slope, below the last level of wall. Yet he'd be just as well hidden there as here – and he could use the old crumbled Priory as a windbreak for his sack tent. Yet he camped here. I borrowed the copper's flashlamp.

The ashes of a good dozen fires, Jake-style, were within twenty feet. Why?

Because he forever brewed up. Find a tramp, find a brew. For which you need water. If fishpools dried often, you'd need a well. Shopkeepers on the street wouldn't give a tramp like Jake the time of day, let alone fill his billycan.

'Here, Craddie,' I yelled. Within yards of where I was.

You go in rings, make circles to search. It was a patch cleared of vegetation that gave it away. A gravestone about six feet long by three wide in the undergrowth, covered loosely by brambles. I hauled them aside. They came easily, which is something brambles never, ever do. They cling and rip your hands. I once rescued a blackbird in my own bramble-riddled hedge from a cat. The blackbird flew off without a word of thanks. I got cut to blazes.

A patch of earth, a crescent, scoured clean of vegetation. Pure dark earth. I tried shoving it, calling. 'Connie? Connie?' Then pulling. I tried knocking on it. Tramps must be tough, if they do this all the time. I was having another go when I got lifted, literally lifted and lobbed aside. Gunge bent, grabbed the stone and flipped it over, nearly driving the constable into the ground like a tent peg.

'Lights! Lights!' Cradhead was shouting.

Big size twelves crushed the earth about my face. I peered over the edge of the well, down. Down into the face of Connie, alive, looking up.

'Lovejoy?'

Inaudible. She was trying to croak out my name, but only managed to move her lips. She was tied to something in a sitting position, maybe on a stool, hands behind her back. Her hair was matted about her face. She was breast-deep in water. A dead rat floated by her shoulder.

There were ominous marks on the well's walling. The stones were shiny to a point some two feet above her head. Even as I gaped down into the fetid chasm, it seemed to me the water rose a fraction.

'We're here, love. Have you out in a trice, eh?'

Then people were bawling for ropes, stand aside, get ladders, and fire engines were wahwahing about the ruins. I only hoped they didn't think it was me this time, or I'd be for it. Suddenly I felt so tired, got up and stepped away. It's times like this I wished I still smoked.

'They found her, then,' a woman's voice said, casual. 'Thanks to you, Lovejoy, I hear.'

A shrug. 'I'm thick. Should have been hell of a sight faster.' Then I looked round, keeping my footing as the Plod milled uselessly about.

'Elizabeth Cassandra Clark, I presume.' I thought a moment, managed dully. 'Descendant of Elizabeth Clark, witch?'

'That's right, Lovejoy.' She looked so pretty and assured. Women never lack confidence, do they? It's us blokes lose heart at the ways of the wicked world. Women are in the thick of things, enjoying it all, good and bad. 'Of course, one hopes Connie Hopkins may not survive even yet. I rather put her through it.'

'Aye. Along the same time-honoured lines.'

'Why not?' Cassandra looked almost winsome. 'Her ancestor murdered mine. He was the most repellent specimen of the human race. Connie deserved at least this.'

She watched as some stalwart fireman was lowered into the well on an impossible array of ropes, pulleys screeching. She chuckled prettily. So very lovely.

'I had to send poor Rye flying – took his little belaying pin out when he least expected it. Very appropriate, don't you think? Death by flying, for Connie's friend?'

'No, love. You can't go about killing folk.'

'But one can, darling, when necessary.' I felt Cradhead come and stand listening. 'Joseph Godbolt's time had come. It was so easy, to become his prison visitor. I was actually fond of him.' She laughed. 'You see how deluded you can become? Fond! Of the spawn of a hanging judge?'

'Connie, though. Your schoolfriend.'

'Don't worry, Lovejoy. I shall get her. You can't imagine the temptation! The times I almost ended her life at the Academy! Only tradition held me back.'

'You still have no right, Cassie,' I said doggedly.

Her eyes filled. She leant and kissed me gently.

Jonathan Gash

'Poor Lovejoy. Always wrong. Knows all, knows nothing.'

Then she drew a knife out of her sleeve, and stabbed me. I looked about, puzzled, thought hey, hang on, then started to die.

Chapter 35

The fact that there was a woman in the bed opposite amazed me. As soon as was I able I asked the nurse, why I was in a woman's ward.

'There's no such thing nowadays,' she scathed. 'How long since you were in hospital?'

'Two years.'

'Things change.' She was gone.

You never see a nurse coming towards you, do you? Only receding at a rate of knots. Where the hell are they all going? Off-duty, I suppose. Sister spent all her waking hours at her desk doing the nurses' Off-Duty Rota, as they cheerfully call their on-duty rotas. You never see the same nurse twice, either. But the noise in hospital's the same. Clash, bang, wallop. All night long the din of nurses playing cymbals. Sirens concentrate on the forecourt below your window. They have lifts that sound like the Brigade of Guards. The trolleys and gurneys whine shrilly, gnats in your earhole the livelong night. Wheels squeak, patients snore and groan.

By the fifth day I was on quite good terms with the woman opposite, in for something excruciating. She was delighted to learn I was the one the papers were on about. She was less excited when the police started taking statements. Several times she asked me what I'd done. Then she went home, made well by some doctoral mismanagement.

Cradhead came to stare about and make oblique references to criminal charges, forgery. Drinkwater never came once, not even to gloat. Miserable sod wouldn't know sympathy if he fell over it.

Early on I'd told a hurtling nurse to clear a table for the flowers all my mates would be sending. She said, 'Clear one yourself!' and sprinted on to rendezvous with her next percussion section. I did, my side hurting from physiotherapy. And waited for the stream of visitors who'd come and give thanks for my deliverance, praise my astuteness, rejoice that I'd tottered from the brink of death.

And waited.

Wai . . . . ted.

It was only in the second week, refused phone access by your friendly surgeons in collusion with your friendly police, the penny dropped. I began to smile. I knew what my friends were doing. They were ringing in to check on my progress, but warning the nurses not to give It away. And I knew what It was.

Surprise party. They'd all jump out of the woodwork the instant I got sprung. Then it would be the inevitable tussle for my body, the women giving me the hard time that I loved deep down. The deeper and downer the better.

'What are you smiling at?' a nurse cried, charging past.

'Nothing, Nurse,' I called, beaming.

'Why've you no flowers, Lovejoy?' I got next morning.

'Get on with you,' I rebuked fondly.

And the great moment dawned, two weeks to the day. The surgeon came round with his entourage, peered shortsightedly at my belly, said hmph, asked Sister did Lovejoy do his physiotherapy.

'Yes, sir. On the hour,' she lied slickly.

'Rum name.' The surgeon strolled affably on. 'He can go.'

Sprung! I dressed, got taken down to Reception. There I waited, smiling knowingly. They would come for me in some daft decorated motor, balloons all over, streamers and banners. I bet Big Frank'd arrange it. He's always keen on barmy jollification at his weddings.

Two o'clock came. No motor. Nobody asking for me. The Reception staff started glancing at me and whispering. I smiled, sure of the loyalty of friends. I'd rescued everybody from everything.

But you can't expect the traffic to ease up just because friends plan a surprise welcome, can you? Maybe some football team was playing, or an accident on the town by-pass interfered. That was it. I got a taxi, and rolled out to the village. I was wearing borrowed stuff. My fireman's uniform trousers cleaned by the hospital laundry. They lent me hospital slippers. I'd had to sign I'd bring them back. I was cold in the taxi.

In the lane I had a row. The driver wanted paying. I had to go in, breaking in because I'd lost my keys, presumably still with the bag of my own clothes in the grounds of the Academy. I found just enough to pay him.

The cottage was empty. No hullooing friends pouring from the wainscoting, no sudden cork-popping. I knew why. They were all waiting at the Ship, or the Welcome Sailor. I knew them. A rough bunch, but they'd all be there: Margaret Dainty, limping in with her gentle humour; Connie Hopkins, shyly suggesting she should come and stay the night; Luna, eager to resume where we'd left off; Jessica, wearing enough perfume to fell an ox at forty yards, every come-hither sign blazing; and the rest, cheering me to the echo – Gunge, Chris Mallon, Sandy and Mel, Liz Sandwell from Dragonsdale, the whole tribe of good friends. Rivals, yes. But friends deep down.

All except Joan. There was a card from her:

> Lovejoy darling,
> I've just heard. Do get better, sweetie.
> If you don't, well, this message won't matter, will it? Del has given me a permanent bodyguard. Geraldo is sworn to obey – if you know what I mean! I'm taking him to Monte Carlo, where we'll marry and live happ. ev. aft. If you see Del, give the poor dear a hand-out. Thanks for the ride, darling.
> Joan.

Which set me wondering. Had Joan Vervain known our noble Mayor, and Luna, before I'd 'introduced' them here? Was the Vervain's party a put-up? And good old Del in cahoots with Oliver Carstairs long before? About Luna: honest, or not? I had a yoghurt aged past its eat-by date.

The bluetits recognised me, though. They started tapping on the windows. I filled their nut-hangers. Indoors, the diet sheet the ward sister had given me made my mouth water. I had no cereals, skimmed milk, oats, bread, bran flakes. I wondered if the birds' peanuts were for human consumption, thought, well, it's those or nothing, and ate handfuls. My belly would have to learn to cope. I have to. There's a limit to the allowances you can make.

Getting on for five o'clock. The pubs would be opening soon. Pleased, I worked it out. They'd have booked the George carvery. My peanut-laden stomach rumbled enthusiastically. I dialled Jacko to come round with his coal lorry and give me a lift. He's been raised on my IOU scheme. Waiting, I composed my speech of thanks and acknowledgement.

'Dear Friends,' it began. 'I never expected . . .'

* * *

The Ship was heaving, but nobody seemed to be in, if you know what I mean. I tapped Gerda for news. Absently she asked if I'd been away. I bit back a rebuke just in time. Of course! All my friends must've warned everybody to act as if nothing was up, my return was an everyday occurrence! I cadged a pint on the slate, then judged the time right to leave.

Naturally, I was getting more excited than I should. But it's unusual, isn't it? To be feted by your friends, a hero, veritable champion of the underdog. I noticed the clock. Getting on for seven. Foolish to turn up too early. A surprise party spoils if the surprise arrives before it's ready.

I timed my exit from the Ship to perfection. Seven o'clock, and the day waning. Walking up East Hill into the town centre was tiring, but I made it.

The Welcome Sailor was practically empty too. No, people hadn't been in – wasn't it Birmingham's Antiques Fair? No Mrs Dainty, no Rebecca from the wharf, no others. The barman supposed there was something on. Maybe the George – he'd heard there was a gathering there.

That was it! The George after all! I was just leaving when a car pulled up, three women inside screaming joyously. The motor was covered in streamers, balloons. At last! I recognised Jenny Calamy. Dressed to kill.

'Lovejoy! You darling!' She raced across the road and bussed me enthusiastically.

'What about Big Frank?' I asked anxiously.

'Wish me luck tomorrow!' she cried.

'Tomorrow?' What was tomorrow?

'My wedding!' she screamed. Her friends in the car screamed along. 'In France! Can you *believe* it? See you when we come back! You really *must* come round! Byeeeee!'

'Bye-eee!' everybody cried but me. The motor sped away.

Well, you can't postpone a blinking wedding, just because the would-be best man's in hospital. Stands to reason.

I made the George, just in time to see Luna descend from the Mayor's grand motorcade. She was positively shimmering. It was coming on to rain.

She seemed to falter as the flash blulbs of our town's three feeble reporters dazzled. Her smile faded. She sized me up. Then she swept inside, mouth tight, hatred in her eyes. I waited until the little crowd dispersed, talking over the Mayoress' lovely dress, then went inside. I'd rather be going to my party than hers any day of the week.

'Party? No.' The receptionist was a tubby girl. She hides a tot of gin under the counter. 'Try the boozer next door.'

The Robin Hood's not my scene exactly, but the Arcade was closed – an hour early. I perked up. A good sign, especially after the way business must have picked up once news of my rescue of Connie broke.

I drew a blank there, except for a sighting of Harry Bateman, who shot off with a scared look in his eyes at the sight of me. Out of the back door. I smirked. Tatty old Harry nearly gave the game away! My surprise party must be in the one remaining waterhole, the Marquis of Granby on North Hill.

Cunning of my friends, to hold the gathering down there, eh? Behind St Peter's Church, where I'd least expect it. It was coming on to rain harder, and black night a-fallen, when I finally entered the thick fug.

Gunge came to meet me. Connie, pale but happy, was on a stool at the bar. Gunge took me across. I can't say I was relieved, because I'd never doubted. I mean, what are friends for? Goodness can't exist alone. It needs people.

'Hello, Connie.' I felt quite shy. Silly, really, after what Connie and me had been to each other. God, but I wanted a woman. I needed one like . . . No good trying to explain. Blokes don't need telling, and women can't understand.

'Hello, Lovejoy.' Her eyes were misty. I wondered how to get rid of Gunge when she said, 'We want you to be the first to know, Lovejoy.'

She did? I thought I already was. 'That's nice, love.'

'Gunge and I are going to live in the Isle of Man.'

'Fine. I'm . . .' I always forget. Do you congratulate the man, and wish the bride-to-be well? Or vice versa? I bussed her anyway, and Gunge gripped my hand to a mince.

'You judge our dollop, Lovejoy,' Connie said, adoring eyes on her man. 'We'll send our address once we're married.'

God knows how long I stayed. They spoke of a little antique shop near the Douglas ferry, shipping stuff Belfast to Liverpool. The Customs Paper re-imports trick, New York via Glasgow. Something in Guernsey with Southampton shippers. Gunge said hardly a thing.

He followed me to the door when I managed to break away.

'Ta, Lovejoy. Pike on, lad, eh?'

'Ta, Gunge. I mean it. Good luck to you both.'

Into the rain, steady now with a stiff breeze. I went slowly uphill into town.

There was no surprise party. I hadn't asked after the mob. Just as, I told myself finally, they hadn't asked after me.

The town centre was almost deserted. Just the George, with its lights. A couple of small restaurants. The Red Lion's upper floor's curtains showing where some vast nosh was taking place. I think hospitals make you tired out just lying abed. Maybe they want it that way, so you can't start injuring yourself again and come back in for more.

'Lovejoy!'

Glad to hear my name, I swivelled so fast I almost dinged myself unconscious on a lamp-post. Miss Turner. And Forage. and Marmalade Emma, with the sleepy Grimes reeling dozily along.

'Hello,' I said. For once I was willing to tell her all sorts of genealogy. As usual she got in first.

'Such excellent news, Lovejoy! We're related! Mr Forage and I! In the sixteen-eighties! First cousins in common. Can you believe it? You were exactly right!'

I looked at Forage, at Marmalade Emma. I would have looked at Grimes, but he can never look back so it's a waste of a look. This was more than a rejoicing of ancient cousins.

'Who's getting wed?' I asked, smiling.

'Mr Forage and I,' Miss Turner said. 'In New Hampshire. We've discovered a branch of our family there.' She plucked me close, whispered, 'I do believe they're very wealthy, Lovejoy!'

'Wonderful!' I said directly to Forage, who had the decency to look away. 'Almost too good to be true, eh?'

'Fantastic!' Miss Turner cried. 'We go tomorrow, Lovejoy.'

Et heartwarming cetera. I heard them out. Wherever love flourishes, let it. Even if Forage was working the old Cousin Horace scam. Maybe in her heart of hearts Miss Turner knew it too. I had the grace to refuse when she offered me some notes she said she owed.

'They were a gift. You can't repay gifts. It's their nature.'

We said goodbye. Off they trogged to the Ship to celebrate. It was all happening tonight. I wondered how I'd get home.

'Evening, Lovejoy.'

'Resisted arrest, old chap. Said he's innocent.'

'Lovejoy,' Acker croaked. 'Tell them, mate. I never

helped Cassie. Only mocked up photos for her to sell to Rye. Honest.'

I halted. God, my belly was stiff. 'Would you have let Connie drown, Acker?'

His face answered me. I limped on, despising him, me, the police for doing him over, every last one of us.

'You not arrested Mayor Carstairs yet?'

'On my way there now.' Cradhead chuckled. 'Drinkwater's at the Mayor's Oyster Feast, guest of honour, I'm wondering what sort of entrance I should make.'

He laughed, wagging his head. I was beginning to quite like Cradhead. Dangerous sentiment. There couldn't be any good in him, because he was the Plod. Logic.

'Sorry, Lovejoy. I'll have to question the Lady Mayoress. Did she *really* not know her husband offed the town silver, Council property from Cornish Place? Cassandra Clark testified Mayor Carstairs put up the money. Hard to believe, eh?'

'Indeed.' I wondered how he'd spotted Oliver's scam.

'I spotted the Mayor's scam by watching your face, Lovejoy,' Cradhead said mildly. 'At Del Vervain's radio show. Good old Del was in it too, of course. Hence the outside broadcast.' He laughed, a surprising sharp baritone. 'We were there to arrest you the instant you cried fake. You being the only true crook in the audience. You had the sense to keep mum.'

'Instinct, Craddie. It lights paths already sure, though some lead daftwards.' Which made me wonder if he'd had the wit to raid Sampney Young Ladies Academy yet.

'I expect you're wondering if I had the savvy to raid Sampney Young Ladies Academy yet.'

'Mmmmh?' This creep was an odious nerk, and no mistake.

'Answer's yes. Found nothing. That Miss Reynolds

shifts fast, what? Pity you can't come and watch me arrest the Mayor.'

He started across the road, towards the George. Two police cars, lights dimmed and sirens mute, crept to meet him.

Good old Miss Reynolds and her all-girl team! Marvellous what women can do when they finally stir themselves.

'Mind you conform to the Police and Criminal Evidence Act, Craddie,' I called. 'Got to be a first time.'

Which left me alone and palely loitering. I imagined I saw Rhea Cousins' grand motor drive by, husband Willis driving, some Continental dealer already mauling Rhea in the rear seat. Willis was some spouse. You don't get many of him to the shilling, not even round here.

There was a bus home in half an hour. The shelters by the post office had all been vandalised, so I decided to wait under the shopping mall arch. As I trudged wearily down Eld Lane I heard the plaintive tones of a cornet. The 'Emperor Waltz'? I'd forgotten: Sandy's dance night.

The square was empty, except for them. It's open to the sky, but for colonnades leading off under the glass-covered ways I've mentioned. The Old Library's a book-shop now. Glossy shops with spread windows look out. A young musician from St Leonard's was playing solo cornet, the waltz too slow but right for the mood. He was stand-ing on top of the fountain, water splashing over his feet, over the side of the ornamental basin. I had to squint to see properly.

Sandy was waltzing in stately fashion with Mel. The latter was attired as a soldier, original shako from Waterloo time, all except his spurs authentic. Sandy looked even loonier. He wore a fantastic silver wig, Carolean tall, with a wide crinoline, an Isabeau corsage dating from about 1846, quite wrong but, since it was white satin covered with pearls and glittering cubic zirconias, accuracy was hardly tonight's theme.

The slowness of the forlorn cornet's melody irritated me. Then I thought, oh well, heaven pardons love's perjuries.

What was I doing here? Wanting to cadge a lift. The pair waltzed gracefully on. I smiled, finally laughed, shaking my head. Who knows why this weird pair did this? Or why any of us ever do anything? Money, love, greed, all motives come nowhere near the truth. Everybody knows nothing.

'Sandy,' I tried for the hell of it. 'Lend us the fare.'

'Loser!' he spat without pausing. 'You almost *ruined* the dolloper. Idiot!'

'To save Connie,' I explained.

'With *her* dress sense?'

They danced on. Well, I had to laugh. I was still falling about twenty minutes later at the bus stop. I don't carry a watch, so have to rely on the town's wayward clocks. I was just beginning to wonder if the last bus had been cancelled when a car drew up.

'Lovejoy?' A girl's voice.

'I'm busy.' Add exhausted. Had enough.

'Get in, you proud fool you.' Sarcasm's the one thing I can take on the chin. I stepped inside, sat with my eyes closed. 'I was going to take you to supper, as a reward.'

'You don't understand.' The car moved off down North Hill. Homeward, thank God. I wondered if I'd any margarine. I could find an apple in the garden, fry some slices. They fill you for about an hour. 'The dolloper you invested in's safe, but a dollop stays inactive for a year after police give chase. It's the rule. No chance of cashing the antiques in for a twelvemonth, love.'

Jonathan Gash

This was where she'd ditch me, fling me out by the old horse trough by the bridge. She just laughed.

'We women are right. Men *are* stupid.'

This was a different car. I opened my eyes. Laura was truly beautiful. Why wasn't she angry? Women are very particular about gelt. They go berserk when bread goes up a penny a loaf. I've actually seen it happen. Yet she was delighted. Seemingly with me.

'Lend us a note, love. I'm a bit short at the moment. I've some money coming tomorrow . . .'

She stopped to buy hot food from a Chinese place at the Middleborough, three great paper sacks of the stuff. I almost fainted from the fragrance. I could remember food, but only just.

We drove to my cottage. I let her carry the nosh inside. There I fell on it, elbows flying. She did nothing, simply observed me like a cat smiling at cream. Except the cream wasn't me. It was something that had happened in town, and very very recently. In normal times I'd have wondered what. Now, in my state of dereliction, I was past caring.

During nosh, the answerphone did its stuff. A familiar husky voice went, 'Lovejoy, darling. It's Vell. Geronimo's on holiday. I'm back. Come soon. Glad it's all over, with those terrible females—'

Laura blocked my reach for the phone, tutting rebuke. I fed on. Who pays the piper.

Two hours later, I managed to stir myself. I noticed she'd locked the door. The curtains were drawn. I saw her erase the answerphone's messages, saw her curl her legs on the divan. They do that when they're settling in.

'Thank you,' I said hesitantly. Fine time to remember I couldn't brew up.

'Thank you, Lovejoy.'

344

Well, you couldn't blame me for asking. 'What for?'

'For having my parents arrested.'

She moved, placed her mouth on mine. Parents? I'd had nobody arrested. Except Mayor Carstairs. And maybe his lovely Lady Mayoress, at the ceremony in town.

'Luna? Oliver?'

Laura's alacrity in replacing Oliver when he withdrew came to mind. And her instant payments for Luna's share . . .

'This means that I'm your boss, Lovejoy. Right?'

'Look, Laura. I didn't know you were, er, her daughter Lola when, er, when we . . .'

'Get them off, Lovejoy.' She reached for me. Lola's their pet name. They try to keep me a baby. And I'm not.'

'Laura.' I tried to back away. 'My side's all strapped up. This bird knifed me. I stink of ether and them yellow chemicals—'

She laughed. 'You mean, be gentle?' She was falling about.

The door pounded, almost falling in.

'Lovejoy? Come right out this minute!'

'Christ! It's Luna!' I'd rather be back in the rain waiting for the bus. 'Your mother!'

'Marvellous!' Laura cooed, pinning me down. I was so weak I just lay there. 'Never underestimate the hatred within families, Lovejoy. Or the ecstasy that comes from assuaging it.'

'Laura. Look, love.' I tried. 'She'll bring the police—'

'There!' She was laughing breathlessly as the hammering continued and I started to be breathless too. 'Not *so* fatigued, are we, darling?' I knew how George IV felt, sprawling helpless in his new Queen's bridal chamber. At least he was drunk. 'Laura . . .'

'Lovejoy!' Luna frantically tried the windows, the door.

I could hear her knocking on the glass. 'I know you're in there!'

'See, Lovejoy?' Laura was moving over me. I was enveloped, entering paradise, bliss-blind. 'Mummy knows you can get her off all charges by refusing to give evidence. But you *will* give it, darling, won't you? Condemn her, Lovejoy. Just a little. Say yes!'

'Ooooh.' I hardly knew what she was on about. Or cared. I was in that helpless phase. All a bloke wants from a bird is everything. Surely everything isn't too much to ask?

'Say yes. Promise me, Lovejoy.' She started to move off me as threat. 'You'll give evidence against her?'

I clasped her close, yelled, 'Yes!' surrendering in a gush of true honest perfect romantic love or something. It's a woman's world, and that's not my fault. 'Oh, yes, love. Anything you say.'

Ecstasy blotted out the entire world to a sound of distant thunder outside on my door.